Stellar

DEA

**A Featured Alternate Selection of
The Science Fiction Book Club™**

"Bill Dietz has taken a diverse—and surprising—cast of characters and woven an extremely intense story. *DeathDay* is a compelling novel of the strength of the human spirit in the face of apocalypse."

—Rick Shelley, author of *Holding the Line*

"*DeathDay* is a classic alien-invasion tale of survival and human triumph—great reading for anyone who loved *Independence Day* or *The War of the Worlds*."

—*New York Times* bestselling author Kevin J. Anderson

"A novel of the near-future alien invasion definitely in the classic line of succession from *The War of the Worlds* to *The Puppet Masters* to *Independence Day* . . . well done. What with breakneck pacing, good action scenes, and unexpectedly strong characterization, alien-invasion buffs should enjoy, enjoy!"

—*Booklist*

"A fast-paced tale of survival and resistance that should appeal to fans of SF action-adventure." —*Library Journal*

"An exciting nonstop-action thriller . . . fast-paced . . . exciting . . . a must-read for sub-genre fans. William C. Dietz provides more than just an opening gamut of a military science fiction thriller along the lines of *V*. He provides a deep social and psychological study of humanity and the Saurons that makes the invasion seem devastatingly real and leaves breathless readers waiting for *EarthRise*."

—*BookBrowser*

continued . . .

Also by William C. Dietz

BY FORCE OF ARMS and BY BLOOD ALONE

"Lots of action, good characterizations, a menacing enemy reminiscent of Fred Saberhagen's Berserker series, and a rousing ending."   —*Science Fiction Chronicle*

"Well-reasoned buildup to the conflict . . . well-thought-out individuals and cultures. A good book."

—*Bibliomania*

LEGION OF THE DAMNED and THE FINAL BATTLE

"A tough, moving novel of future warfare."

—David Drake

"A complex novel . . . scintillating action scenes. . . . A satisfying, exciting read."

—Billie Sue Mosiman, author of *Widow*

"Rockets and rayguns galore . . . and more than enough action to satisfy those who like it hot and heavy."

—*The Oregonian*

"Exciting and suspenseful . . . real punch."

—*Publishers Weekly*

DeathDay

William C. Dietz

ACE BOOKS, NEW YORK

This is a work of fiction. Names, characters, places, and incidents either are the product of the author's imagination or are used fictitiously, and any resemblance to actual persons, living or dead, business establishments, events, or locales is entirely coincidental.

DEATHDAY

An Ace Book / published by arrangement with
the author

PRINTING HISTORY
Ace hardcover edition / September 2001
Ace mass-market edition / October 2002

Copyright © 2001 by William C. Dietz.
Cover art by Edwin Herder.
Cover design by Pyrographx.

All rights reserved.
This book, or parts thereof, may not be reproduced in
any form without permission.
For information address: The Berkley Publishing Group,
a division of Penguin Putnam Inc.,
375 Hudson Street, New York, New York 10014.

Visit our website at
www.penguinputnam.com
Check out the ACE Science Fiction & Fantasy newsletter!

ISBN: 0-441-00981-6

ACE®
Ace Books are published by The Berkley Publishing Group,
a division of Penguin Putnam Inc.,
375 Hudson Street, New York, New York 10014.
ACE and the "A" design
are trademarks belonging to Penguin Putnam Inc.

PRINTED IN THE UNITED STATES OF AMERICA

10 9 8 7 6 5 4 3 2 1

To Ginjer Buchanan,
for many years of friendship, and good counsel.
Thank you for the great ideas,
the feedback, and continued support.

1

DEATH DAY MINUS 155

FRIDAY, FEBRUARY 28, 2020

> And the fifth angel sounded, and I saw a star fall from heaven unto the earth: and to him was given the key of the bottomless pit. And he opened the bottomless pit; and there arose smoke out of the pit, as the smoke of a great furnace; and the sun and the air were darkened by reason of the smoke of the pit. And there came out of the smoke locusts upon the earth: and unto them was given power, as the scorpions of the earth have power.
>
> —REVELATIONS 9:1–2,
>   Holy Bible

NEWPORT, OREGON

The cities of New York, Paris, Moscow, Madrid, Cairo, Beijing, Sydney, Lima, Rio de Janeiro, Johannesburg, Tehran, and New Delhi were already in flames by the time the people of Earth realized they were under attack. Skyscrapers toppled, apartment buildings exploded, bridges collapsed, housing tracts were incinerated, forests were consumed by fire, and pillars of black smoke speared the sky.

The nations of Earth wasted precious minutes hurling accusations at each other, and two actually launched missiles before they realized the nature of their mistake and tried to abort. But it was too late . . . and the cities of Bombay and Islamabad vanished in the twinkling of an eye.

The truth was that the attack originated from space, from the great blackness that started just beyond the planet's atmosphere, and extended past the edge of the galaxy. Monsters, the same ones that children so wisely fear, had finally arrived. And they were bad, *very* bad, which was why more than three billion people died in less than three days.

Those who survived, who lived to endure the days ahead, would remember Black Friday in a variety of different ways. For Jack Manning it was the noise, the sound of sonic booms that rolled across the land, each one overlapping the last, like the hammers of hell.

He was on vacation near Newport, Oregon, when the thunder started to roll and contrails clawed the sky. The wind caused his eyes to tear as Manning looked upward. There were others on the beach, not many given the time of year, but a thin scattering of tourists salted with locals. They shaded their eyes against the glare and pointed toward dots that raced out over the Pacific. Most assumed it was some sort of military exercise—role-playing for the kind of war that no one expected anymore.

The first hint of what was actually taking place came from an older man in a yellow windbreaker. The words "North Face" were emblazoned over his left breast pocket. A cloud of windblown hair danced around his ruddy face. He waved his unicom like a high-tech talisman. His voice was hopeful, as if the tall, lean stranger might be able to explain the news, or make it go away. "Have you seen this nonsense? These idiots claim Portland is under attack! But that's impossible! My daughter works there . . . not far from Powell's bookstore. Here . . . look at this."

Manning looked at the little screen and was amazed by what he saw. The video quality was pretty good considering where they were. The old Pittock Mansion was on a hill west of downtown Portland. A guy named Frank had gone there to get a better view. Now, thanks to a home videocamera and his wireless connection to the Web, Frank's video was available worldwide. The footage managed to be both horrible and awe-inspiring at the same time. The two men watched as three aircraft, one the size of a city block, systematically destroyed the city. The attackers used energy weapons, high-explosive bombs, and a variety of missiles to do their bloody work. The new fifty-story Willamette office tower took a direct hit, folded like a tube of wet cardboard, and fell on the Morrison bridge. The span collapsed into the river. Boats, barges, and other debris were swept downstream and into the wreckage, where they were trapped. A dam started to form.

"Jeez," the man named Frank said feelingly, "somebody needs to stop these bastards."

A windblown shout carried down the beach. Manning looked up into the sky. One of the black specks wheeled, did a nose-over, and dove for the beach. He could have run, *should* have run, but there was nowhere to go. The nearest cover was more than half a mile away. Manning had never felt so exposed—so vulnerable. The blob grew into a delta-shaped hull and roared overhead. It was so low they could feel the wind created by its passage and read the hieroglyphics on the fuselage. Engines howled. Both men turned to watch it depart. The ship pulled up, climbed at an amazing rate of speed, and was gone. The boom followed a few seconds later.

"Damn!" the man said. "Did you see that? It looked like the ones on TV. Who are they? The Chinese?"

As with most members of his particular profession, Manning knew a thing or two about military aircraft. "No," he answered slowly. "The Chinese don't have anything like that."

"Then who?" the older man demanded desperately. "*Who* do the planes belong to?"

"I don't know," Manning replied grimly, "but I doubt they're human."

The older man's jaw dropped, and remained that way, as Manning turned and walked away. Thunder rolled—and the human race continued to die.

McCHORD AFB, WASHINGTON

The conference room was long and narrow, like the table that ran its length, and looked out over a semicircular space. There wasn't much doubt who the facility belonged to, since the Air Mobility Command's shield dominated the front wall. It consisted of a globe, wings, and a clutch of arrows.

Like the rest of the AMC, McChord's team was dedicated to putting equipment and supplies wherever the rest of the military wanted them to go. That included airborne refueling for the air force, navy, marine corps, and allied aircraft as well. The areas to either side of the AMC shield were covered with the new Sony-manufactured "video wallpaper" that allowed the thirty-six officers and enlisted people who staffed the Tactical Operations Center, or TOC, to "post" images in any manner they chose.

Though the Air Mobility Command was headquartered at Scott AFB in Illinois, the functions of the Tanker Airlift Control Center, or TACC, could be duplicated elsewhere, and McChord was one of those places. And, while they were doing the best job they could, their efforts had been hampered by a lack of what computers need most: reliable data.

In spite of the fact that the TOC was more than five stories below ground level, and was hardened against nuclear, biological, and chemical attack, those individuals lucky enough to be there—and that included Alexander Ajani Franklin, the governor of Washington State—could still feel the reverberations of the powerful subnuclear explosions. They shook dust out of the light fixtures, made coffee shiver in cups, and sent a stylus tumbling to the highly polished floor.

General Charles "Coop" Windgate bent to pick it up. He'd been up for more than forty-eight hours, but his uniform looked like it had just come off a hanger, and his shoes were mirror-bright—just as they had been every day for the twenty-seven years he'd spent in the air force. He surfaced with pen in hand. "Damn the bastards anyway. . . . How many bombs do they have?"

Others were present as well: Jina Claire Franklin, the governor's wife; Major Linda Holmes, the general's adjutant; and Michael Olmsworthy, secretary of the air force. None of them replied. None had to. The answer was obvious. The extraterrestrials—or XTs, as many had taken to calling them—had enough bombs to reduce the entire country to burning rubble, and assuming the reports from abroad were reliable, the rest of the world as well. Why? Nobody knew. If the aliens had the means to communicate, they hadn't bothered to do so.

Holmes sat in front of an IBM "Cyber Warrior" field-ready portable. It was waterproof, shockproof, and damned near bulletproof. She touched an earplug and cocked her head to one side. Holmes had short black hair, serious brown eyes, and a thin-lipped mouth. She listened for a moment, murmured an acknowledgment into the boom mike, and bit her lower lip. Governor Franklin had never seen an air force officer cry but sensed she was about to.

"Well?" Windgate demanded. "Spit it out."

Holmes struggled to control the tremor in her voice. "Sir, that was the com center. They caught a relay from a nuclear sub. *Air Force One* went down near Kansas City. Some sort of energy weapon was fired from orbit. *Air Force Two* was attacked and destroyed on the way back from Panama City. No known survivors."

"Were the planes targeted?" Windgate asked. "That would tell us something."

"No," the major replied. "It doesn't sound that way. Preliminary reports suggest that the XTs have downed thousands of civilian and military aircraft. Average life of a fighter after launch is just twenty-five seconds. They kill anything that moves. The missile command tried to launch nukes—but every silo was plastered before they could get a shot off."

Jina Franklin tried to swallow the enormous lump that had formed in her throat. The president and her husband, the vice president and his wife, all of them dead. She felt a terrible sense of loss—for the country, for their families, and for herself. Tears trickled down her cheeks. Her husband's hand closed over hers. The grip was tight, *too* tight, but she made no attempt to escape it. His voice was controlled. "And the Speaker? Do we have any word on him?"

"No," Holmes replied, "I'm afraid we don't. That's not too surprising, though, since Washington, D.C., was almost completely destroyed. If the Pentagon issued any orders, they haven't reached us."

There was a long moment of silence as they absorbed the news. "So," Windgate said finally, his eyes swinging to Olmsworthy, "who's holding the bag?"

The secretary was a onetime CEO of Boeing, an old friend of the president's, and a grandfather three times over. That's where his mind was—with his children and his grandchildren. It was chance, pure chance that his plane had landed at McChord to refuel, and been on the ground at the moment of attack. He should be dead by now, blown to bits, or fried to a crisp. More than that, he *wanted* to be dead—if that's what it would take to be with his family. Olmsworthy's eyes were red with fatigue, fields of white stubble covered both cheeks, and his suit was badly wrinkled. He forced his mind to focus. "No, I don't think so. I'm an appointee. I'd say the governor's the one you want. People *voted* for him."

Slowly, but with the surety of a compass needle seeking true north, all eyes went to Franklin. He had good hair, cut short without a trace of gray, medium brown skin, even features, and a mouth that was normally ready to smile. Not now, though, and not for some time to come. He shook his head. "Thanks, but no thanks. I'm no expert on matters of succession—but it seems to me that I'm in the wrong branch of government."

Holmes tapped the last few keys and waited for a response.

The XTs had neutralized most of the government's considerable inventory of com and spy sats during the first five minutes of the attack. There was still plenty of buried cable, however, and in spite of the fact that some had been cut, there was plenty of redundancy, and that, plus her high-priority military "push," got Holmes through to the State Department's home page. She cleared her throat. "It looks like the governor is correct, sir: The secretary of defense is fourth in line after the Speaker of the House, and, in a situation where the attorney general and the other secretaries are killed, responsibility devolves to the next level of administrators. You're fourth . . . right after the secretary of the navy."

Olmsworthy held his head in his hands. "Tell me this is a dream . . . some sort of horrible nightmare."

Windgate didn't seem to hear. He held up his hand. "Listen . . . the bombing has stopped."

There was a moment of silence as everyone sought to verify what the general had said. A minute passed but nothing was heard. Satisfied that he was correct, Windgate turned to Holmes. "Get Jeski on the horn . . . tell him to activate roamers one through five. We need a sit rep."

Holmes looked alarmed. Sealed in their underground command post and with no satellites to rely on, the high-flying drones were the only sources of visual input they had left. All had been launched immediately after McChord came under attack, and they seemed to have escaped notice. "The XTs could home in on the signals, sir, and blow the roamers out of the sky."

"The thought had occurred to me," Windgate answered sarcastically, "but so fucking what? The roamers will run out of fuel in about two hours and we'll lose them anyway."

Not roamers four and five, Holmes thought, because they're solar-powered. But there was only one response she could properly give—and the officer gave it. "Sir, yes, sir."

"Step over to the window," the general ordered, "and let's take a look." A motor whined, and the Plexiglas barrier fell as the civilians lined the newly created opening. Jina marveled at the discipline of men and women below. Here they were, doing their jobs, knowing that wives, husbands, mothers, fathers, sisters, brothers, and in some cases sons and daughters were most likely dead. It was the most courageous thing she had ever witnessed.

There was a stir on the floor as new images appeared on the gently curved wall. For all their professionalism and attention to duty, the TOC's staff were just as curious regarding "out there" as their commanding officer was.

Each rectangle of video was identified by the name of the drone from which it came, a plain English description of the area under surveillance, and a line of zeros where precise coordinates should have appeared. Like so much of the technology they had come to rely on, the Global Positioning System (GPS) was a thing of the past.

So, due to limitations of range and the fact that the drones had been launched at McChord, none was more than about three hundred nautical miles away—that in spite of ranges that could extend to fifteen hundred nautical miles under OTH (over-the-horizon) operational procedures. But without sats to link everything together, line-of-sight transmission was the best that any of them could hope for.

Two of the units were solar-powered Gnat 1150s, both having a 250-pound payload, capable of staying aloft for up to a week, assuming they received enough sunlight. Something in short supply, what with fires burning all around the globe.

The other three were heavier craft, direct descendants of the General Atomics "Predator" series, each having up to sixty hours' worth of endurance at an altitude of thirty thousand feet.

Windgate signaled to Holmes. "Tell Jeski to give us whatever he's got."

Holmes murmured into her mike. Down on the floor, in what was generally referred to as "the pit," Captain "Jaws" Jeski nodded and tried to concentrate. He had brown hair, hazel eyes, and a strong, jutting jaw. It was badly in need of a shave. He'd been on duty for more than thirty-six hours and couldn't stop thinking about his girlfriend. Was she alive? Or lying dead under a pile of debris? His voice was deceptively serene. The words boomed over the PA. "If you would direct your attention to the real-time image on the far left . . ."

Franklin did as the officer suggested and found himself looking down at what was, or had been, the city of Seattle. Smoke boiled up from a multitude of fires and served to blanket the metroplex. There were holes, however—and Predator Five took full advantage of them.

The first thing the politician looked for and couldn't see was the 605-foot-tall Seattle Space Needle with which the city had long been identified. He assumed the problem was a matter of perspective at first, till Jina squeezed his hand. "Alex, look! The Needle is down!"

Franklin realized the truth, that the tower had fallen to the east and lay pointed toward the foot of Capitol Hill. The landmark had survived the quake of '09, in which dozens of buildings had been flattened. Now it was down.

But that wasn't all—not by a long shot. The new Aurora Bridge, completed only two years before, had collapsed into the Lake Union ship canal. Roughly half the downtown area had been slagged, although the top five stories of the Microsoft tower, including its much-discussed transparent dome, still poked up through the roiling smoke. A two-mile stretch of the partially elevated I-5 freeway was down, the "condo farm" that dominated the Denny Regrade area was burning, and nothing moved.

Jeski chose that moment to order an increase in magnification, and the streets seemed to leap upward. There were M&M–colored cars, plenty of them, but most were stationary. A slowly winding river of people snaked along the main arterials, surging toward the heavily damaged freeway.

Habit? Because that's the way they normally moved around? Or pragmatism, because damaged or not, highways offered the fastest way out of town? It didn't matter.

Another picture appeared. Rather than circling as the first drone had, this one was headed south, right over McChord, Fort Lewis, and the capital in Olympia.

Windgate, who expected the worst but was still eager to see how badly his base had been damaged, was appalled by the extent of the destruction. It appeared as if the XTs *knew* the military bases were a threat and had been careful to target them. The administrative buildings, housing, and hangars had all been leveled.

Worse, from a pilot's point of view, the runways were so torn up that none of the general's tubby Lockheed Martin "Load Warriors" would be able to take off or land. Assuming any were left— which seemed doubtful. Those not destroyed on the ground had been forced to ditch at sea or land on any kind of airfield they could find. They were theoretically capable of landing on a 750-foot strip, but that was under ideal conditions, which didn't apply here.

"Holy shit!" someone said. "What the hell is *that?*"

Holmes couldn't believe her eyes. The object in question was huge, *so* huge that it obliterated the Gnat's view of the ground as it nosed into the picture.

"It's one of their ships," Windgate said dully. "One of their *smaller* ships."

Franklin stared in wonder as the alien vessel slid in under the drone's belly. Though it was too large to see properly, the politician had the impression of a delta-shaped hull, along with various fins, fairings, and other structures that gave texture to a surface otherwise aerodynamically smooth. The sight of the ship inspired both awe and terror. How could the human race possibly survive the onslaught of such machines? Was this the end?

Light winked from the top of the black matte hull. "Uh-oh," Holmes exclaimed. "We need to break it off.... They know the roamer is up there and—"

The sentence went unfinished. The Gnat exploded, the video vanished, and the other images winked out one after another. The drones were gone.

Silence reigned for only a moment, as a technician broke into tears. Windgate swore and shook his head. "Damn the bastards, anyway. If only—"

"Sorry to interrupt, sir," Captain Jeski said over the PA, "but we have an incoming transmission."

Windgate looked hopeful. Could help be on the way? "Really? Who is it?"

Jeski looked up at the window. "It's *them*. The aliens. The message is in English."

The general struggled to conceal his disappointment. There would be no help . . . just aliens who spoke English. The "how" seemed unimportant. "All right, then—what do the bastards want?"

Jeski liked old movies and would have smiled if the circumstances had been different. But they weren't, so what might have been funny wasn't. "They want to meet our leader, sir. Up top in thirty minutes."

NEWPORT, OREGON

The Agate Beach parking lot was only half full. A group of people stood next to an RV, shaded their eyes, and pointed into the sky. It was cold . . . and all of them were bundled up. Manning fumbled for the Hertz remote and pointed toward the maroon SUV. The motor started, the lights flashed, and the door popped open. Lots of conveniences. More than he needed.

Manning climbed inside, opened the United Nations–issue Kevlar soft-sided briefcase, and removed the phone. It was linked to an entire fleet of low-orbit satellites and would work from anyplace in the world. Some very heavy stuff was coming down, and the secretary-general would need protection—*had* protection, since the team he led would be at her side. Comforting, but not the same as being there himself, which, in spite of the accusations leveled against him, was where Manning wanted to be.

Manning pressed the power button, entered an access code, followed that with a three-digit priority "push," and waited for the call to connect. Nothing.

The security officer swore, switched to the terrestrial PCS system, and entered another sequence of numbers. There was no dial tone, and a "no service" message appeared on the screen. Something cold filled his gut. The XTs, because that's what they obviously were, had destroyed the entire communications system in what? Hours? It didn't bode well.

Manning secured his seat belt, pulled out of the lot, and headed north on Highway 101. The United States wouldn't cave without striking back, he felt certain of that, and there would be a need for people like him. People who could fight.

There wasn't much traffic, not at first, and the security chief made fairly good time up through Lincoln City, and on toward Tilamook. Then he hit Winenna Beach, saw what looked like a parking lot up ahead, and hit the brakes.

Three alien fighters, miniature versions of the ship he'd seen earlier, flashed overhead. Bright blue energy beams stuttered toward the north, a tanker truck exploded, and a ball of fire floated upward. The booms came so close together they were nearly indistinguishable.

The tanker was blocking the highway, which made it impossible to move. Not only that, but the fighters could return at any moment. People bailed out of their vehicles and started to run.

Manning considered heading in the opposite direction, checked his rearview mirror, and discovered that fifteen or twenty vehicles had pulled in behind him. It was hopeless. Even if he could turn around, even if he fled toward the south, there would be other traffic jams.

The security officer turned the engine off, got out of the SUV, and opened the back. He had a single suitcase and no intention of lugging it around. Most of the contents were what he thought of as "vacation crap," meaning clothes he wouldn't normally wear, books he wouldn't actually read, and postcards he wouldn't send. All part of a vacation he'd been ordered to take in the wake of what the press called "The Pretoria Massacre," a fifteen-minute gun battle in which Manning and his team had gone head-to-head with eight heavily armed assassins and killed every one of them. That made him a hero to some . . . and a villain to others—especially since he was white, the assassins were black, and there were rumors that some of them had been "capped." An allegation no one had been able to prove—but it now stained his reputation. That's why he was in Oregon instead of New York on this day.

There were some useful items among the "vacation crap," however, including the Smith & Wesson .40-caliber sidearm he was authorized to carry in most nations around the world, two backup mags holding fourteen rounds each, an anodized Tecna Lite-3, a small first-aid kit, and the day pack he used as a carry-on. Those items, plus a sweater and gloves, completed his kit. Not exactly combat-ready—but better than hauling the TUMI around.

The plan, such as it was, involved a hike to Portland, some sort of high-priority flight to New York, and a reunion with the rest of his team. People who, along with his seldom-seen sister, provided his connection with the world. At least Marta would be safe—given where she was.

There didn't seem to be much chance that the Hertz Corporation would be able to recover the SUV, not anytime soon, but it was in his nature to lock the doors.

That accomplished, Manning swung the pack onto his back, turned toward the north, and started to walk. The exercise felt good.

DENVER, COLORADO

The Abco Uniform company maintained a locker room for the convenience of its male employees. The door opened, and a man entered. He had dark hair, long sideburns, and a carefully trimmed mustache. A small goatee completed the look. His features were even, some said handsome, but lacked warmth. Perhaps it was the hard, cold eyes—or the mouth that rarely smiled. A woman had tried to figure that out once but given up, a decision her family heartily endorsed.

The man's chrome-toed combat style boots clacked as he walked down an aisle guarded by two rows of lockers. His feet were small—*too* small, according to the boys in the sixth grade—and the lace-up boots helped to compensate for that fact.

Ivory wasn't his *real* name, but it was the one he had chosen, both because it was more attractive than Kreider, and because it made a statement about his Christian identity, and the essential whiteness that marked him as special. The color of purity, of truth, of goodness.

Still, it said "Kreider" on his Social Security card, which meant that it said "Kreider" in the company's records, which meant it said "Kreider" on his olive-drab locker. The letters were picked out in white.

Ivory looked left and right, assured himself that he was alone, and opened the padlock. The door squeaked as he pulled it open. The interior was arranged with military precision—one of many things he admired about the army, even if they had kicked him out. The pen was right where he'd left it. Or was it a sword? Yes, any instrument capable of inflicting damage on the enemy qualified as the righteous sword of God.

Quickly, so as to beat the rest of the shift out of the locker room, Ivory removed the company's blue overalls and donned his street clothes. Then, when everything was ready, he took the pen and closed the locker. With that accomplished, it was time to take one last look around. Nothing. Good. He needed the money—and didn't want to get fired. Not again. Not so soon.

Ivory moved with the surety of a man who knows exactly what he's doing. The black man's locker was next to the door. The letters said "Jones," as if African slaves were from England and entitled to Anglo-Saxon names. Ivory stepped up, drew a much-practiced swastika, and wrote "nigger" below it. The cap made a satisfying "click" as it mated with the marker.

Ivory wanted to run, wanted to fill the hole at the bottom of his stomach, but forced himself to stay. The black man was big and strong. There was little doubt about what would happen if he and his friends arrived. Ivory would suffer, as he had suffered before, and wake up in the hospital. But if he ran, if he surrendered to his fear, the nigger would win. Right now, right here, Ivory was the most powerful man in the world. Especially since he knew that the great Yahweh was watching and measuring his worth.

For five long, excruciating seconds the laundry worker forced himself to stand there, to admire his own handiwork, before turning away. The doorknob felt cold, his heart raced, and his mind was supernaturally clear. He felt invigorated, powerful, and important.

The door opened, a bomb detonated one block to the north, and the ground shook. Another person might have stood there, might have wasted precious seconds wondering what was happening, but not Ivory. He ran, cut left at the first corner he came to, and ran some more. The front of the building was more than eighty years old. Mortar cracked, bricks came loose, and masonry tumbled into the street.

Warned as if by some sixth sense, Ivory sprinted for safety but didn't quite make it. Something heavy hit his shoulder, his feet went out from under him, and the sidewalk smacked his face. He experienced the full weight of the debris, felt the air leave his lungs, and knew he was going to die. Dust filled his nostrils, another explosion shook the city, and a siren started to wail.

Ivory felt hands grab his wrists, heard his belt buckle scrape along the pavement, and was pleased when the weight disappeared. Then, amazingly, unbelievably, he was free, and standing unsupported. The African-American's hair and face were coated with light-colored mortar dust. He looked like a street mime. He held Ivory's arm. "Are you okay? Damn! That was close."

"Yeah," Ivory replied, surprised to find that it was true. "Thanks."

The black man looked as if he were going to say something more, but his wife spoke first. "Come on, honey. We've got to get the kids."

The man nodded, waved to Ivory, and was swallowed by smoke.

Stunned by his brush with death and still in shock, Ivory stumbled down the street. His car, a twenty-year-old Toyota, had been crushed by a light standard. It was totaled. He continued to move. People ran for cover, explosions threw columns of debris into the air, and aircraft crisscrossed the sky. They looked different, foreign somehow, but it was hard to see.

A wino lurched out of a doorway, asked for spare change, and got the finger instead. After all, if there was anything worse than a nigger or a Jew, it was a white man who had failed his race. A blood-sucking parasite who, along with the homosexuals and drug addicts, should be erased for good.

A pickup loaded with injured schoolchildren lurched over a curb, circumvented a pile of concrete blocks, and bounced into the street. A man stood crying on a corner, a bike messenger wove his way through traffic, and thunder boomed.

The world had gone mad, totally mad, and Ivory blocked it

out. He walked head down, ignored everything but the pavement in front of him, and left the worst of the chaos behind. Traffic lights were out, cars smashed into each other, and battery-powered burglar alarms bleated their warnings.

The weather was clear but cold, and Ivory regretted the fact that his coat remained in the Toyota.

Ivory made his way to Speer, followed that to I-25, and looked down onto the freeway. It was packed bumper-to-bumper, side-to-side, and nothing was moving. Some of the cars had burned themselves out, some were on fire, and most were abandoned. Thousands upon thousands of people were climbing over wrecks, winding their way among the still-burning hulks, trying to escape the danger. Most were headed south, toward their homes in 'burbs such as Englewood, or to escape the bombing to the north. There was little choice but to join them.

Ivory followed the flow down onto the freeway, ignored the Hispanic woman who struggled to deal with three children, and started to walk. Someone had left their dog in the backseat of their car. It yapped as he passed. A teenager, his face alight, smashed a windshield. The state-of-the-art entertainment console would fetch top dollar *if* the idiot could find a buyer. A man, fully loaded backpack firmly in place, nodded and smiled. He'd been ready and was enormously pleased with himself. Screw the world, screw the boss, screw the job. *He* was free. Ivory trudged on.

It was dark by the time he made it to the Arapaho exit, followed a mob down the off ramp, and turned east. Two additional moons had appeared in the sky and threw a strange blue-green glow across the land. Fires burned for as far as the eye could see. The power grid had been destroyed, and outside of a few hardy souls stupid enough to run portable generators, there was no electric light. But they learned quickly enough—oh, yes they did—as the glows drew looters. The intermittent pop, pop, pop of small-arms fire signaled a dozen backyard wars. Ivory avoided such places, preferring the shadows to confrontation, moving as quickly as he could.

Finally, nearly dead on his feet, he approached the tacky little storefront that served as headquarters for the nascent White Rose Society. It was untouched. Luck? Certainly, although the fact that four heavily armed skinheads, or "skins," stood in front of the building might have something to do with it as well.

A smallish group, fewer than the seven described in Ezekiel 9:

1–2, but adequate, and consistent with the principle of leaderless resistance that had protected his brothers and sisters for so long.

A flashlight bathed him in white. Two men rushed forward, grabbed Ivory's arms, and practically carried him inside. The walls were covered with Hitler posters, black swastikas, and racist epithets. Two battery-powered lamps threw shadows toward the door.

First aid came in the form of an ice-cold Coors—the skins' remedy for almost any injury. It tasted cold and crisp. Parker, who functioned as the group's master at arms, raised a bushy eyebrow. He'd been a boxer once, and his nose was nearly flat. The word "Rahowa," an acronym for "racial holy war," had been tattooed across his forehead so that anyone who encountered him was forced to encounter his belief system as well. "Hate to say it, boss—but you look like hell. Where you been?"

So Ivory told them the story, except the way he told it, the black couple were white, and *he* rescued *them*. "So," Ivory said, bringing the report to a close, "have you seen the news? What the hell is going on?"

The skins looked at Parker. He shrugged. "Cable went down more than two hours ago. The last thing they said had something to do with aliens. They dropped out of nowhere, took a notion to kick our ass, and proceeded to do so."

Ivory looked from one face to the next. "Don't bullshit me, Parker . . . this is serious."

"I ain't bullshitting you," the skinhead replied stolidly, "it's for real."

"What about the air force? What are they doing?"

Bonner, better known as Boner, gestured with a can of beer. Some slopped onto the much-abused floor. "They ain't doin' shit, not so far as we can tell, but who knows? Could be that they're in on it."

Ivory had done everything within his power to foster that kind of paranoia while avoiding such thinking himself. Why go for some complicated answer when the simple ones were generally right? No, the flyboys were outgunned, and that was that. The ZOG, the Zionist Occupational Government, was tits up, along with the police, military, and other structures created to support it.

Then it dawned on him: This was it! Armageddon, the fire from which the new order would be born! The very thing he had prophesized but never really believed in. From the ashes the true

Israel would rise, Yahweh's kingdom would be born, and Jesus would finally return.

Ivory was about to say something, about to share his insight, when he looked into their faces and realized they were ahead of him. What they wanted were orders. He nodded. "All right, then—this is the day we've been waiting for. What's the status on the war wagon?"

"Out back," Parker said proudly, "ready to rock 'n' roll."

"Supplies?"

"On board."

"Fuel?"

"Both tanks full."

"Weapons?"

"Locked and loaded."

Ivory downed the last of his beer, wiped his mouth with the back of a hand, and got to his feet. He felt dizzy but managed to hide it. Strength, or at least the perception of it, was critical to leadership. Hitler said so. "Let's haul ass."

Boner gave a whoop of pure joy, Parker grinned, and the others slapped each other on the back. Unseen, a cockroach emerged from the woodwork, decided the room was too bright, and retreated to his hole. His kind had been around for millions of years and would be for millions more. Darkness would fall . . . and he would feed.

ABOARD THE SAURON SHUTTLE *OR SU*, OR *USEFUL*, FIVE THOUSAND UNITS OVER THE PLANET NOW DESIGNATED AS HAVEN

The ship shuddered as it dropped through some choppy air, and the Sauron pilot, a Kan named Hol-Zee, waited for the almost inevitable reprimand. A Zin master named Hak-Bin occupied the single thronelike passenger seat and would almost certainly interpret the momentary discomfort as a personal affront. The Zin were like that, a fact that Zee had never bothered to question. After all, *his* chitin was a rich brown color, and while not as good as black, it was superior to white, or—and the Sauron could barely imagine it—light-colored *fur*. Such as Ra 'Na slaves were born with.

Disgusted by his own imaginings, the warrior waited for the expected rebuke, gave thanks when nothing happened, and turned his attention to the landing. There were winds to contend with—not to mention layers of thick black smoke.

Hak-Bin, comfortably ensconced in a seat that had been

custom-molded to his body, sat at the exact center of the cabin. He felt a series of bumps, considered the possibility of a reprimand, but couldn't muster the necessary *vil*, the negative energy he would need to properly chastise the Kan. Things had gone well, *very* well, and try as he might, the Zin found it difficult to be anything but happy. The long, tension-filled journey was over. An appropriate planet had been located and would soon be ready.

The indigenous population represented something of a threat, especially since they outnumbered the Saurons thousands to one, but that problem had been addressed. The challenge was to control the Kan, who, though skilled at killing things, often resembled newly hatched Nymphs where their mental processes were concerned. Left to their own devices, the warriors would destroy *all* the humans, leaving no one to construct the citadels. Yes, there was little doubt that the great architect understood the nature of his creations, wisely setting Zin over Kan, Kan over Fon, and the Saurons over all other species.

The shuttle made an approach from the north, hit the surface of Spanaway Lake, and coasted toward the south. There was some sort of structure to the left, the purpose of which didn't matter to the pilot, who was focused on landing the ship. Zee dropped the ship's spoilers, allowed the ship to slow, and retracted them again. The impact was negligible, Hak-Bin's mood remained intact, and the pilot gave thanks for his extraordinary run of luck.

None of the ships within the Sauron fleet had been designed by the aliens themselves. The shuttle was an excellent example. The Ra 'Na came from a water-dominated world and engineered their ships accordingly. That being the case, the Saurons were accustomed to landing on water, which was fine so long as it was available and reasonably calm.

The shuttle slowed, Hak-Bin waited for a Fon functionary to unlatch his safety harness, and clacked his tripartite pincers. "Mok! Where are you? Come here immediately!"

Mok, who knew better than to come without being summoned, seemed to materialize at the Sauron's side. Like most of her kind, she stood about four feet tall. She had a round head, a short muzzle, jet black eyes, and pointy ears. Short, blond-colored fur covered most of her body. Her hands, with webbing between each finger, were small and delicate.

Though not allowed to wear anything more elaborate than a simple uniformlike jerkin, Mok, along with many of her female friends, wore fancy underwear—an act of rebellion that the Zin was unaware of and would have regarded with lordly contempt. She kept her face carefully neutral. "Yes, master? What do you wish?"

"I wish to stand, and having done so, to leave the ship," Hak-Bin said crossly. "You will attend me to ensure that technical matters are taken care of."

"Yes, master," Mok replied evenly. "Will you require a translator?"

The humans were a voluble race, and clever beings that they were, the Ra 'Na had recorded countless variations of their mostly meaningless blather, analyzed the results, written the necessary programs, and downloaded the resulting software to thousands of wearable computers. The reply was nothing if not predictable. In spite of the fact that most of their claims to superiority were clearly specious, the Zin did have an unusual facility with spoken language, and had already mastered Haven's dominant linguistic system. "No," Hak-Bin snapped. "Such devices are intended for less capable beings such as the Kan, Fon, and Ra 'Na."

"Of course," Mok replied smoothly, knowing full well that the Sauron might well have been furious had she failed to offer him the device he didn't need. "I meant no offense."

The Zin clacked his pincers impatiently. "Here—help me up."

Hak-Bin was quite capable of standing unassisted, and both of them knew it. But by demanding such attentions, and receiving them, his position was continually reinforced.

Mok moved in, touched the release on the Zin's safety harness, and took the Sauron's chitin-covered arm. Hak-Bin levered himself to his feet. His long, oval-shaped head was crowned by three triangular plates that ran from front to back. As with all of his kind, the Sauron had large, light-gathering eyes; a wide, meat-eating mouth; and slits rather than external ears.

The rest of the Zin's body consisted of a pod-shaped torso balanced on two deceptively slender legs, which were ideal for jumping. But this means of locomotion was rendered impossible due to the way Ra 'Na ships were designed; so, that being the case, Hak-Bin was forced to engage in an awkward shuffling movement. A necessity that the Sauron and his peers not only resented, but found ways to punish the Ra 'Na for. Their insistence on heavily decorated sedan chairs as a means of ground transportation was an excellent example of this. But no chair was available, and Hak-Bin would have rejected it regardless. He felt like walking—and proceeded to do so. The lock was aft and to the right. A milk-white Fon waited to assist him.

Meanwhile, a few hundred yards away, Alexander Franklin, along with his wife, General Windgate, and Secretary Olmsworthy, stood at the south end of Lake Spanaway, a small body of water adjacent to McChord. It was cold, damned cold, and the overnight frost had only recently surrendered to the wintry sun.

There was a snack bar on the right, complete with a sign that advertised "Sundaes, Cones, Bars, Hamburgers, and Fries," plus a window placard that read "Open," except that it *wasn't* open, and never would be again.

A dock reached partway out into the lake from the left, as if eager to embrace returning boats, which were retrieved via the ramp sloping down into the dull gray water.

The humans watched in awe as the alien vessel came in for a landing. They had been summoned to the surface, met by more than fifty heavily armed alien troops, and transported to the lake. During the trip they learned there was a second set of XTs, smaller creatures who spoke via brooch-sized translators and seemed more than a little subservient.

The whole thing boggled the politician's mind. After all the conjecture, the religious debates, the scientific pondering, the unmanned probes, the books, the movies, and the TV programs, here they were, the life forms everyone had speculated about, hoped for, and in some cases feared. Correctly feared, as things turned out.

Water foamed away from the spaceship's bow as it touched down and coasted toward shore. Houses, still intact, could be seen on the far shore. They looked incredibly mundane with the alien space vessel plowing through the water in the foreground. It came to a stop about fifty yards from the beach, where it was met by a bargelike water craft that appeared to have been imported for that very occasion.

Intimidated by the presence of alien troops, the humans stood at something approaching attention as one of the XTs departed the confines of the ship, stepped onto the barge, and was transported to shore.

Jina noted that the newly arrived alien was insectoid. She was, or had been, a teacher, and that particular part of her persona was busy analyzing the aliens, or trying to, in hopes of deducing what sort of environment had given shape to them, and more importantly, how that might shape their psychology.

Windgate, his face a study in stony intransigence, ignored the alien dignitary and eyed the troops. Like most officers in his particular branch of the military, Windgate didn't know a whole lot about infantry tactics, but some things were obvious.

The XTs had roughly the same mass as a human male, appeared to be somewhat less flexible, but possessed built-in body armor. Tough enough to stop a bullet? He would have welcomed the opportunity to find out.

It was too early to render any judgments about their weaponry, but, assuming that their small arms were on a par with their ships, it could be quite powerful indeed.

Secretary Olmsworthy eyed the approaching barge with a feeling of deep apprehension. What, if anything, could he do? He had read books about statecraft, hundreds of them, but most had one thing in common: They were written by winners. *Human* winners. What about losers? What could they teach him? The dead were mute.

The hull grated on the concrete ramp and crunched to a halt. Rather than jump the intervening gap, as either a Fon or a Kan would almost certainly do, Hak-Bin chose to make use of the makeshift gangplank that a gang of energetic Ra 'Na hurried to put in place. Slow and deliberate—those were the hallmarks of good leadership.

Jina watched the alien's awkward slide-step motion, concluded that it was not the optimum way for the XT to get around, and wished she could see more of its physiology.

But that was impossible, due to the pleated black skirt that hung from the creature's waspish waist and swished around knobby knees. The rest of the alien's clothing consisted of a heavy necklace made of what looked like stainless steel mesh, leather straps that crisscrossed an otherwise bare chest, and a pouch-belt decorated with metal studs.

Of nearly equal interest were the alien's retainers—assuming that described the relationship. Two were of equal height and had an equivalent body mass. But their exoskeletons were light, almost white. The other alien's chitin ranged from black—the obvious leader—through various shades of brown. A smaller and apparently unrelated alien stood off to one side. Like the group that handled the gangplank, he, she, or it was a good deal less intimidating.

Jina wanted to comment on these matters but knew the timing was wrong. She looked at her husband, saw his pleasant but rather bland expression, and knew his mind was churning. More than that, looking for some way to adapt, to survive, because Franklin was a born politician, and a man for whom the doing of deals was more than a way to get things done. It was an art plus a pleasure in and of itself. Would the aliens negotiate? There had been little sign of that—but there must be some purpose for the meeting. That's what she hoped, anyway.

A crow cawed as Hak-Bin and his retainers made their way up the ramp. It was uncomfortably cold, but Hak-Bin had no intention of requesting additional clothing, as that would signal weakness.

Olmsworthy drew himself up and stepped forward. He didn't expect the alien to understand his words but hoped that raised palms would be interpreted as a sign of peace. "Hello, my name is Michael Olmsworthy, secretary of the United States Air Force."

Hak-Bin listened, made the necessary translation, and felt a rising sense of anger. He had prepared himself for a variety of possibilities, ranging from sullen resistance to fawning acceptance. This intentional insult was an unpleasant surprise. He turned to the nearest Kan officer, switched to the coarse dialect appropriate to that group, and issued an order: "Kill the one who spoke."

The Kan raised his t-gun and fired two rocket-propelled darts. The human staggered, backpedaled, and collapsed. Blood splashed the ramp and trickled down toward the lake. The soldier felt good. His brothers would be jealous.

Windgate made a strange, inarticulate noise and threw himself forward. A second Kan fired—three projectiles this time—and the general went down.

Jina made a sobbing sound and grabbed her husband's arm. Franklin, who fully expected to die, braced himself for the impact. Nothing happened.

"So," Hak-Bin said in his only slightly accented English, "your insult was wasted. Two perfectly good servants are dead—and you have nothing to show for it."

Franklin was stunned by the violence and the alien's facility with the English language. He looked left and right. Who was the XT talking to? That's when the politician understood the truth, realized that the alien was speaking to *him,* and more than that, waiting for a reply. But what to say? Something was happening here—something he had failed to grasp. Franklin performed a mental two-step and took a chance. It wasn't something he would be proud of, not later when he reviewed it, but it probably saved their lives. "I'm sorry. It was a foolish thing to do."

Mollified, and in need of a malleable human, Hak-Bin waved a pincer. "Your apology is accepted. We, too, have our pride."

Franklin, who couldn't think of anything to say, chose to remain silent. The alien seemed to expect as much and continued to speak. "It may interest you to know that we arrived in your solar system some twenty-five planetary rotations ago, and, rather than announce our presence, chose to observe your civilization instead. We monitored thousands of audio-video broadcasts, absorbed your major languages, mapped your technology, and drew some conclusions regarding your culture. You are a talkative species, much given to meaningless babble, and we are not. Please keep that in mind while I outline my proposal."

Franklin nodded mutely, wondered if he was trapped in some horrible nightmare, and fought the desire to say something meaningless.

"My name is Hak-Bin," the alien continued, "and I, along with my fellow Zin, rule the Sauron race. We attacked your planet for an extremely important reason. We are a nomadic people destined to roam the stars in search of a planet called Paradise. Our religion, a philosophic structure so highly evolved that you would never be able to comprehend it, requires that we construct what you might refer to as 'temples' along the path of our journey."

The last statement was an out-and-out lie, but the Zin had no intention of revealing that. "Labor will be required to build these temples," the Sauron continued, "which explains why some of your population will be allowed to live.

"However, in order to control the slaves and ensure maximum productivity, a native leader is required. Someone who understands the nature of the situation, has his people's best interests at heart, and has the requisite experience. You are what is referred to as a 'governor'. . . . Is that correct?"

"Well, yes," Franklin began, "but I don't understand how—"

"Of course you don't understand," Hak-Bin interrupted. "Inferior beings seldom do."

The alien directed a pincer at the smaller being who stood to one side. "The Ra 'Na have full access to the somewhat primitive computers in which your personal data are stored. They ran a search, and three thousand one hundred twelve names appeared. Many of the candidates are dead. You survived. Will you accept the position or not?"

Jina, who didn't like what she was hearing, squeezed her husband's arm. "Don't do it, Alex. . . . They plan to make you into a slavemaster, a puppet, someone they can manipulate."

The politician knew his wife was correct but couldn't help himself. Here was power, or the promise of it, plus an opportunity to make an important difference. Perhaps he could negotiate improvements, help those under him, and make things better. Besides, even if he refused, someone else was sure to agree. His voice was hoarse. "Yes, I accept."

Jina gave a gasp of surprise, the Sauron clacked his pincers, and the Fon turned toward the barge. "Excellent. We will locate suitable quarters for you and your mate. Training will be necessary. We will meet in orbit."

So saying, the Sauron turned his back and shuffled toward the water. He had boarded the barge, and was halfway to the shuttle, when six powerful explosions shook the ground. Waves crossed the lake. Smoke boiled up into the sky. McChord AFB ceased to exist.

THE COAST OF OREGON

The secretary-general had been a field worker once and still liked to "get out and about," as she referred to her trips to the world's current trouble spots. So, given the fact that her security detail went where she did, Manning had *seen* plenty of refugees. But he had never been one himself.

People joined or dropped out from time to time as the security chief found himself walking with a group of people all of whom moved at the same pace. Among them were an older couple who wore matching parkas and seemed way too cheerful. Both were extremely fit and seemed to take pleasure in walking younger people into the ground.

Slightly to the rear, trudging head down, was a middle-aged businessman. He tried his cell phone from time to time, frowned when it didn't work, and shook his head. He wore an overcoat, suit, tie, and tasseled loafers. They wouldn't last very long, and Manning gave thanks for his boots.

Ahead, and a little to the right, were a mother and her two children, all dressed in puffy coats. The older of the two, a boy of seven or eight, walked, while the younger, a girl of three or four, sat in a well-equipped stroller. Manning couldn't see the woman's face but guessed that she was pretty.

But there were others as well, predators who watched the

stream of humanity with hard, glittering eyes, sifting the flow for those who might have something worth stealing, or, as in the case of the young mother, might offer some recreation.

Manning, who was trained to scan his surroundings for signs of trouble, noticed them right away. A group of three men, all standing around the back end of a stalled pickup truck. They looked more like weekend football fans than people who feared for their lives. Perhaps that was because they didn't get it yet, and wouldn't until they were forced to do so, or ceased to exist.

Well aware that his pack could attract the wrong sort of attention, and hoping to avoid trouble, the security chief edged toward the other side of the highway.

The older couple made a similar move, and Manning waited for the others to do likewise. But much to his surprise, they didn't. The businessman, who seemed oblivious to the threat, walked right past them. The predators might have interfered, might have gone for the briefcase, but the young mother was there to distract them.

The girl started to cry, so the woman didn't immediately notice when the men sauntered out onto the two-lane highway and stood in her path. She saw them and turned to the left, but it was too late.

Their leader had long, stringy hair, two days' worth of dirty-blond beard, and a Colt .45. It was stuck into the top of his pants. He sneered. "Hey, baby, what's happening?"

The woman tried to go around, but Stringy Hair stepped in close, put a hand on the stroller, and said something Manning couldn't hear. Her hand made a cracking sound as it connected with the side of his unshaven face.

The security chief did a quick 360, realized that the flow of refugees had bent out toward the ocean, and that no one planned to help. He couldn't really blame them. The predators were armed and looked barroom mean.

Manning sighed. Here was the kind of trouble he really didn't need. But what choice was there? Stringy Hair delivered a blow to the woman's face, the boy tried to hit him, and the girl cried harder.

The security chief pulled the Smith & Wesson and held it down along the side of his right leg. He was no more than ten feet away when the threesome finally took notice.

The biggest, a beer belly with a 12-gauge duck gun, turned to deal with the interloper. "The bitch belongs to us—go find your own."

Manning had a healthy respect for scatterguns *and* men with beer bellies. Some are soft, and fold when you hit them, while others are rock hard. He shot the big man twice. Once in the chest and once in the head. Brains flew back and spattered the pickup.

The body was still in the process of falling when the security chief nailed the second backup in the throat and turned to Stringy Hair. His eyes were big, his mouth was open, and the .45 was stuck. The would-be rapist jerked on the handle, shot himself in the thigh, and collapsed like a sack of potatoes. He screamed as he went down. The pistol skittered away. Manning bent to retrieve it. Stringy Hair curled up into the fetal position, grabbed his bloodied leg, and muttered an obscene prayer—"O Jesus, motherfucking God, O Jesus, motherfucking God . . ."—over and over again.

One side of the woman's face had started to swell. The boy clung to her leg. Manning offered the .45 grip-first. She took it. He pointed. "The safety is there. . . . Squeeze to fire. Any questions?"

The woman shook her head. "No. Thank you."

Manning nodded. "You're welcome. That's one brave little boy you have there. His father would be proud."

The security chief remembered the other weapons and turned to find that they were gone. Scavengers had snapped them up. He shrugged, turned toward the north, and resumed his journey.

Stringy Hair was crying by then—begging for help. No one listened.

SALEM, OREGON

George Farley—*Staff* Sergeant Farley to those who had known him in the Rangers, and "Popcorn" to his friends—took advantage of his considerable knowledge of Salem, Oregon, pushed his '06 Ford pickup down a series of back roads, pulled a hard right-hand turn, passed under the cedar crosspiece that Deacon Smith and he had hung a little over two years before, and churned his way up the gravel drive. Linda would be mad, what with his speeding and all, but Deac would understand. Aliens had landed, and the whole world was in the shitter.

A well-kept two-story house appeared up at the end of the drive. It was gray with white trim, and looked normal except for the fact that the ten-year-old Suburban was missing, and Ralph,

Deac's one-eyed Lab, was nowhere to be seen. Of course, Deac could be down at the store, buying some last-minute supplies, or topping the four-by-four's dual tanks.

Farley killed the engine, opened the door, and jumped to the ground. Gravel crunched under his army-style combat boots. Had anyone been watching, they would have seen a middle-aged black man who walked with a slight limp, had the beginnings of a paunch, and wore a .44-caliber wheel gun in a custom holster. They might have underestimated Farley, might have written him off. And been very, very wrong. The ex-noncom paused in front of the house. "It's me, Linda! George Farley." Not mandatory, but not a bad idea—since Linda kept a 12-gauge by the front door.

But there was no reply, no sound of footsteps, and no rug-rats exploding around the corner of the house as they shouted his name and tackled his knees. What there was amounted to a single sheet of folded paper attached to a clip on the front door. Farley pulled the sheet loose and turned into the light. The words were typewritten.

Dear Friends,
Linda and I have gone to be with her parents in Ashland—
and we'll be back soon. May God bless and be with you.
                                        Deacon Smith

Farley gave a snort of derision, restored the paper to the clip, and ran his hand over the top of the door frame. Linda's parents were dead, they weren't from Ashland, and the whole thing was bullshit. Everything except the blessing. *That* was serious.

The key was where it had always been. It slid into the lock, turned the tumblers, and, when turned another full rotation, disarmed Deac's homemade burglar alarm—a system complete with its own standby battery in case the power failed, which it sure as hell had.

Farley entered the house, took note of the fact that it was neat as a pin, and conducted a lightning-fast tour. Looters, and they'd be along soon, would believe that the place was untouched, and, if asked, would testify to the fact. The ex-noncom knew differently.

The family photos were missing, *all* of them, as were all but two of Deac's guns, neither one of which would shoot worth a damn, plus the Ranger plaque, the one that General Mosho had awarded him, which bore words taken from paragraph three of the Ranger Creed: "Never shall I fail my comrades. I will always keep myself mentally alert, physically strong, and morally straight and I will shoulder more than my share of the task, whatever it may be . . . Deacon Smith . . . a Ranger through and through."

Also missing were the patchwork quilt Linda was so proud of, a sandalwood cross, and half the books in the living room.

Farley paused for a moment, put his hands on his hips, and shook his head. "I don't know where it is, you sneaky bastard— but I know it's out there. The place you never told anyone about, not even me, 'cause they can beat information out of anybody, and your family's on the line. Good for you, Deac, good for you. I've got my own little hidey-hole, but I reckon you know that, and I'm gonna climb in and button things up. *Vaya con Dios,* old buddy, and watch your six."

That being said, Farley hitched his gun belt up, locked the front door, and drove away. He and his wife were gone an hour later.

Elsewhere, all across the country, thousands of survivalists, nature freaks, cult members, diehard loners, and just plain wackos faded into the wild. Everyone else continued to die.

WEST OF LINCOLN CITY, OREGON

Manning was on Highway 18, headed east toward Portland, when he walked into the Sauron trap. He had traveled more than twenty-five miles during the past twenty-four hours, spent the night curled up in the back of a decrepit '03 Dodge van, and consumed the only food he had: a single Mars bar. It left him thirsty. He should have considered food, should have bought or stolen some, but it was too late. Every store he passed had been looted and completely cleaned out. Most of the convenience stores were easy pickings, since they belonged to huge conglomerates, and the employees ran rather than defend them. Others— mom-and-pop enterprises—showed signs of violence. The facades all looked the same. Smashed glass, bullet holes, and stupid graffiti.

The security chief forced himself to inspect a couple of stores, hoping for an overlooked candy bar or a can of Coke, but the only merchandise that remained were things like floor mops, racks of magazines, and rotting produce. That and some pitiful bodies.

Manning ignored the stores after that, telling himself that Portland was the goal, while trying to ignore the rumblings in his stomach. The security chief and roughly thirty others topped a hill and approached the intersection without knowing exactly where they were. The Hertz map, the only guidance Manning had, didn't show anything beyond major highways, towns, and landmarks.

The group of walkers had evolved by then. The older couple had continued north toward Tilamook, the businessman had last been seen trying to use a pay phone, and the woman with the two children had turned toward home.

New recruits had joined, however, and while different in many respects, all shared one common trait. They liked to walk fast, and that being the case, often overtook and passed slower "pods," a fact that led some of the more loquacious members of the group to adopt a group name.

Manning didn't care for that sort of thing but made no attempt to fight it, and was among the self-styled "Jets" when they topped a hill and approached an intersection. There were some tired-looking buildings, the still-smoking remains of a gas station, and a clutch of half-slagged tractor-trailer rigs.

There was no one in sight, not so much as a dog, and, if Manning had been a little less tired, he might have wondered why. But he didn't, which meant that he was as surprised as everyone else when a hundred Kan warriors shuffled out of the surrounding structures, ordered the humans to place their hands on their heads, and marched them up a graveled side road.

Manning considered the Smith & Wesson, knew it would be suicide, and did what he was told. He eyed the guards. They were heavily armed, which meant that a good deal of their bodies was covered by straps, pouches, and other gear. They looked like huge insects and walked upright. Their skins were brown, if "skin" was the right word, and it shifted to match the background. Not perfectly—but to a significant extent. That meant the surface of their bodies looked a lot like army camos, only animated, because the effect continued to change. Born soldiers then, evolved for war, and doing what they did best.

Still, seeing the aliens made them less frightening somehow. They looked tough, no doubt about that, but far from invincible, not to *his* eye, anyway, which offered a small ray of hope.

There wasn't much time for evaluation, however, as the humans were forced through a cattle gate and out into a field. Some equipment had been established near a metal water trough—and a group of small fur-covered aliens seemed to be in charge of it.

They looked nothing like the warriors and were clearly part of another species.

The aliens spoke via electronic translators, ordered the captives to remove all objects from their pockets, and pointed to a large pile of belongings. It stood head-high and served as mute testimony to the fact that a number of refugees had already been processed through the trap. Manning looked back over his shoulder and realized that trees screened the field from the highway. The next pod of hikers would have no way to know what had befallen the Jets. The town, if that's what it was, had been transformed into a simple but effective processing center.

Manning looked at the pile as he shrugged the pack off his back. He saw child carriers, purses, umbrellas, unicorns, a shovel, a camp stove, a crutch, and other items too numerous to identify. It reminded him of pictures he'd seen of the World War II Holocaust, and his spirits plummeted.

He had hoped—no, *assumed*—that a battle was being fought, that the human race had a chance, but here was what looked like irrefutable evidence to the contrary. To be *this* organized, *this* sure of themselves, the aliens had already won.

The others must have felt the same way. Dull eyes met his as they threw what few belongings they had onto the pile.

Manning contributed the pack, the handgun, the Hertz access device, his pocket change, and, after another moment's thought, his Buck pocketknife. The one his father had been carrying the day a heart attack brought him down. It was a hard decision but a good one.

Shortly thereafter the entire group was poked, prodded, and pushed toward a metal framework. A line formed, jerked its way forward, and paused when a beep sounded. One of the aliens grabbed a woman by the arm, jerked her out of the file, and passed her on. Another held the human, put a t-shaped weapon to her head, and blew her brains out. She crumpled to the ground.

None of the XTs showed the slightest bit of interest in finding out what had tripped the alarm. Had the female been so foolish as to retain a weapon? Or—and Manning judged this to be more likely—had she forgotten some keys? Or a PDA? Or a ballpoint pen? No one would ever know.

A pair of aliens, white—not camo-brown, like the soldiers—moved in to drag the corpse toward a prefab outbuilding. A path of bent blood-smeared grass led the way.

Manning stepped through the gate, felt a sense of relief when nothing happened, and felt something jab him in the side. A pincer? A weapon? It hardly mattered. He hurried to catch up.

The group was chivied across the field and down a slope. A sizable man-made drainage pond lay at the bottom. A shuttle, similar to the ones the security chief had seen earlier, floated on the dark gray surface.

Manning studied the ship, looking for clues that might tell him something about his captors, but didn't learn much. The hull metal was dark gray in color, nearly black, and looked worn.

The ship's design puzzled Manning. Why would what looked like land-based life forms build ships oriented to the water? Or could it land anywhere—and the pond had been a matter of convenience? Just one of many unanswered questions.

The humans tramped through a watering station, where they were allowed to scoop one and only one cup of reasonably clean water out of a metal trough before being herded toward the ship.

A metal ramp extended from the shuttle to the shore. It bounced as the humans made their way on board. It was warm inside, too warm from Manning's point of view, and rather strangely proportioned. Everything seemed just a little *too* small, including the hatches, which forced the aliens to stoop, and the more obvious fittings.

Metal paneling lined the interior of the ship. Each rectangle was embossed with hundreds of shapes and patterns, some of which reminded the ex-geologist of the fossils found in certain kinds of sediment, only different in shape.

The cargo compartment was relatively large. It was already half filled with frightened humans and the stink of their sweat, feces, and urine. There was an almost universal moan of misery as the newcomers were ushered in and as those who had been squatting, or in some cases lying on the metal deck, were forced to stand or be trampled.

Some effort had been made to use one particular corner of the space as a makeshift toilet. Manning edged away from that, found himself jammed against a gaunt-looking mail carrier, and heard the hatch slam shut. The lights went out a few seconds later.

The cargo compartment was full, so full that no one could do anything but stand, and there was no need for safety harnesses. Each and every human would serve as padding for the rest, and if he or she died, then so what? There were plenty more to call upon.

A voice issued from the darkness. "Welcome to Bug Air."
No one laughed.

PURDY, WASHINGTON

The Washington State Women's Correctional Facility near Purdy
hunkered low and gray. With the exception of the new four-story
maximum-security block constructed in 2014, and the bulbous
gray water tower, the rest of the buildings were only two or three
stories tall. A cyclone fence topped with razor wire circled the
perimeter. A fringe of trees sought to conceal the complex, but
no amount of green camouflage could disguise the fact that even
now, after decades of steadily declining crime rates, the human
race still produced individuals so amoral, so dangerous, that they
were best kept confined.

Marta Manning, a.k.a. "the bitch in cell 147," was only vaguely
aware of external events, but that wasn't the prison's fault—no,
not by a long shot. Not only was the inmate population allowed
to watch television, they were *encouraged* to do so, in the belief
that a steady diet of soaps and sitcoms would help keep the lid
on. But the news shows weren't very popular, not unless something relevant was on, which meant something about *them*. Maybe
that's why nobody took the alien stuff very seriously until it was
too late.

Marta was focused on something she considered to be a good
deal more important, and, if allowed to go unchallenged, might
disturb the hard-won status quo.

The inmate population had been segregated for a long time,
not as a result of policies put in place by prison administrators,
but by the prisoners themselves, who, led by the likes of Marta
Manning, had allowed themselves to be defined by the color of
their skin, divided into racially defined gangs, and set at each
other's throats.

The authorities disapproved, or said they did, although there
was very little doubt that the racial divides helped keep the overall
population weak, making their jobs that much easier.

That being the case, certain things were tolerated, including the
way that women of the same race clustered together during meals
or out in the yard. So it was obvious when someone crossed the
line.

The girl named Angie had arrived two days before, and for
reasons known only to herself, had chosen to associate herself
with Las Chicas. Something that *their* leader, a tough young

woman named Trena, had decided to tolerate as a way to pull Marta's chain. An obvious offense and one that had to be addressed. Not with the other gang leader, not right away, but with Angie, because for segregation to work everyone needs to know his or her place and stick to it.

Marta watched thoughtfully as the white girl took a tray, passed through the chow line, and made her way across the cafeteria. Las Chicas made room for her; Trena waved and laughed out loud.

Marta endured the insult, turned her attention to the food, and let the sisters talk. Most were spineless sluts who didn't actually believe in the cause, but a few were hard-core bad-to-the-bone female warriors who cared as much as she did. Women who understood that struggle is the price of survival, that competition is nature's way, that the end justifies the means. They knew that the white race had been chosen by God and that the nonwhites, also known as "mud people," or "muds," were the descendants of "pre-Adamite" races created by Satan. The true-blue believers ate in silence; the rest worked their jaws.

Lunch ended forty-five minutes later and, as the population was allowed to go out into the yard, a carefully conceived plan was put into play.

Angie had never been very good at picking friends. The boy who talked her into robbing the convenience store and the woman named Trena were only the latest examples of this flaw.

As the "fish" followed Las Chicas out into the cold, Angie was blissfully unaware of the movements around her until hands grabbed her arms, bodies closed around her, and she was frogmarched toward a corner of the exercise area. A poorly conceived overhead walkway built the year before had created a tiny blind spot, or "safety," where the inmates could have a few moments of privacy. The word "Femskin" had been painted on the wall, using the same type style favored by World War II Nazis.

The Hispanic women had disappeared, and Angie found herself surrounded by a wall of flinty-eyed white chicks. She tried to cry out, tried to call for help, but a fist slammed into her ribs. Words were transformed into inarticulate croak. Someone smelled of cheap perfume. Angie fought to breathe.

The "painters" were waiting. The feces, which had been donated by one of Marta's most trusted lieutenants and stored in a plastic bag, were brown in color, and though slightly more dense than Marta would have preferred, adequate for the task.

Two of the sisters held Angie's arms while two more, both equipped with disposable gloves stolen from the kitchen, went to work. Marta waited until the first gob of excrement had been smeared across Angie's mouth before stepping in close. Her voice was deceptively quiet. "So, bitch, you want to be brown? Well, you'll be *real* brown in about thirty seconds. Brown and smelly—just like the hos that hang with Trena. Is that what you want to be? One of Trena's hos? Or maybe you'd like to spend some time with your *own* kind? If so, join us for dinner tonight. The choice is yours."

Angie gagged on the smell, tried to keep her mouth closed, but was unable to do so. The recently consumed lunch came up and spewed outward.

Marta sidestepped and laughed. The rest of the group did likewise.

Angie, her face covered with feces and her chest splattered with vomit, was propelled out into the yard. The whole thing had taken less than a minute and a half.

Tears ran down Angie's face as she stumbled, regained her balance, and made for the patch of ground that Las Chicas referred to as *la casa*.

But rather than the sympathy she expected, the fish was treated with contempt instead. Like Marta, Trena's power flowed from the racial divide, and she saw no reason to give it up for some *gringa*. Besides, everyone knew the Femskins were not only crazy but dangerous as well. The Hispanic pointed, held her nose, and laughed.

Angie, totally friendless, and humiliated beyond belief, was trapped. Even she knew better than to go to the guards or to rat Marta out. She sensed that there were worse things than the "facials" and was determined to avoid them.

A full half hour elapsed before the inmates were allowed to leave the yard and Angie returned to her cell. A single glance in the mirror was sufficient to ascertain that her efforts to wipe the disgusting substance from her face had been futile. Patches of dried excrement still clung to her skin. She opened the tap on her small metal sink, grabbed a bar of soap, and scrubbed till her skin was raw. Then, clean at last, she collapsed on her bunk and wished she were dead.

The inmates might have spent more time discussing Angie's predicament, and taken bets on what she would do, but that was the afternoon when the external world managed to penetrate the prison's walls. They heard the dull thump, thump, thump as bombs hit Bremerton Naval Base, saw some of the last television feeds before the networks went off the air, and complained as raw, acrid smoke made its way into the prison's ventilation system.

Everybody had people on the outside, even Marta Manning, and was scared for them. Those with children had it worst, desperate to know if they were okay but with no means to find out.

The staff had similar concerns and, lacking the discipline expected of military personnel, started to desert their posts.

The warden, terrified of what might happen as her people melted away, instituted a full-scale lockdown, issued weapons to the guards who remained, and wondered what to do next. Her name was Martha Anne Farraday—*Miss* Farraday to the staff, and ma'am to the inmates. There were rules, plenty of them, regarding everything from prisoner hygiene to the color of paint on the walls, but none that covered this. Not only that, but the phones were dead, her Internet connection was down, and there was no way to pass the buck to Olympia. Passing the buck was something Miss Farraday was known for.

She accepted a note brought by one of the remaining guards and actually read it. The message was short—and brevity was a virtue. Some of the cons made a hobby out of writing long and largely meritless missives complaining about the way they were treated, requesting special privileges, or trying to earn the kind of suck points that would influence the Parole Board. This one was different. It read: "I can help," and it was signed by Marta Manning.

Farraday made a point out of knowing who the leaders were, out of keeping the gangs in some sort of balance, so she was well acquainted with the individual in question, knew about Angie's "facial," and approved of it. The prison was like a kettle of tea . . . the steam it produced needed a place to go. She controlled some of that steam, but so did Marta, Trena, and a couple more. Maybe, just maybe, the woman could help keep the lid on. Yes, Marta was dangerous, the fact that she had beaten a man to death attested to that, but so what? Farraday had dealt with hundreds of dangerous offenders over the years and always came out on top.

The warden sent a guard to get the inmate, turned the high-backed chair toward the window, and watched the world go up in smoke.

Marta offered Dedra and the rest of the blacks a one-fingered salute as the guard escorted her through the cell block. They shouted the usual insults, but their hearts weren't in it. Some shit was coming down, some *heavy* shit, and the white bitch was small potatoes.

Marta made note of the fact that at least half the staff appeared to be missing, followed the guard through a heavily secured door, and eyed his sidearm. He wore the weapon high and tight, the way street cops do, and tilted toward the front. His name was Marvin, Marvin Pesko, and he lived by himself. That's why he was still here, because there was no one to go home to, no one who cared.

I'll bet you practice in front of the mirror, Marta thought, and I'll bet you never lose. Every time that bad boy comes out of the holster, somebody has to die. Except that nobody has—and nobody will.

They entered the elevator, the doors closed, and Marta opened her blouse. Her breasts weren't especially large, but they were firm, and plenty good enough. Especially for mooks like Marvin.

The guard looked, realized his mistake, and was reaching for his weapon when Marta kicked him in the balls. Marvin grabbed the pain, left his head open, and paid the price.

Marta had been victimized by a long string of boyfriends till one of them introduced her to kickboxing and soon lived to regret it. She took to the sport like a duck to water, kicked his ass the first night she found him with someone else, and never took shit from a man again. Including the one she killed. Marta practiced in her cell and tried to stay in shape. She put Marvin down for good.

Farraday heard the knock and said "enter," but didn't turn. It was a trick, one of many she used to keep the upper hand, especially where mind-gaming inmates were concerned. Body language could be a tool and her position signaled superiority mixed with disdain. The warden heard the door close, gave the inmate a moment to cross the wooden floor, and swiveled around.

Marta waited for eye contact, brought the Glock out of hiding, and held it barrel up. She was tall for a woman, about five-nine, very lean. So lean that her brother called her "stringbean," or "SB" for short. Her hair was crew-cut short. She managed to look good in prison blues—like a model at a dude ranch. Her eyes were blue, *ice* blue, and disturbing somehow. They looked hard, unyielding, as if made of stone. The kind of stone on which the Kingdom of God would eventually be built. The rest of her face was attractive in a stiff, angular sort of way.

Farraday eyed the weapon. This was not the way she had planned to die. "So," she said, "your mind is made up? There's nothing I can say or do?"

Marta shook her head. "Nope, I don't think so."

"You won't get far, you know. The aliens kill anything that moves."

"Not *everything*," Marta answered calmly. "Not the things that are stronger and meaner than they are."

"And that's you?" the warden asked skeptically, her hand drifting toward the .32 clipped to the underside of her desk.

The Glock jumped twice, the noise bounced off paneled walls, and casings tinkled to the floor. Farraday jerked, looked surprised, and slid to the floor. "No," Marta said with an air of certainty, "that's *Yahweh*."

It took little more than a minute to find the .32, shove it down the back of her jeans, and grab the warden's plain black purse. The inmate took the administrator's key card, some money that was already worthless, and a remote with the name "Honda" embossed on it.

Marta thought about releasing some of the others, her lieutenants if no one else, but decided not to. Once free, they would want to hook up with their families, do some drugs, and generally waste time. No, it didn't make sense. The only things she would take with her would be the pictures of her mother and her brother plus the stuff she had stolen. Everything else could stay.

Marta draped Farraday's jacket over the Glock, marched down the hall, and left through the staff entrance. Even more of the guards had deserted by then, and she could hear the inmates yelling. No one tried to stop her. Cold air hit her face, the smoke made her cough, and something went "boom" in the distance. Rows of mature trees marched across the parking lot, their recently fallen leaves crunching underfoot.

There were at least three Hondas in the lot. The remote started the second. She got in, released the brake, and pulled out of the lot. The motor, which was electric, made a soft, whining sound. Was it evening? She wasn't sure. Marta turned the lights on and headed for the highway. It felt good to be free.

HOWARD UNIVERSITY, WASHINGTON, D.C.
The attack was only hours old, and most of the television networks were still on the air when Professor Boyer Blue returned

to his office, laid his lecture materials on an already cluttered wooden desk, and searched for the remote. It was hidden beneath the copy-edited manuscript for his latest book: *White, Yellow, Black, and Brown: A Study in the Symbology of Race*. It was due back to the publisher in three days—which meant he'd have to work all weekend.

The following moment, the one in which he lifted the remote and pressed the power button, would remain burned into his memory for the rest of his life.

Later he would wonder how such a thing was possible, how God could be so cruel, until finally, shivering under the remains of a freeway overpass, he would realize the truth: Horrible though the image was, he *knew* the fate of his wife and child, while thousands did not. There was a blessing in that—and a strange sort of emotional freedom. Death mattered no more.

The old outdated HDTV screen popped to life, and the shot showed a beautiful African-American woman with a child at her side. Not just any woman, but *his* woman, and not just any child, but *his* daughter.

Loretta looked poised, as she always did, like royalty, or the way royalty should look, calm, confident, and almost impossibly serene. Especially given the smoke that rose in the background, the people who ran every which way, and the persistent sound of sirens.

Snowflakes, only a few, drifted, as if exempt from the law of gravity. The school, his *daughter's* school, was in the process of being evacuated. That meant they were a good twenty-five miles away—a reality he had only begun to consider. His wife was in midparagraph: ". . . So it makes sense to send the children home, though I'm worried about—"

Loretta never finished her sentence. There was a flash of light, the 150-year-old school seemed to leap off its foundation, and the picture snapped to black. It stayed that way until a shaken anchorwoman appeared, mumbled something about having lost the feed, and started to cry.

Blue cried, too, big, wet tears like he hadn't cried in years. Tears for himself, for his family, for the entire human race.

Later, when he found himself huddled under the overpass, the historian couldn't remember leaving the office, or walking in the vague direction of home. He had learned some things, however . . . things he should have known all along.

First was the fact that "home" wasn't so much a place as a set of relationships, now snatched away.

Second was the fact that life is fleeting—here one moment and gone the next.

Third was that deep down in his hypothalamus, the marrow of his bones, or the twisted pairings of his DNA dwelled the very thing he had studied for so long. The thing that defined who he was. *Man.* *Black* man. African-*American* man. An African-American *hu-man.* And they, the things that killed his family, were the *other.* The *other* group, the *other* tribe, the *other* race, the *other* color, the *other* religion, the *other* team, the *other* by which Blue and people like him would now come to define themselves.

A scholar named Vamik Volkan had written about the phenomenon, about the way in which people ignore their breathing until they contract pneumonia and start to notice each breath, and how people don't concern themselves about group identity until it is threatened. And now, as the world caved in around him, Blue's identity seemed very important indeed.

What did it mean? It meant that in spite of all his training, all the civilized notions he believed in, the academic wanted something so primal, so base, that his great-great-great-grandfather would have understood it. He wanted revenge.

NEAR THE COAST OF OREGON

The Sauron shuttle lifted off the surface of the man-made lake more by means of brute strength than by whatever lift the stubby wings were able to generate. Once aloft, the alien aircraft started to climb.

The humans, packed cheek to jowl in the shuttle's cargo compartment, felt the additional gs, heard their ears pop, but were powerless to move. Manning was reminded of Styrofoam pellets. Only these pellets were made of flesh and blood.

Making an already uncomfortable situation worse was the fact that most if not all of the humans were from North America, a place where people value "personal space" and go to considerable lengths to establish and maintain it.

The security chief, who had spent time in other cultures, understood the problem but discovered that understanding didn't make much difference. Soft, warm flesh pressed in from all sides and threatened to engulf him. That, combined with total darkness, was extremely claustrophobic, and Manning fought to maintain his composure.

Manning remembered his watch and how the woman had died over something equally mundane. He'd been lucky. He realized how ironic the thought was and suppressed a chuckle.

It was difficult to drag his arms up in front of his face, but the security chief managed to do so. He touched a button, saw the circle of light appear, and felt better somehow. Others weren't so easily comforted.

Voices came out of the darkness, crying, pleading, desperate for relief. They were tolerated at first, but each voice seemed to trigger another, until those with more control started to assert themselves. They lashed out verbally, instructing the voices to "shut the hell up," and, when that failed to elicit the desired result, inflicted punishment via their knees and elbows.

The "voices" complained, tried to move away, and, like a bowl of gelatin, sent shock waves rolling from one side of the compartment to the other.

That resulted in reprisals both against the voices and the largely innocent "transmitters" who tried to defend themselves.

Finally, after what Manning estimated to be ten or fifteen minutes of such activity, it finally wound down. The voices were reduced to an occasional sob, the enforcers let up, and peace reigned. Conversations had a tendency to die, somebody muttered the Lord's Prayer, and another person started to snore.

Now, with nothing beyond his own thoughts to occupy his time and energy, Manning thought about Marta, felt the usual sense of guilt, and realized that he'd been wrong. She *wasn't* safe. Not in prison—not outside. None of his attempts to protect to her, to guide her, had made any difference. Something, he wasn't sure what, had gone terribly wrong during the years after their mother's death. Years during which their father would trudge off to work, put in his eight hours, and trudge back home. His was a life of duty, of doing what "Mary would want me to do," but empty of joy.

Marta, who had been a rambunctious little girl prior to her mother's death, had started to wilt, to fade, until the smiles disappeared.

At some point she turned to boys, and when they failed to deliver what she was looking for, to groups of people. Scumbags for the most part—who tried to transform their largely meaningless lives by hating others. Self-proclaimed soldiers of God who dreamed of a Christian nation free of mosques and synagogues, and a culture based on Aryan values.

And it was there, in the context of hatred, that his little sister found the support she'd been looking for. A fact that came back to haunt Manning after he and his team were accused of racism after someone named him "The Butcher of Pretoria," and his picture appeared on the World Wide Web, plastered right next to one of his sister dressed in full Nazi regalia.

That had been it, the end of the end, and he still couldn't hate her. Only his father, for giving up, and himself for doing the same.

The transition to weightlessness came with very little warning. There was a good four feet of space between their heads and the ceiling—or what navy personnel would refer to as the "overhead." It wasn't long before some of the captives were squirted upward, and swore as they hit their heads on bare metal. It was natural to flail about. Boots connected with faces, victims sought revenge, and chaos prevailed. The security chief entertained the notion of trying to restore order, but only briefly, because although he saw himself as something of a leader, he had no talent for *that* kind of leadership, the kind that volunteered itself.

Not everyone felt that way, however, which was good not only for the prisoners, but for humanity in general. A deep bass boomed through the compartment. It was loud enough to be heard over everything else. The syntax had a military ring. "All right, people—that'll be enough of that. Those of you who wound up as floaters need to control your movements. Go horizontal, gently now, and stay that way. Use the overhead to orient yourselves. Everyone else—as you were. You'll have increased elbow room, so go ahead and enjoy it. Keep one thing in mind, however: The chits could activate some sort of artificial gravity system, or put us back on Earth. The floaters will fall either way. We need to be ready for that, so pay attention. The moment you feel gravity, reach up, grab some ankles, and pull 'em down. It's that or a broken head."

Everything the man said made perfect sense. Manning was grateful to the unseen pragmatist—and so, for the most part, was everyone else. Only one voice suggested that the pragmatist could "shove it," but the owner took a well-aimed elbow in the ribs from the person to his right.

There was one thing the levelheaded advice *couldn't* protect them from, however, and that was the fact that a significant amount of the previously static waste materials were suddenly airborne, and, thanks to the fact that at least 20 percent of the prisoners were spacesick, a fog of vomitus misted the air. Manning choked on the taste, fought the nausea that threatened to overwhelm him, and momentarily wished he were dead.

That was the moment when his inner ear signaled some sort of change, the shuttle slowed, and gravity started to return. "Now!" the pragmatist boomed. "Reach up, find some ankles, and pull them down. Quickly, before they fall on our heads!"

The security chief did as directed, located a pair of feet, and worked his way back to a pair of thick ankles. The next step proved more difficult, however, since there was nothing beyond the friction of the bodies around Manning to anchor him in place, and each attempt to pull the floater down served to lift him *up*.

A dramatic increase in gravity served to resolve the matter, however, and the "standers" were soon struggling to reintegrate the "floaters" into their midst, a task only barely accomplished when the shuttle touched down. It hit with a thump that was felt throughout the ship's hull. Were they back on the surface? And if so, where? There was no way to know.

A full fifteen minutes passed before an exterior hatch finally opened and light flooded in along with a blast of cold, ozone-tinged atmosphere. The humans just stood there, blinking into the glare of the cargo lights, until the alien warriors began to shout. Their translators doubled as amplifiers, and the words punched through the hard, cold air. "Out! Out! Out!"

Metal clanged, hydraulics whined somewhere nearby, and the prisoners shuffled down a ramp. It shivered under their weight. They weren't on Earth, that was for sure, which suggested artificial gravity.

Manning saw his own breath, eyed his companions, and knew he looked as they did. Most had matted hair, filthy skin, and dirty clothes.

The environment was of even greater interest, however, and like most of those around him, the security chief turned his attention to the inside of the alien spaceship. The first thing that struck him was how large the vessel's interior was. The hangar deck, if that's what it could properly be called, was easily the size of Seattle's Safeco Field. A steel deck stretched in every direction. Shuttles crouched at thirty-yard intervals, and carts whined in every direction. He could see other groups of humans in the distance. One such group appeared to be Asian. And that suggested the alien attack had been a worldwide effort.

Manning allowed his eyes to drift upward. What looked like

galleries rose on three sides and were served by a fleet of small
sledlike vehicles, some of which carried the insectoid aliens, although most were piloted by the small fur-covered XTs the human had noticed earlier.

The fourth bulkhead was dominated by a huge blue disk, or
what *appeared* to be a disk, that rotated in a counterclockwise
manner.

The security chief scanned the area around him. The overall
impression he received was one of calm, well-organized activity—
an observation that did nothing to make him feel any better.

Suddenly there was a loud "pop," which the aliens ignored and
the humans responded to. Manning looked in the direction of the
noise just in time to see the blue disk complete its transformation
to light turquoise. A shuttle nosed through the very center of the
steadily rotating pinwheel, circled the blast-scarred deck, and settled in for a landing. Another "pop," and the disk turned dark
blue again.

Manning was a geologist by training, but it didn't require a
degree in physics to realize that the blue disk represented some
sort of force field, which functioned as a semipermeable lock—a
level of technological sophistication far in advance of anything
humans had achieved. If the security chief had been depressed
before, he was even more so now.

But there were even more immediate concerns to be dealt with,
such as staying alive, which Manning was determined to do. He
looked over the shoulder in front of him and realized that the line
had started to split. It didn't make any sense until he realized that
people with darker skin were being separated out.

The security chief's first reaction was to feel a sense of concern
for them, until he saw the table full of refreshments, and realized
that his sympathies were misplaced. Or were they? Manning
looked again, confirmed the fact that no such accommodation
awaited people such as himself, and wondered why.

Four of the small fur-covered aliens trotted by. They carried
an elaborately carved sedan chair occupied by one of the insectoid
aliens.

"Hey," one man said, waving his arms. "What about *us*? We'd
like some water, too."

"Yeah," a woman agreed stoutly. "It isn't fair!"

One of the warrior aliens took exception to the unauthorized
verbalization and laid a shock baton along the side of the

woman's head. She dropped like a rock. The complaining stopped as suddenly as it had begun.

The security chief saw a man dressed in a badly soiled army uniform, noticed the sergeant's stripes on his sleeves, and pegged the noncom as the voice from the darkness. A no-nonsense type who might make an effective ally. There wasn't anything he could do about the idea, not right then, but Manning made a note to follow up if the opportunity came.

With no refreshments to slow it down, the line he was in moved more quickly than the other lines did. Nothing was said—that level of hostility would come later—but some very nasty looks were directed toward those who had benefited from the alien favoritism. Never mind the fact that at least a third of the darker-skinned humans refused to partake in the refreshments on principle—and never mind the fact that many of the others would have accepted such favoritism had it been offered to them. A wedge had been driven, and North American society, or what was left of it, started to split.

The line jerked forward. One by one the humans stepped up to a long metal table. It was laden with what looked like a jumble of electronic equipment and staffed by four of the small fur-covered aliens. The security chief wondered who they were. Slaves? Or willing participants? Dominated by the bugs but feeding off their conquests? There was no way to know.

The man in front of Manning exchanged words with one of the diminutive aliens and stepped out of the way. Manning moved forward. The table, which had been designed to meet the needs of those who were using it, hit him above the knees. The voice had a hard, mechanical edge to it. The request took the human by surprise. "Social Security number, please."

Manning looked at the equipment arrayed in front of him, realized that some of it was human, and gave the appropriate response. There was little point in doing otherwise.

The technician's name was Da Dwa—and he hated the job to which he had been assigned. Processing sentient beings into slavery—what could be worse? And yet, shameful though the procedure was, the Ra 'Na couldn't help but feel proud. After all, who but *his* people had the technical expertise necessary to marry modern cutting-edge computers with the unsophisticated junk manufactured by the natives? Nobody, that's who, not that the Saurons showed the least bit of appreciation.

Da Dwa entered the number verbally and touched one of the

twenty-eight digit-sized depressions that lined the keyboard in front of him. The data display shivered and changed. A picture of the human appeared. It was the same one associated with his chipcard-encoded passport, his U.N. ID badge, and his international driver's license. Biographical information pulled straight out of the United Nations' highly secured computer system flooded the Dell XX-3D Holotank. The translation was a little ragged in places, especially where acronyms, abbreviations, and U.N.–specific jargon were concerned, but the essence was clear enough. Dwa looked almost straight up. "You were trained as a geologist?"

Manning felt completely helpless. The bastards had his personnel file! Or his résumé, or his school records, or a credit report. Not that it made much difference. "Yeah, I have a master's in geology."

Dwa felt sorry for the human—but not as sorry as he felt for those who lacked relevant skills. They were being ejected from the ship's locks in groups of fifteen. The Saurons saw no reason to expend the time or the energy necessary to return surplus humans to the surface. Not when there were plenty of natives running around loose.

The Ra 'Na turned toward one of the omnipresent Kan. On any matter that was technical in nature, or required the ability to read and write, the slaves had the upper hand. The words were in Sauron. "Send him to the mines."

Manning was shoved in the direction of a twenty-person cluster. All of them were Caucasian. The same noncom he had noticed earlier stood at the periphery of the crowd. The security chief drifted in that direction. The soldier wore a name tag that read: "Vilo Kell." He was handsome in a rugged sort of way, with a blond crew cut, blue eyes, and square jaw. "So," Manning said by way of an opener, "nice job aboard the shuttle. We were in need of some organization."

The noncom looked surprised. "Thanks, but the credit belongs to someone else. I had *you* pegged as the man in the dark."

Both men laughed. It seemed natural to shake hands and introduce themselves. The soldier explained that he was a member of the 2nd Battalion (Ranger), which had originally been activated at Fort Lewis, Washington, back in 1974 and was still there. He'd been in Oregon for a conference and walked into the same trap that Manning had only six hours earlier. "So," Kell finished, "what do you make of the whole table thing?"

"Some sort of sorting process would be my guess," Manning responded, scanning the people around them. "What does this group have in common, anyway?"

"They're young, meaning less than fifty years old, and mostly male. Everybody's in reasonably good shape."

Manning nodded. "Right on every count, but I've got a hunch that there's something more, a factor we can't see."

Kell shrugged. "You're probably right, but it beats the heck out of me."

The conversation ended as an alien barked a series of orders. The group formed a line and marched toward a distant corner of the deck. The security chief sensed motion off to the right and turned to look.

A brown bug had taken up a position next to the humans and carried one of the smaller aliens on his back. The well-designed saddle appeared as though it were well made and suggested that such rides were fairly common, a conclusion that raised even more questions regarding the nature of the relationship between the species. The little furry guys carried *black* aliens—but the brown bugs carried *them*. The whole thing was screwy.

The rider looked a lot like the individual who had asked Manning for his Social Security number. For some reason, he wasn't sure why, the security chief felt a connection with the alien. He took a chance. "Hello there—what can you tell me about where we're headed?"

Dwa considered the question and decided that there would be no harm in answering it. He liked looking down on someone for a change. "This group will be transported to an orbital asteroid, where they will work in the mines."

An asteroid! Holy shit. There had long been talk about such things, but no one had actually accomplished it. The geology thing suddenly made sense. The bugs wanted knowledgeable miners. If given a chance to interview them, the security chief would find that he was shoulder to shoulder with a bunch of mining engineers, equipment operators, and other experts. "So," Manning said, searching for the bright side, "how long before we come back?"

Had Manning been better acquainted with Ra 'Na facial expressions he would have recognized the ears-forward position for what it was: an expression of surprise. "Back?" the technician asked rhetorically. "None of you will come back." So saying, the alien urged his mount forward and made for the head of the line.

Kell, who had monitored the interchange, looked back over his shoulder. "Way to go . . . you really know how to lift a guy's spirits."

"No problem," Manning replied. "It was the least I could do. By the way—I was a geologist once. What do the bugs want with you?"

"I'm not sure," the Ranger replied soberly, "but it might have something to do with things that go boom."

"You're a demolitions expert?"

"Yup. When I'm sober."

"So you could help me blow myself up?"

"I'm your man."

"Thanks."

"Think nothing of it."

SEATTLE, WASHINGTON

The fancifully named Neptune Hotel and Entertainment Complex sat at the end of a man-made peninsula a full half mile out into Seattle's Elliott Bay. Controversial from its inception, the project had been built by a consortium of international hoteliers on fill generated by the 6.3 quake of '09.

Though devastated by the considerable loss of life, and more than five billion dollars' worth of property damage, Seattle's citizens had been determined not only to rebuild, but also to make the Emerald City bigger and better than before.

The Neptune Project had taken a negative—the collapse of the elevated highway that ran along the east side of Elliott Bay—and turned it into a positive: sufficient fill to construct an artificial island and connecting causeway.

Though it had been completed long before he had taken office, Alexander Franklin was quite familiar with the complex. In addition to having attended countless political functions there, he and his administration had inherited two lawsuits filed by enraged environmentalists. Not that their efforts had much relevance anymore.

The Sauron shuttle circled the bay, providing the politician and his wife with an only partially obstructed view of their new home. Significant parts of the city were still on fire—but the prevailing winds blew most of the smoke toward the east. The hotel, which a reporter for the *Seattle Times* had described as "a cross between a wedding cake and a Moorish fortress," rose in tiers, each succeeding layer smaller than the one below. It was white, and judging from above, largely untouched. Whether that was by chance or design there was no way to know.

"It's grotesque," Jina whispered, "and people will hate us for living there. Especially when they have so little."

Franklin shared his wife's concern, even going so far as to wonder if Hak-Bin *wanted* the population to hate him, but with characteristic optimism, saw the issue as a challenge rather than an insurmountable barrier. He patted her arm. "It's not as if we were given any choice, babe. Let's see if we can open the hotel to injured children or something. That would take the edge off."

Though more than a little cynical, the comment did represent an attempt to take her concerns into account, and Jina decided to accept the peace offering. More than that, to take her husband at his word—and the sooner the better. The shuttle touched down, threw a bow wave, and coasted toward the three-hundred-slip marina.

Elsewhere, many miles above, a Zin master sat in a thronelike chair and examined the image that rotated in front of him. The text, which only he and his peers were able to read, amounted to a biological calendar, a blueprint for the coming months, and an outline of what he was expected to accomplish—*would* accomplish, no matter the price. Not that he was worried. Things had gone well, very well, and there was reason to be pleased. The planet Haven was ready—and the *real* work could now begin.

2

DEATH DAY MINUS 151

TUESDAY, MARCH 3, 2020

> Divisions among large groups, whether they were called tribes or ethnic groups, were encouraged and kept alive by the colonial powers, who also impressed on the masses the idea that their chiefs were effective leaders—as long as they administered to their people to the satisfaction of the colonial masters. This encouragement of distinction and division among groups, and the creation of a dichotomy between the tribes whom the colonial powers considered "backward" and those they judged "advanced," was essentially an effort to divide and conquer. . . .
> —VAMIK VOLKAN,
> *Bloodlines: From Ethnic Pride to Ethnic Terrorism,* 1997

SEATTLE, WASHINGTON

Thanks to more than twenty-four hours of steady Seattle rainfall, most of the city's fires had been extinguished, and, thanks to an equally persistent wind from the southwest, both the smoke and the clouds had been pushed off toward the east. The sun rose over the Cascade Range, threw early rays of orange-pink light across Elliott Bay, and signaled a brand-new day.

Franklin, clad only in his underwear and one of the hotel's white terry-cloth robes, slipped out onto the balcony. It was chilly, and he shoved his hands into deep patch-type pockets. The smell of salt water, tinged with smoke, filled his nostrils.

The room, which was considerably smaller than the Presidential Suite they had been offered, was a concession on his wife's part, since Jina felt they should refuse any accommodations whatsoever.

Franklin understood her point, but would have accepted more generous quarters had the decision been left up to him.

Still, the veranda was nice, if cold and windy. The breeze whipped the robe around his legs, sent formations of whitecaps racing across the bay, and allowed the seagulls to float suspended over the water. For one brief moment Franklin felt elated, high on the oxygen that flooded his lungs, and the optimism that was integral to his nature.

It wasn't till the politician turned toward the east, and gazed at the half-slagged ruins of the state's largest city, that reality reasserted itself. He could see no movement, no signs of life, beyond the unusual number of crows. They rose in groups of thirty or forty, circled booty beyond his line of sight, and settled again. There were bodies—thousands of them—rotting in the ruins.

How could he forget? Even for a moment? Jina didn't. A smile rarely touched her lips anymore, and she couldn't stop crying. Crying for relatives, crying for friends, crying for people she didn't even know.

That's how Franklin would feel *if* he really cared. The politician felt guilty because he couldn't hold on to the sorrow the way Jina could. Plans got in the way. Stupid plans, mediocre plans, and good plans all mushed together. Franklin wanted to *do* something, wanted to find ways to improve the situation, wanted to help people in some palpable way. But to *do* that, to really make a difference, would require some degree of accommodation. Not a pleasant prospect—but that's how things were. The Saurons were real—which meant you could deal with them or die.

As if summoned by the human's thoughts, an alien shuttle appeared from the north. It flew low and slow over what remained of Seattle Center and south along the waterfront. What looked like a flurry of late snow fell from the aircraft's belly, was gathered up by the wind, and scattered far and wide. The Saurons were dropping leaflets. *Thousands* of leaflets.

The ship passed over the man-made island two minutes later. Curious as to what the leaflets might say, Franklin shaded his eyes, watched a likely-looking cluster slip in his direction, and managed to grab one before it fell to the rocks below.

At first glance the politician thought the paper was blank. Half a second later, the heat-activated image appeared, and Franklin was looking at a full-color image of himself. It started to speak. The voice was perfect if a little thin. "Greetings, fellow citizens.

My name is Alexander Franklin, governor of Washington State, and head of the provisional government.

"As you know, a race of beings known as the Saurons have taken control of our planet. The purpose of their invasion is to construct what we might think of as temples along the route of a long galaxy-spanning pilgrimage. Labor will be required to build these structures—which means that we have an opportunity to speed our own recovery."

The image shrugged matter-of-factly. "Like it or not, the simple fact is that the sooner the temples are built, the sooner the Saurons will leave. That being the case, I urge you to volunteer your help. Those who do will be fed, housed, and allowed some degree of personal freedom. Those who ignore the common cause, or attempt to hinder construction, will suffer punitive measures.

"So," the electronic Franklin concluded, "which would you prefer? Life in the ruins? Or an opportunity to better yourself—and the rest of humanity as well? I chose the latter course—and hope you will, too."

The visual faded to white, and words appeared. "Bring this document to any Sauron-sponsored processing center and receive six cans of Spam."

A minute passed while Franklin stood transfixed by what the aliens had done to him. In one stroke the Saurons had transformed him into a spokesperson and collaborator. It meant he had three choices—cooperate, wait for someone to kill him, or kill himself.

Shaken, and more frightened than he'd ever been before, the politician reentered the hotel suite and closed the door. His first impulse was to go to Jina, to tell her what they had done to him, but she was asleep. The sheet had slipped down to expose soft brown skin. One arm was outstretched, as if reaching for him, or pushing something away. He knew what his wife would say, or *wouldn't* say, since she never said "I told you so." Not to him, anyway. Not in more than ten years of marriage. Franklin fell into an easy chair, threw a leg over one arm, and watched Jina breathe. It was the most beautiful thing in the world.

EARTH ORBIT

The dreadnought was 4,492 feet long; 1,028 feet wide; incorporated more than 12,000 compartments; possessed a flight deck large enough to park, launch, and recover up to 95 smaller vessels; and carried a combined complement of 20,800 Saurons and Ra

'Na. It was called *Hok Nor Ah,* or *Pride of the People,* and functioned as the heart of the Sauron fleet.

Sunlight played across the surface of the space-black hull as it rotated around a hollow axis. Unlike hundreds of lesser craft that hurried to and fro, the *Hok Nor Ah* and her sister ships would never land on lake or ocean. They were far too big and heavy to cope with most planetary atmospheres.

Deep within, protected by heavy curtains, a Sauron was carried down a gleaming corridor. Yes, Hak-Bin thought as the sedan chair swayed from side to side, our power is great. Will *always* be great—so long as we take the necessary precautions. That's what I must tell them . . . that's what I must emphasize.

Any sort of delay would be intolerable—which was why the Ra 'Na in charge of Hak-Bin's transportation sent a runner ahead. The youngster glanced back over his shoulder to ensure proper spacing between the conveyance and himself, paused at an intersection, shouted at the top of his lungs, "Chair! Chair coming through!" and continued on his way.

What occurred next stemmed from long-established tradition. Carts swerved toward bulkheads, pedestrians scurried to get out of the way, and a corridor was formed. The bearers, four sturdy males, puffed as they passed down the center. Everyone stared—but the curtains remained closed.

The bearers were tired, *very* tired, and starting to slow. They were close, however—and took comfort from that knowledge. A hatch hissed open, the chair passed through, and Hak-Bin was delivered to a small compartment. It was there, within the privacy of the smaller room, that the Zin would make his final preparations.

Once inside, the chair was lowered to the deck, and the slaves were ordered to leave. It was then and only then that Hak-Bin eased his way out of the conveyance, shuffled toward a waiting chair, and pushed his torso into the docklike slot. Sensors were activated, and the richly decorated piece of furniture came to electronic life. Others had occupied the position before him. Hak-Bin could feel their power, *his* power, and savored the moment.

Meanwhile, beyond the partition that separated the Zin from the meeting space, preparations were well under way. The chamber, originally designed to accommodate up to a hundred Ra 'Na, had long since been retrofitted for use by the Council of Clans. So, given the fact that there were thirty-three clans or "lines," there also were thirty-three U-shaped chairs or cradles designed with Sauron anatomy in mind. Not by *them,* since the warrior race had no tradition of furniture-building, but by the Ra 'Na, who sought to please.

One member of that race, a rather elderly individual by the name of Na Nas, had been in charge of the compartment for more than seventeen shipboard years. It was an easy job, what amounted to a sinecure, for which the oldster was grateful. The problem was that his left leg, which had been injured years before, kept him from performing other, more highly regarded activities. Something that had bothered him at first, but not for a long, long time.

The attendant hummed while he worked. The deep thrumming sound, which comprised an important part of the Ra 'Na musical tradition, was similar to a cat's purr. The requirements for the gatherings were always the same: Check the chairs for alignment, ensure that the refreshments were close to pincer, test the sound system, monitor the temperature, and see to security. An important responsibility given the highly confidential nature of the governance meetings.

With the single exception of Nas, no one except the Zin themselves knew what transpired during the meetings, and neither party was likely to talk. The Saurons because they didn't want to—and the Ra 'Na because he was afraid to. He *could* have told stories, however, some real whoppers, and the knowledge felt good.

In the meantime, almost directly over the elderly slave's head, another Ra 'Na settled in for what promised to be a rather entertaining lunch. His name was Pas Pol. *Fra* Pas Pol, since he was an initiate, if a somewhat wayward one.

The space over the chamber was too small for a Sauron to enter, and had been left there "to facilitate maintenance," which was the phrase the Ra 'Na routinely used to justify what amounted to a complex system of secondary passageways, corridors, and tunnels reserved for their exclusive use.

Some of the undocumented "maintenance ways" functioned like public thoroughfares, while others, the gallery over the Sauron meeting room serving as a case in point, were off-limits to anyone not on official business.

Not that such restrictions were likely to deter an individual whose personnel file occupied a lot more memory than it should have, who had recently been disciplined for "willful disregard of the order's rules, guidelines, and traditions," not to mention "the unauthorized removal of stored equipment," and ". . . an unseemly focus on issues beyond the scope of his duties and responsibilities."

The fact that Pol had visited the space before was evidenced by the equipment he had cobbled together and a sizable pile of trash. Food containers for the most part, which the initiate intended to carry off, but never got around to. Foolish really, since the entire fleet was infested by some rather nasty vermin, all of which were attracted to unprocessed waste. But, with so many things to do, Pol never found the time.

The eavesdropping equipment was set up on a table "borrowed" from Logistics, the chair had been "salvaged" from Engineering, and the lunch had been "liberated" from the Droma's private larder. A rather sizable locker stuffed with seafood had been harvested from the planet below.

Not the inbred tank-raised organisms which the Ra 'Na ate day to day, but *wild* protein reminiscent of the species native to the Ra 'Na home world, a nearly mythical planet that lay hundreds of years back along the fleet's zigzag course. Rumor had it that some of the local organisms were poisonous, but others were not, and made very good eating—an assertion that the plump little cleric wanted to test for himself.

And where better to do it than right there? While listening to a lot of pretentious blather—and laughing himself sick? Not that there weren't nuggets to harvest, factoids to swell his ever-growing store of information, all of which were dedicated to one purpose: *freedom*. A concept the Ra 'Na hierarchy hadn't given much thought to for a very long time.

Pol brushed a scattering of crumbs off the chair, settled into place, and flipped a row of switches. Six tiny cameras came online, and video blossomed on the same number of oval screens. The initiate watched Nas limp across the room, heard the oldster's humming, and noticed it was the same tune as last time.

Then, with all systems functioning appropriately, Pol reached for his lunch box. It had an internal cooling system and was heavy with exotic protein. He opened the lid, waited for the vapor to clear, and eyed the contents. More importantly, he *smelled* the contents—which caused the saliva to flow. The top layer of food consisted of half shells—each filled with what looked like brain tissue. The bouquet was interesting, however—which augured well.

The initiate lifted one of the shells, tilted the contents into his pink-lined mouth, and immediately fell in love with the planet below. Any place capable of producing such heavenly delights was worthy of his affection. A second shell followed the first—and the meal was well under way by the time the Zin entered the chamber below.

In keeping with his personal tendency to arrive early for nearly everything, Lak-Tal was the first to enter. Not only that, he also arrived under his own power, a rarity for Zin.

Unlike those who arrived behind him, Lak-Tal made a point out of saying hello to Na Nas. The Ra 'Na was pleased—and took extra care with the Sauron's tray of personalized refreshments.

Watching the slave, and the difficulty with which he moved, served to remind the Sauron of his own aches and pains. Some had been rather acute of late. The natural result of a long, active life? Or signs of something more ominous? He hoped for the former—but feared the latter. The Zin took his place, and the chamber continued to fill.

Hak-Bin monitored the arrivals via the screen in his private quarters, waited till everyone had settled into their cradles, and touched one of five buttons in the right arm of his thronelike chair. A series of three tones sounded, and the Zin, many of whom were engaged in conversations with their neighbors, turned toward the front of the room.

A relay closed, and the heavily embossed metal partition whirred as it rose into the well above. Hak-Bin waited until he had everyone's undivided attention and opened the meeting. There was no need to explain or comment on the ritual, since everyone present had been entrusted with their clan's names— *every* name, of *every* ancestor, stretching back for thousands of years. Names that they now started to chant, the syllables flowing together into long, complex passages, then woven into a multilayered song, voice over voice, lyric over lyric, until the entirety formed a complex tapestry of sound.

Fra Pol had heard the chant before, and much as he hated the Saurons, couldn't help but feel moved, because here, buried within an otherwise execrable culture, was a reverence for lives lived. The initiate even stopped eating, a prawn halfway to his mouth, listening with rapt attention.

Finally, after the last name had been chanted and Fra Pol had taken his long-delayed bite, Hak-Bin tackled the issue at pincer: "Greetings, my brothers—and congratulations on your recent victory. Not just any victory, but *the* victory, since Haven is the planet upon which *we will die* and the next generation will be born."

Only forty feet away, but hidden by a layer of steel, Fra Pol choked on the latest bite of seafood. *"Die? Born?"* This was the first time the initiate had heard such matters mentioned. Issues that he and his more inquiring friends had long wondered about. How old were the Saurons, anyway? Old, that was for sure. . . .

Working backward from the fleet's supply stats, the initiate figured there were approximately 1,896,000 Saurons in the fleet. Of that number, about 13 percent were Zin, 37 percent were Kan, and 50 percent were Fon. Except for lives lost to accidents or to battle, the *same* individuals meeting in the chamber below had been among those responsible for enslaving his grandparents more than two hundred years before.

So how *did* the hard-shelled bottom-feeders reproduce, anyway? Since they were all of one sex—or so it seemed? Maybe, just maybe, the mystery was about to be solved. The Ra 'Na leaned forward, his lunch momentarily forgotten.

"Only one hundred fifty-one local days remain until the change will carry us away," Hak-Bin continued, "until the nymphs emerge and sing our names. Then, when they are ready, the journey will resume. Perhaps they will be the ones to find the Paradise mentioned in the Book of Life, or the *next* hatching, or the one after that. It hardly matters. *Our* task is to prepare the way by building the citadels in which the change can take place, by ensuring their safety, and by replenishing the fleet."

Hak-Bin paused for a moment to let his words sink in. Na Nas, who, like the rest of the Ra 'Na, spoke fluent Sauron, tried to merge with the nearest bulkhead. He had heard Zin secrets before—but nothing like this. Were they conscious of the fact that he was present? Had he earned their trust? There was no way to be sure.

Hak-Bin took inventory of the faces in front of him. "The planet is ours—but threats exist. Knowing that our lesser brethren are weak, and, if faced with the certainty of death, could lose all reason, the great architect passed the burden of racial memory along to *us,* the all-powerful Zin, secure in the knowledge that we would care for the Kan and Fon as they have cared for us." ·

Lak-Tal stirred uneasily. Referenced but not said—not directly, anyway—was the widely held belief that because the Fon and the Kan were unable to remember anything beyond a few years back, they were clearly inferior. That made the Zin superior . . . and justified the Sauron social structure. Something that he, though privileged himself, was not entirely comfortable with.

Hak-Bin, satisfied with the content of the nonverbal olfactory feedback provided by his audience, continued to speak. "There are other threats as well—some of which are seated around you."

Hak-Bin raised a pincer as heads swiveled back and forth. "What I mean is that some of our population, approximately three percent, are likely to change early. Should this occur, *when* this occurs, it could serve as an unintentional warning to our lesser brethren, not to mention the slaves.

"Imagine," the Zin master continued, "what could ensue. Once we enter the citadels, once we are incapacitated, the entire race will be vulnerable. That's why early changers must be identified— and why harsh steps will be necessary."

Lak-Tal felt a sudden sense of warmth, as if his internal organs were on fire, and burning their way out. The sensation was psychological, he knew that, or thought he did, but disturbing none-theless. Was *he* one of them? An early changer? What if he was? Should he identify himself? For the good of the race? And what would happen then?

The Zin's thoughts were interrupted by the clan leader seated to his right. His name was Mal-Hiz. "Surely you jest. We are Zin—not Fon or Kan."

Hak-Bin, who had expected something of the sort, touched a button. Video flooded the wall screen to his left. "What you say is true, Mal-Hiz—but the change spares no one. Please observe."

The ensuing time-lapse video had been shot in a laboratory setting and showed the last moments of a Zin named Raz-Pak. The audience watched in horror as the Zin's body expanded by 50 percent, large plates of chitin broke away, and sections of the natal sac expanded to fill the recently created gaps.

Due to the manner in which he had been betrayed by his body, Raz-Pak lacked the naturally produced painkillers that would otherwise have protected him. He soon started to scream. Another Zin appeared, pressed an injector against the unfortunate Sauron's neck, and squeezed the trigger. Raz-Pak spasmed, went limp, and the video came to a merciful end.

"The nymph was only partially developed," Hak-Bin said sadly, "which means that an entire lineage has been lost."

Lak-Tal wondered about the origins of the video. Had Raz-Pak turned himself in? Or been discovered by one of his peers? And what about *him?* Was *he* under surveillance? No, he didn't think so—not yet, anyway. But it would pay to be careful.

Meanwhile, in the space above, Pol sat in stunned silence, shocked by what he'd heard. Here, delivered as if on a platter, was the sort of information he'd been looking for! The Saurons were going to die, and then, just before a new generation was born, the entire race would be vulnerable! That was the moment when his people could strike. *If* they had the vision, courage, and resolve.

The Ra 'Na felt a sudden stab of fear. What if the Saurons discovered his presence? Suddenly, what he had heretofore regarded as something of a lighthearted adventure, an act of symbolic superiority, was transformed into a moment of vast importance. *If* he could get the information back—*if* they would listen to him—everything would be different. The fleet could turn, retrace the meandering course it had followed, and return home. To Bal'wur. The very name filled the initiate with emotion.

"So," Hak-Bin concluded, "there's a great deal to consider and do. Each one of us will play an important role. Remember what is at stake, do what you must, and all will be well."

The Zin were a subdued lot as they withdrew from their respective cradles, turned, and shuffled toward the hatch. Most had departed the chamber by the time Hak-Bin raised an imperious pincer. "Slave, come here."

Nas jerked as if stabbed with a knife. His bad foot made a scritching sound as he dragged it across the deck. "Yes, master?"

Pol, his eyes locked on the tableau unfolding below, felt the bottom drop out of his stomach. He wanted to do something, wanted to help, but knew anything he did would result in his death. And if *he* died—the secret died with him.

Hak-Bin freed the t-gun from its clamps and aimed the handgun at Nas. "Place your head in front of the weapon."

Nas had been a slave all of his life, and while afraid to comply, was afraid not to as well. Perhaps this was some sort of test . . . a way to gauge his loyalty.

"No!" Pol wanted to shout. "Don't do it! Run! Hide!"

But it was too late. Nas positioned himself in front of the gun, and there was a loud crack as the dart blew the top of the oldster's head off. The body toppled over backward and crashed into some seats.

Hak-Bin restored the weapon to its clamps and touched a button. A Fon came online. "Yes, master?"

The Zin spoke in the dialect reserved for inferiors. "The slave made a mess. Clean it up."

"Yes, master."

That was the end of it—for Hak-Bin, at any rate, but not for Pol. He swore a terrible oath and went to work. The first task was to remove the trash. Then, when that effort was complete, he would return for the equipment. The Saurons couldn't fit into the space, but their Ra 'Na spies could, and there must be no sign that anyone had observed the proceedings below.

The initiate gathered the trash into a pile, filled two sturdy bags, and dragged them away. He was a good hundred feet down the maintenance way before the scent of nicely aged garbage wafted its way through a ventilation shaft and entered some very sensitive nostrils. Eyes popped open, claws scratched on metal, and the harakna formed a sound deep in its throat. *More* eyes opened, *more* bodies unwound, and the pack was ready. The scavengers launched themselves in the direction of the only thing they really cared about: food.

ASTEROID AR-309

After a relatively short shuttle flight, and a zero-g transfer to an elongate asteroid that the humans immediately named Turd, the slaves were pushed, shoved, and in some cases towed through a flexible tube and into a generously proportioned lock. From there they were herded down a tunnel into a rock-lined cavern, where they floundered about in a mist of vomit and urine.

The rock, which was dark in color, made the perfect background for the structures that Manning recognized as chondrules, spherical bodies no more than half an inch in diameter, which glittered when the light struck them.

Not that such matters were of much importance to the slaves, who spent much of their time hoping for food, fighting nausea, and literally bouncing off the walls. Finally, after what seemed like an eternity of discomfort, they were herded out into the tunnel. Metal handholds had been anchored in the rock. By grabbing them in sequence, the humans could pull themselves along. It was a challenge to "close it up" and not take a foot in the face.

Eventually, after numerous twists and turns, the slaves propelled themselves into a brightly lit chamber. It smelled of plastic and contained row upon row of injection-molded orange chairs.

Looted, Manning wondered, or manufactured for the occasion? Judging from the odor and the rough-and-ready construction, the second possibility seemed more likely. Each chair was piled high with equipment and clothing. What looked like harnesses held the materials in place. A pair of the furry aliens sorted the slaves as they entered. Their voices were hard and mechanical. The words had the quality of a chant. "Small to the front, medium in the middle, large to the back. Small to the front . . ."

Jack Manning and Vilo Kell used the well-anchored seats to pull themselves toward the rear of the cavern. Once in place, they discovered that what looked like oversized metal slippers had been secured to the floor in front of each chair. By inserting their boots or shoes into the fittings, the humans were able to "stand."

The security chief was impressed by the manner in which everything had been thought through. The aliens had invested a lot of energy in the effort. Why? They would know soon enough.

Three rows forward, and toward the center, a man released his equipment and took a seat. What looked like a bolt of blue electricity stabbed his chest. He convulsed, lost all expression, and floated face up. Hands pushed him away—but no one tried to help.

"You will sit when you are told to sit—and not a moment before," a voice said. "The consequences for disobedience are quite painful."

The source of the voice, a ratty-looking Ra 'Na, hovered at the front of the chamber. "Now," the diminutive being said, "pay close attention. My name is Baz, *Instructor* Baz, and you will address me as such. You are about to receive *valuable* training on how to remove ore from this asteroid, earn your keep, and stay alive. Those who fail to demonstrate a sufficient amount of enthusiasm, or fall short of my exacting standards, will be ejected from an auxiliary lock. The choice is yours."

"I *know* this guy," Kell said *sotto voce*. "Big mouth—little head. Just like a Ranger instructor I used to know at Fort Benning."

Manning struggled to keep a straight face, ducked as the still-unconscious body threatened to connect with his head, and wondered how long the insanity could last. Twelve practically nonstop hours later, he knew the answer: Too damned long. There was, it turned out, a lot for the newly inducted slaves to learn—starting with some basic information about the asteroid itself.

Turd, or AR-309, as Baz referred to it, was approximately four hundred feet long and two hundred feet in diameter. That being the case, the object weighed more two million tons, with a surface gravity that approached zero. Or, as Baz put it, "should you manage to get yourself killed—the better part of five minutes will pass before your body hits the ground."

Unlike most asteroids, AR-309 was equipped with externally mounted engine pods—a refinement that enabled the aliens to steer raw materials to the fleet rather than the other way around.

There were, Manning learned, various ways to process asteroids, including the spacegoing equivalent of strip mining, blowing the planetoid into manageable chunks, or, as was the case where Turd was concerned, tunneling into the rock's iron-silicate guts.

The process, as outlined by Baz and illustrated with computer-generated graphics, involved a number of steps: Bore a hole in the rock, suck the resulting gravel into crushers via powerful vacuum tubes, sift the ore through vibrating screens, grind the materials that come out the other side, feed the stuff through magnetic fields to separate nickel-iron granules from the silicates, bag the proceeds, and ship the high-grade ore to another asteroid for final processing.

Then, after a much needed bio break followed by lunch, it was time to get acquainted with the gear secured to their chairs. The first items were one-piece orange coveralls, which they were ordered to don without regard for personal modesty, a concept of dwindling significance.

After that the humans had an opportunity to acquaint themselves with personal hygiene kits that appeared to have been looted from Wal-Mart, a variety of odds and ends, and last, but certainly not least, some specially manufactured spacesuits.

Baz explained that sample suits had been obtained from Boeing's Sky Hab III orbital habitat, enhanced with their advanced technology, and duplicated in their shipboard factories.

Each suit had a multiplicity of parts, each of which came in a variety of sizes. Some items didn't matter too much, but gloves were considered critical. The alien instructor gave his students an hour to try things on, trade parts, and construct a workable suit. Finally, after haggling with his neighbors, Manning assembled something that looked and felt like it might work. He looked for Kell and got the thumbs-up. Others, including a few who refused to take the exercise seriously, continued to bargain.

A voice sounded in their helmets. It belonged to Baz. "Time's up. Seal your faceplates."

Powerful pumps started, oxygen was sucked out of the cavern, and the slackers started to yell and scream. Manning couldn't hear them, though, not through the well-insulated helmet, but was happy to see that most of them managed to close their suits.

Two people failed, however—which Baz took in stride. His space armor was lime green in color. He steered with jets of air. People moved as if to assist their fellow slaves, but a warrior bug in black space armor fired a shot over their heads. Sparks flew where the dart bounced off rock. The humans had little choice but to back off. Baz supplied the narration.

"Please turn your attention to the half-wits located at the center of the cavern. One individual wasted an excessive amount of time; the other received a defective suit. One deserves to die and the other doesn't. There's nothing you can do about bad luck—but there's no reason to be stupid."

Manning watched the contorted faces, "heard" the silent screams, and closed his eyes. Even then he could see them, gasping for air, bodies fighting the change in pressure. How, he wondered, could the furry aliens be so cruel? Especially since they seemed to be slaves themselves? Or was that the answer? *Because* they were powerless, or had been up till now, the XTs could elevate themselves by oppressing a new subclass: humans.

Manning opened his eyes, was nauseated by what he saw, and turned away. A sense of helplessness filled his gut.

"All right," Baz said matter-of-factly, "see the Kan by the door?" He gestured toward the warrior bug. "Follow him. The lesson will continue while we move to the next location."

Most of the slaves launched at the same moment. Suits collided, bodies tangled, and voices swore.

Manning and Kell allowed the crowd to sort itself out, joined the gently undulating line, and followed whatever set of boots happened to be in front of them. The lecture continued. "Each suit incorporates twelve functional layers. The first two layers consist of tubing sandwiched by flexible fabric. Liquid flows through the tubing and cools the suit. An overheated suit can kill you—so watch the indicator above your faceplate. If the temp indicator turns amber, notify your shift boss.

"Next comes a pressure bladder made of what humans refer to as urethane-coated nylon and Dacron. You saw what can happen, so watch for punctures. Mining is a highly physical and therefore traumatic activity. I know because I survived more than nine years of it. Take care of your suit and it will take care of you."

Manning noted the fact that Baz had been a miner himself, realized that the sudden availability of humans had given the Ra 'Na race what amounted to a promotion, and realized how insidious slavery can be. The instructor continued to speak. "The outer layers of your suits consist of aluminized Shim, a material we use in *our* suits, protected by an outer skin that consists of Gore-Tex, Kevlar, and Nomex.

"Your support equipment includes primary as well as secondary oxygen supplies, regulators, sublimators, temperature controls, tool jacks, an on-board computer, battery packs, radios, lights, and TV cameras that link you with your shift boss."

The group passed through a large air lock and entered a tunnel. It was approximately twenty-five feet in diameter and sloped downward—although the concepts of "up" and "down" were less meaningful with each passing hour. Manning grabbed a metal handhold and floated beneath what he considered to be the ceiling. A mass of cables, hoses, and tubes were draped along the opposite wall. The floor had been scored by multiple sets of heavy-duty treads, blue-green lights followed the passageway down into the asteroid's depths, and a thick pall of gray dust floated through the light from his headlamp.

"This is it," Baz announced, "the entrance to what my people refer to as 'Domar' and you call 'hell.' Welcome to my world."

ABOARD THE SAURON DREADNOUGHT *HOK NOR AH*

Fra Pol didn't even know he was in trouble, that the harakna were after him, until he heard the chittering sound. He dropped both bags of garbage and ran for his life. Maybe, just maybe, the scavengers would settle for the trash and leave him alone.

But harakna hunt for more than food, they hunt for pleasure, and ignored the garbage. It would be there when the chase over, the animals knew that, and skittered around a corner.

The initiate heard the sound of claws on steel, redoubled his efforts, and cursed his short, stubby legs. The amulet, the one his mother had given him, came loose and bounced into his face. The initiate tucked the pouch away and decided to call upon the Great One.

Pol apologized for his many shortcomings, and promised to chant all 111 stanzas of the Water Prayer each and every day, if only the supreme being would spare him long enough to deliver the message that the fates had entrusted to him.

Perhaps the Great One had heard such promises before, and, having never seen one of them kept, was feeling a bit cynical that day. Or, and Pol knew this was more likely, he had other more important matters to attend to. Whatever the reason, the harakna continued to pursue him . . . and the initiate continued to run.

The chittering was louder now—and the cleric's breath came in short, ragged gasps. There was a hatch ahead, *if* he could make it, *if* he could close the door in time. Damn the Saurons, anyway. . . . If it hadn't been for the fact that the Kan liked to hunt the harakna, and intentionally allowed the species to survive, the vermin would have been exterminated long before.

The hatch appeared. The initiate accelerated down the straightaway and heard a harakna squeal in glee. It saw the hatch as a dead end, a barrier against which the food would be trapped, and started to salivate.

A sensor detected motion, another sensor confirmed the necessary amount of heat, and the hatch hissed open. Pol threw himself through the gap, hit the emergency close switch, and heard something scream. He turned to discover that the door had sliced the lead harakna in two. The animal's eyes glared—and its teeth snapped in frustration.

Pol shuddered and hurried away. The use of the emergency close switch would activate an alarm, a technician would come to investigate, and the initiate would be elsewhere.

Meanwhile, in a distant part of the ship, two Ra 'Na males met in a well-appointed compartment. The corners were guarded by exquisite wood carvings executed by the Fras of the ship *Pas Hak Tur*. The bulkheads were hung with glow paintings that, if somewhat circumscribed where subject matter was concerned, were nonetheless beautiful to look upon.

A conference table occupied the center of the compartment. Dro Tog, the larger of the two Ra 'Na, sat with his feet on a stool, his heavily ringed fingers laced over his well-rounded tummy. P'ere Has, the prelate's assistant, was shabby but earnest. His voice became a drone as he read summaries of reports submitted from throughout the fleet. The number of services held, number of prayers said, on and on until the prelate lost the narrative thread and allowed his thoughts to drift.

The Ra 'Na weren't allowed to have a government of their own, but they *were* allowed to worship as they pleased, as long as the church did nothing to undermine the Saurons, their goals, or their daily operations.

A proposition that *sounded* easy enough, but was actually quite difficult, given the number of hotheads, iconoclasts, and rebels with which the Ra 'Na race had been saddled. Dangerous types who, if left to their own devices, would soon destabilize the delicate machinery of accommodation and thereby trigger some sort of disaster.

That's not how *they* saw things, of course, believing as they did in all sorts of naive nonsense having to with personal freedom, self-determination, and a return to Bal'wur. No, Tog consoled himself, my role is far from easy, but critical to the well-being of the Ra 'Na race. While others speak of absolutes and flirt with anarchy, I must remain objective. Compromise, conciliation, and appeasement. *Those* are the keys to survival. Not only survival, but now, with the advent of a second client race, the possibility of something more. A step up, perhaps? Time would tell.

The prelate's stomach started to growl, an unpleasant reminder of the manner in which the recently stocked ecclesiastical larder had unaccountably begun to melt away, and a far more important matter than the drivel pouring from his assistant's mouth. Tog cleared his throat in a clearly portentous manner, and the priest, who made his living from understanding such signals, paused in midreport. "Yes, your excellency?"

But Tog's question regarding his food supply went forever unasked as a tone sounded and a clerk entered the room. She was a comely creature—and a pleasure to gaze upon. The prelate was single, determinedly so, but far from celibate. "Excuse me, excellency, but Fra Pol is here to see you. He says the matter is urgent."

Dro Tog was surprised, to say the least. Never, so far as he knew, had the famously wayward cleric entered a superior's office of his own volition—so the matter must be urgent indeed. Some foolishness or other, the prelate supposed, but sufficient to rescue him from his assistant and therefore welcome. He raised a permissive hand. Light winked off a jeweled pinkie ring. "Thank you, P'ere Has, we can finish this later."

Has, who knew of the low esteem in which Fra Pol was generally held, felt a sudden sense of resentment. Here *he* was, doing most if not all of the old reprobate's work for him, and not a word of thanks. But no sooner had Has experienced the emotion than it made him feel guilty. He made the bow deeper than necessary—and backed out of the study.

No sooner was the priest gone than the initiate appeared. Though never fastidious about his appearance, Fra Pol looked even more rumpled than usual. His robe hung askew, food stains decorated the front of it, and his ears were laid back. The cleric was afraid of something—but what? Pol scurried forward, dropped to one knee, and made the formal obeisance. "Greetings, excellency . . . and thank you for seeing me on such short notice."

Tog frowned. Humility? From Fra Pol? The prelate was intrigued. He flicked a finger in the direction of the recently vacated chair. "Please . . . take a seat."

Pol hurried to obey. The Dro's nose twitched. That odor—what was it? And the stains. . . . Then he had it. Bivalves! Stolen from his private cooler! Here was the thief, then—ready to confess. What would the penalty be? Something very, very unpleasant. But that was for later. Now was the time to savor Pol's discomfort, watch him squirm, and thank the Great One for such a marvelous treat. The cleric took his seat and Tog formed a steeple with his fingers. "So, Fra Pol, a matter of some urgency, I believe? A confession perhaps?"

Pol was both shocked and amazed. Was Tog smarter than he seemed? "You know about the space over the chamber? And the way I spied on the Saurons?"

Tog felt ice water trickle into his veins. "Chamber? Saurons? What in the names of the six blue devils are you talking about?"

So Pol plunged in, described the nature of his hideaway, and provided a detailed account of the Sauron meeting. Finally, when the report was complete, Pol dropped his eyes. "I am sorry, excellency, truly sorry, but felt sure that you would want to know."

The unruly cleric was wrong, of course, since Tog not only didn't want to know, he didn't want *anyone else* to know either, lest the Saurons learn of such duplicity and blame the whole matter on him.

For one brief but heartfelt moment the prelate actually considered murder—no, not murder, but a *sacrifice*—made in the name of the Ra 'Na people and dedicated to the greater good. No one would miss Pol—no one in his or her right mind, that is—and the status quo would be preserved.

But what if the initiate vanished, the Saurons got wind of the matter, and came looking for someone to punish? There would be no one to sacrifice, no one beyond himself, that is, and Tog was not about to countenance such a horrible possibility. He struggled to control his voice. "I cannot condone your methods, Fra Pol, but you were right to bring this matter to my attention. Did you share this information with anyone else?"

"No, excellency."

"Good. Under no circumstances should you do so. I will discuss the matter with my peers, solicit their counsel, and proceed accordingly."

Pol, concerned by the prelate's tone, looked up from the deck. "You'll tell them that the Saurons plan to kill us?"

"I will tell them everything you told me," Tog lied.

Pol felt relieved. He stood, bowed, and started to back away. Maybe, just maybe, he could escape without punishment.

Dro Tog cocked both ears. "Just a moment, Fra Pol. There's the issue of your unauthorized activities, not to mention certain thefts from my kitchen."

"Thefts?" the initiate asked innocently. "What thefts? Surely you don't think that *I*, one of the Great One's servants, would stoop to—"

"Save it for someone more gullible than I am," Tog interjected. "P'ere Has needs someone to teach devotionals to the fourth form—and you're perfect for the job. Who knows? Some spiritual activity might do you some good. It certainly can't hurt. None of your funny business now. . . . Has is no fool, and he won't stand for it."

Pol, happy to get off with what he considered to be a light sentence, bowed submissively. "Yes, excellency. Thank you, excellency."

Tog waved dismissively and the initiate was gone.

Then, alone with his thoughts, Tog took a moment to consider. What if Pol was correct? What if the Saurons were about to die? *Should* he take action? No, not on the unsupported word of a single eccentric. He would monitor the situation and await further validation. Then, if that was forthcoming, *that* would be the time to share the matter with his peers.

Satisfied that his judgment was correct, and still in throes of hunger pangs, the Dro touched a button. Some of those bivalves would be good—along with a glass of nicely aged fa.

ASTEROID AR-309

The crew room was little more than a thirty-by-fifteen-foot box carved out of solid rock, pressurized, and equipped with some rudimentary furniture. It was olive drab in color and bore the initials "USMC."

Dim red lights cast a ghostly glow over three rows of cocoon-like sleeping bags suspended bat-style between webbing secured to floor and ceiling. The highly recycled air stank of ozone, plastic, and unwashed flesh.

The Klaxon made a harsh squawking sound. Manning awoke with a jerk, opened his eyes, and wondered where he was. He remembered and swore. He'd been on a beach with the sun against his back.

Now, having been on Turd for—what? Three? Four days?—he knew what to expect—and none of it would be a walk on the beach.

Men and women groaned, shoved their arms up through openings, and began the process of getting up or, more accurately, "out." Tired though all of them were, no one lingered in "bed." The twelve-person group had seventy-three minutes to rotate through two one-person showers, gobble the contents of an MRE (meal ready to eat), and don their spacesuits before their shift began. Once the time elapsed, the air would be pumped out of the room. A more than adequate incentive for even the most recalcitrant slave.

Manning tagged onto one of the lines that snaked toward one of the small cubiclelike showers, took note of the rather attractive nude woman who floated ahead of him, and pulled a check on his own libido. Was he interested? No, and that was depressing.

Others were more enterprising, however, and zero-g liaisons were common after dinner, particularly among the "what the hell, we're all going to die crowd," which neither Manning nor Kell considered themselves to be part of. Unlikely though such a possibility was, they hoped to escape.

It was a full quarter of an hour before Manning got his three-minute turn in the shower and ducked out again. That left barely enough time to towel off, gobble his ham and limas, and suit up—a process best carried out with help from someone like Kell, who could be trusted to look for external damage and check seals.

Once the crew were ready they left as a group and pull-pushed their way to Shaft No. 1, where they were met by a shift boss.

The shift boss was named Sig. He was a Fon, which Manning now knew was the way in which the white bugs called themselves. None of the Fon struck Manning as especially charismatic. Sig seemed especially unimaginative, going about his duties with all the flair of an inveterate sleepwalker.

Still, one benefit of Sig's somewhat plodding approach was that he was predictable, and not given to gratuitous acts of sadism, something for which many of his peers were known. That being the case Manning, Kell, and others on their team had agreed to make Sig look good as long as he treated them well.

None of which was of the slightest interest to Fwa-Nal. He was the top bug—the Zin to whom all of the shift bosses reported. *He* focused on three things: making or exceeding quota, producing the raw materials necessary to maintain the fleet, and making way for his nymph.

Given the realities of the cultural divide, plus the fact that the humans had no leverage whatsoever, there was no need for a crew meeting. Sig grunted his acknowledgment, waved the crew on, and waited for work to begin. Orders would be passed by radio, functions were dictated by which tool interface had been built into each slave's suit, and the objective was simple: Make Fwa-Nal happy. Nothing else mattered.

The preceding crew had been off for the better part of forty-five minutes by then, a break that allowed the equipment to cool and that provided Ra 'Na technicians with an opportunity to perform preventive maintenance.

The hose teams, which were timed to come on shift at the beginning of the break, used the interval to catch up. When everything was working correctly the tool teams produced more ore than "the suckers" could keep up with, which meant that extra time was required.

Dust swirled as the hose teams inserted powerful suction tubes into duct-filled hoppers, struggled to find a dependable purchase, and fought the kickback as the gravel rattled through. That's where they were, and that's what they were doing, when the tool teams "swam" past.

For reasons not entirely clear to Manning, the aliens believed that a higher level of intelligence was required to operate the hoses, and that being the case, consistently assigned darker-skinned humans to the job.

Most of the whites, or those arbitrarily classified as whites, understood the fact that the decision was capricious, and knew that the other humans played no part in making it, but some were resentful nonetheless. They grumbled, offered rude gestures, but stopped short of open conflict.

Due to the fact that the "black group" also included people who considered themselves to be Hispanic, Asian, and Native American, it was actually quite diverse. This meant that their attitude toward the "white group" was diverse as well.

One of the team's leaders, a man named Alvarez, understood

the nature of what was taking place and tried to play the schism down. Some of the team listened and some didn't. All he could do was try.

The tool pushers followed the harsh blue-green lights deeper and deeper into Shaft No. 1. The machine to which the humans had been assigned seemed to squat in murk. Viewed from a distance, the floods mounted on its frame reminded Manning of animals that live so deep beneath the surface of the ocean that they generate their own light.

The Ra 'Na had a largely unpronounceable name for the machine, but form often follows function, and Duncan, one of two mining engineers on their team, said it bore a striking resemblance to a single-boom, sixty-ton, Dosco NM2500 roadheader with four integrally powered drill rigs for roof and side bolting, on-board computer, power takeoffs, operator's cage, and horizontal stelling jacks to hold the unit in place—a rather important function under zero-g conditions. Someone had referred to the roadheader as "the Gopher," and the name stuck.

Though just starting to familiarize himself with mining jargon, Manning had no difficulty understanding that the main components of the rig or "tool" consisted of a track-driven platform, a "boom," or extension on which the cutter was mounted, massive intake ducts into which loose ore was pulled, and side jacks that held the entire machine in place.

The crew consisted of an operator, who should have been Duncan, but for reasons known only to the Saurons was Manning, plus four "jack men," or women, as the case might be; three "bolt shooters," who nailed tightly knit fabric or "curtains" to the ceiling and walls; two "goo gunners," who ran the injectors that blew lining in behind the curtains; and two "duct jockeys," who followed along behind and "dressed" the tubes through which the raw materials flowed. They spent half their time clearing blockages and the other half floating around.

The weird part, which Manning was careful to keep to himself, was that he actually *liked* running the Gopher, for the first three or four hours anyway, until fatigue started to pull him down. The work was direct and easy to understand. There were no politics to deal with, no directives to respond to, and no time-wasting meetings.

So he felt mixed emotions as he grabbed the tool's superstructure, pulled himself along the hull, and entered the specially modified cage. It was easy to see the welds where a smaller Ra

'Na-sized control station had been removed and a larger version dropped into place.

Now, as the security chief managed to maneuver himself into the big black chair, the sixty-ton tool sensed his presence, removed itself from standby, and started to make demands. Video blossomed as the human fastened his safety harness, a touch-style control panel came to life, and the words "Plug yourself in" flashed yellow on the middle of the primary screen.

He took what he thought of as the "umbilical," inserted the plug into a round receptacle, and gave one turn to the right. Additional data cascaded onto the screens along with a new message: "Crew check."

Manning obediently checked to ensure that the crew was ready, received the usual range of mostly obscene responses, and watched new words appear. The sentence was short and to the point: "Start work."

The human checked the control screens, took a joystick in each gloved hand, and pressed the decelerator all the way to the floor. Then, by letting up on the pedal, he sent the machine forward. Moments later the cutter made contact with the workface, rock began to fly, and the shift officially began.

Not far away, in Shaft No. 2, another tool bored into the asteroid's core. In spite of the number assigned to it, this tunnel actually predated the one Manning was working within. It ran deeper, too. Ra 'Na slaves had started the shaft—and been replaced by humans. That's why the No. 2 hose team was working almost side by side with No. 1's tool pushers when the ceiling collapsed.

Later, during a rather perfunctory investigation, various theories would be advanced to account for the cave-in, but the reason didn't really matter. Not to the half dozen men and women who survived the initial "fall" but were trapped in what amounted to a freshly made tomb.

Now, as thick dust swirled through the light mounted on his helmet, Jamal Johnson activated his radio. He was a high school science teacher, or had been before the chits arrived, and wasn't very knowledgeable regarding radio procedure. "Hey, can anyone hear me? The roof caved in!"

Manning took his foot off the decelerator, pulled the cutter off the face, and put Gopher in neutral. "Who's speaking? Where are you?"

"My name's Johnson," the teacher replied. "I'm part of the

hose team working Shaft Two. The ceiling collapsed in two different places—and we're caught in between them."

"Roger that," Manning replied as he punched some buttons. "I have you on my displays. It looks like you're right next to us, maybe a hundred feet away. Shore up the ceiling if you can, give aid to your crew, and conserve oxygen. We'll see what we can do from over here."

"Thanks," Johnson said fervently. "Who's speaking?"

"Manning, Jack Manning," the security chief replied. "I'm the tool operator in Shaft One. By the way—how 'bout the folks on your tool team? What's their status?"

"We're getting the hell out of Dodge," a new voice answered. "The back tunnel is blocked, but a vertical access shaft intersects Shaft Two about fifty feet aft of the tool, so we're headed for the surface."

Manning frowned as he shrugged the harness off. "You're kidding. . . . What about Johnson and his people?"

"Screw 'em," the voice answered caustically. "Let their friends save them."

"He has a point," the engineer named Duncan said over the Shaft 1 intercom. "They skate while the rest of us do the work."

Manning knew the hose team was working its ass off, but he also knew that nothing he could say would convince the Duncans of the world, so he didn't bother to argue. "Suit yourself—I'm going to try to help them. Anyone who wants to help can meet me next to the starboard power takeoffs."

Manning half expected to hear from Sig right about then—but the Fon chose to remain silent. Time and energy had been invested in the slaves, which meant they had at least some value. Not a sufficient amount to justify the use of outside resources—but enough to justify an internal rescue attempt.

Thus encouraged, the human pulled himself back along the machine, saw that three headlamps were there waiting for him, and knew that one of them would belong to Kell. The Ranger had removed a T-shaped drill from the clamps that secured it to the Gopher's much-scarred hull and was connecting the power supply. "Make way for the army . . . I'll drill while you civilians move rock."

Manning grinned, nodded to the others, and the four of them went to work.

Johnson did his best to sound nonchalant, but couldn't hear

anything said over the other team's intercom, and wondered if anyone remained. "Manning? Are you there?"

The drill bit bored into rock, and the work began. "We're here," Manning replied grimly. "See you shortly."

But it wasn't shortly—not by a long shot. Hour after hour went by while the four of them took turns on the drill, evacuated rock from the newly formed shaft, and sweated into their already fetid suits.

Meanwhile, trapped in a pocket no bigger than a standard Earthside bathroom, Johnson and his coworkers turned off everything they could to conserve their batteries, sat in the dark, and watched their oxygen supplies dwindle toward zero.

Finally, after what seemed like a stint in hell, rock crumbled, dust swirled, and headlamps bobbed through the fog. Johnson, along with four of his companions, were free a few minutes later.

A fresh crew, summoned by Sig, went in to clear the rubble. Maybe, just maybe, some of the missing were alive but pinned beneath the debris.

The Shaft 2 hose team "swam" toward the surface along with their rescuers. "So," Johnson said, "why did you do it?"

The question took Manning by surprise. Truth was that he had never stopped even to think about it. He eyed the lights ahead. "Hell, I don't know. 'Cause it needed doing."

Elsewhere, the Fon named Sig listened, wondered if *he* would do the same thing for a group of Zin, and couldn't come up with an answer.

ABOARD THE SAURON DREADNOUGHT *HOK NOR AH*

The shuttle received the necessary clearance, nosed through the light blue force field that guarded the *Hok Nor Ah*'s cavernous flight deck, and settled onto one of three illuminated high-priority triangles.

A tubeway snaked out to mate with the shuttle's lock. The flight deck was pressurized, but the lock-to-lock connection would speed the transfer. The Ra 'Na named Lin Mok made her way out to the waiting spacecraft. The descriptor "slave dignitary" sounded like an oxymoron to her, but that's how Hak-Bin referred to the human, so that's what he was. Not that Mok really cared, since the meet and greet was just one of her many chores.

The hatch opened and Franklin stepped out. Here he was, leaving one spaceship for another—a memorable moment for anyone who had never been outside of the atmosphere before—and the main thing he noticed was how funky the larger vessel smelled. It reminded the politician of walking into an unfamiliar apartment house, the sort of place where the odors produced by people living in close proximity to each other had blended into what amounted to an olfactory fingerprint so unique you'd know where you were with a blindfold over your eyes. It made the human wonder how *he* smelled to the aliens.

Franklin had an excellent memory for faces and names, an asset where a political career is concerned, and he recognized the Ra 'Na female the moment he spotted her. Not knowing her culture, he bowed and hoped that was okay. "Hello, we meet again. My name is Franklin, Alexander Franklin, here to see Lord Hak-Bin. Am I allowed to know your name?"

Though it ran counter to her better judgment, Mok found herself charmed by the fact that the human clearly regarded her as an individual rather than one of Hak-Bin's many appendages. That, plus the fact that one so dark would want to know who she was, won the female over. The translator turned her words into what she heard as incomprehensible gibberish. "They call me Lin Mok. Master Hak-Bin sent me to greet you."

Franklin smiled, realized the facial expression might not mean anything to her, and nodded. "It's a pleasure to meet you. Please lead the way."

Mok led Franklin out into a busy corridor. Humans were still something of a curiosity on the *Hok Nor Ah,* which meant that many of the Ra 'Na, Fon, and Kan turned to stare. Franklin tried to ignore it but felt uncomfortable nonetheless.

The politician was thankful that Jina had remained on the surface. Partly because she was safer there . . . but also because he didn't want his wife to witness what he might have to say or do. Her faith in him, in what she sometimes referred to as the "higher" part of him, was something Franklin had never really understood, especially since the profession he had chosen forced him to slap backs, cut deals, and accept tradeoffs. Very little of that was pretty.

Nevertheless, the politician treasured her faith in him, even if it was misplaced, and wanted to nurture her illusions as long as possible.

The twosome turned a corner and someone yelled, "Hey, mister!"

Franklin turned in time to see the fall of the whip and hear the sound it made as the finely braided harakna hide sliced into a young human's back. The boy staggered. The high-tech cargo pallet to which he was harnessed rocked in response.

The politician took a full step forward, but Mok grabbed his arm and pulled him back. "No! You musn't. There's nothing you can do."

The boy saw Franklin hesitate, started to speak, and flinched as the whip fell again. Both blows had drawn blood and left a crimson cross on the young man's pale skin. He closed his mouth, turned, and stumbled forward. The heavily laden platform bobbed along behind. Something, Franklin didn't know what, allowed the pallet to float three inches off the deck.

The politician had seen the boy's expression, however, seen the unmitigated hatred. He knew it was nothing compared to what the air-dropped "talkies" might generate. The Saurons had set him up, *were* setting him up, and he had to do something. He needed an agreement of some sort, an accommodation that would allow him to *help* his people, and live long enough to do so. He turned to Mok. "Let's go," he said grimly. "I have a meeting to attend."

*   *   *

The compartment was one of the largest on the ship. It had once served as private quarters for a prosperous Ra 'Na merchant, which was why the bulkheads were so heavily decorated. But the original owner had been dead for a long time, and the present occupant had no interest in bas-relief metalwork—or any other form of art, for that matter.

Hak-Bin stood naked at the center of a shallow basin while a Ra 'Na slave worked aromatic oil into his coal-black chitin. The ostensible purpose of the oil was to make the Sauron's exoskeleton more pliable and less prone to the tiny hairline cracks that, if left untreated, could lead to fracture lines and an uncomfortable course of treatment. But the rubdown *felt* good as well—and seemed to lubricate the Zin's thought processes. He closed his eyes.

The reaction to the meeting had been positive, as evidenced by the sort of feedback he had received from his peers. But that was to be expected. The hard times lay ahead—no, *were* already here, given the content of the reports from the planet's surface.

Although a significant number of humans had been taken into slavery, and already labored on behalf of nymphs to come, some continued to resist. Most of the "wild" nondomesticated natives were too busy foraging for food to present the Kan with much of a problem, but there was evidence that groups had started to form. *Militant* groups, some of which had actually managed to disrupt the construction process; had diverted supplies; and, in one disturbing incident, freed more than fifty slaves.

What if such activity increased? What if construction of the citadels was delayed? Not by days—but by months? The Zin envisioned Saurons roaming the surface, searching for places to hide, at the mercy of feral slaves.

The very thought of it sent an unexpected shudder through his body, and the Ra 'Na, a male named Rek, waited for some sort of punishment. Nothing happened. The Zin pointed toward his clothes. "I will dress now."

Both surprised and thankful, the slave scurried toward the rack on which garments were hung, and brought them one at a time.

The key, Hak-Bin thought, is to give the humans some hope, an alternative to armed rebellion, to which they can willingly submit. That, combined with harsh lessons taught by the Kan, would provide the stability that Saurons required. Not forever, but long enough, until the citadels were complete. The human named Franklin seemed pliable enough, and like Dro Tog, would make an excellent tool. Yes, some maintenance was in order, along with minor concessions. But the bargain was a good one. Why fire a thousand darts when one fool will serve just as well?

Fully armed Kan warriors stood to either side of the hatch. It was difficult to see them clearly because of the manner in which their chitin shifted to match the steel bulkhead. They were motionless and remained so as Mok and Franklin passed through the entranceway.

The human looked for Hak-Bin, failed to spot him, and took a moment to survey his surroundings. Almost every square inch of wall space was occupied by bas-relief artwork. There were thousands of impressions, all taken from alien leaves. No two were alike.

The rest of the space was quite spartan. The only furniture consisted of a U-shaped desk and cradle-chair combination plus a pair of guest slings for use by visiting Zin. Some sort of mechanism hummed as two silver globes rose from their pedestals and hovered over their heads. Thin shafts of light nailed them to the deck.

The slaves heard Hak-Bin before they actually saw him. There was the whine of servos followed by the shuffle of flat Sauron feet. Franklin noticed that the Zin looked shinier than the last time they had met. No word was spoken until the alien had settled into his chair and consulted his tabletop computer screen. There was no preamble or preliminary chitchat.

"Your job is to visit our construction sites, urge the supervisors to drive the rest of the slaves harder, and thereby control the population. You will start immediately. Are there any questions?"

Franklin had never felt so intimidated by anyone in his entire life, not even by his father, who could make an entire house tremble with his anger. That being the case, it was a struggle to get his much-rehearsed sentence out of his mouth. "The plan won't work—not the way you describe."

Mok closed her eyes, hoped none of the human's brain tissue would splatter on her clothes, and waited for the sound of the t-gun. The silence stretched thin . . . and when Hak-Bin spoke, the words dripped with sarcasm. "Oh, really? Perhaps the *slave* would care to enlighten me?"

Franklin knew that his great-great-grandparents had sold like cattle and still managed to survive. The knowledge gave him strength. He stood ramrod straight and called on the same voice he had once used to address the legislature. "Your goal is to build certain structures, and having done so, to continue your pilgrimage.

"The fact that you plan to leave, to release us from slavery, means there is still reason to hope, more than that, to cooperate, knowing that the sooner the work is completed, then the sooner you will leave."

The human understood! Hak-Bin was pleased but gave no sign of it. And he believed the cover story—and would help to sell it. "So? Rather than counter my thinking, you seem to support it. My time is precious—please don't waste it."

"The strategy has merit," Franklin added hurriedly, "but the suggested execution is flawed. For me to play the role you envision, I must deliver *real* benefits to my people. Benefits that make everyday life better, benefits that stand in marked contrast to what it would be like living in the wild, benefits that build credibility."

It gets better and better! the Zin thought. Though appalled by the notion of a society in which slaves were accommodated in any manner, he knew human norms were different and would have to be taken into account. The words were at variance with his thoughts. "Benefits? What sort of benefits? Slaves are slaves. There's no need to mollycoddle them."

"Simple things," Franklin answered quickly. "Shelters to live in, medical care, and plenty of food."

"Or?" the Sauron asked provocatively. "What will happen if I don't?"

The human shrugged. "Assuming you plan to build in the area where we first met, there will be organized resistance. Not by a few holdouts, but by professional warriors who have plenty of weapons."

Hak-Bin was further impressed. The human knew what he was talking about—especially where the resistance movement was concerned. "So the 'benefits' you speak of will eliminate armed revolt?"

"No," Franklin replied honestly. "That's impossible. But the policies I recommend will reduce the conflict to more manageable levels."

Mok, who had followed the conversation via her translator, was totally amazed. No one talked to Hak-Bin that way—not even Dro Tog. Her respect for the human went up a notch.

Hak-Bin let the silence build—knowing it had power. Finally, when Franklin's knees were almost ready to give, the Sauron spoke. "It shall be as you say."

Franklin was quick to follow up. "And I can have the support I need? Vehicles for transportation? Security for me and my wife?"

"Transportation will be arranged—and a team of Kan will be assigned to protect you."

"Thanks," Franklin responded, *"but no thanks.* How credible will my words be if I'm surrounded by Saurons? It will look as though I'm acting under duress—or as a full-fledged collaborator. Neither of which will get the kind of results you're after. I want a human security detail, approved by *me,* and armed with whatever weapons they deem necessary. Furthermore, I want to use Terran aircraft and ground vehicles with humans at the controls."

The Zin struggled to keep his anger in check. The knowledge that this human would be executed along with all the others in less than 150 local days helped Hak-Bin maintain his composure. The measures the human wanted would make the other slaves somewhat more difficult to keep track of—but there were remedies for that. The Sauron leaned forward to add force to his words.

"I hereby approve your requests—but *not* the manner in which they were framed. You would do well to show more respect in the future—or I will find other, more appropriate work for you to do. Do I make myself clear?"

Franklin wanted to tell the Sauron to screw off, to shove it up his ass, assuming the alien had one, but knew that such a course would be suicidal. It was a struggle, but he managed to make his voice sound submissive. "Yes, Lord. It shall be as you say."

"Excellent," the Zin replied, his composure restored. "We are in full agreement. That concludes our discussion for today. Mok will show you out."

Franklin bit his lower lip. There were more things to discuss, *many* more, but there was nothing he could do. Hak-Bin had granted him some concessions, important concessions, and that was a victory of sorts.

Mok bowed, the politician followed her example, and together they backed out of the room. The interview was over.

ASTEROID AR-309

Manning didn't expect trouble, but it came anyway. Thanks to the time lost while helping the Shaft 2 hose team, Shaft 1's production quota had gone unfulfilled and a punishment had been levied. Not by Sig, who approved of the rescue, but by Fwa-Nal, who saw the slaves as expendable.

The fine—half their evening ration of MREs—was a blow to those who not only needed the calories but who also looked forward to dinner, no matter how spartan, as one of the few pleasures left to them.

That, combined with a growing sense of resentment toward those who appeared to have privileges, had started team members talking. Talk fueled anger, and it wasn't long before the more militant types wanted blood. *Manning's* blood, since he'd led the rescue and showed no signs of regret.

Manning was in the communal lavatory when they entered. He had just washed his face with a wet wipe and turned to shove it down the waste chute. The attack, which was led by a 250-pound ex-linebacker named Podo, came without warning.

However, since Podo had never fought anyone under zero-g conditions before, his unanchored lunge packed very little punch.

Manning felt the impact, realized it was intentional, and sank his elbow into the larger man's gut. And thanks to the fact that the security chief's feet were anchored by a footrail, his blow had force.

Podo let out a whoosh of expelled air, struggled to obtain more, and drifted away. But his partners *had* anchored themselves in place—and entered the battle.

The first, a goo gunner named Reems, wrapped his legs around one of the pipes that ran the width of the overhead and attacked from above. He had small, bony fists, and they worked like pistons.

The second, an enterprising sort known as "Smoker," grabbed a handhold some five feet away, went horizontal, and used his boots like pile drivers. One of them struck Manning in the shoulder. His feet came free. Reems slipped an arm around his neck, and Smoker proceeded to kick the shit out of him.

That was the intent, anyway. And they might have succeeded if Kell hadn't chosen that particular moment to intervene.

Smoker didn't know the Ranger was there until the belt passed in front of his eyes, a noose tightened around his neck, and it became impossible to breathe. He stopped kicking and grabbed for the makeshift garrote.

Freed from one attacker, Manning dealt with the second. Reems was still pounding his face steadily. Capillaries broke, blood flowed, and a universe of red planets spun through the air.

Manning used the goo gunner as an anchor, brought his legs up, and placed his boots on the overhead. One strong kick was sufficient to break his assailant's hold.

Diving toward what would normally be regarded as the deck, Manning saw his opportunity. He executed a full somersault, pushed off, and shot upward.

Reems, still clinging to the pipes, saw the danger but couldn't move in time. Manning drove his fist into the other man's unprotected genitals, heard him grunt, and barely got his feet up in time. They hit the ceiling as he grabbed for a pipe.

A stun grenade went off, as two Kan warriors entered the compartment on self-propelled battle platforms. Those not rendered unconscious by the concussion froze in place. Servos whined as frame-mounted automatic weapons probed the room.

In spite of the fact that no one had ever been able to locate anything that resembled a camera or a microphone, everyone assumed that the Saurons had some way to monitor their activities. That being the case, it seemed logical to suppose that the Kan intended to stop the fight.

One of the aliens, a file leader named Mim-Bor, eyed the slaves through his multipurpose battle goggles. They resembled blobs of red-orange heat. Targeting parameters rippled down the right side of his field of vision. Mim-Bor's voice boomed through a speaker mounted on the front of his platform. "Human Manning—identify now."

Reems clutched his genitals with one hand and used the other to point. The motion put him into a forward spin. "That's the bastard—he started the whole thing!"

The Kan turned his platform on its axis. Alien eyes examined Manning. "Is this true?"

Hundreds of blood droplets orbited his head. Manning used an arm to wipe his face. "Which? The Manning part? Or the other stuff?"

"We have no interest in what slaves do to each other," the warrior said flatly. "Are you the one called 'Manning'?"

There wasn't much point in denying it—so the human nodded. "Yes, I am."

"Position yourself on the rear of my platform," Mim-Bor ordered. "You will come with us."

"Can I clean up?"

"No. You will come with us."

Manning shrugged, dove toward the battle platform, and grabbed a side rail. It took a moment to maneuver his near-weightless body into a "standing" position, and he discovered that the Sauron-sized "slippers" were way too large for his feet. It felt strange to "stand" behind the alien, with the Kan's backsloping body extending down between his calves, but that's the way the platform was configured. Kell looked concerned, and Manning waved. "Don't wait up! We're going for burgers after the dance."

Kell laughed—but the others remained silent.

Jets hissed as Mim-Bor backed the platform out of the compartment, paused, and waited for the other warrior to do likewise. The hatch thudded into the closed position, steel bolts shot into place, and the platforms sped away.

ABOARD THE SAURON DREADNOUGHT *HOK NOR AH*

Franklin, who had been summarily woken from a fitful sleep, dragged out of his tiny Ra 'Na–sized cabin, and marched through the ship's busy corridors, tried to look alert. A human-style chair had been provided this time—and that made him feel better.

Hak-Bin, still shiny from the oiling five hours earlier, appeared unchanged. As was his peremptory manner. "In keeping with your wishes, I chose a highly qualified human to take charge of your personal security. He will have the freedom to select up to twenty-five additional staff."

Franklin swallowed to moisten his throat. The last session was fresh in his mind. He chose the words with care. "Thank you. May I inquire as to his background?"

"Yes," the Zin acceded, "you may."

A three-dimensional image seemed to boil up from the surface of the Sauron's U-shaped desk. Franklin saw a woman whom he immediately recognized as the secretary-general to the United Nations, a tiny, almost childlike female aide, and a tall, intense-looking male who stood with his back to the Secretary. His eyes were focused on something beyond the range of the camera. The earplug was a dead giveaway.

"That's him?" the politician asked. "On the right?"

"Yes," Hak-Bin answered. "His name is Manning, Jack Manning, and he was in charge of the larger female's security."

"Was?"

"She was killed when the building she worked in was destroyed."

Franklin wondered if that meant the U.N. building and was fairly sure that it did. He would never forget what the aliens had done to McChord—and the city of Seattle. The next words were something of a surprise—even to him. "He's white."

Hak-Bin's eyes were huge. Was that amusement in his voice? "Yes," the Sauron responded, "that's true. *I* might find such a development to be somewhat disturbing, especially in light of the fact that the Fon are something less than competent where matters of violence are concerned, but *you* hold other views. I respect that."

Franklin started to speak, started to reply, but stopped when a second holo appeared. This footage was of *him,* taken at a political rally, addressing the problem of latent racism. The aliens had not only analyzed human culture in a very short period of time, they also had archived materials that might be useful, and were ready to call on them when the need arose. Digital technology at its best and worst. The politician's face felt warm. "Point taken."

The Sauron touched a symbol, and the video collapsed. The human was easy, *extremely* easy, and therefore instructive. The issue of race was a sensitive one, subject to hypocrisy, and potentially useful.

Mok appeared in the entranceway. "Slave Manning has arrived, excellency."

Here it was—*another* surprise. Like most professional politicians, Franklin had "faces" for every occasion. He took refuge behind what Jina referred to as the "show me" expression.

Manning entered the compartment. Franklin was disheartened. The man chosen to lead his security detail had been badly beaten. His face was blotchy with dried blood, one eye had swollen closed, and his lower lip was cut. Was the man's condition a message of some sort? An implied threat? Or a matter of chance? Anything was possible.

Manning, still in the dark as to what was going on, scanned the compartment. He saw a black Sauron—and a black human. The man was familiar somehow, but Manning couldn't quite place him.

The fact that the human had been provided with a chair and allowed to sit grabbed the security chief's attention. A full-blown collaborator? Or just a guy sitting in a chair? There was no way to know. He resolved to pay close attention to whatever happened next.

Hak-Bin was becoming more and more adept at reading human facial expressions. He saw the manner in which Manning looked at Franklin and knew his plan was working. Neither human trusted the other. The goal was to achieve enough alignment to get the job done—but keep them wedged apart. With that in mind the Zin became much more solicitous than usual. "Welcome, slave Manning. . . . I assume you know Governor Franklin?"

Franklin's head came around. Did the Saurons really believe that all humans knew one another? Like the old racist stereotype about African-Americans? Or was the comment indicative of a blind spot? An inherent contempt for *all* humans regardless of ethnicity?

Yes, Franklin decided, the bastard *believes* we're inferior, and that's a weakness. One that I will find a way to exploit.

Now Manning knew where he'd seen Franklin before, on the evening news, where he was often described as an "up-and-coming politician with potential for even greater things." By which the commentators meant the Senate or the presidency itself. So what did the two of them have in common? And where was the meeting headed? Caution was in order. He nodded. "Governor."

Franklin nodded in return. "Mr. Manning."

Had the Sauron's knowledge of the culture in which both men had been raised gone a little bit deeper, he would have detected a certain chilliness in the air. But he didn't, so he went straight to the point. "Governor Franklin has agreed to lead an interim human government. The primary goal of his administration will be to ensure the timely completion of certain construction projects. There's a distinct possibility that feral humans may try to interfere with his activities. Your job will be to protect him and his wife and thereby further our goals.

"Now," the Sauron continued, without soliciting any sort of response from Manning, "there is the matter of your qualifications. Which were under discussion just prior to your arrival."

The Sauron touched his desktop and turned his coal-black eyes to Franklin. "Watch this . . . it should put your concerns to rest."

Manning recognized the footage from the moment that the first picture coalesced into a three-dimensional image. As well he should, since he'd seen it on the news, as part of the investigation, and during his dreams.

Seeking to gain as much notoriety as possible, the would-be assassins had staged their attack where the cameras would be most numerous, which meant the nets had the action from multiple angles. For what seemed like the millionth time the secretary-general's motorcade pulled into the kill zone and came to a stop.

Responsibility for securing the area had been assumed by the South African security apparatus, which, jealous of its prerogatives, had refused to provide Manning and his team with prior access.

Doors opened and about twenty-five suits exited their various vehicles. Plenty of targets for a team of trigger-happy fanatics. But not this lot, who were cool, *very* cool, and held their fire like the disciplined troops they were.

The secretary-general's heavily armored Mercedes was third in line on that particular day, so Manning knew where to look. He saw himself exit the vehicle first, followed by a flash of mocha-colored thigh as the chief executive, code-named Oracle, swung her long, shapely legs out through the door and stood in one smooth movement. She'd been a model once and could still turn heads.

Then, as she stepped up onto the curb and the first dignitary came forward to greet her, the top of his head flew off. Blood, bone, and brain tissue splattered the secretary-general's cream-colored suit and thereby saved her life.

Experts, and there seemed to be plenty, testified that the appearance of blood on the front of Oracle's suit, followed by the speedy manner in which Manning threw her to the ground, may have played an important role in convincing the lead triggerman that he had taken out his primary target and could redirect his fire. That's when his associates cut loose as well. Three government officials, a street vendor, and a limo driver were killed in seconds.

People screamed, ran for cover, and in the case of South Africa's finest, fired in the wrong direction and shot an innocent bystander.

What happened next was described by a *Newsweek* reporter as "the most efficient public execution ever carried out."

If the assassins were counting on confusion and miscommunication to raise the kill ratio, they were badly disappointed. Working like the machine they were, aided by information provided by a recon drone they weren't supposed to deploy, the security team nailed the killers with ruthless efficiency. Subsequent investigations would suggest that at least two of the assassins had been severely wounded when follow-up head shots silenced them for good.

The feces hit the fan. The would-be assassins were black, Oracle was on the political make, and the press was starved for violence. It wasn't long before an entire subcontinent wanted Manning on a freshly sharpened stick.

His defenders, all two or three of them, said, "No, the lad may be a tad overzealous, but who's to judge? Bullets were flying and people were dead."

Which was where the matter stood until a reporter located the security chief's sister, arranged for a cell block interview, and spread her incendiary comments across the front of *USA Today*. "'He should have killed *more* of them,' sister says. '*I* would have.'"

"So," Hak-Bin said, as the video caved in on itself, "I assume you're satisfied as to the particular slave's capabilities."

The comment was directed to Franklin—but it was Manning who answered. "Thanks, but no thanks. Maybe the governor has the hots for your puppet government, but I don't. Send me back to the mines. My spacesuit may stink, but it smells better than this."

Hak-Bin came very close to killing the recalcitrant human then and there, but managed to control himself and touched another symbol. Video, shot and stored against that very possibility, boiled to life.

Once the holo locked up it took Manning the better part of a minute to understand what he was looking at. The scene looked like something straight out of an old-fashioned Hollywood epic, complete with a recently denuded hill, overseers with whips, and thousands of raggedly dressed slaves. As they pulled on thick nylon ropes, blocks of stone inched their way up a thirty-degree slope. A thick layer of blood-streaked mud greased the way.

Franklin was appalled. "What's going on? Why do the work by hand? Machines could cut the time by seventy-five percent."

"The Book of Cycles is quite specific about the way in which the work will be carried out," Hak-Bin said truthfully, "and only certain kinds of tools are permitted."

Franklin remembered the Amish, their prohibition against the use of electricity. What the Sauron described was similar.

"Okay," Manning put in, "but what *is* it?"

"That," Hak-Bin said proudly, "is the site of our new temple complex. Once work is completed, a central hall and various support structures will occupy the top of the hill."

For the first time, the politician truly questioned his decision to cooperate. What made him think *he* could help? And what were his *true* motives? The question hung unanswered as the scene changed.

Now, rather than the panorama they'd seen before, the humans found themselves staring at a tight shot. A man—no, a woman—strained at the end of a heavy nylon rope. Her blue denim shirt hung in tatters, and she staggered as a whip fell across her already bloodied back.

Many people would have screamed, many would have cried, but *this* woman was tougher than that. She grimaced, swore, and fought for a better purchase. Others strained as well—and their load jerked forward.

The security chief had seen that expression before, especially during the years immediately after his mother's death, and knew who the woman was: his sister Marta.

"Yes," Hak-Bin confirmed, "your sibling was captured by the Kan. She lied about her identity and paid the price. What happens now depends on *you*."

Memories flickered through Manning's mind. The too-sweet smell of his alcoholic mother's breath, his father's impassive stare, and the sounds of little-girl sobs in the room next to his. The words were soft—as if voiced by a man a million miles away. "Let her go. I'll do what you ask."

Franklin started to say something and thought better of it. Hak-Bin had gone to considerable lengths to recruit Manning—objections would be pointless.

Hak-Bin touched the desktop, and Marta seemed to crumple. "Excellent. She will be released within six hours. Now, if it isn't too much trouble, we have work to do. Mok, fetch another chair. President Franklin's chief of security would like to sit down."

NEAR BELLINGHAM, WASHINGTON

The finger of land called Governor's Point had been the site of a stone quarry as early as 1857, and sandstone from that location had been used to construct the Portland, Oregon, Customs House in 1876, the Whatcom County Courthouse in 1890, and many other structures prior to its closure in 1913.

Viewed from the north, the point rose to form a softly rounded hill, once covered with evergreens, now stripped to make way for the Sauron temple complex.

Like the slaves around her, Marta Manning knew next to nothing about the structures she was working to build, including what the structures would look like when complete, or how they would be used.

What she *did* know was that while she hated the chits, she hated the collaborators even more. They were human, or claimed to be, but were quick to accept positions of privilege from which they could dominate those with lighter skins. Like hers. Somehow, in some way, the ex-con was determined to get her revenge.

But that would have to wait. Right then, on the slippery slopes of what the slaves had already dubbed "Hell Hill," she, along with eight of her companions, struggled to carry a large piece of stone up a recently cleared path to a flat area where the temple would be built. The raw split-log steps were crude and still under construction.

The load consisted of a slab of sandstone roughly six feet in length, four feet wide, and four feet thick. Other slaves, those working in the quarry itself, had spent sixteen hours cutting the block free, and two more to trim and shape it.

For reasons no one understood, they'd been forced to use hand tools, in spite of the fact that power tools were available.

Now, lashed on top of an H-shaped litter, the quarter-ton stone was on its way to a staging area, where it would wait for actual construction to begin.

One of the other humans, a graduate student from the University of Washington, assured Marta that the process was similar to the one the ancient Mayans had employed to construct their centers north of Petén, Guatemala—as if that made the whole thing more palatable somehow. She was surrounded by dumb shits, even more than in the joint, and that was saying something.

Here, straight out of the Bible, were Satan's beasts.

Marta's boot slipped, the slab lurched, and someone swore. She found better footing, told them to screw off, and helped move the block another three feet up Hell Hill. That's when someone shouted, "Watch out below!"

Marta looked up, saw one of the teams scatter, and watched their burden tumble down the slope. It flipped end over end, hit a bump, and took off. The ex-con watched the five-hundred-pound block of stone cartwheel through the air, land in the middle of the team ahead, and explode as rock met rock. Sharp-edged shrapnel whirred across the hillside, cut a work party to bloody shreds, and fell into the bay beyond.

But Marta and her coworkers had stood their ground, had escaped untouched, and were ready to proceed. The bovine stupidity of that made the ex-con sick.

"Well?" a black supervisor demanded caustically. "What are you waiting for? Get those asses in gear." He stood on a crudely constructed platform more than a hundred feet away. Power tools were forbidden, but bullhorns were okay. The Saurons were nuts.

The escaped convict gritted her teeth, felt the load shift as the others pushed upward, and put her shoulder into it.

The makeshift pad that she'd shoved up under the remains of her Eddie Bauer shirt had slipped. The pole made contact with her shirt, pushed the filthy cotton down onto her already raw skin, and hurt like hell. Marta ignored the pain, forced herself to concentrate, and eyed the ground ahead. One foot at a time—that's how she would survive.

The morning passed slowly. But the team—if that's what the group of slaves could properly be called—transported two additional blocks of stone from the bottom of the hill to the top.

Then they were allowed to eat their MREs while sitting on some rocks, gazing out over Chuckanut Bay and the spaceships moored there. One of them was fairly large, about the size of a cross-sound ferry; the other two were smaller, maybe a quarter as big.

Dozens of smaller watercraft, some alien, some human, plied

back and forth. Their wakes left white streaks on the gray-blue water.

Farther toward the north, Marta could see the larger expanse of Bellingham Bay, where even more spacecraft lay at anchor. And off to the east, the city itself, which, from her vantage point, appeared entirely untouched, as if the chits knew exactly what they wanted and where to find it. Trucks growled their way south along the twisty two-lane highway. They were loaded with pastel cargo mods, many of which were piled at the foot of the hill. Roads that would spiral toward the top were under construction.

The sky was blue, fading to light brown where it touched the horizon, and smoke clutched the land. A breeze pushed its way down from Canada and sent whitecaps racing toward the base of the hill, cooling Marta's sweat. It would rain soon and add to their misery. She shivered, cupped the self-heating can in her hands, and wished she had a jacket.

But that, like her momentary freedom, had been left north of Tacoma. Once across the Narrows Bridge and headed north on I-5, traffic had moved quickly—*too* quickly, she now realized—though it had been welcome at the time.

There was damage, lots of it, so the detour signs made sense, and it wasn't until the escaped con left the freeway and was directed into an amusement park that she had realized the truth, that the parking lot was a trap, and she was a prisoner. Again.

The fugitive *could* have fought, *could* have killed someone, but she chose to live instead. Others had taken a different course. Their bodies were stacked to one side of the parking lot, nearly invisible beneath a seething cloak of jet-black crows. The birds squawked and cawed as they fought over choice morsels.

Marta had shoved her weapons under the driver's seat, plastered a shit-eating grin on her face, and eased her way out of the car. She kept her hands visible and moved in a slow, deliberate manner. Just as Larry, her ex-husband, had taught her.

Three alien warriors watched, weapons ready, faces expressionless. Unlike the cops, who were subject to some rules, the chits could do anything they pleased. Kill, not kill, it made little difference to them.

Once outside the car, Marta had been chivied into a line where she was forced to wait for the better part of an hour. The people around her were a wild-eyed, teary-faced, babble-mouthed mess. Some were frightened for themselves, but many spent their time worrying about others, baggage Marta didn't have. Except for Jack . . . and *he* could take care of himself.

Finally, after reaching the knee-high table, it had been her turn. The alien looked up. It demanded Marta's Social Security number, ran it on the computer, and said something unintelligible.

One of the gray-green aliens stepped forward, jabbed Marta with a baton, and squeezed the weapon's handle. Electricity crackled, Marta fell to her knees, and the odor of ozone scented the air.

"Now," the small alien said firmly, "let's try that again. What is your Social Security number?"

Marta had provided the real number, was jerked to her feet, and shoved through a makeshift portal. Two men, both of them white, seized her arms. A third held some sort of tool. He grabbed her right ear, and there was a clacking sound as an alloy tag was fired through the cartilage.

It hurt and the escaped convict tried to grab her ear but the men held on. The guy with the tool had bad breath. "Sorry, lady, but we ain't got no choice."

Marta wanted to say something, *would* have said something, but they shoved her on. She stumbled, felt the metal tag, and was reminded of dairy cows she'd seen. Others, processed before her, stood in sullen groups, their tags marking them as what they were: slaves.

She'd spent the night with a pathetic collection of business-women, truck drivers, schoolteachers, sheetmetal workers, and every other kind of honest, upstanding citizen, all of whom would have been shocked by Marta's background. None of them was as prepared for the dog-eat-dog world of slave life as she was. The irony of it made her smile.

The next four days had been spent walking north on what remained of I-5. The original crowd of maybe three hundred people soon swelled to at least three thousand as more and more humans were captured, processed, and marched down on-ramps and onto the freeway.

The humans with darker skin were segregated—but were allowed to rest more frequently. That fact caused Marta to seethe with anger. Still another grievance for which the aliens would have to answer.

"The herd," because that's the way Marta thought about them, was frequently forced to leave the interstate to circumvent collapsed overpasses and slagged bridges. But they always made their way back. Difficult though it was, I-5 made the best path north.

Many of the humans were out of shape, which led to casualties, *lots* of them, but the Saurons had planned for that, and been careful to capture more slaves than they would actually need. Those who fell by the wayside, or couldn't keep up, were shot and left for the crows. The popping sounds had grown more and more common. By the third day, no one even turned to look.

Some of the now filthy captives had attempted to bond with Marta, tried to tell her about their husbands, wives, children, brothers, and sisters, but she didn't want to know, and she shook them off. Knowing made you think, knowing made you care, knowing made you weak. Prison taught her that.

There were others, men mostly, who, in spite of how stupid it was, wanted to have sex with her—or anyone, for that matter—and didn't know why. All of them understood pain, however, and having received some, gave Marta a wide berth.

That was how it went. A long, exhausting march had been followed by a night in Bellingham's makeshift slave pens, then day after day of backbreaking work.

Marta heard a noise and turned ready to snarl at anyone stupid enough to invade her personal space. She knew one alien from another now. The offenders were a Fon-mounted Ra 'Na plus two gently morphing Kan. It was the Fon who spoke. His voice was hard and flat. "Slave Manning?"

Marta considered a lie, remembered the last attempt, and thought better of it. Attention, any sort of attention, was generally bad, which explained the empty feeling at the bottom of her gut. She stood. "Yes?"

The Fon turned to one of the Kan. "Take the slave's tag—and escort her to the gates."

Marta was still analyzing the words, still trying to make sense of them, when a Sauron seized her throat. His pincer was strong, *very* strong, and cut her air off. She grabbed his wrist and tried to break the Kan's grip. The second warrior stepped in, used his combat knife to take her right ear, and tossed it away. The tag went with it.

The first Kan released her throat, and she inhaled enough air to scream, grabbing at what remained of her ear. It felt warm and wet.

"Here," the second Kan said, "press this against the wound." Marta did as she was told, felt a sense of warmth as the self-sealing bandage formed a temporary bond with her skin, and felt her head swim. Only one Kan had been detailed as an escort, but that was plenty. The world whirled. She stumbled, and struggled to stay upright.

But there was no time for shock or anything else as she was herded down a trail, past a dull-eyed work party, and toward the protective palisade. It had been constructed from logs harvested on the hill itself and was little more than a temporary measure till a stone wall could be built.

The gate, which remained open to accommodate a steady stream of sandstone blocks, was guarded by six heavily armed Kan. The ground dipped at that point, which meant that a certain amount of water had collected, and they stood shin-deep in mud.

Marta's escort said something, his peers responded in kind, and she was shoved toward the opening. The muck sucked at the soles of her boots. She was free to go. . . . But why? She turned. "What's going on? Who cut me loose?"

But the Kan didn't know, or if they did, weren't willing to say. They turned their backs, worked to pull their podlike feet up out of the mud, and moved toward drier ground.

Marta backed away, nearly tripped over a rock, whirled, and ran. Then, heart pounding, she ran some more, fearful that the whole thing was some sort of mistake, that the Kan would chase her.

Finally, lungs on fire, she followed a ribbon of ancient blacktop toward some fire-gutted homes, spotted an outbuilding that stood unscathed, and headed in that direction. The door had been kicked in, and there wasn't much left inside, but Marta didn't care. The shed was a sanctuary, a place to hide while she recovered, a place to cry.

Tears were a privilege, a release she had never allowed herself while in prison, nor during her time as a slave. Now, safe within four musty walls, sunlight forcing its way in through a dirty window, she finally let go. Her sobs lasted a long time.

Then, when she could cry no longer, when it felt as if every bit of moisture had been wrung from her tear ducts, Marta lay down on the pad from an old chaise lounge, grabbed her knees, and immediately fell asleep.

Outside, beyond the weathered walls, day faded to night, and stars appeared. The world continued to turn.

3

DEATH DAY MINUS 148

FRIDAY, MARCH 6, 2020

Anarchy is the stepping-stone to absolute power.
—NAPOLEON I,
Maxims, 1804–15

SALMON NATIONAL FOREST, IDAHO

The night was pitch-black, with a low overcast, and a steady drizzle of rain. It gathered along the leading edge of the roof, divided into rivers, and zigzagged across the badly cracked windshield. The much-abused truck lurched as the front right tire dropped into a large pothole. A skin named Jonsey swore when a dollop of hot coffee slopped into his lap, and Boner, who had the wheel and who didn't like anyone to criticize his driving, told the other man to "shut the fuck up."

Ivory, who sat in the passenger's seat with a dog-eared copy of the 2019 *Rand McNally Road Atlas* spread across his knees, bit the inside of his cheek. The map light had burned out long ago and been replaced by a flashlight on a string. The blob of light swayed wildly as the war wagon swerved from one side of the road to the other. He stared out into the darkness.

The journey north from Denver to Salt Lake City, from there to Pocatello, and west along Highway 33 had been rough. Ivory and his followers had fought their way out of an ambush, raced through a forest fire, used a train trestle to cross a river, been strafed by an alien fighter, and replaced a faulty starter all while foraging for food, gas, and beer. Not pleasant, but understandable, and therefore acceptable.

What *wasn't* acceptable was all the complaining and just plain bullshit. The skinheads made Ivory crazy, and if the trip lasted much longer, he'd have to shoot one of them. Not a good idea, since he needed their support, *would* need their support, especially during the days ahead.

Boner stood on the brakes as the beams from the carefully masked headlights washed over a sturdy metal gate. The sign, which consisted of a black swastika against a red background, spoke volumes. "Damn!" Jones said enthusiastically. "Look at that shit! We're here."

Confirmation came in the form of two handheld spotlights. They caressed the truck like a pair of soft white hands. There was a thump and the truck rocked as a man dropped out of the tree above them. He landed on the hood, pointed a twelve-gauge pump at Boner's face, and grinned. A gold tooth gleamed in the light.

The heavily amplified voice came from the surrounding darkness. "Leave the headlights on. Open the doors. . . . Keep your hands in sight. . . . Move to the front of the vehicle. Kneel facing east. This would be a good time to make your peace with Yahweh."

The last part was pure intimidation, Ivory hoped, as he opened the door and stepped into a mud puddle. The group's leader could see his breath, and the rain felt especially cold after the foggy warmth of the cab. The wipers squeaked as they slapped back and forth. A dog barked, and a woman seemed to materialize out of the darkness. She was pretty in a calculated sort of way. Her eyes were knowledgeable—as if she already knew what made him tick. She cradled the ancient AK-47 in the same way another woman would hold a baby. "You heard the man . . . get a move on."

Ivory turned, walked to the front of the truck, and prayed the skins would do likewise. He'd prepped them for this, or something *like* this, and he hoped they were ready. One mistake, one wrongheaded move, and all of them were dead. He watched from the corner of his eye as Parker appeared, followed by Jones, Boner, and Hopkins. They lined up next to him, knelt when he did, and kept their heads up. Cooperative but proud. The soldiers of God.

Bodies approached from behind, and hands patted them down. Wallets, knives, and handguns were confiscated. "So far so good," the voice said. "Now place your hands behind your backs and cross your wrists."

The newly arrived men did as they were told. Plastic ties were used in place of handcuffs. Hands jerked them up out of the mud. Their pants were wet and muddy. "Good," the voice said. "Start walking."

Ivory did as he was told, heard someone put the war wagon in gear, and thought about what he had observed so far.

The center seemed well organized, but he had questions. The group's founder, old man Howther, had been dead for the better part of six months. Ivory had read about it in the *Denver Post,* been to the group's web site, and dispatched his condolences via e-mail. So who had taken control? And what were they doing? Building an Aryan nation? Or hiding in the woods?

Ivory would support the first possibility but not the second, which led nowhere. If ever there was a chance to build a new nation, this was it. He'd have to be careful, however, *very* careful, lest he unintentionally reveal the full scope of his ambition.

The darkness made it difficult to scope the place out, but the handheld spots drifted here and there, highlighting various aspects of the property. The road swung past what looked like a machine-gun emplacement, snaked between some well-kept sheds, and fronted the remains of a once substantial log building.

The woman with the AK-47 appeared at his elbow. She nodded toward the ruins. "Old man Howther inherited the lodge from his father—and lived there all his life. He's buried over there ... under that arch. The chits nailed the place from orbit. It burned to the ground."

"From *orbit?*" Ivory asked. "You're sure of that? They have fighters, you know—and larger ships, too."

"We've seen 'em," the woman confirmed grimly. "They started a forest fire about twenty miles west of here. But this bolt came out of the blue, not a cloud in the sky, and that pretty well speaks for itself."

"Yes," Ivory agreed, "I suppose it does. But why pick on you?"

" 'Cause we were careless," the woman said matter-of-factly. "The aliens can detect heat from orbit, and anytime they spot anything bigger than a campfire, they zap it. Long as they do that, people will be forced to live in the boonies. Add the fact that they're working with the Jews—and you can see why we were targeted."

The last statement was uttered as if such a conspiracy were a matter of documented fact—something that Ivory found easy to believe. The ZOG was powerful, *very* powerful, and wanted to stay that way.

The combined group, some fifteen individuals altogether, followed the road across a timber-built bridge, past some old mining equipment, and back to the base of a cliff. Shadowy figures came out to meet them, words were exchanged, and the woman motioned Ivory forward. "Old man Howther's grandfather staked a claim here and took a quarter million in gold from the mountain, back before the government stole most of the surrounding land. We had our supplies stored here anyway—so it was natural to move on in."

"What about the aliens?" Ivory inquired. "They attacked once. Why not again?"

"We're smarter now," the woman answered simply. "We heat the place, to the extent we can, but control how much leaks out."

Ivory saw what the woman meant as they passed through a thick door followed by a succession of heavily insulated "rooms," each slightly warmer than the last. Finally, after stepping through one last door, they entered a large, rock-lined chamber. It was about the size and shape of a medium-size hotel lobby.

Most of the light originated from a damaged but still functional crystal chandelier. It had been salvaged from the lodge and hung suspended from a length of rusty chain. A generator purred in the distance.

There was furniture, too. Massive pieces that still looked small within the cavern's rocky embrace. They were grouped around what looked like an old boiler, which, with its curved metal door removed, made a sizable fireplace. Something popped as sparks flew upward and disappeared into a makeshift chimney.

Flags hung at regular intervals around the walls, one for each of the white nations that Howther had envisioned. Interspersed with the flags were Nazi swastikas and larger-than-life oil paintings of chiseled white people, all posed in front of verdant fields, Art Deco cities, and majestic mountain ranges. It was Howther's vision of the way the future would be if the white race controlled the planet. The "muds," assuming they were permitted to live, would be relegated to the least desirable climes. "Damn," Boner said admiringly, "these dudes have their shit together! Just look at this place."

Though not as easily impressed as Boner was, Ivory knew class when he saw it, and some of that must have shown on his face.

The woman smiled. "Not bad, huh? Hold your hands away from your body."

Ivory did so, felt a jerk as the tie was cut, and rubbed his wrists. "Go ahead," the woman said, "take a seat. I'll be back in a moment." The newcomers did as they were told.

The woman vanished behind a tapestry that bore a likeness of the Norse god Thor, his hammer held high. She was replaced by a teenage girl bearing refreshments. The guards remained where they were, chatting among themselves, but vigilant nonetheless. The skins looked uncomfortable but kept their mouths shut, a blessing for which Ivory was truly thankful.

Ten extremely long minutes had passed before the woman returned sans AK-47, shucked her waist-length jacket, and dropped into a well-worn leather chair. A leg dangled over one well-stuffed arm. Though concealed by black denim, the leg was long and shapely. A second girl brought coffee. Her eyes were downcast as she hurried from the room. The woman sipped and watched Ivory through the steam. He'd seen the look before . . . at a cattle auction.

The silence grew. It seemed as though everybody were waiting for someone. . . . But who? The answer arrived ten seconds later.

A hand-hewn wooden door groaned open. An elderly woman entered the chamber. She was thin, extremely thin, like a bundle of sticks covered with translucent white skin. Her long, disconcertingly blond hair hung down her back in a single thick braid. She moved under her own power, with assistance from twin girls, who supported her arms.

The younger woman stood and crossed the room. She kissed a brightly rouged cheek. "Hello, Mother. How are you?"

The voice was thin and reedy. "A little tired, my dear . . . but otherwise fine."

Ivory, who had been waiting for some hint of who he was dealing with, literally sat up and took notice. Mother? As in *Mother Howther?* So the family was in control . . . the *same* family a *New York Times* journalist once referred to as "the first family of American racism." Not "racialism," which would have been accurate, but "racism," which was Zog-given code intended to promote racial mixing and undermine the white race.

Ivory knew he should have been offended, should be angry about the manner in which the younger woman had manipulated him, but discovered that he wasn't. He stood out of respect and motioned for the skins to do likewise.

The younger woman saw and smiled. She took a skeletal arm and escorted the oldster toward the visitors. "Mother, there's someone I'd like you to meet. Mr. Kreider, this is my mother, Marianne Howther. . . . Mother, Mr. Kreider came all the way from Denver to join us. Isn't that right, Mr. Kreider?"

Ivory, momentarily shocked by her seemingly miraculous knowledge of who he was, remembered the missing wallet and felt a bit silly. Marianne Howther extended a fragile, liver-spotted hand, and he took it. He looked into her eyes and saw that they were opaque. Mrs. Howther was blind. "It's a pleasure to meet you, Mr. Kreider. . . . My husband spoke of a great ingathering, and now it has finally begun."

"Mr. Kreider was kind enough to send his condolences the day after Father died," the younger woman said matter-of-factly. "One reason why he and his men are still alive. All sorts of people want to join now . . . many of whom are scum."

Ivory felt a sense of panic. How in the hell did she know that? What the woman said was true enough, but the note had been signed "Jonathan Ivory" rather than "Jonathan Kreider." Then he remembered. The e-mail would have displayed his real name at the top. Within a very short time after his capture the group had compared the name on his driver's license to their records and established a positive match. Very impressive and very wise, given the manner in which the Zog attempted to infiltrate such groups.

"That was very considerate of you," Mrs. Howther said, moving even closer. "I was touched by the great outpouring of sympathy that came our way."

The old woman had invaded Ivory's personal space by then . . . and it required an act of will to stand his ground. Even more so when her hands came up to caress his face, smoothing his brow, tracing the length of his nose, petting his goatee.

Then, as if satisfied with what she had discovered so far, Mrs. Howther dropped her hands to his torso. They slipped inside his shirt, found his skin, and slid down along his flanks. Ivory met the younger woman's eyes, saw the challenge there, and knew something important was taking place.

Ivory stood absolutely still as the old woman slid her soft, cool hands down across his hard, flat stomach, found his belt, and released the buckle.

Then, with a surprising amount of dexterity, she cupped his genitals. The reaction came with embarrassing speed. Mrs.

Howther nodded and withdrew. "My apologies, Mr. Kreider, but I had to be sure. Homosexuals are a constant threat. We have a race to build, and each man must do his part. Not to mention the fact that Yahweh hates them just as we do. We've been expecting you. Welcome to Racehome."

Ivory wondered if he should refasten his pants, decided to do so, and took a chance. "I'm sorry, Mrs. Howther, I don't understand."

It was the younger woman who replied. "My father prophesized that the white race would receive three presents . . . he said the first would arrive on Christmas Day. One would prove to be a leader, the second would be an assassin, and the third a saint."

"And I am?"

"The leader."

"And you are?"

The woman smiled. "My name is Ella . . . and I'm your race wife."

GUTHRIE, WASHINGTON

It was dark, the last patient had been seen, and the entire town was heading for the old community church. Flashlights danced like fireflies as people filtered toward the center of town.

Dr. Seeko Sool closed the door behind her, checked to ensure it was locked, made her way down the wooden steps, and turned to look at the hotel. Well, not a hotel, Guthrie hadn't had one of those for a long time, but the Orchard Bed and Breakfast, which, thanks to the aliens, was full for the first time since it had opened. Not that Mrs. Blake was making any money—or that the currency would be worth anything anyway.

No, the locals, like country people everywhere, had long depended on each other for help. So when the nation went to hell in a handcart, they wasted little time switching to a barter-based economy.

That meant Sool received things such as eggs, vegetables, and meat in place of her usual fees. She passed them on to her landlord, who proceeded to serve them in the form of breakfast, lunch, and dinner.

The Victorian-style house had been constructed by the town's foremost banker back in the 1920s and stood three stories tall. Carefully shielded candles had been placed in each of the front windows, which, along with the Coleman lantern beside the front door, made for a festive feel.

It reminded the doctor of the house she had grown up in, of her parents, and their probable fate. Mr. Chong, who shared the room just down from hers, had escaped from Seattle and walked east over the mountains. He said that with the exception of the Neptune Hotel and Entertainment complex, the entire metroplex had been leveled. The chances that her parents had survived ranged from slim to none.

Sool had been lucky, assuming there was something to live for, which was open to question. No fewer than three patients had taken their own lives during the past few weeks. Two had run out of their medications and figured they'd die anyway, and the third was too despondent to keep going.

That's why the celebration was so important, why she had encouraged people to get involved, why she was headed for church. For the first time in ten years? Yes, at least that long. The knowledge fueled feelings of guilt.

Sool turned, pulled her collar up around her ears, and headed toward the center of town. Houses, most of which were old and tired, squatted on both sides of the street. A few sported candles. Candles were precious now and, with the exception of free spirits such as Mrs. Burke, were hoarded for more important purposes.

The town, which boasted 2,000 souls back in its heyday, had shrunk to fewer than 100 by 2020. Now, with the addition of refugees such as Sool, it had swelled to about 450, with more arriving every day. *More* mouths to feed, *more* medical issues to deal with, and *more* voices to be heard. Voices that had already skewed local politics, reset the community's priorities, and stirred resentment.

Of even more concern—to Sool, at least—was the possibility that the steadily growing population would attract the wrong sort of attention and trigger an attack by the aliens, or even worse, by human looters who preyed on small communities. A militia had been organized to resist them, but the doctor had doubts regarding their effectiveness.

Someone yelled, "Hey, Doc!" and waved from half a block away.

Sool waved in return and continued toward the church. It was amazing how her life had changed. She'd been born at Swedish Hospital in Seattle, gone to public schools, attended the University of Nebraska at Lincoln, received a B.S. in biology, applied to medical school, and been accepted. Then came year after year of hard work until finally, in what felt like an anticlimax, Sool finished her residency in 2015.

Then the newly minted doctor took a long-deferred vacation, traveled through Europe, and made an important decision. Rather than work for an HMO or join a partnership, she would open a practice of her own. Not right away, since she lacked the necessary funds, but as soon as she could.

That's what the years in Minneapolis were about, saving money, polishing skills, and building her dream.

A dream that came true on September 12, 2018, when she opened her practice in Spokane, Washington. And it came crashing down on February 28, 2020, when the aliens attacked from space.

She'd been in her car, driving west on Highway 2, when the first reports filtered in. Sool thought the whole thing was a joke at first, a put-on *à la* Orson Welles and *The War of the Worlds* back in 1938.

But it soon became apparent that this was *real* as radio stations dropped off the air. She ran into a traffic jam east of Dry Falls Dam and Coulee City. Even more disturbing was the huge column of black smoke that billowed up toward the sky.

Traffic had come to a complete standstill by then; many people had left their vehicles and were standing around, talking to each other. There was no eastbound traffic beyond a few folks who had pulled U-turns and were headed back east. Because of whatever caused the smoke? Yes, that seemed logical.

Sool had decided she would get out to see what, if anything, her fellow motorists knew about the situation ahead. Should she continue? Or turn around? Any information would help.

Additional vehicles had already pulled in behind her, and Sool hadn't taken more than a dozen steps before a man on a fancy high-tech touring bike came from the direction of Coulee City. He wore street clothes rather than cycling togs and looked frightened. The doctor had called to him, asked him what was wrong.

"Spaceships!" he'd replied. "They attacked the dam!"

Sool had started to think about what that meant when a woman screamed, "Look! Here they come!"

Sool looked, saw some specks low on the horizon, and ran toward the side of the freeway, where she tripped and tumbled down a gravel-strewn bank.

The fighters positioned themselves two abreast to ensure that nothing would escape their overlapping fields of fire. Their energy cannons burped coherent light, and a tsunamilike wave of destruction rolled east. A tanker truck exploded, a red Mercedes cartwheeled through the air, and a group of people were incinerated where they stood.

Anyone who had remained in their vehicle, went back for their luggage, or stood on the freeway died.

But Sool, like the others who survived, had relied on instinct. Already at the bottom of the bank and bleeding from numerous cuts and scrapes, she'd scrambled for the mouth of a large culvert. She had ducked inside, plunged into the dank interior, when the fighters passed overhead. There had been a loud bang as something exploded, followed by screams and the crackle of flames.

Sool had turned, waited for the worst of the noise to die down, and stumbled into thick, black smoke. She'd felt for the culvert's opening and followed the dry creekbed forward until the smoke thinned and she found herself standing next to the supports for a short train trestle that paralleled the highway. In the meantime a gas tank exploded, a horn started to bleat, and a woman screamed in pain.

That's when Sool climbed the railroad embankment and stood on the track.

The wind changed direction, blew the smoke toward the south, and the doctor spotted her Honda. It seemed to be intact, but it was trapped between two heavily damaged vehicles. The first was burning, and the other was leaking what appeared to be gas.

Sool skidded down the railroad embankment, climbed the one that led up to the highway, and hurried forward. The physician opened the car door with her remote and grabbed her purse and the medical bag that sat on the passenger-side floor. A man yelled at her from the top of the neighboring railroad embankment, "Hey, lady! Get the hell out of there!"

A piece of burning upholstery hit the pool of gas, and it exploded into flames. Sool backed away, tripped, and recovered. There was a whoosh as fire consumed her car. It had taken four long years to pay for the Honda, and the doctor wondered if alien attacks were covered by her insurance.

That was the last personal thought she'd had for next three hours. She went to where the screaming was loudest, opened her bag, and went to work. An off-duty EMT and a retired nurse appeared, offered to help, and rolled up their sleeves.

The three-person trauma team sorted the patients into categories: those who would almost certainly die of their injuries, those who might stand a chance, and those with minor cuts and abrasions.

Bystanders were recruited to give comfort to the dying so that Sool could focus on those for whom there was still some hope.

An insurance agent called for volunteers, managed to get the worst of the patients loaded onto a nearly empty tractor-trailer rig, and sent them east to Spokane. The EMT and the nurse went along. Maybe the city was still there, maybe the hospitals were open, maybe things would be okay.

Sool could have gone along, but still hoped to reach her parents. If they were still alive, they would need her help.

So she joined the ragtag column of people and marched toward the west. Some followed the highway, weaving their way among still-smoldering vehicles, while others walked along the side of the road. Their faces were grim, and they were silent for the most part, all except for a baby who wouldn't stop crying and a man with a radio. He'd held it to his lips and begged for someone to "come in." No one did.

The refugees soon discovered that rather than a single traffic jam, as many supposed, there were actually many, interspersed with stretches of open pavement. Pieces of flaming debris, carried south by the wind, had sparked a grass fire.

They were in farm country, which meant that long, low farm buildings could be seen off to the right and the left, some naked to the elements, others encircled by protective vegetation.

Like most of those around her, Sool walked quickly, curious as to what lay ahead and eager of find out. An old building bearing the sign "Coulee Stove & Collectibles" passed to the left, and the now deserted Coulee City campground passed to the right.

Viewed from the approach east of Coulee City, the dam and the two-lane blacktop that ran along its top made a long, straight line that stretched toward the west. That alien spacecraft had been there was evidenced by still-smoking clusters of burned-out vehicles that dotted the highway.

In spite of the fact that Sool had passed that way dozens of times before, she saw it differently now. To the right of the highway, which was to say the north, lay the silvery waters of Banks Lake, its surface interrupted by a few low-lying islands.

The dry side of Dryfalls Dam, which consisted of a marshy area dotted with ponds, lay to the left of the highway. Either obstacle could be dealt with—but only with difficulty.

A group of overnight desperadoes had established a roadblock complete with armchairs looted from a local motel, six cases of beer, a stereo complete with loud country and western music, and some dusty pickup trucks.

They waved pistols, invited the refugees to come forward, and checked them over. Tolls varied according to what people had with them. The bandits were in the process of accumulating a wild variety of what would soon be worthless junk. They'd favored things such as cash and jewelry, while the *real* valuables, the bullets in their guns, were fired willy-nilly into the air.

The yahoos didn't know how stupid they were, which meant people could either deal with them, find a boat, or swing to the south and be forced to negotiate the marsh.

Sool, along with a scattering of others, chose the latter course. She had walked south, along the western edge of Coulee City, down past the silvery grain silos, then west through low-lying scrub, down onto a section of hardpan, between two ponds, across a sandy land bridge, and toward the bank of gray lichen-spotted shale that rose to the west. It formed a cliff to the right but sloped down on the left.

Others had pioneered the route before her, and Sool had followed their footprints through some mud, up a rock-strewn ravine, onto a plateau, and down the other side. From there it was possible to parallel the dam, cross the dry lakebed, and make it to the other side.

There Sool had passed the still-smoldering remnants of Larry's Diner and started the long climb up Highway 2 toward Waterville to the west. Two of the huge transmission towers that carried power across the state had gone down along with the cables they carried. Fires, started by sparks from the black, snakelike cables, headed for the southern horizon.

By the time Sool had topped the long incline that led up out of the valley, a number of things were apparent: Night was coming, she was hungry, and the odds of successfully crossing the Cascades equipped with a light jacket and running shoes were not especially good.

Not only that, but the scumbags back in Coulee City were but a sample of things to come. A woman alone would be extremely vulnerable. Like it or not, Sool figured she would need some help. But where to find it?

The physician had driven that particular route many, many times before and knew that the next town of any size was Waterville. If it was not already overwhelmed by refugees, it soon would be.

So rather than follow the herd to Waterville and the inevitable confrontation with its hard-pressed citizens, Sool had decided to turn either north or south and try her luck in an even smaller community. One that could use a doctor.

All of which was fine, or would be, once she reached a turnoff. There was a night to get through first, however—and that had the higher priority. There were no houses, sheds, or barns in sight, which meant Sool had three choices: She could sleep in one of the abandoned cars, sleep next to the road, or sleep in a field.

The last two alternatives were clearly unattractive, especially on a night when the temperature would drop into the low fifties, so the car was best. Not that she wanted to be alone, not if she could help it.

She continued to walk until she spotted two women walking side by side, approached, and asked if they would join her. They were quick to agree.

The women introduced themselves as the Landy sisters, both of whom were from Tacoma. They pointed to a stalled minivan. It had three flat tires and a badly scorched fender but seemed otherwise intact. Sool had agreed, the vehicle was appropriated, and the doors were soon locked behind them.

The Landys had two loaves of bread looted from a delivery truck, and they were kind enough to share.

Sool used a first-aid kit that the owner had stupidly left behind to tend the blisters on their feet and then dumped the rest of the contents into her nearly empty medical bag.

The three women talked for a while. But due to the fact that none of them wanted to discuss their real concerns, not in front of strangers, they stuck to the safer stuff. An hour elapsed, the number of people who passed the van dwindled to little more than a trickle, and darkness descended.

They slept after that, or tried to, although Sool awoke several times—once when someone tried to open a door, once when one of the Landy sisters talked in her sleep, and once to escape a nightmare.

Finally, when her watch told her it was 4:00 A.M., Sool opened the back door, took her bag, and locked the van behind her.

It was cold, and the physician's teeth chattered as she headed west. Sool wished she had a toothbrush, toothpaste, and a piping-hot cup of vanilla-flavored coffee—trivial, everyday comforts she had long taken for granted.

Others would be up soon, the moment the sun broke over the eastern horizon. But now, until the rest of them crawled out of their holes, the doctor had the highway to herself.

Now, looking back, the medic realized how critical that seemingly unimportant decision had been. Because Sool was the first one up, and because of her early start, the physician was all by herself when she topped a rise and saw the work party below.

Ten or twelve men and women had been clustered around the point where a farm road connected with Highway 2. A power saw screamed and sparks flew as the steel blade sliced through metal supports. Sool had seen the sign topple, watched people carry it toward a waiting dump truck, and realized what they were up to.

They were from a town, a *small* town. They were afraid of refugees. So they were busy removing signs, erecting barriers, and blocking roads.

Sool felt her heart beat faster as she ran down the road, approached the work crew, and slowed to a stop. She had noticed they were armed—and anything but friendly. A man helped a woman position a freshly painted "Road Closed" sign so that it blocked the two-lane highway. His voice was hard and cold. "Something I can do for you?"

"Yes," Sool had said earnestly. "Take me with you." She eyed one of the signs already loaded into the back of a pickup. "Take me to Guthrie."

The man's eyes had narrowed. His mouth made a straight line. "I'm sorry, lady, but Guthrie is full up. Try Waterville . . . it's a few miles west of here."

Sool refused to back down. She was five foot five and tried to look taller. "I understand the problem . . . but I'm a board-certified surgeon. How many doctors have you got in Guthrie?" she'd asked.

"One," the woman had answered, "*if* you count ol' Doc Peterson, and he's retired."

The man looked at the woman and then back to Sool. "You're telling the truth? 'Cause I'll shoot you if you're lying."

"I'm telling the truth," she had replied.

The woman had stepped forward to take the physician's arm. Her eyes were friendly. "Of course you are. . . . Don't mind Tom . . . his bark is worse than his bite. Would you like some coffee? I have a thermos in the truck." She'd led Sool toward the vehicle.

Which was how Dr. Seeko Sool came to be a resident of Guthrie, Washington.

"Hey, Doc," someone called. "Here, let me get that door."

A rectangle of buttery yellow light appeared, the smell of food floated on the air, and Sool entered the church. It was warm . . . and she felt safe.

THE THREE SISTERS WILDERNESS AREA, OREGON

The woods were almost completely silent as Deacon Smith made his way up the steadily rising trail. Fir trees, many more than a hundred feet tall, rose to either side. It was snowing, not hard, but in a steady sort of way. A late snow that would soon disappear. Each flake seemed to materialize from thin air, hang as if from an invisible string, then twirl to the ground. Bootprints could be seen here and there, but the hiker had a pretty good idea who they belonged to and wasn't especially concerned.

The ex-Ranger exhaled puffs of lung-warmed air, marched through them, and knew they were coming faster of late. That's because he was forty-six, almost forty-seven, and starting to feel it.

Smith paused at a turn in the switchback trail, tilted the barrel of his weapon up, and allowed the military-grade Remington 7.62mm M42A1 sniper's rifle to rest against his right shoulder. Then he listened—carefully, as if his life depended on it. Which it did.

Smith's hair, which he wore short, was dark but peppered with gray. His serious brown eyes punctuated a face that was too strong to be classically handsome. His legs, planted like tree trunks, supported a barrel-like torso.

The ex-Ranger's attire, which, with the exception of his combat boots, was based on that worn by the original mountain men, was made entirely of handsewn buckskin.

His pack was equally authentic, but the contents, like his weapon, were strictly contemporary. They included an expedition-quality down sleeping bag, a selection of freeze-dried meals, and a high-tech first-aid kit.

The period clothing had to do with the fact that Smith, like hundreds of other men and women, had long been part of a loosely organized group that staged gatherings similar to those that real trappers held 180 years before. To that end they wore historically accurate garb, fired black powder rifles, and bartered for handmade usefuls such as tomahawks and knives.

That had been for fun, whereas this was real, which meant there was no room in the ex-noncom's pack for anything but the best that the present had to offer.

Smith allowed the silence to settle around him, ignored the sounds that belonged, and listened for those that didn't. It came as a simple *clink*. The sound of metal on metal, natural elsewhere, but false here.

The ex-Ranger brought the rifle down from his shoulder, flicked the safety to the "off" position, and backed into the rocks that marked the point where the trail turned.

Then, resting the weapon on the top of a boulder, he peered through the Redfield twelve-power scope. In a minute, perhaps less, a face would appear. What happened then would depend on who the person was, or conversely wasn't, since Smith knew every individual who had been invited to the rendezvous. He'd warned them against bringing friends, relatives, or acquaintances. His finger rested on the trigger. He took a deep breath and let it out.

A branch twitched, a face appeared, and Smith removed his finger from the trigger. It felt good to breathe again. The ex-Ranger waited till George Farley, better known to his friends as "Popcorn," was only ten feet away before he stepped out onto the trail. The other man showed no visible sign of surprise. "It's good to see you, George, even if you are ugly as the back end of a dog."

Farley wore a dark blue watch cap, a matching REI Gore-Tex jacket, and a much-used backpack. The Mossberg 12-gauge pump he carried didn't have much in the way of range, but it was a damned good brush cutter. The ex-noncom grinned. "I might be ugly, but I sure as hell dress better than you do. Where did you get that outfit, anyway? At a garage sale?"

Both men laughed, embraced, and took the next section of trail together. It was second nature to delay the small talk, open up some distance between them, and pay close attention to their surroundings. There were occasional piles of horse dung in the middle of the trail, deer tracks, and in one case, a patch of pee-melted snow. Nothing threatening, though—at least not yet.

The trail climbed, took a turn to the right, and crossed a split-log bridge. Lake water gushed, gurgled, and leaped toward the slopes below. It had a date with the Pacific and seemed eager to keep it.

The bridge terminated on a muddy embankment. Smith added some tracks to the already well-churned muck, savored the tang of wood smoke, and pushed his way up over a rise. Farley followed.

The scene that greeted them was part 1840 rendezvous and part on-line equipment catalog. True to the standards of the group to which they belonged, roughly half of the "trappers" had elected to erect tepees, wigwams, and other historically correct shelters along the shore of a half-frozen blue-black alpine lake.

Others, conscious of the reason for the gathering, opted for the latest in ultralight, self-erecting, stormproof blue, green, and occasionally orange tents.

The combination was a bit strange, but Smith didn't care. Only one thing was of interest to him: Were the people gathered in front of him willing to fight the bugs, and if they were, could they get the job done?

He saw at least fifty different shelters, many of which were large enough to accommodate two or three people. That, plus the number of bodies gathered around various fires, suggested a minimum of seventy-five people. Not enough for what he had in mind, but an excellent start. Especially given the *kind* of people they were. Tough, independent, and more than a little paranoid. That's why they were breathing while millions weren't. Some of them waved, and the newcomers waved in return..

The two men followed the well-churned trail across a snow-covered meadow, past a half-buried miner's cabin, and over to the ice-rimmed lake. Like most of the reenacters, Smith had a handle or nickname—the same one given to him while serving in the army: "Deacon" Smith. It wasn't long before greetings flew back and forth. "Hey, Deac! Good to see you!"

"Popcorn, how's it hangin', man?"

"Over here, guys—you can throw your gear in my tepee."

The next hour was spent talking to old friends; commiserating over relatives, friends, and acquaintances lost to the aliens; and speculating on the future.

Then, as if summoned by a group mind, the would-be trappers gathered within a triangle formed by three substantial fires and waited for Smith to speak. Not because they had to, but because they respected the ex-soldier and wanted to hear his opinions.

Like most professional noncoms, Smith wasn't one for speeches, figuring that's what generals were for, and knowing that 86 percent of what *they* said was standard-issue bullshit, meant more for their superiors than for the men and women who reported to them.

So the man who had seen close combat in the U.N. police action called "the war that wasn't" and who received two decorations for valor was scared. What if he blew the opportunity? Screwed everything up? The thought scared the crap out of him.

But nobody knew that, except for George Farley, and *he* believed in his friend.

Smith stood on a chunk of snow-encrusted rock and scanned the people in front of him. Most were white, but there were some darker faces, like Farley's, visible as well. They stood in clumps, or by themselves, leaning on long-barreled flintlocks, snug within their Gore-Tex, or draped in furs. These were good people, *strong* people, who survived when many perished.

However, Smith thought, *if* they have a flaw, *if* they share a weakness, that's what it is—a focus on *individual* rather than group survival. Could he, or someone more qualified, take this group of rugged individualists and forge them into a hard-core cadre? The kind that could spread out, recruit more people to the cause, and push the bugs off the planet? Or would they refuse to submit themselves to the kind of discipline required by successful resistance fighters, and scatter like a pack of cats?

Smith hoped for the former but feared the latter, and called on God for help. Then, with snowflakes kissing the hard planes of his face, the ex-Ranger made his case. His voice, still parade-ground strong, echoed off the surrounding slopes.

"Information is hard to come by right now, but it's likely that millions, if not *billions*, of human beings are dead. Not as a result of some horrible disease, or a series of natural disasters, but because they were murdered. Not somewhere else, in some other country, but right *here* in the good old U.S. of A. There isn't a man or a woman among you who hasn't lost a relative or a friend. That means that you're involved whether you want to be or not, it means you have a stake in what happens next, and it means this is *personal*."

"You tell 'em, Deac!" someone shouted. "Tell 'em how it is!"

"So," Smith continued, "what are you going to do? Hide in your holes and hope those MREs will last your family the next thousand years? Or are you ready to fight? To track the aliens down—to kick their butts?"

"We're ready!" a woman shouted. "Tell us what to do!"

Smith held his hand up. "Thank you! It's good to hear your enthusiasm. But this ain't no movie. Some of you, people like George Farley over there, have been in combat, seen a buddy go down with a bullet in his belly, and heard him call for his mommy. But most of you haven't . . . and don't have the foggiest notion of what combat is like."

"So what are you saying?" a man in a coonskin hat demanded. "You telling us to fight or not?"

Smith waited for the echoes to die away before nodding his head. "I'm asking you to fight—but only if you know what to expect. A long, bloody campaign, lots of casualties, and not much thanks. So give it some thought. Ask God what to do. Then, after the potluck tonight, cast your vote. Not with a paper ballot, or some kind of machine, but with your lives. Thank you."

GUTHRIE, WASHINGTON

Guthrie didn't have a hospital, clinic, or doctor's office, which explained why Sool's patient, who was still very much alive, was laid out in the back of the Berry Brothers Mortuary when the slavers attacked.

Their leader, a woman named Horsky, had been among fifty candidates put forward by the Ra 'Na and interviewed by a Fon named Mor-Duu. Finally, after a good deal of thought, Horsky was chosen because of her expertise, hard-nosed attitude, and skin color. Dark brown skin that would have been considerably lighter if it weren't for her regular visits to the tanning salon. Now, as her artificial tan started to fade, she had taken to rubbing what amounted to dye into her face, neck, and hands.

Though not especially thrilled about the opportunity to hunt "feral" humans, Horsky was a pragmatist. She believed that order, almost any kind of order, was superior to the anarchy that claimed most of the land.

That being the case, she had been allowed to create a "posse" of more than a hundred men and women. She used the knowledge gained during eight years with the Washington State Patrol to hit a long list of small towns, many of which had managed to survive the initial attack virtually unscathed.

Though impressed by the fact that the townspeople had removed all the signs that pointed toward the refuge, she knew where the town was and knew how to take it. The keys to success were absolute surprise, brute force, and ruthless efficiency.

"Horsky's Hounds," as the rank-and-file cutthroats liked to refer to themselves, preferred to strike just prior to dawn, a time when trained infantry usually stand to but when bored farmers, ranchers, and truck drivers have a tendency to doze.

Thus the lead element of their assault force, a heavily reinforced Kenworth truck, was only half a mile away, and traveling at better than sixty miles per hour when Dave Robbins heard the unmistakable roar of the big diesel and elbowed his father's side. "Wake up, Dad, someone's comin'."

Dave Robbins, Sr., awoke to find that "someone was comin'" indeed and immediately opened fire. Others joined in. The crack, crack, crack of their hunting rifles was lost in the roar of the oncoming semi. A pair of high beams came on, Robbins threw an arm across his eyes, and knew it would have been better to run.

But it was too late. An air horn sounded, the driver shifted into a lower gear, and the steel tubing mounted on the front of the truck hit the first set of obstacles. The carefully constructed barricade, which consisted of two pickup trucks and a line of water-filled fifty-gallon drums, were swept away in the twinkling of an eye.

Horsky loosed her "hounds," and a double column of "liberated" National Guard vehicles penetrated the lightly defended perimeter and entered the center of town. There was some resistance, snipers mostly, but they were dealt with in minutes.

Sool, who was engrossed in the first stage of a rather primitive appendectomy on a middle-aged woman named Miller, was unaware the invasion had taken place until the door slammed open and a half-dozen slavers burst into the room. The man in the lead motioned with his weapon. "Everyone out."

Sool eyed him over the top of her mask. She was more angry than scared. "I don't know who you are, but get out of my surgery. Whatever you want can wait."

Conscious of the fact that the others were watching, and worried lest he lose some of his tenuous authority, the man crossed the room.

Frank Berry, who had volunteered to administer the ether, the only general anesthetic Sool had access to, backed away. The surgeon stood her ground. The slaver looked down at the incision then up at her. "So, what's the problem?"

"Acute appendicitis."

The man fired his handgun. The slug took Mrs. Miller under the chin, traveled up through the roof of her mouth, and took the top of her head off. "She's cured. Get your ass in gear."

Sool, too stunned to speak and still cloaked in a makeshift gown, was pushed, shoved, and prodded out the door and into the parking lot. Once there, she was fitted with a Ra 'Na–manufactured collar and chained to the local real-estate agent.

Then, with tears flowing down her cheeks, Sool was marched away.

WASHINGTON, D.C.

Though he was emotionally numb by the time he had been processed and loaded into the back of a semi, there was nothing wrong with Professor Boyer Blue's mind. There was a collective moan as the doors closed and what little bit of light there was, disappeared. A man swore and a woman began to weep. These were professionals for the most part, men and women who like Blue lacked street smarts and were easy pickings for the alien soldiers. But every one of them was African-American. *Why?* What did that mean? Their captors weren't redneck humans, they were insects.

As the tractor-trailer combo jerked away from the makeshift processing plant, people were thrown toward the back. Someone said "Excuse me," and incongruous though it was, Blue heard himself say "No problem."

The manner in which they had been packed into the trailer, plus the fact that all the people around him were black, couldn't help but remind the history professor of the slave ships on which many of their ancestors had been transported to North America—his own great-great-grandparents among them.

They had been chained, of course, and laid in rows like human cordwood, forced to endure endless days of agony while a sailing ship made its long, uncertain way across the Atlantic.

But was the analogy real? Or did the aliens have something different in mind? There were signs that they might. Though cognizant of the fact that conditions might vary from place to place, Blue had no choice but to work with the data at hand, much of which seemed to support a rather interesting hypothesis—namely, that onerous though present conditions were, the aliens demonstrated a marked bias *in favor of people with more pigmentation,* and an equally marked bias against those who had less of it.

For example, there was the fact that those herded into the trailer had been selected from a larger group, all of whom had tan, brown, or black skin. Significantly, or so it seemed to Blue, those having the darkest coloration had been chosen for the truck.

All of this could be read to infer that like the Europeans who colonized central Africa 150 years in the past, immediately took a liking to the tall, light-complexioned Tutsi cattle lords, and subsequently put them over the Hutu farmers, who tended to be shorter and darker, the aliens were biased in favor of humans who looked like they did. Well, not exactly, but in terms of color.

Or was that too fanciful? Perhaps he was generalizing from an inadequate amount of data—a potentially serious error for any academic.

Suddenly the darkness, plus the feel of bodies pressed in around him, threatened to overwhelm the historian, and he fought a growing sense of claustrophobia.

The trailer lurched as it passed over something in the street— and a single flame popped into existence toward the center of the cargo area. It was like a candle in the dark, a beacon on which Blue could focus his eyes, and he was thankful.

The trip lasted roughly twenty minutes and terminated with a screech of brakes and plenty of invective as the entire group was thrown toward the front of the trailer.

Not long after that metal clanked, the doors were thrown open, and the humans were ordered out. It was dark, *very* dark, without any streetlights. The aliens used cone-shaped light wands to show the way.

Blue paused, allowed others to precede him, and scanned the surrounding area. Was this his chance? His *only* chance to escape? No, not with heavily armed aliens all about.

The academic marveled at the way in which their chitin morphed to provide them with camouflage. They did not become *black,* like the members of the seldom-seen insect ruling class, but *gray,* which worked almost as well and didn't violate the demarcations of what Blue saw as castes.

Functional castes, similar to those common to India, where the circumstances of a baby's birth still determined whether it was Brahmin or Untouchable.

Except here was a situation where social stratification led to functional specialization—which led to physical adaptation. Or had the process worked the other way around?

The whip struck Blue's back with considerable force, pushed the air out of his lungs, and drove him to his knees. Only his thick tweed jacket prevented the tightly braided leather from cutting him to the bone. A voice, amplified to the point of distortion, originated with one of the guards: "Move or die."

Hands helped Blue to his feet, gripped his elbows, and carried him forward. A voice muttered in his ear, "Better get a move on, bro—these suckers mean business."

The column wound its way through a warehouse and emerged on a nicely appointed platform. The sleek-looking Maglev train consisted of six coach cars, two first-class cars, and a lounge car. All of them were powered by current that passed through propulsion coils mounted on the bottom surface of the U-shaped track and held aloft by superconducting magnets.

The train could travel at speeds in excess of 250 mph, and, like the city of Bellingham, had been preserved for use by the Saurons.

Doors hissed open, the humans were ordered to enter, and they had no choice but to do so. It was warm inside—a fact for which many were grateful.

Blue, who felt a little better, thanked those around him and managed to board without assistance. There were seats, plenty of them, all covered with gray upholstery. The history professor took one and was glad to get off his feet.

"This is more like it," someone said, and a woman burst into tears. A stranger patted her arm and looked like *she* needed comfort herself.

Blue watched the doors, waited for the guards to board, and was surprised when they didn't. The reason became apparent a few minutes later, when the doors slid shut. A man attempted to force one of them open and discovered that it was locked.

The train slid away from the platform, and a voice came over the PA system. There was no way to be sure, but Blue theorized that it was prerecorded and belonged to one of the small, furry aliens rather than the large, more threatening species. The fact that the invaders had translation devices suggested the possibility of other, even more sophisticated technologies.

"My name is Mon Lon. I am permitted to inform you that all of the individuals on this train have been selected to serve as slave supervisors, a position of considerable responsibility and one that entails numerous benefits. You will receive extra food, comfortable quarters, and access to a well-equipped medical facility.

"The train will carry you to a place called Bellingham, Washington, where you will participate in the construction of a Sauron temple complex. Military rations are available in each car, as is water."

There was no "Thank you, have a nice day," just a click as the PA system went dead.

"Damn," someone said, "it took a long time, but I'm a manager at last."

There was laughter, but it was brittle, and a woman put Blue's thoughts into words. She stood and scanned the compartment. She had beautiful medium-brown skin; large, luminous eyes; and dreadlocks salted with gray. "You think that's funny? Well, *I* don't. My ancestors came to this country the hard way, in the hold of a slave ship, and there's some things I won't do. Becoming a slavemaster happens to be one of them."

The woman pointed a long, bony finger at Blue. "Everything we do matters. Professor Boyer Blue taught me that—and he's sitting right there. Ask *him*."

Then and only then did the academic recognize the matronly-looking woman as a fortysomething version of young Amanda Carter, just one of more than three thousand students who had passed through his classrooms over the years.

Every eye in the car swiveled toward Blue, and the teacher recognized the moment for what it was. He could remain what he had been up till then, a well-trained observer, who though possessed of many opinions, left the doing to others. Or he could take the plunge and actually *do* something, knowing even as he did so that doers make lots of mistakes. Perhaps he could make a difference or, failing that, exact some sort of revenge.

The professor stood, grabbed a luggage rack, and felt the train start to accelerate. They were on the main line now headed for Pittsburgh. Rather than the lights one would expect to see, darkness ruled the external world. "Amanda is correct. Everything we do matters. *Now* more than ever before."

"So?" a man in a badly ripped business suit demanded. "What would you have us do?"

Blue was surprised by the strength of his own conviction. "I suggest that we escape from the train, find some weapons, and fight back. This is *our* country, *our* planet, and *our* solar system."

There was a moment of silence, followed by the sound of two hands clapping, followed by general applause.

Passengers from adjoining cars forced their way in as someone yelled, "Let's kill the bastards!"

The man in the ripped business suit waited for the noise level to drop and said what many were thinking. "Grandiose plans are one thing—making them happen is another. The train is in motion. How do you propose to stop it?"

Blue experienced a moment of complete hopelessness as the

man's words blew his fantasy to smithereens. What was he thinking, anyway? The entire notion was stupid.

Then a young man stood up and cleared his throat. "That would be *my* job. My name is Jared Kenyata. I work for the company that built the train. All the operating systems are tied together by a bundle of wires and fiber-optic cables that run through the center of each car. All we have to do is remove an access panel, cut the correct cable, and voilà—this baby comes to a stop."

The effect was magical. In one miraculous moment Blue's plan was transformed from a wild-eyed scheme into something that might actually work. The academic hadn't known about Kenyata, but the engineer's comments made it sound as if he had.

"So let's get to it," an older man suggested. "What the hell are we waiting for?"

All eyes went to Kenyata. The young man pointed toward the deck and smiled. "The access panels are secured against unauthorized access. We need a quarter-inch hex key. Does anyone happen to have one?"

NEAR WINTON, WASHINGTON

The sun rose, tried to penetrate the thick gray overcast, and produced a sickly yellow glow.

The "feral" humans, who had been allowed to bed down in what had been a rest area, were covered with four-by-eight tarps they had been issued in lieu of tents. They huddled in misery below.

Not that Norm Vecky spent much time worrying about such matters. That was his gift—not knowing, not thinking, not caring. It was a talent that stood him in good stead when the state shuttled the younger version of himself into one foster home after another. One of the social workers had nailed it in a memo to file: "Much like a cat or a dog, Norman seems to dwell in the eternal now, having little or no concept of the past or the future."

So he could pass the night in the comfort of a forty-foot RV, boil oatmeal in a pan, sprinkle brown sugar on top, make coffee, consume both, slip into the heavily insulated parka, step out into the cold morning air, and produce a guilt-free belch. Life was good—for him, at any rate—and that's all that mattered. Horsky was supposed to find the ferals—and he was supposed to move them. That was that.

The RV's headlights served to illuminate the scene in front of him. There was nothing sadistic about the manner in which he moved from one tarp-covered mound to the next, kicking slaves with his boots and lashing out with his tongue. It was efficient and nothing more.

Sool, who, cold though she was, had finally managed to fall asleep, felt the boot connect with her side, heard the slavemaster say "Up and at 'em," and cursed the man with every swear word she knew.

The object of her hatred never took such insults personally. He grinned and continued on his way.

Bodies stirred, rose like zombies, and shook showers of dew off their nylon shrouds. Human guards, all armed with rifles, stood like statues. During the course of the day Vecky would allow each one of them to visit the RV, have some coffee, and take a break. Thus he was reasonably popular.

It took the better part of two hours to prepare a rudimentary meal for the ferals, chain them together, and resume the march.

Sool, whose feet felt numb in spite of two layers of socks in her much-abused running shoes, knew what the day would bring. Seven miles before lunch; some thin, watery soup; and eight miles before dinner. Not that it mattered, not that *anything* mattered, not anymore.

The RV lurched into motion, the ferals were ordered to move, and they shuffled forward. The concrete led them on. The only sounds were those made by the motor home's engine, the rattle of neck chains, and the occasional comment from the ever-present crows.

Later, after the column had cleared the area, the crows, seeming even blacker against the snow, fluttered down out of the trees. Seven bodies lay half covered by windblown tarps. Eyes glittered; caws cut the cold, crisp air; and beaks went to work. The feast would last for days.

SALMON NATIONAL FOREST, IDAHO

Most of the high-altitude smoke had blown away, the sun was out, and the temperature had risen a bit. Everything was wet, however, and the slightest encounter with a tree could produce a momentary shower.

Marta didn't mind, however, because after 350 miles of travel she was stronger than she'd ever been before, well equipped, and within a mile of her final destination: the compound known as "Racehome." Assuming the center was intact, that is—and remained in friendly hands.

The possibility that it wasn't, that the compound had been compromised, accounted for her slow, circuitous approach. Marta wanted to know who and what she was dealing with before she made herself vulnerable.

Having been freed for reasons she still didn't understand, Marta had hung around Bellingham for a few days, gradually acquiring the things she needed to survive. The obvious targets, such as sporting goods stores, had already been looted, but there were plenty of isolated homes, cabins, and trailers to choose from, and, given the fact that millions had been killed or enslaved, less competition for supplies than she expected.

She was able to accumulate a good backpack, three sets of winter clothing, two pairs of boots, cooking gear, a one-burner butane stove, medical supplies for what remained of her still-healing ear hole, lots of valuable odds and ends, a compass, stainless steel wire, road maps, a Leatherman folding tool, water bottles, and—oh, yes—three rolls of three-ply toilet paper, which, along with a stash of Hershey bars, were her only indulgences.

Thanks to America's long-standing love affair with guns, weapons were less of a problem than she had imagined. They were so plentiful, in fact, that she had acquired, then abandoned, no fewer than four long guns prior to happening across a collection of firearms in an out-of-the-way farmhouse. The fully automatic Uzi was illegal, or had been when there were laws, but fit her needs to a T.

Yes, rifles were more elegant, and certainly more accurate, but the submachine gun offered more firepower per pound, which made it the better trade-off. The Uzi could throw a lot of lead in a short period of time—six hundred rounds per minute—which made it the perfect accessory for this postapocalyptic female. A .9mm Glock served as her backup. The fact that both weapons fired the same ammo didn't hurt, either.

The gear, and the comfort it brought, served as ends in and of themselves for a while. But eventually—she couldn't remember exactly when—other needs started to make themselves manifest. The need to do something about the aliens and the mud people who worked for the aliens. And yes, much as she hated to admit it, the need for human companionship.

Marta had been invited to Racehome during her fifteen minutes of fame, as Jack's "racist sister." She'd been in prison then. But now it seemed like the natural place to go. She'd be welcome there, maybe something of a celebrity, part of the new order. So, confident of her choice, she had set out.

The Kan stopped her twice, but the ear, or what remained of it, served as a pass. They released her on both occasions.

She'd had other adventures, including two confrontations with bandits who turned out to be far less violent than Marta was, a running two-day battle with some feral dogs, some scary moments in a town decimated by disease, a close call with a group of westbound slavers, one heart-stopping occasion on which a Sauron fighter caught her in the act of crossing a field, and worst of all, food poisoning, suffered as a result of eating some canned chili.

But those were behind her now, and snow crunched as Marta followed a gravel road up the side of a hill. The area had been logged two or three times, but that was a long time ago. The current crop of trees was at least thirty years old.

Strangely enough, they—along with an untold number of other plants and animals—had benefited from the alien invasion, suppressing as it did their most rapacious enemy: man.

The road turned and followed the contours of the hill. A slide blocked the path ahead, but Marta didn't care. She'd come as far as she needed to. Assuming her navigation was good, and that the Howther family had survived the initial attack, Racehome should lie in the valley below. A notorious place that had survived rumors, infiltrators, raids, lawsuits, and all the other weapons the Zog infrastructure could bring to bear.

Careful not to break the skyline, Marta slipped among some boulders, felt for the small pair of 9 × 25 Nikon Travelite binoculars that she wore around her neck, and brought them to her eyes. The binoculars were surprisingly powerful, and the valley seemed to leap upward. She saw the road, the burned-out lodge, a group of well-maintained outbuildings, a jumble of rusty mining equipment, and there, against a gray rock wall, what looked like the entrance to a mine.

There weren't any people around, not at the moment. But judging from the heavily churned mud, there had been a considerable amount of activity in and around the complex in the recent past.

Marta's nostrils had become a good deal more sensitive since she'd been forced to give up smoking. She caught wind of the man a full second before he rammed the gun into the base of her skull. Her father had worn Old Spice, a lot of it, on the day they buried her mother, and she would never forget the scent.

"What a naughty girl! Spying from the rocks! You should be ashamed." The voice was amused.

Marta *was* ashamed. Not for spying, which made perfect sense, but for getting caught. How could it have happened? There had been no sign of tracks—no sign of anyone in the area.

"Keep your hands on the binoculars and stand up," the voice said. "I'll take the hardware."

It was difficult to rise without using her hands, especially with the weight of the pack to contend with, but Marta managed to do it.

She heard a knife snick open, felt the sling tug at her shoulder, and knew the Uzi was gone. The man found the Glock without difficulty, ordered her to drop the pack, and tossed it aside. "Now," he said, "that takes care of the more obvious stuff. Let's see if there's anything else. I'm not alone. Keep that in mind."

Marta kept it very much in mind as hands sorted her hair, ran the perimeter of her collar, fondled her breasts, slid the circumference of her waistband, squeezed her butt, probed the crevice between her thighs, and wandered down the contours of her legs.

Most women would have been furious, many would have squirmed, and a few would have fought. Marta was the exception. She had been searched, felt up, and generally violated by so many people over such a long period of time that it no longer mattered.

The man, who had hoped for some sort of reaction, was disappointed. His companion, silent till then, finally spoke. Her voice dripped with sarcasm. "Now that you've had your jollies, let's take her in."

The hands were withdrawn, and then, without the slightest hint of embarrassment, the man invited Marta to turn. "All right, my dear, you *feel* good, so let's have a look at you."

Marta turned to find herself face-to-face with a thin, almost skeletal man. He had a swastika tattooed on his forehead, another dangling from his ear, and a large shit-eating grin. He held a sawed-off shotgun. It was pointed at her midriff. "Welcome to Racehome, sweetie. My name's Limey."

The woman, who appeared to be thirty or so, had short black hair, brown eyes, and well-applied makeup. *Her* weapon, an M-18, hung from a shoulder. The Uzi, Marta's Uzi, was pointed at the ground. She shook her head in apparent disgust. "Sorry about that, but the limey enjoys his work, and you can't fault him for that. Grab your pack and head thataway—we'll bring up the rear."

Meanwhile, in a room not far away, Ivory had a hard-on. Not remarkable in and of itself, but something to be nurtured. He allowed his mind to drift—rather than focus on the woman above him.

The room had been cut from solid rock. No one knew for sure, but, judging from the rails that led in through the arched entryway and terminated somewhere under Ella's queen-size bed, the chamber had once served as a siding, a place where her great-great-grandfather could remove an ore car from the line and slip another into its place.

Now, with the addition of some hangings plus an enormous armoire, the space had been transformed into a bedroom, an Aryan bedroom with a mural painted on the wall opposite the bed. It featured a faceless warrior framed with the wreath of the German knight's cross, all on a field of red.

Springs squeaked and the frame creaked as Ella built toward her climax. Ella liked to have sex at least twice a day. Partly because she enjoyed the process, but partly because she wanted to produce a son, or failing that, a daughter, who, according to one of her father's prophecies, would lead the race into a new age of power and prosperity. Of course, Ivory had to do his part, which, thank God, he had so far managed to do.

Ella, who preferred to be on top, where she could control the pace of their lovemaking, was a sight to see. Her hair flew, sweat fell like rain, and her hands cupped small, hard-tipped breasts. The sheer wantonness of her movements kept Ivory hard.

In spite of his enjoyment, however, part of Ivory's persona remained eternally on guard. Rather than lose himself in lust, he preferred to perform some analysis. Even if Mother Howther was correct, and he had been sent to "father the great white hope," problems loomed, not the least of which was the manner in which the old lady controlled her daughter, and even worse, the extent to which Ella governed *him*. It wasn't fitting, not according to Aryan doctrine, but that didn't change how things were.

Ivory's "wife" made a noise deep within her throat, increased her speed, and screamed. His signal to let go.

Ivory did so, and the intensity of the orgasm served to silence his internal voice and grant him a moment of peace.

Five minutes later, after the glow had dissipated, both were up and around. Unlike the women he'd been with before, Ella felt no need for prolonged cuddling. Slam, bam, thank you, sir. Women like that don't come along every day, Ivory thought. It was as if God had taken a guy and dumped him into a female body.

Together the twosome made their way up through a series of galleries to the room where he had first been interviewed. It was warm—relatively so, at any rate—and filled with the rich odor of slowly roasting meat.

The fact that a stranger was standing there, waiting for their return, was in no way surprising.

The average day brought five potential recruits. Some held promise; some were Jews, or what Ella called proto-Jews—meaning they weren't actually Jewish but couldn't be trusted—and some were obvious halfbreed muds, bent on polluting the race.

So Mrs. Howther maintained, although Ivory figured a lot of them were just plain hungry, and would have been willing to join damned near anything to get some food. After all, if one drop of black blood made someone into a mulatto, then who was safe? And how would you know? Especially without sophisticated testing procedures.

Still, according to the seedline doctrine laid out by the American Institute of Theology (AIT) Bible study guide, the muds had been created *before* Adam and Eve, and after the Adamic or light-skinned race was conceived, it was with them and *only* them that Yahweh formed the Holy Covenants.

Generally, when five people showed up, it seemed like one of them always wound up being classified as a mud or a Jew regardless of how they looked. That being the case, the other four, those whom Mrs. Howther had blessed as "founders," would be instructed to shoot their less fortunate companions. Those who obeyed were "in." Those who didn't were killed. The process was cruel, but functioned to separate the weak from the strong, and made for a memorable initiation ceremony.

Ivory had popped a few, just to prove that he could, but generally left that sort of thing to the skins.

It seemed that this particular day was a bit slow and that only one potential recruit had been caught in the security net that encircled the steadily growing compound.

The moment the woman met his eyes, Ivory knew she was a far cry from the fertile-hipped "race mothers" that old lady Howther took such an interest in. No, this female was a hard-assed take-no-prisoners warrior of the type *he* wanted to recruit, and if Ella hadn't sucked him dry, hit the hay with. The missing ear, which she made no effort to conceal, gave the woman a piratical air.

Ivory kept his face blank, collapsed into a chair, and watched his "wife" accept a folder from an assistant.

She opened it, scanned the contents, and handed the file to Ivory. Old man Howther had been a stickler for good records, a predilection that paid off in numerous ways, not the least of which was the area of recruitment.

Ivory opened the folder, saw the newspaper clippings, verified that the woman standing in front of them was Marta Manning, skimmed the accompanying text, noted her credentials as a bona fide white supremacist, and found a copy of the letter old man Howther had sent to Purdy.

Howther followed the stories about Jack Manning, had heard the sound bite in which Marta defended not only her brother but also white separatism in general, and had taken the opportunity to send his respects, a copy of the AIT study guide, *and* an invitation to Marta to visit Racehome when she was released.

The paperwork was impressive, *very* impressive, and barring some off-the-wall reaction from Mother Howther, made the woman a natural.

Ella, who was as impressed as Ivory was, invited Marta to sit, and left to fetch her mother. The two of them returned a short while later.

Ivory watched the old woman conduct her now familiar "reading" of Marta's body, took note of the way the candidate took the process in stride, and waited for the old crone's "finding." It arrived with considerable speed.

Mrs. Howther stepped back, felt for her daughter's arm, and used a nod to convey her pleasure. "Ella! Jonathan! Another prophecy has come true. Please welcome the assassin!"

Ivory continued to have serious reservations regarding not only the prophecies themselves but also Mrs. Howther's rather convenient pronouncements. Still, having benefited from one such edict himself, he could hardly object. That being the case, the racialist made all the right noises, and shook Marta's hand, but resolved to test her mettle.

Ella, who rarely if every questioned her mother's judgments, had no such qualms. She had gone into what Ivory thought of as the "Howther hospitality mode," a sort of heavy-handed version of the generosity for which the American South had once been famous. She gestured toward the meat roasting over the fire. Fat popped as it hit the coals. "Would you join us for dinner? There's plenty of meat."

Marta, though puzzled by the "assassin" comment, was pleased by the warmth of her reception and eager to fit in. Besides, the roast smelled wonderful. "Why, yes, thank you."

Marta was escorted to a dormitory-style cavern, assigned an empty bunk, and introduced to four women already in residence. Breeding stock mostly, waiting for Mother Howther to match them with appropriate mates. Or, in the case of those not deemed suitable for reproduction, to be assigned to useful activities. It made no difference to Marta. She had bunked with worse, much worse, and looked forward to a night spent indoors.

It took the better part of an hour to set the long plank-style table, bring the side dishes out from the kitchen, and remove the roast from the spit. The meat continued to steam as Marta reentered the chamber, was introduced to six additional guests, and shown to the heavily laden table.

Mrs. Howther offered a long, loopy prayer, finished with a stiff-armed Nazi salute, and waited for Ella to cut her food.

Marta helped herself to a large portion of meat, mashed potatoes, and canned peas. The other guests peppered her with questions, especially about her time in the slave camp, and Marta answered as best she could.

Then, with an intensity that spoke of her time as a slave, Marta dug in. She noticed that the meat was white rather than red, and while flavorful, a bit too chewy. Marta looked up from her plate, realized everyone was staring at her, and knew something was up. "What? Did I do something wrong?"

Ivory smiled. "How's the roast?"

"It's chewy," Marta answered truthfully, careful to omit how greasy it was, "but I like it. What is it?"

"Well," Ivory answered deliberately, "it's something of a delicacy, a dish we hope to enjoy more often."

"Don't tease her," Ella said crossly. "Have you seen the spaceships? The little ones?"

"I sure have," Marta admitted. "One caught me in the act of crossing a wheat field. I thought the party was over, but the pilot ignored me."

Ivory nodded. "You were fortunate. It happens that one of their fighters crashed about fifteen miles north of here. One of our patrols happened to be in the vicinity, captured the pilot, and brought him back. It takes quite a bit of work to bust one of those suckers open—but they make for some mighty fine eatin'."

Marta knew they were waiting for her to gag or something, but she had consumed worse things, *lots* worse, and would never forget the way the chits cut her ear. The ex-con speared another piece of meat and raised it into the air. "My compliments to the chef—and may his larder remain stocked."

Everyone laughed, Marta grinned, and Ivory nodded. This woman was special. What if the old hag was correct? What if the assassin *had* arrived? A weapon to be aimed? The meal continued, and it was Ivory who picked at his food.

BELLINGHAM, WASHINGTON

By the time the ragtag column of ferals made it to the outskirts of Bellingham, Sool had lost track of how many days had passed during the long, arduous trek up over Steven's Pass, down through Skyhomish, Gold Bar, and Monroe, and north through Everett, Marysville, and Mount Vernon. Not that names meant much anymore.

Emptied of people and left to the depredations of looters, fires, and feral dogs, once-bright cities had been transformed into rubble-strewn labyrinths.

Danger lurked in those dark, smoke-blackened ruins, and the slavers were careful to avoid them, steering their charges up I-5, well clear of the horribly ravaged cities.

But Bellingham was different. Emptied of people, all of whom had been enslaved, the community possessed a brooding quality. As if the inhabitants were asleep—and might emerge at any moment.

Sool looked left and right as they tramped down Meridian and ran her tongue over dry, cracked lips. The woman in front of her stumbled, fell forward, and, thanks to the neck chain that linked them together, nearly took Sool with her. Her name was Martha, and she had pneumonia. Sool caught her, murmured some words of encouragement, and managed to get her going again. Some of the guards relished any opportunity to use the whip and would gladly lay into her.

Martha coughed up a big glob of yellow-green sputum and spit on the white line.

Sool looked ahead. They were close, very close, and maybe, just maybe the Saurons had established a medical facility of some sort. Martha would die otherwise, like so many others.

Thanks to the fact that the wind was blowing from the west, in off Puget Sound, Sool could smell the camp long before she saw it. The stink, which she would later learn was derived from untreated sewage, rotting garbage, and decaying flesh, was worse than anything she had experienced before. It filled her nostrils, caught at the back of her throat, and triggered her gag reflex.

Sool's spirits sank even lower. She didn't even have to enter the enclosure to know that there were no medical services ahead, that Martha was slated for death, and that her own worst fears were about to be realized.

The ferals rounded a bend, passed an immaculate Texaco station, and got their first look at the slave camp.

A wall constructed of telephone poles interspersed with tree trunks had been erected to keep the slaves in and the raiders out. It ran north and south for as far as the eye could see. Kan warriors, their chitin constantly shifting between the gray sky and the tan wall, patrolled the top. They were heavily armed and looked invincible. Houses, strip malls, and everything else had been leveled to create a free-fire zone.

Later, after she knew more, Sool would learn that the camp was little more than a receiving area and that the *real* center of activity lay about five miles to the south.

Still, the fact that a group calling itself the "Free Taggers" had spray-painted graffiti onto the wall below them served as mute testimony to the fact that at least some humans remained stubbornly, and in this case stupidly, free.

The gates, which stood a good twenty-five feet high, were closed at the moment. To keep slaves in? Or to keep others out? It was impossible to know. They were guarded by a detachment of Kan who pulled the slabs of wood open and watched impassively as the ferals marched through. Two prefab buildings formed a passageway of sorts. There had been plenty of rain, and the dirt between them had been churned into ankle-deep muck. It sucked at the soles of Sool's shoes.

Someone shouted, "Make way! Make way!" A horse-drawn cart appeared in front of them. Though once a flatbed truck, its engine had been removed to reduce weight, and a makeshift seat had been mounted in its place. It was occupied by a scabrous-looking man of indeterminate ethnicity. He slapped the team with his reins. His voice was high and querulous. "Get a move on, you worthless, four-footed shit throwers—we ain't got all day."

Above the man, ensconced in the cab, a Fon rode in dignified silence.

Sool, forced to the side along with the others, turned to watch the wagon pass. The back was piled high with dead bodies. It was a horrible sight, so she turned away. A hand flapped as if waving at her. A sign caught her eye. It had been nailed to a post. The lettering was large but crude: "Welcome to hell."

■ ■ ■

The fires, which were almost certainly detectable from space, leaped high. A log crumbled, sparks spiraled upward, and Smith prayed that the Saurons had bigger fish to fry.

No, the fires weren't absolutely necessary from a physical perspective, but the psychological value was considerable. How many raids, attacks, and full-scale wars had human beings plotted while crouched around a fire's reassuring warmth? Backs to the darkness, faces lit by the flames? Thousands? Millions?

Yes, Smith decided, given the full run of human history, the number could be in the millions. First as families, then as clans, tribes, peoples, religions, and nations. Now, for the first time ever, humans were gathering as a *species,* regardless of their membership in other groups, to consider an attack on another species. Were other, similar meetings taking place around the globe? Smith hoped so—and wished them luck.

Slowly, conscious of the way his middle-aged body ached, the ex-Ranger stood and made his way out into the space between the fires. The reenactors formed a rough-and-ready circle. There were clusters of friends, and loners who liked a bit of personal space, but every eye was upon him. There was no point to a lot of preliminary talk, so Smith took the plunge. "Okay, you've had time to think, and the issue is clear. Do we sit back and let the bugs take our planet? Or do we kick their butts back into space? I believe in option two. Who's with me?"

There was silence for a moment as heads turned and people looked to their friends. Smith, his heart in his throat, feared the worst.

Then a tall man, his body draped in a facsimile of a Hudson Bay trading blanket, got to his feet. He had dark skin, white teeth, and a square chin. A flintlock lay cradled in his arms, a tomahawk was thrust through his heavy leather belt, and the handmade mocs reached all the way to his knees. The man looked like a ghost, a visitation from the past, and his voice carried clear across the camp. "There ain't nowhere to run, there ain't nowhere to hide, and there ain't no choice. We can fight or die. I plan to fight."

Without the cheers or yells that Smith might have expected, the people rose in groups or one at a time. Finally, when no one remained on the ground, a circle had been formed. There weren't very many of them, not compared to the force they were planning to battle with, but had the Saurons known more about the human race's long and bloody history, and had they been less arrogant, they would have, *should* have, been extremely worried.

NEAR WENATCHEE, WASHINGTON

The Maglev train rocked slightly as it passed through a long, gentle curve, roared through the remains of a half-slagged city, and accelerated down a section of elevated track.

A cluster of raggedy shelters marked the spot where some free humans had camped next to the track. They stood clustered around some rusty brown burn barrels. Heads turned as the first train roared past. A woman waved.

The journey had been under way for more than fourteen hours by then. If Jared Kenyata was correct, and the Maglev was traveling at more than 250 mph, that meant that Boyer Blue and the rest of the contingent had traveled some 3,500 miles and would arrive in Everett, Washington, before darkness fell. Assuming the slaves remained on board, that is, which they had no intention of doing.

The plan, if it could be dignified as such, was to stop the train short of its final destination, find a place to hide, acquire some weapons, and launch a resistance movement. Or, if one already existed, find a way to join up.

Blue, who had become the group's leader more by acclamation than by democratic process, knew that while the majority of his so-called followers supported the plan as being, in the words of one cynic, "better than nothing," at least 25 percent had serious doubts. Had they been able to do so, they would have abandoned the train earlier, hoping to make contact with loved ones, or, failing that, to fight on more familiar ground.

The logic for waiting, for going to ground in the vicinity of their final destination, had nothing to do with self-preservation and everything to do with the overwhelming sense of anger that most of them, including Blue himself, felt deep inside. They wanted revenge, and, based on what little information they had, the Pacific Northwest was the place to get it.

Would their resolve hold? Especially when confronted with the grim realities of protracted guerrilla warfare? Blue had serious doubts. About the group, about his own leadership abilities, about the possibility of success. He hoped that a more qualified man or woman would step forward, someone with military experience and the right sort of personality. In the meantime, until that day came, all he could do was fake it and hope for the best.

Kenyata, who, with the assistance of a computer technician, had used three nail files to convert a safe-deposit box key into the functional equivalent of a number five hex key, sat in the subfloor utility run and caressed a snakelike cable. His grin was contagious. Others—as many as could crowd into the car—were gathered around. They smiled and weren't sure why.

"This is the one, Doc. We cut this baby and the ride is over."

Blue nodded. He didn't like it when people called him "Doc" but decided to let the matter pass. "Excellent. Will it coast for a while or come to a sudden stop?"

"Think sudden," the engineer replied, "as in hang on to your seat or kiss the front bulkhead."

"Good," the academic replied. "That gives us more control." Blue turned toward a window. "Hey, Mr. Foley, how're we doing?"

Orlon Foley—*Mr.* Foley to everyone but his family—had been raised in Seattle and traveled the route many times. Though retired, he still wore a suit and tie. Not a bolo tie, like young people did, but a *proper* tie with a Windsor knot. The ex–high school principal looked back over his shoulder. "We passed Wenatchee a while back. Given the way the train's climbing, we should cross Steven's Pass before too long and start down the other side."

Blue realized that the Maglev had slowed a bit. He looked out a window, saw granite race by, followed by a group of sturdy fir trees, and a flash of an emerald-green valley. The train crossed a high-tech trestle and followed the track as it wrapped itself around the side of a snow-clad mountain, then turned the other way. "Good. The bugs will be waiting for us in Everett, so we should stop in the vicinity of Gold Bar. Mr. Foley will make the call, Mr. Kenyata will cut the cable, and the rest of us will hang on.

"Then, when the train comes to a halt, we run. Not in every direction, but in groups, according to which car we occupied during the trip.

"Now I would appreciate it if those of you who agreed to function as car coordinators would return to your constituents, remind them of the plan, and ask them to brace themselves. Questions? No? Let's go, then—and good luck."

A number of people left, as coordinators and onlookers alike returned to their seats.

With that accomplished, there was nothing more that Blue could do, nothing but wait and hope the plan would work. There were plenty of things that could go wrong. Kenyata appeared to be competent, but what if he wasn't?

Or what if the plan worked, but half the passengers were injured during the process?

Or what if everyone survived the stop, only to be attacked by the Kan?

And where were the Kan, anyway? In one of the locked cars? Up toward the front of the train? Waiting on a platform in Everett, Washington? There was no way to be sure.

Five minutes passed, followed by ten, followed by five more. With each passing moment Blue found it more and more difficult to maintain his composure. Was Mr. Foley awake? Did the older man know what he was doing? Was it stupid to trust such an important task to someone he barely knew?

Blue, unable to stand the pressure, was about to say something when Mr. Foley broke the silence. His nose was plastered to the window, and his voice was clear. "Okay, pass the word. Cut the cable one minute from now."

Blue discovered that there was no need for him to speak as the message raced from person to person. Those in the forward cars, like those in the rearmost cars, would have less than a minute to respond, but it couldn't be helped.

Blue looked around, was surprised by the number of people staring at him, and knew what they wanted. He forced himself to smile. "So, Jared, are you ready?"

The engineer was wedged into the trough-shaped utility run. He raised a thumb. "Ready, Doc."

Blue winced internally and was about to make some sort of reply when Mr. Foley gave the order.

Some of the passengers had been searched, and forced to divest themselves of everything they had, while others, all part of a different draft, had been allowed to bring whatever they happened to have with them.

It didn't make sense, but Kenyata was thankful, because the side cutters were part of a tool kit that the computer tech lugged around with him. They sliced through the half-inch cable with ease.

Data stopped, a computer took notice, emergency programming kicked in, signals were passed, current ceased to flow to the propulsion coils, mechanical brakes were triggered, and the passengers were thrown forward.

Even though they were prepared, people still swore, yelled, and in one case screamed.

Metal screeched, the train shook as if palsied, and a preprogrammed announcement came on. The voice was female and soothing in a condescending sort of way. "The train is coming to a stop. Please remain in your seats. There is nothing to worry about. The train is . . ."

The Maglev shuddered to a stop, a computer opened all the doors to facilitate emergency egress, and Blue shouted at the top of his lungs, "This is it! Everyone out!"

Mr. Foley followed a group out the nearest door, checked to ensure that his coat was properly buttoned, and took pleasure in the sign: "Gold Bar." Not only had he halted the train in the right area, it also had stopped in front of the train station. Not bad for a retired school administrator!

Blue passed through the door, noted that a fire had ravaged the ersatz train station, and guessed that the town was in equally bad shape.

Of more immediate concern was the question of Kan. Had any of the aliens boarded the train? If so, they would show up soon.

But there was no sign of the aliens as Blue, Kenyata, and a handful of others herded their fellow passengers away from the train, across a wreck-strewn four-lane highway, and into the town beyond. Most of the fakey-looking "old-time" buildings had been destroyed, but a few survived. They leaned on each other like drunks.

There were bumps and bruises but no serious injuries, a fact for which Blue was grateful. He waved a group forward. "All right! We made it! Follow me!"

Some of the people grumbled, a doubter wondered where the hell Blue thought he was headed, but everyone obeyed. Kenyata hurried to catch up. Blue set a brisk pace, and the engineer fell into step. "So, Doc, we're free. What's next?"

"The basics. We need food, shelter, and weapons."

"And then?"

"And then you and I are going to talk. I spent a lot of time and energy earning my doctorate, which means you can call me a lot of different things, but 'Doc' isn't one of 'em. Got it?"

Kenyata grinned. "No problem, Pops, I've got it."

Blue sighed and hurried the group along.

A Sauron shuttle arrived twenty minutes later, landed, and dis-
gorged four heavily armed Kan and a Ra 'Na technician. It took
him fewer than five minutes to search the train, locate the cut
cable, and arrive at the appropriate conclusion. Having done so,
the Ra 'Na passed the information to the ranking warrior, was
thankful that the screwup couldn't possibly be blamed on him,
and faded into the background.

The NCO, a not especially enterprising Kan named Paz-Hab,
gave the matter some thought, concluded that one of his peers on
the other side of the continent would eventually be found culpa-
ble, and carried out a halfhearted search of the immediate area.

Yes, the matter was annoying, but humans were stupid and
would soon be caught. If not by the Kan, then by the slavers.

The aliens reboarded the shuttle, circled the area three times,
and turned toward the west.

Darkness fell a few hours later. Another day had passed—and
the clock continued to tick.

4

DEATH DAY MINUS 140

SATURDAY, MARCH 14, 2020

The history of liberty is the history of resistance. . . .
—Woodrow Wilson,
Speech to New York Press Club, 1912

BELLINGHAM, WASHINGTON

Waves formed orderly rows as the wind marched them into Bellingham Bay from the southwest. The breakwater took the brunt of the attack, but some of the swells found their way among three fingerlike projections of land previously home to a variety of commercial enterprises, and rolled all the way in to break white along the waterfront.

The dock on which Manning stood, along with the marina that it was part of, had been home to hundreds of small craft, most of which had been destroyed or simply cast loose. Some could be seen heaped along the shore like abandoned toys. Others, their masts poking up through the steely-gray waves, sat on the bottom. Fuel from their tanks gave the water an oily, rainbow-like sheen.

In place of the pleasure boats, dozens of tugs, barges, and Sauron spaceships crowded around the docks like maggots feeding on a corpse. The shuttles, lighters, and transports rolled sluggishly, as if uneasy at their moorings.

Even as the security chief stood there, watching one of the delta-shaped spacecraft make its final approach out beyond the breakwater, a newly arrived contingent of Kan warriors filed out of the transport docked below him and shuffled their way up a metal grating. Manning could feel the deck vibrate. He steeled himself against the possibility that his presence would be challenged, and was relieved when it wasn't.

A red tag dangled from his right ear, a tag that authorized him to go where he pleased, though not with total impunity. Unlike Ra 'Na technicians, "authorized" humans were a rarity and subject to harassment. Not this time, however. Perhaps it was his apparent self-confidence, or—and this seemed more likely—the noncom in charge of the file had spotted the brightly colored ear tag and understood what it meant.

Whatever the reason, the warriors continued on their way, and Manning, whose entire body was rigid with tension, forced himself to relax. This is how it must have felt to be a Jew in Nazi Germany, he thought, or a black in pre-Mandela South Africa, or a Palestinian in Israel: frightened, paranoid, and vulnerable. The experience was worse than he would have imagined because the possibility of abuse hung over his head twenty-four hours a day.

There was a splash as the incoming shuttle belly-flopped into the bay, followed by a flurry of activity as small craft were sent to meet it. Though highly maneuverable in the air, the larger spaceships were a good deal less agile on the water and were routinely towed to the dock.

A recently constructed box sat on stilts at the far end of the dock. Six-foot-high alien pictographs had been spray-painted onto the raw, unpainted wood; a wraparound window provided 360-degree views of the surrounding area; and a thicket of antennas sprouted from the shed-style metal-covered roof. Manning thought he could see the Fon harbormaster pacing back and forth inside.

Was the Sauron *really* in charge? Or just pretending to be, while a fur ball stood in the shadows and told the other XT what to do?

There were parallels, he knew that, human cultures in which slaves exerted a great deal of influence on their supposed masters. But history wasn't something geology majors spent much time on, and he couldn't remember the details.

An engine roared and water churned white as a Ra 'Na operator put one of the Saurons' bargelike boats into reverse and nudged the landing stage below. A tall, lanky human wearing a ragged-looking one-piece orange coverall stepped onto the floating dock. Manning went down to meet him. The ramp bounced under the impact of his boots. The remnants of shells, dropped there by the ever-wheeling gulls, crunched underfoot.

Vilo Kell looked up, saw Manning, and grinned. The men embraced, slapped each other on the back, and laughed. "So," Kell said, looking his friend up and down, "what's the scoop? There I am, living it up on Turd, when the chits haul my ass away . . ." Kell tugged at the red ear tag. "Your doing?"

Manning nodded. "Sort of . . . with help from our so-called president."

"Thanks. Half our team died when the tool's power coupling overheated and a condenser blew."

Manning grimaced. "I'm sorry to hear it. None of them deserved that. Not even Reems. As for pulling you out, well, don't thank me yet. Not till you hear what we're up against. This job could make life on Turd look like a walk in the park. Come on, let's get out of here. There's plenty to discuss."

Manning brought Kell up to speed as the two of them made their way up the ramp and walked the length of the dock. "So," he concluded as they approached the one-time parking lot, and negotiated their way among stacks of Sauron cargo modules, "I don't have a whole lot of choice."

"You could run," the other man said pragmatically. "Your sister should be free by now, assuming the chits did what they said they'd do, so where's the downside?"

It was cold, and Manning rammed his hands deeper into his pockets as they passed a group of slaves. They wore blue ear tags and had been assigned to load bundles into a cargo net. If looks could kill, both men would have dropped dead on the spot. Any human who was free was labeled a collaborator. The security chief nodded in their direction. "*There's* the downside. Franklin is a collaborator, but he's all we've got. He's a power freak, but reasonably human, and one can hope. Who knows? Maybe, just maybe, something will break our way."

"So we protect him?"

"Yeah, for the moment, anyway."

"And if he gets weird?"

"Then we cap him and run."

Kell's eyebrows shot up. "We get weapons?"

"Yup," Manning answered. "Anything we can requisition, scrounge, or steal."

"Excellent," Kell replied earnestly. "I like this job already."

A Kan named Bik-Hok had been assigned to sentry duty high atop a pile of light blue cargo modules. It was a boring job, and the humans made a welcome diversion. He gathered his powerful hindquarters and sprang into the air. His body traveled through a fifty-foot arc and landed with an audible thump. Manning took an involuntary step backward, saw the t-gun, and froze in place. The warrior was of average height and wore a light combat harness and something similar to a grin rippled the full length of his sharklike mouth. The electronically generated voice grated on their ears. "Slaves should be working. Not walking around."

Manning resisted the temptation to test the alien's speed. Could he pull the .40-caliber semi? And do it fast enough to keep the Kan from firing? Or would he lose? The t-gun was already aimed at Kell's head, so the answer seemed obvious. Besides, even if he won, there were more Kan, *lots* more, and the battle would be over before it began. He kept his voice level and therefore respectful. "If you examine our ear tags you will see that we are authorized to go wherever we need to."

Bik-Hok, who had seen the red tags from the very beginning, gave a snort of derision. "On your knees."

The humans looked at each other and went to their knees. Manning felt his face burn with the humiliation of it, marveled at the extent to which the Saurons had mastered human culture, and realized how little he knew about them.

"Good," Bik-Hok grated. "That's where all humans belong. No matter what kind of tags they wear. You can leave now—but on all fours. Like the animals you are."

The humans had no choice but to scuttle away, hand-walking across the gravel-strewn concrete, till they rounded a pile of crates, where it was safe to stand. Kell wiped his hands on his overalls. "Reminds me of boot camp. Does that sort of thing happen often?"

"Yes," Manning replied, "it does. Not to the Ra 'Na. To us."

Kell nodded. "Did you see that leap? Imagine fighting those bastards one-on-one."

"Yeah. I did and I have. Come on, my truck's up ahead. Well, *somebody's* truck, till the chits took over."

"Where are we going?"

"The so-called temple complex. More like a city, really. And growing every day. That's where most of the slaves live—and we can find some recruits."

"Recruits? What kind?"

"The kind who know how to shoot straight. Unless you'd like to handle all the assassins yourself."

Kell grinned. "Hell, no. Why should I have all the fun? Please lead the way."

ABOARD THE SAURON DREADNOUGHT *HOK NOR AH*

The compartment, which was part of the extensive medical facilities established by and for the Ra 'Na, was tolerated because healthy slaves get more work done. It was well equipped. Cabinets containing specimen jars, instruments, chemicals, and all the other paraphernalia necessary for dissections lined the walls. The lighting was perfect, and the stainless steel work table was the correct height. All blessings that Fra Pol planned to thank the Great One for as soon as he found the time.

But that would have to wait, since all of his attention was presently focused on a half-dissected arm. A *Sauron* arm, which, until very recently, had been attached to a Fon named Wol-Wul.

There had been an accident of some sort, the details of which held very little interest for the initiate, who had gone to considerable lengths to liberate the limb from its owner prior to the moment when that unfortunate being's corpse had been ejected from Lock 16. Not a pleasant chore but a necessary one. After all, how could the Ra 'Na defeat an enemy unless they knew him? And what could be more basic to *knowing* the Saurons than a study of their physiology? A highly dangerous avocation punishable by the usual penalty: death.

Which explained why, with the exception of the med tech who allowed the cleric to use the lab, Pol was unaware of anyone else engaged in this sort of activity. Certainly not the church, which, led by prelates like Tog, was focused on accommodation rather than revolt.

Still, never one to let orthodoxy stand in his way, Pol was determined to learn all he could. Especially since the Saurons, who allowed the Ra 'Na to serve them in every other possible way, never failed to provide their own medical care—even when that was unpleasant. Pol had long wondered why.

Now, in the light of the new information regarding their reproductive cycle, the initiate thought he knew the answer. Should the Ra 'Na become acquainted with the most intimate details of Sauron physiology, they would inevitably stumble across the master race's secret and use it against them. The very thing Pol had in mind.

The arm, which was secured to a plate of the initiate's own

design, had been slit along a line from grasper to elbow, and from elbow to armpit, or where an armpit had once been.

Then, with the aid of tiny hooks linked to stainless steel wires, each layer of the Fon's anatomy had been peeled back and connected to metal pegs.

Taken as a whole, the limb consisted of a coxa located up near the Sauron's armpit or axillary, a trochanter, femur, tibia, tibial spur just posterior of the grasper, and the tripartite grasper itself, which though adequate for the manipulation of rudimentary tools, lacked the finesse natural to fingers and tentacles. This explained at least to some extent the fact that while intelligent, the Saurons had failed to master the intricacies of high-tech equipment and were dependent on slaves to do that for them.

Inside, within the arm itself, Pol discovered a thin layer of subepidermal fat, a tight cluster of nerve fibers, and a petal-shaped grouping of chemical receptors at the point where the grasper and tibia came together. This was not too surprising, since it was common knowledge that the sense of smell was an important component of the interpersonal communication among Sauron castes.

Still, the location of the receptors was noteworthy, and explained why the aliens waved their extremities over food prior to ingesting it. They were *smelling* the meal rather than blessing it, as many had assumed.

Would Zin and Kan anatomy prove identical to what he was looking at? Or be different in subtle ways? The cleric was eager to find out.

A hand touched Pol's arm, and he gave an involuntary jerk. "Shu? What are you doing? How many times have I told you? *Never* bother me while I'm working."

The med tech had a strange, inexplicable soft spot for the intense, rumpled, and, some said, worthless initiate. A weakness she regretted but seemed powerless to overcome. That didn't prevent Shu from expressing herself, however, and in no uncertain terms. "*Never?* Not even when Dro Tog sends P'ere Has to track you down? Well, my mistake, then . . . I'll nip out into the corridor, inform the good father that Fra Pol is too busy to be disturbed, and suggest that he return later."

Pol felt an immediate sense of remorse followed by panic. "I'm sorry, Shu. You surprised me, that's all. . . . Hide the arm, tell Has I left, and I'll see Tog. I'd rather show up on my own than have his pet priest drag me there."

Shu tried to remain annoyed but found she couldn't. The way she felt about the initiate was plain to see—to anyone but Pol, that is, who, had someone informed him that the med tech had feelings for him, would have been shocked. He had never been attractive to females, and to the extent he could, the cleric sought to avoid them. "Okay, but take care of yourself."

"Of course," Pol replied carelessly. "Don't I always? See you later."

The initiate left by means of a maintenance hatch, and was a good distance away by the time Shu lied to P'ere Has and wondered if the Great One would forgive her.

■ ■ ■

The lights in the rectory were low out of respect for Dro Tog's hangover, a horrible affliction that made his stomach queasy and sent daggers of pain through his head.

The dinner, which had been sponsored by the College of Dromas, had been a convivial affair that featured no fewer than eight courses of fresh seafood accompanied by dozens of toasts and the usual amount of self-aggrandizing puffery.

The fa, a rather nice vintage that the Frahood acquired during the siege of Deeth, had gone down with considerable ease. Which explained both Tog's headache and momentary loss of judgment.

But what was he supposed to do? Especially on the heels of Dro Gor's boast that the quality of intelligence flowing from *his* initiates clearly surpassed anything available to his peers, and proceeded to reveal the not so surprising news that the Zin planned to hold a surprise inspection eight days hence.

An interesting tidbit, to be sure—but far from world-shaking. No, Gor's claim of superiority was spurious and therefore demanded a rebuttal. Tog rose and, with a tongue lubricated by fa, proceeded to hold forth for the better part of five full units.

Then, feeling a tad dizzy, he sat down again. It was only when the compartment stopped spinning that the Dro realized the extent of his indiscretion. He had not only spilled his guts regarding the Sauron reproductive cycle, he had praised Fra Pol during the process, and turned the rapscallion into something of a hero. A hero his peers wanted to interrogate firsthand. It was horrible, just horrible, and the prelate had only himself to blame. Well, not *only* himself, since the entire episode stemmed from Pol's nefarious activities. Clearly he had been *too* compassionate, *too* lenient, *too*—

"Fra Pol has arrived, excellency."

Tog, who normally took pleasure in eyeing his sleek, well-groomed assistant, answered without turning his head. "Send the cretin in. Secure the door. Allow no one to enter."

Truth be told, his assistant, whose name was Mys, took a certain amount of pleasure in her superior's obvious discomfort and found subtle ways to torment him. "Not even P'ere Has?"

"*Especially* P'ere Has."

"Yes, excellency." Mys bowed and withdrew.

Pol, out of breath, entered. He approached the prelate, bowed, and went to one knee. "You sent for me, excellency?"

"Yes," Tog said with a growl, "I did. Do you remember our last conversation?"

Pol, conscious of the fact that he had yet to minister to a single youngster, bowed his head. "Yes, excellency."

"And you remember the matter we discussed?"

Pol felt his heart beat just a little bit faster. Did this mean what he thought it did? That Tog had kept his word? That he had discussed the threat with the College of Dromas? "Yes, excellency, I remember."

Tog coughed, felt pain lance through the front lobe of his brain, and motioned for the initiate to move closer. As with all good lies, this one felt natural. "I raised the topic. Some of my colleagues indicated interest and wish to question you directly."

"Of course," Pol replied evenly, barely able to contain his joy. "I will help in any way that I can."

"Good," Tog said somewhat lamely, "very good. Please join us here, in my chambers, four units from now. And Fra Pol . . ."

"Excellency?"

"Please be aware that in an effort to protect you and your reputation I allowed the other prelates to believe that you were acting under my instructions."

Pol bowed his head in gratitude. "Thank you, sir. That was kind of you."

The Droma nodded in agreement. "Yes, it was. Answer their questions honestly—but take care with the manner in which you do so. We understand each other?"

"Yes, excellency, we do."

"Good. You may return to your duties."

"Yes, excellency—thank you, excellency."

Pol backed into the doors, felt them open, and found himself in the waiting room. The doors closed behind him. Mys looked up from her desktop screen. "So, Fra Pol, how did it go?"

The initiate smiled. "Well, *very* well."

Mys had her doubts about that, but, as with so many things, she kept her thoughts to herself.

NEAR BELLINGHAM, WASHINGTON

Rain lanced down out of a dark gray sky, drummed across the surface of the pastel-colored cargo modules, saturated the recently denuded earth, and formed new streams that rushed, gushed, and gurgled their way down the side of the hill, thereby ripping the planet's skin away. The newly born rivers leaped obstacles, cut channels through roads, and transformed dirt into glutinous mud.

All of these were lost on the carefully sheltered, almost skeletal Zin, who, along with his entourage of Kan, Fon, and single Ra 'Na functionary, shuffled through the daily rounds. Grouped as they were, with black umbrellas held over their heads, they looked like mourners on their way to a funeral. But the Zin's thoughts lay not with the weather but the task that confronted him.

While the Sauron Book of Cycles was very explicit regarding some matters, such as the layout of the "temples," the manner in which they were constructed, and the tools that could be used, the tome was a good deal less helpful where adjunct activities were concerned.

For example, while it was clear that the temples were to be grasper-built, using nothing but approved tools, what of the structures the slaves lived in? The roads over which supplies were to be brought in? The bridges that carried the roads? And on and on.

Truth was that the ancients who had written the book had assumed that future generations would carry out these tasks *themselves,* never dreaming that their distant descendants would rule alien stars. All of this meant that the questions generated by these ancillary issues had to be answered by someone. Which was where the hereditary stonemaster came in. His name was Ras-Rak. He, with input from the great Hak-Bin, made the necessary judgments.

It was a demanding job, and one for which the Sauron had been preparing for hundreds of years. Not that he had need of extensive study, since in addition to the Book of Cycles itself, the Zin had been born knowing/remembering most of what his ancestors had learned. That being the case, many aspects of the City of Life, as Ras-Rak chose to call it, bore the imprint of his cumulative personality.

Satisfying though grasper-built structures were, there simply wasn't enough time or resources to construct everything that way. This was why slaves had been employed to prepare sites for the "temples," and to quarry the rock from which they would be built, but earthmoving equipment had been used to carve semicircular plateaus into what had been known as Governor's Point. It now had the appearance of what one of the indigenous heavy-equipment operators had described as an "elongated wedding cake."

The tiers, or levels, were connected by a road that started out beyond the protective palisade, branched into countless dead ends, and spiraled its way to the top of the hill. The lowest levels of the city were reserved for huge piles of stone, cargo modules loaded with the hardware required to equip the birth chambers, and the supplies necessary to sustain the slaves.

Once the cargo modules had been emptied, as many already were, it seemed natural to put them to further use, stacking one atop another in stair-stepped piles so that the slaves could take shelter inside.

Which human claimed which module was of no interest to the stonemaster, who preferred to let lower life forms sort themselves out, as long as they showed up for work and followed orders.

In an effort to ensure discipline, minaretlike watchtowers were being constructed at regular intervals around the circumference of the hill. Each was equipped with powerful spotlights, infrared surveillance gear, and long-range weaponry. The Kan, who staffed the towers, had orders to shoot at least one human a day, just to prove the efficacy of their nestlike perches.

Based on experience handed down from his predecessors, Ras-Rak knew that random killings, plus the knowledge that they were under constant surveillance, would go a long way toward keeping the slave population in line.

Ras-Rak paused in front of a "stack," as each of the piles of cargo modules was known, turned to the Fon who carried the waterproofed copy of the Book of Cycles, and checked to ensure that his memory was correct. As with so many things, the ancients had devoted very little space to matters of runoff and drainage. Major problems in this cursed latitude.

The Zin looked up, speared the Ra 'Na overseer with his eyes, and pointed to the top of the hill. "Have some slaves dig a trench from down the side of the hill. Move that pile of cargo modules. Lay drainage pipe all the way to the bay. Bring smaller conduits in from both sides."

Like all his people, the Ra 'Na technician had a body adapted to life in and around the sea. Because of the fact that special oils acted to keep the water away from his skin, the diminutive alien was not only comfortable, but somewhat smug because he had no need for an umbrella.

He made a note, felt sorry for the humans who had established themselves in the path of the pipe, and knew that no attempt would be made to notify them. "Yes, my lord."

Satisfied that his instructions had been understood and properly recorded, the Zin shuffled forward. His retinue followed. A column of slaves trudged by. Their chains rattled, a chain saw whined off in the distance, and a crow cawed from one of the few remaining trees.

Meanwhile, toward the top of the just-condemned stack, two humans sat in a nearly empty module and watched the aliens depart. The walls were bare, the floor was covered with mud, and rain blew in through the open door. Five-gallon buckets served as stools.

"So," Kell said, his breath fogging the air in front of him, "what was that all about?"

"Beats the hell out of me," Manning replied. "Bastards."

"Yeah," Kell agreed. "So how are we doing?"

The two men had interviewed dozens of people. The candidates had been recruited by word of mouth and posters taped to walls. The text read: "Bodyguards wanted. Must have military or law-enforcement background. See Jack Manning, Tier 3, Stack 31, tomorrow only. Don't come unless you are off-duty."

Rather than the fifty or sixty people they expected, more than two hundred showed up. Most of the mob were wishful thinkers with a sprinkling of lunatics. But there were bound to be some *real* candidates, too—assuming the security chief could properly identify them.

Manning began by creating a process in which each person met with him first, and then, if he or she had the right qualifications, was referred to Kell. A sequence that left them with the mistaken impression that the ex-Ranger was in charge. The purpose of the deception was to determine how their attitudes would change, something Manning considered to be much more important than how tough they were.

The candidates who swaggered into the room, bragged about their martial arts experience, or had difficulty meeting the security chief's eyes were immediately rejected. So were those refused to strip, had prison-style tattoos, or recent whip marks. Not because Manning sided with the Saurons, but because he needed people smart enough to get along with the aliens, regardless of how they felt about them. After all, one of the easiest ways to get Franklin killed would be to offend a Kan.

Those who managed to make it into the interview itself were quizzed about appropriate experience, tested as to their knowledge of security-speak, and relevant technology. Those who failed— and that included most—were sent packing. Those who survived made the list.

Manning consulted the data pad he had rescued from a box filled with confiscated PDAs. The screen welcomed its owner back, notified Toni Tosco that today was her mother's birthday, and offered a blank agenda.

Manning knew that the owner, assuming she was alive, would have very little say about the way in which her day would be spent. He made a note to reprogram the device, brought the list up for review, and read the entries aloud. "Here's the ones that I marked as keepers: Rafik Alaweed is a foreign exchange student who was caught here when the shit hit the fan. He's a reserve member of the Egyptian Security Force, helped retake Flight Two Thirty-five two years back, and appears to have a level head on him.

"Then we've got Garly Mol. She's an experienced border agent and martial arts expert, with a master's in psychology.

"The next one on my list is Orvo Orbin, geek's geek, and technoid extraordinaire."

Kell frowned. "Wait a minute. I rejected that one. How did he get back in?"

Manning grinned. "He ignored your rejection, waited till you were busy, and came to see me. I gave him points for that. Plus his sales pitch."

"Based on what? If memory serves me correctly, he wouldn't know a nine-millimeter from a cup of coffee."

"True," the security chief conceded, "but he *did* work for Dell, and claims he can build a first-class computer system that will enable us to track threats, inventory supplies, and jack the chits around. To provide what the U.S. Secret Service refers to as 'defense in depth,' we need to establish concentric rings of protection. The outermost ring, and in some ways the most important, consists of intelligence. Getting the information, organizing it in the correct manner, and using it. That will make the critical difference."

Kell shrugged. "You're the boss, boss. Who's next?"

"Juma Parlo. No security experience, but he's marine recon and a good, all-around troop. He doesn't care for us white folk, however, which could be a problem."

Kell raised an eyebrow. "Yeah, but he's got good creds though, assuming he told me the truth. That's the problem with this process. There's no way to verify what people tell us."

"That's where Orbin comes in," Manning observed gently. "He's already at work. As for Parlo, well, the chits offered to make him an overseer and he refused."

"Which is more than Franklin can say," Kell said grimly.

"So," Manning continued, "you add Morley Rix, Sanjiv Sidhu, and Sandi Taglio, and we have the core of a team."

"So, you took Taglio."

"Yeah, as a driver. Motorcycles, race cars, and Humvees. She knows 'em all."

"We need pilots."

Manning nodded. "We'll find 'em."

"Okay, so what's next?"

"The president will have to spend some time here. That means we need to find the most defensible stack we can, fortify the sucker, and fill it with supplies. Once that's out of the way, we open for business."

"Oh, goody, I can hardly wait."

Manning grinned. "Me, too."

ABOARD THE SAURON DREADNOUGHT *HOK NOR AH*

Though still a little woozy and therefore off-balance, Tog felt better. Much better. He, with the assistance of P'ere Has and the comely Mys, welcomed the Dromas to chambers, ensured they had seats, and urged their guests to sample spicy weed cakes and piping hot tea. The golden liquid, which had been filtered through wonderfully porous blu wood, had analgesic qualities. Some of the prelates, who had hangovers of their own, were most appreciative.

Not Dro Rul, however, who, in addition to being a continual

pain in Tog's posterior, *never* imbibed, and saw those who did as irredeemingly weak. More than that, it was *he* more than anyone else who had locked on to Tog's ill-considered statements and insisted on an interview.

Now, as the freshly bathed Pol huddled in a corner and waited for the interrogation to begin, much was at risk. If any of the rather conservative prelates could be considered a radical where matters of species relations were concerned, Rul fit the bill.

What if Rul actually believed Pol? What if the others followed? What if they took action? The relationship with the eternally touchy Saurons was iffy at best—and not something to mess around with. No, Tog didn't approve of slavery, but it was better than being human. *A lot better*.

Rul coughed, fastened Tog with one of his hard, cold stares, and blew steam off the surface of his tea. The message was clear.

Tog rang a silver bell, produced a beatific smile, and scanned the compartment. It had been swept for listening devices. The Saurons weren't very skilled where things electronic were concerned, but one never knew. One leak, one mistake, and their lives were forfeit. He cleared his throat portentously. Twelve sets of eyes locked with his.

"Thank you for coming. In case you haven't met Fra Pol—please allow me to introduce him. He brings news, which if true, is more than a little disturbing. Fra Pol?"

Pol stood, was careful to keep a steel bulkhead at his back, and struggled to breathe. The prelates were fallible, the cleric knew that, but the males assembled before him were the closest thing to a government that the Ra 'Na were permitted to have. Like the rest of his race, the initiate had been raised to respect and emulate them. Which explained not only his choice of professions but also the profound sense of disappointment he felt. Rather than *lead,* most of them seemed determined to follow. Still, they *were* Dromas, and he couldn't shake a sense of awe.

Slowly, haltingly, Pol told his story. Not the part about the illicit lunch, or the fact that he had been monitoring the Zin for an extended period of time, but the essence of what he had learned: All of the Saurons were going to die within the next 140 days, making way for a new generation. A brand-new crop of oppressors who would hatch within the "temples" and emerge to redomidate what remained of the Ra 'Na race. But only a relatively small population would be spared for that purpose.

Pol spoke calmly, rationally, and respectfully. Once he was

finished, the chamber fell silent. It remained that way for what seemed like a long time. Dro Rul was the first to speak. His voice was solemn. "There are two possibilities: Either Fra Pol is deluded, or he's correct. Given the fact that Dro Tog speaks highly of him, and sought to bring this information to our attention, we must assume the latter. That being the case, the *real* question is how to proceed."

Pol, for whom the answer seemed obvious, was amazed as his superiors debated the matter for the better part of two units, eventually coming to what amounted to a nondecision.

In spite of Rul's more activist stance, the conservatives, surreptitiously led by the likes of Tog, called for scientific verification of the initiate's claims, slyly suggesting that matters of such importance require considerable intellectual rigor.

That's what they *said*. Their true goal was to delay any sort of potentially dangerous action in hopes that the whole mess would go away.

Though disappointing, the outcome did produce a single ray of sunshine. By suggesting that Pol be assigned to lead the scientific investigation and be given the resources necessary to carry out the assignment, Dro Rul placed the conservatives in something of a bind. Unable to fault a recommendation so clearly in line with their group position, the Tog contingent could do little more than concur and hope the results were inconclusive.

In an aside that occurred as the meeting broke up, Pol found himself nose to nose with Dro Rul. The initiate tried to kneel, but a hand prevented him from doing so. It felt heavy. Rul's voice was pitched low so no one else could hear. "Speed is critical, Fra Pol. Let no one block your efforts. Call me should that become necessary."

Pol was about to thank Rul, about to assure him that he would do his best, when the prelate turned and walked away. The meeting was over—but the *real* task lay ahead.

NEAR BELLINGHAM, WASHINGTON

The weather had turned clear but cold. Jina Franklin was dressed in three layers of REI backpacking togs and carried a heavily loaded pack. It threatened to ruin her balance as she stepped off the boat and onto the metal gangplank. A Fon stood on the dock but made no effort to help.

The plank bounced under Jina's weight, and she felt frightened. The trip, which had begun as something of a lark, was turning serious now as she left the aura of privilege that surrounded her husband and entered the real world.

Alexander was absent most of the time, and sitting around the hotel was boring, which was why Jina, over the objections of the Ra 'Na "adviser" assigned to assist her, had decided to venture out on her own. Well, not *entirely* on her own, since the female Ra 'Na called Lin Mok had insisted on coming with her. Thanks to the rather authoritarian nature of Sauron society, the actual process had proved easier than she thought it would.

The Fon, who had responsibility for such matters, viewed the Franklins as members of a small but distinct caste, which, though of less importance than the most humble Sauron, had certain privileges. Freedom of movement was one of them.

That being the case, Jina discovered that she could demand things and actually get them. Well, *some* things, anyway, since the Fon ignored orders they didn't want to comply with, such as Jina's instructions to load a shuttle with supplies for the slaves.

Mok followed in the human's footsteps, kept one eye on the group of Kan who stood clustered on the dock, and wondered how much trouble she was in. Some, that was certain, but what could she do? Lacking the authority to tell the president's wife "no," and with no precedent to rely on, the Ra 'Na was forced to acquiesce.

That explanation was unlike to satisfy the female's mate, however. He, in contradiction of all that was right and fair, had authority over *her,* a member of the *first* slave race, and therefore Franklin's obvious superior.

Now, as Jina passed the Kan and started up the steeply sloped ramp, Mok gave thanks for the human's somewhat exaggerated egalitarian instincts.

Though she was not required to wear an ear tag like the rest of her kind, Jina Franklin had insisted on doing so. And much to Mok's amazement, convinced her husband to do likewise.

Now, as the Kan eyed the human's quickly departing back but made no effort to challenge her, the Ra 'Na felt sure that the red tag was working in Jina's favor.

Yes, Mok could have explained the matter to the Saurons, or tried to, but not before a certain amount of unpleasantness had occurred.

Relieved, but still concerned regarding the difficulties ahead, the small alien quickened her pace and wished humans had shorter legs. She liked the sea smell, however. She wondered if the nearly mythical Bal'wur smelled the same way.

The twosome passed through a canyon comprised of multicolored cargo modules and emerged into what had been a parking lot but now served as a transfer area.

Jina turned to see if Mok had caught up, only to discover that the Ra 'Na had corraled some local transport. The three-wheeled conveyance was of Ra 'Na manufacture, which meant Jina was too large to ride in the cab.

She dumped her pack into the cargo bed, climbed in after it, and grabbed the side rails. The truck bounced over frozen ruts, swerved to avoid a ragged-looking work party, and sped through a checkpoint.

Jina felt a strange sense of elation, knew it was wrong, but couldn't help herself. It felt good to be alive.

■ ■ ■

Manning stood with hands on hips and watched as Parlo rotated the handle of the Ra 'Na power wand into the "on" position and gave a grunt of satisfaction when a bar of bright blue energy appeared. Masking tape had been used to describe a four-by-seven rectangle on one of the cargo module's beat-up walls. Juma Parlo was a big man, about 250 pounds, with hands to match. He held the Ra 'Na–sized torch like a pencil and ran the cut next to the tape. Metal glowed, beads of perspiration appeared on Parlo's forehead, and the stink of ozone filled the air.

A hard black line appeared as the edges cooled. It wasn't long until the big man sliced through the last few inches of metal, stood back, and gave the panel a well-aimed kick. It hesitated, fell free, and clanged as it struck the floor in the neighboring cube.

Parlo looked from the tool to the newly created door. "Damn! Black & Decker oughta sell some of these babies!"

"They're slick," Manning agreed. "Now, if you would be so kind as to tackle the tape over there, we'll have a door to the ops center."

Parlo nodded happily and was halfway across the floor when Kell entered the module. The standard-issue military PRC-200, plus two dozen just like it, were among the many things Manning had requested and was starting to receive. The ex-Ranger handed the device over. "It's the boss-man . . . something about his wife."

Manning grimaced, accepted the pocket-sized radio, and held it to his ear. "Manning here."

Franklin had just spent four hours listening to a collection of

Fon functionaries lecture him about their endless expectations. And he had another four hours to go. That made him cranky. It came through in the sound of his voice and the intentional lack of front-end small talk. "Have you seen my wife? Five minutes ago I learned that she left Seattle headed for the camps."

Manning frowned. That's all he needed—a wide-open target with a wayward wife. It was important to cover them, and quickly, too. "No, sir."

"Well, get out there and find her! Lord only knows what could happen in that shithole."

Manning had been yelled at by everyone from the secretary-general of the United Nation to a camel driver in the Sudan. He knew that the yellers, with the possible exception of the camel driver, were generally running their egos. But something, he wasn't sure what, told him this was different. Judging from the catch in Franklin's voice, the politician was genuinely concerned. Manning took note of the fact, filed it away, and tried to sound soothing—something he had never been especially good at. "If she's here, we'll find her."

Franklin took comfort from the obvious sincerity of his security chief's words and felt a twinge of guilt. "I'm sorry, Jack, please ignore my tone."

"No problem, sir. We're on it. I'll call the moment we locate her."

"Thank you."

The radio went dead and Manning made a note to come up with some sort of authentication code, and a list of code names. But that was for later. Manning handed the radio to Kell. "The missus is on the loose. Let's go find her."

■ ■ ■

Jina braced her feet against the side of the cargo bed and looked up over the cab. The much-excavated "Hell Hill" rose beyond, the natural lines of its slopes interrupted by the hard angularity of the stacks. Viewed from a distance, they were reminiscent of the ancient sheer-sided cliff dwellings found in certain areas of the American Southwest.

Watchtowers, their bulbous turrets rising like alien mushrooms toward the sky, added an exotic and somewhat ominous note. And there, up at the very top, barely visible as yet, the Sauron temples had started to rise, their foundations just breaking the skyline.

That's where the slaves would be—and that's where Jina was determined to go.

The vehicle rocked from one side to the other, and she held on.

■ ■ ■

Occasional rain squalls assaulted the hill, squandered their energy, and died away. That made it all the more cozy within the make-shift "com center" where Orbo had set up shop. He was a small man with a halo of brown hair, intelligent eyes, and a determined mouth.

The technician cocked his head as the transmission came in, jotted a couple of lines on a piece of paper, and hurried off to see the boss.

Manning read the note and swore. It seemed Mrs. Franklin had commandeered some ground transportation and was on her way up the hill.

"This is truly screwed up," Manning complained as he backed out of the cargo module, swung onto a ladder fabricated from metal tubing, and lowered himself to the ground. Kell followed.

"Roger that," the ex-Ranger agreed, "but *which* part did you have in mind?"

"The part where the people we're supposed to protect don't tell us jack shit," the security chief replied. He pointed. "Look, here she comes now. I've had enough of this bullshit. It's time to give the Franklins a piece of my mind." Manning stepped out onto the road, waved his arms, and waited for the vehicle to stop.

Then, with Kell in place to ensure that the three-wheeled truck stayed where it was, the security chief walked toward the back. He saw the back of a gold ski parka, had opened his mouth, and was just about to speak when Jina turned his way.

What happened next took Manning back to the sixth grade when he had fallen hopelessly in love with Linda Hanson from the far side of the cafeteria. His eyes locked with hers, something strange happened to his stomach, and the words caught in his throat.

Jina Franklin was beautiful, all right, but, based on what he could see in her eyes, she was much more than that. She was intelligent, and, in spite of the insanity that surrounded her, in-explicably serene. A smile touched her lips. "Yes? Can I help you?"

Manning realized that his mouth hung open. He felt himself

blush. "Mrs. Franklin? My name is Manning, Jack Manning, and I'm in charge of your security detail."

Jina stood, climbed out of the truck, and offered her hand. The handshake was warm and firm. "It's a pleasure to meet you, Mr. Manning."

"Jack."

"It's a pleasure to meet you, *Jack*. I hope my presence here isn't creating some sort of problem for you. I would have contacted you and your people in advance had I known how to do so."

"Yes, ma'am. We'll remedy that—starting today. I'll provide you with a radio *and* a bodyguard. *Two* of them once we get more people on board."

Jina reached for her pack. "Thank you. Please recruit as many people as the Saurons will permit you to take. Not for my husband or me, but to better their living conditions. I want to visit the slaves. Can you help me?"

Manning, who saw any such activity as an unnecessary risk, heard himself say, "Yes, of course."

Ten minutes later, as a heavily armed Manning and Kell prepared to escort the president's wife up multiple flights of stairs toward the top of the hill, the ex-Ranger spoke from the side of his mouth. "Nice work, boss. I guess you straightened her out."

Manning jacked a shell into the chamber of the 12-gauge Mossberg. "Hey, Kell. Screw you."

The other man smiled. "Sir, yes, sir."

Manning scowled, turned his attention to the trail, and continued to climb.

NORTH OF MARYSVILLE, WASHINGTON

The underground room was dark except for a rectangle of blue lights that defined the ceiling and lit the space with a ghostly glow. The fact that the spots functioned, along with nearly everything else electrical, was thanks to the emergency backup systems installed by the Boeing Corporation, and expertise supplied by Jared Kenyata. A wizard of sorts, who, along with a few surviving members of his ilk, could summon power from diesel generators, bring dead screens back to life, and, to some small extent at least, restore a lost civilization to its former glory. A culture built on electrons rather than bricks.

Boyer Blue sighed. His thoughts veered toward his wife, but he steered them back. The facility was north of Marysville, Washington. It had been used for a variety of purposes over the past eighty years, the latest having something to do with a system of orbital energy weapons.

So had Orville Hamby claimed, anyway. And *he* should know, since it was he who stepped forward back in Gold Bar, announced that he was a physicist, and knew where the group could hide.

Hamby had been in Washington, D.C., attending a series of meetings at the Pentagon, when the Saurons attacked. Fortunately for him, the scientist had been out in the suburbs visiting a friend when the Pentagon was destroyed from orbit. Hamby tried to get out, tried to find transportation home, but, like Blue, was caught in an alien sweep.

There had been discussion, lots of it, but given the fact that most of Blue's group were from the East Coast and knew next to nothing about the Pacific Northwest, the possibility of a well-protected, well-equipped sanctuary sounded very good. Almost *too* good, since there was no reason to believe that the facility had survived, or if it had, was available for their use. That was something that bothered Blue right up to the moment the group finally arrived. It was late afternoon, nearly dark, when the ragtag band of fugitives approached the eight-foot-high security fence and followed it to a well-secured gate. It was dented but still intact.

There had been more than one break-in attempt, which, judging from the ragged remains of a corpse that hung draped over the top of the inner fence, had all been equally unsuccessful.

Hamby, who appeared as cheerful as anyone had seen him, walked up to what looked like a large aluminum mailbox, opened the cover, and stuck his hand inside. A laser scanned the surface of his hand while a needle performed a painless biopsy. DNA was checked, matched, and verified. He, and *only* he, was allowed to enter.

There was a long, nervous wait while the balding physicist entered the facility, went directly to his wife's desk, and confirmed what his heart already knew. She was gone, looking for him most likely, or captured by the aliens.

Tears flowed unchecked as the scientist hurried through the halls, confirmed that the place was empty, and entered the security center. Only three people possessed the codes necessary to effect a security override: the facility's director, assistant director, and head of security. Hamby, who, in addition to his other responsibilities, served as assistant director, made the necessary entries. The group entered.

Now, days later, they had converted office cubes into bedrooms, accessed the emergency supplies stored in the first subbasement, and generally made themselves at home.

But it was the third subbasement, where Blue and a group of his colleagues now sat, that served as the group headquarters. Heat could give them away. Hamby and Kenyata kept harping on that, so most of their time was spent deep underground.

In fact, the facility was *so* comfortable that it was tempting to settle in and wait for things to get better. Except there was no sign they ever would, which was the reason for their gathering.

Leaders had emerged during the train trip and the subsequent march. Blue looked the length of the conference room table and saw Jared Kenyata, Amanda Carter, Dr. Orville Hamby, Mr. Orlon Foley. And just back from a trip up north, an ex-marine corporal, ex–scam artist, and ex-convict whose actual name was Arthur Tremby but who was better known as "Shoes." A nickname that stemmed from his affinity for high-quality footwear.

Though a bit unsavory in some respects, Shoes was intelligent, shrewd, and courageous, qualities that had everything to do with his successful recon mission.

Shoes, who seemed to have eyes in the back of his head, turned to meet the older man's gaze. "So, Professor, are you ready for my report?"

Blue rankled at the tone but forced himself to ignore it. "Please proceed."

Shoes nodded to Kenyata. A digital still photo filled the far wall. It had been taken with a long lens on a reasonably clear day. The group saw a raw tree-stripped hill, roads lined with stacks of pastel cargo containers, and a flat area on top. Spindly towers rose here and there. People could be seen, along with piles of stone, and a low, dark line. A structure? Or the beginning of one? So it appeared. Rather than the rambling, semicoherent account that Blue expected, Shoes delivered his report Marine Corps style, using short, clipped sentences.

"This is the south side of the hill on which the alien structures are being constructed. A place called Governor's Point. I couldn't get any closer. Kan patrols were everywhere. But a number of things are clear: One, even though they use heavy equipment to move those cargo modules around, the bugs use slaves for everything else.

"Two, the vast majority of the slaves are white, while most of the overseers are dark-skinned. That's what most of us would be doing had we remained on the train.

"Three, any person of color who refuses to serve the Saurons is subject to punishment."

Carter frowned. "Punishment? What sort of punishment?"

Shoes nodded, and the shot changed. Unlike Christian crosses, the Sauron version featured two crosspieces, one toward the top, and another near the bottom. The chief advantage of the alien design was that the aliens could not only spread-eagle their victims, but hang them upside down as well. At least four of the crosses were occupied, but there were an awful lot of crows, so it was hard to tell. Carter shuddered and looked away.

Blue was reminded of the Billie Holiday song "Strange Fruit," which referenced an earlier time, a time when poplar trees had been used to lynch African-Americans, and the crows were, ironically enough, black themselves.

There were *more* pictures, most of which served to reinforce what they already knew. "That's about it," Shoes concluded, "except for this—the aliens drop them from the air. They make better fire starters than ass wipes."

The leaflet played as it was passed from hand to hand. Blue placed the object on the table in front of him. He watched the image of Franklin not only come to life but also start to speak. "Like it or not, the simple fact is that the sooner the temples are built, the sooner the Saurons will leave. That being the case, I urge you to volunteer your help. Those who do will be fed, housed, and allowed some personal freedom. Those who ignore the common cause, or attempt to hinder construction, will be subject to punitive measures."

Blue felt the anger start to build. As if the aliens weren't bad enough, here was a human, an African-American, helping the scum to maintain their rule. He brought his fist down on the ex-governor's face. The table jumped. "You rotten sonofabitch! We've seen *your* punitive measures—now you'll see *ours!*"

Shoes raised his eyebrows. The historian was pissed, that was for sure. "What have you got in mind, Doc? What should we do?"

"Find the bastard," Blue said with a growl, *"find the bastard and kill him."*

■ ■ ■

The rain was back. It drummed along the top of the cargo module–sized clinic, soaked the bedraggled slaves who waited outside, ran down the recently placed stairs, and gushed through a drainage pipe. It was broken and delivered a torrent of water onto an already devastated hillside.

Inside, working by the light of four battery-powered lamps and assisted by a gaunt-looking R.N., Dr. Seeko Sool prepared to examine her next patient. The process was something of a ritual: wash her hands in the basin, dictate notes to a volunteer, and take a sip of black-market coffee. The key to staying awake.

For reasons known only to the Fon, the doctor had been assigned to the night shift. Her job, and that of the others on the six-person team, was to dig drainage ditches. That meant the physician was available to see patients during the day, but left her short of sleep, hence the coffee. She stifled a yawn. "Okay, who's next?"

The nurse, a woman named Dixie, gestured toward the makeshift examining table that claimed the center of the room. Her voice was level but her eyes were filled with pain, the kind that stems from seeing so much misery and being unable to alleviate it. "We have a seven-year-old male with severe diarrhea. He has been vomiting for the past six hours or so."

Sool took one look at the youngster and knew she could make the diagnosis from ten feet away: cholera. The onetime scourge of countries such as India had long since been brought under control. Though one of the oldest and most infectious diseases to plague mankind, it was also one of the easiest to treat. *If* one had some basic medical supplies.

The cause, a bacterium called *Vibrio cholerae,* typically found its way into the patient's intestinal tract via contaminated food or water.

Most infections tended to be mild, resulting in little more than a bout of diarrhea. But in some cases, like the ones Sool was seeing with growing frequency, patients would experience the rapid onset of severe diarrhea, which, when combined with incessant vomiting, resulted in the loss of fluids and electrolytes, leaving the victims thirsty, weak, and dehydrated. Some would experience stomach, arm, and leg cramps. And none of this had to happen if there were only some preventative measures taken. Some attempt at proper sanitation.

Sool produced a smile and approached the examining table. The boy was barely conscious. His clothes appeared to be reasonably clean, as were his feet, which was highly unusual. A man, his hat held in his hands, stood on the opposite side of the up-ended crate. She knew without asking that he had carried the boy to the clinic in his arms and waited for hours in the cold and rain. She met his eyes. They were brown and filled with concern. "Hello, I'm Dr. Sool. Is this young man your son?"

The man shook his head. His voice was gruff. "No, he's an orphan. Far as we know, anyway."

So few words and so much meaning. There were very few children among the slaves. Millions had died during the first few days of the attack, but thousands upon thousands had been captured during the sweeps, categorized as "substandard labor" by the Fon overseers, and eliminated.

A few had slipped through the system. Many, those who did best, were "adopted" by people like the man across from her. Sool nodded. "He's lucky to have you. Thanks."

The man shook his head. "He's a good boy—the privilege is mine. Can you help him?"

Sool nodded, explained that while she didn't have any way to administer IV fluids, the man could boil water, add some sugar and salt, and give the ORS solution orally. More than that, he could spread the word that people should boil all drinking water, damn near burn their food, and see to their own cleanliness.

The man listened attentively, used a pencil stub to take notes, and accepted the necessary ingredients from Dixie. They were sealed in squares of plastic wrap and secured with blue rubber bands.

With the packets stowed in his pockets, the man lifted the boy off the table. "Thank you, Doctor. Assuming there's a heaven, they're holding a place for you."

And for *you,* Sool thought, as the man turned and stepped into the rain.

The next hour was little more than a blur. Sool, who prided herself on knowing her patients as people, was forced to abandon such niceties in favor of treating as many people as possible in the shortest period of time.

That being the case, the doctor remembered the procession of ragged-looking people as a broken tibia, followed by a laceration of the hand, another case of cholera, what might have been an impacted tooth, a sprained ankle, and a case of flu.

There was a stir outside, the sound of voices, and a tall man entered the clinic.

The man held a young woman in his arms. She appeared to be in her teens. Rain had plastered her hair across her face. Her body was limp and apparently unconscious. His eyes were filled with anger. "She was injured in some sort of construction accident. The Saurons left her by the road to die."

Sool nodded. "Place her on the table. Dixie, check the line to make sure we don't have anything worse waiting in the wings."

The stranger did as he was told. There was something infinitely tender about the way he placed the teenager on the recently scrubbed table. Something that Sool liked. "Do you know her?"

He shook his head. "No. My name is Jack Manning. I serve as chief of security for President Franklin and his wife. We found her lying in a ditch one level up. People mentioned your clinic, so we brought her down."

Sool placed a makeshift pillow under the patient's knees, noticed the way one of her legs was bent, and began the examination. The teenager's skin was cold, *too* cold, and Dixie started to warm her. The blankets got in the way, but Sool managed in spite of that. "You said 'we'?"

"Yes," a new voice answered. "I'm Jina Franklin, Governor Franklin's wife."

Sool looked up to discover that a woman had entered the module. An extremely attractive woman, who, judging by the cleanliness of her clothes and the heavily armed bodyguard who stood behind her, was some sort of collaborator. A breed for which the doctor had nothing but contempt.

"Nice to meet you," Sool said sarcastically. "We don't serve tea till four. Perhaps you could wait outside."

Jina jerked as if slapped and felt the blood rush to her cheeks. "Yes, of course. Here, it isn't much, but it's all I could carry. There will be more, however, *much* more, now that I know where to send it."

Manning opened the pack, and Dixie's eyes lit up as she peered inside. "Supplies! Drugstore-type stuff for the most part, but wonderful nonetheless. Thank you."

Sool felt her anger melt away. The woman had been carrying a pack, for God's sake, looking for people to help. "I'm sorry about what I said. It was uncalled for. My name is Sool, Seeko Sool, and I'm a bit cranky."

Jina smiled. "No, it's quite all right. The simple fact is that I'm going to hear a lot worse during the coming weeks and months. By working with the Saurons, my husband hopes to help people. That may be a bit naive, but that's how he is."

The comment was revealing, *very* revealing, for Sool, and for Manning, who had noticed the manner in which Jina Franklin used her husband's *former* title rather than the one bestowed on him by the Saurons.

The patient moaned and attempted to move. Sool gestured toward the teenager's head. "Hold her still while I finish my examination."

It was a peace offering of sorts, and Jina accepted it as such.

Manning checked to be sure that Kell had his back to the room, and was watching the entrance, before stepping forward to lend a hand.

Sool cursed the lack of diagnostic tools, found passageways in through Dixie's wraps, and tried to "see" with her fingers. Finally, when the examination was over, Sool motioned to Jina and Manning. They joined her in a corner. "She has two broken legs—and there is the very real possibility of internal injuries. We'll have to wait and see."

Jina looked at the battered walls and mud-streaked floor. "Where will you put her? Who will take care of her?"

Sool shrugged. "Excellent questions. I wish I had answers. We will set her bones. As for the rest, well, Dixie and I go back on duty in fewer than three hours."

Jina was shocked. "They make you work on the temple?"

Sool looked the other woman in the eye. "We dig ditches. Good, honest work, which, if properly carried out, will help control the cholera epidemic."

"Cholera epidemic?"

"Yes, I'm afraid so. Tell your husband—maybe he can help."

Jina nodded. "And the girl?"

"We'll park her against a wall and see if we can find a volunteer to stay with her."

Manning watched Jina, and Sool watched him. She wondered if the other woman knew. No, the doctor decided, she doesn't have a clue. Not really. And he, judging from all appearances, is wasting his time. Which is too bad, or would be, if life were normal and I liked alpha males, which I don't.

Jina looked out toward the people in the rain. "I don't know how much the Saurons will allow us to do, but you have my word that we will push it to the limit."

Sool smiled and wiped her forehead with the back of her hand. "Thank you. Anything would help."

The two women shook hands, Jina turned to go, and Manning

pulled something out of a pocket. "Here, Doc, you look a little on the thin side. Eat some of these."

Sool accepted the package, discovered that it consisted of five Hershey bars held together with a red rubber band, and felt the warmth of his hand. It lingered long after he was gone.

NEAR SALEM, OREGON

The hawk was a creature of both instinct and habit. And it was habit that caused the bird of prey to launch itself from the light standard, beat its way higher into the air, and circle the mile-long stretch of I-5. The sun was out, and the raptor threw a cross-shaped shadow on the ground.

The thermal, created by hot air rising off the concrete below, provided extra lift. The hawk seemed to float. Its eyes searched for food.

There were bodies below, *large* bodies. Too large to attack, so the vigil continued. Perhaps they would scare a food thing out into the open.

Meanwhile, directly below, and concealed against notice by eyes out beyond the edge of the atmosphere, Deacon Smith brought the binoculars up, leaned back, and allowed the concrete overpass to accept most of his weight. By resting his elbows on his knees, he could steady the binoculars. With the exception of some carefully repositioned wrecks, the freeway stretched empty for as far as the eye could see. Humans, those with enough smarts to escape capture, knew better than to use it. To do so was to invite an energy bolt from orbit or to attract one of the fighters that crisscrossed the sky.

No, the freeway belonged to the bugs now, and, as with many occupying armies, especially those that believe all resistance has been crushed, the aliens were increasingly predictable. Radio traffic rode the same frequencies every day, recon drones patrolled identical vectors, and the I-5 supply convoy ran like clockwork. Tanker trucks mostly, filled with chemicals. Why? Who the heck knew? The important thing was that the bastards were predictable. *That* was a weakness, and one that Smith planned to exploit.

The ex-soldier shifted the binoculars to his immediate surroundings. There was the freeway itself, which was littered with rusting hulks. There were eight lanes. Four north, four south, and a heavily planted median strip that ran straight down the middle. He expected the bugs to arrive from the south traveling at approximately sixty miles per hour, slow as they were forced to thread their way among the labyrinth of wrecks, and run right smack into his ambush.

At least some of the action would take place under the same overpass at his back, which because of the six-lane highway it supported, would screen the ensuing activities from orbit. Could anything go wrong? Heck, yes, hundreds of things. But that's why war sucks.

Smith scanned both sides of the northbound lanes. Thanks to the fact that the vast majority of "Deac's Demons," as they had chosen to call themselves, had either served in the military or spent a lot of time outdoors, they knew how to make themselves comfortable. And after some coaching from experts such as George Farley, they were very well camouflaged.

More than fifty heavily armed men and women had infiltrated the ambush area during the night, used two small tractors to reposition the wrecks, and retired to their places of concealment.

Smith could see them—some of them, at any rate—sitting in carefully dug foxholes, lying in shallow trenches, or concealed by half-destroyed vehicles. They had been there for more than six hours, careful not to move more than a few inches, struggling to keep their bodies ready for action.

The aliens might have spotted them, if they had been looking. But they hadn't. There hadn't been any widespread resistance, so why look for it? Arrogance for which the chits were about to pay.

Of course Smith knew that the *next* attack, if there was a next attack, wouldn't be so easy. A voice whispered through his ear plug–sized receiver. The transmission was scrambled and originated with a woman named Ross. She was stationed on top of a low-lying hill two miles to the south of the ambush site. "Eyeball One to D-One. Over."

Smith made note of the fact that Ross was making use of something that resembled correct radio procedure and gave thanks. "This is D-One . . . go. Over."

"I have *six*—repeat, six—enemy vehicles northbound at approximately fifty miles per hour. ETA thirteen twenty hours."

"Classifications? Over."

"Alien armor, tanker, tanker, tanker, tanker, armor. Over."

"Air cover? Over."

"Negative at this time. Over."

"Roger that. Hold for ten, watch for tail-end Charlies, and haul fanny. Over."

"Roger. Eyeball One over and out."

Smith switched to the team freq. "D-One to D-Team. We have six northbound vehicles. Implement Plan One. Lock and load. Over."

Most of the team *were* locked and loaded, but it didn't hurt to make sure, especially with so many amateurs about. There was a chorus of clicks as the team acknowledged the transmission and readied themselves for combat.

Smith looked to his own weapon, the same Remington 7.62mm sniper's rifle he had carried into the mountains, and felt his stomach start to churn. He hadn't been in combat for a long time. Did he still have what it took? The ability to acknowledge the fear, accept it, and still continue to function? There was only one way to find out.

Smith used the Redfield scope to look down the freeway. The hawk circled above. Both predators waited for their prey.

■ ■ ■

The Sauron convoy had made excellent progress, and Ank-Oon, the Fon with responsibility for the high-priority cargo it carried, was in a good mood. He liked to ride up top, where he could see, and preferred to leave the hatch open. A violation of combat protocols—but so what? The Kan could worry about such mundane matters. *He* had better things to do.

The Sauron allowed the webbing to accept his full weight, watched the alien landscape roll past, and tried to remember the last planet he had served on. Was it called Deeth? Yes, he thought it was, although the information hung at the very edge of his memory and would soon slip-slide away.

The never-ending memory loss was both annoying and comforting, since knowing involved bad memories as well as the good.

Besides, remembering things, such as the names of the ancestors, was the responsibility of the Zin. Poor creatures, who in spite of the privileges attendant to their caste, spent far too much time attending meetings. Yes, there were worse things than being a Fon. Like being Ra 'Na or human.

Lower down, in the vehicle's belly, the driver, a Kan named Sit-Tos, eased the grasper-controlled throttle and allowed the combat car to slow. He turned the handlebar-style control yoke to avoid the remains of a burned-out truck, and nosed into the maze.

Sit-Tos had negotiated this particular obstacle course half a dozen times before and knew what to expect. But things looked different today. Not much—but a little. The blue wreck was closer to the side of the road, the red vehicle had been shifted to the right, and a sort of corridor had been created. Why?

The Kan checked his rearview monitor, confirmed that the first tanker was tucked in behind him, and looked forward again.

The driver was about to go on the radio, about to share his impressions with the noncom named Dor-Buk, when strange things started to happen. Electromagnetic detectors went off, a heat sensor beeped, and automatic weapons systems came on-line as at least some of the wrecks came to life! More than that—they started to close around him.

Part of what made the Kan such good warriors, and helped explain how they had been able to subjugate races that were technologically superior to their own, was the fact that they were born knowing how to respond to most tactical situations. They could do so with the confidence that their hatchmates would react appropriately, and thus were free to attack non-Saurons with complete impunity. Well, not *complete* impunity, since the penalty for killing a slave was identical to the punishment suffered for a lost canteen: one unit of extra duty. That being the case, Sit-Tos opened fire with every weapon he had, and knew that Dor-Buk would order his driver to do likewise.

Energy weapons lashed outward, a Ford pickup exploded, and a human was tossed high into the air.

Meanwhile, up top, Ank-Oon was so foolish as to waste a precious second wondering what Sit-Tos was firing at, and paid the ultimate price.

The handloaded experimental "bug-killer" round left the Remington's barrel, punched a hole through the front of the Fon's skull, and blew his brains out through the back of his elongate head. A definite success.

Smith watched the Sauron die through his telescopic sight and nodded his satisfaction. One chit down—and at least a million to go.

Sit-Tos steered around one of the smaller wrecks, passed under the overpass, and was forced to squeeze the grasper-operated brake when a hoverbus lurched out in front of him. The combat car skidded to a halt. More than an ambush, it was a trap! The humans planned to take the entire convoy!

The Kan had released his harness and was backing out of the driver's sling when Farley dropped through the open hatch and landed on top of Ank-Oon's body. The .38 Magnum barked twice. The Sauron jerked as the bullets bounced off his chitin, turned, and lashed out. A razor-sharp wrist spur passed within an inch of the human's face. He swore, fired two additional slugs into the Kan's torso, and felt a sense of relief as one of them managed to punch its way through. The alien toppled to one side, and the entire combat car shuddered as something exploded and shards of shrapnel rang against the hull.

The last vehicle in the column jerked to a halt. The driver, a Kan named Rel-Dek, saw the tanker blow as a shoulder-launched missile struck it halfway back. The Sauron slammed the vehicle into reverse and felt the rear crash guard slam into something extremely solid. It seemed that a burned-out hulk, completely immobile only moments before, had blocked the only escape route.

Rel-Dek's superior, a rather stern noncom by the name of Dor-Buk, was as cool as space itself. He requested air support, checked his t-gun, and issued the only orders he could. "It appears that the soft skins have the means to destroy this vehicle. Drop the rear ramp, form on me, and kill anything that moves."

They were "good orders," meaning orders that were consistent with his subordinate's instincts, experience, and training. The warriors freed themselves from their harnesses, grabbed their weapons, and followed Dor-Buk out into the cold alien atmosphere.

The move was far from unexpected. Mary Trantor had been looking forward to and dreading that moment for a long, long time. The Saurons had killed everyone she ever loved, and it was payback time. The only problem was that she still had the instincts of a housewife rather the soldier she sought to become.

The onetime mother of three hesitated for a fraction of a second, and checked to ensure that her safety was off, before squeezing the trigger. The TAR-21 Israeli "Bullpup" submachine gun's barrel jerked upward, and she forced it back down as a stream of .233 NATO SS109 ammo raced through the space the Saurons had occupied only one second before.

But they were gone by then, having leaped high into the air.

Dor-Buk eyed the enemy from his vantage point fifty feet over their heads. He fired *three* separate bursts at *three* separate targets and knew every dart would strike its target. Heads mostly, totally unprotected.

Trantor never knew what hit her. The projectile entered through the top of her skull, traveled down through her neck, and buried itself in her left lung. Her eyes rolled back in her head, blood gushed out of her mouth, and she fell backward into some Scotch broom. The rest of the fire team died with her.

Smith, who had hoped to keep the Saurons *in* their vehicles and thereby keep casualties low, knew his entire plan was starting to come apart. He watched the Saurons hit the ground and bounce back up. Once they reached apogee, the aliens seemed to hang there as if suspended by invisible ropes. They maintained a diamond-shaped formation and wreaked havoc on the resistance fighters below. Smith wanted to shout orders but knew there wasn't time. Someone would do what needed to be done—or the whole group would go into the shitter. The lead Kan fired, and a man named Hatch was thrown off the back of a truck.

Unlike the parking lot on the freeway below, there was only one vehicle sitting on the overpass. It was a yellow school bus with the name "Bright Stars Preschool" emblazoned along the side.

The door opened, a man named Luis Rallos stepped out, flipped a cigarette away, and brought the rocket launcher up to his shoulder. There were only two things he'd ever been good at: high school football, and the use of heavy weapons. Crew-served machine guns, mortars, and light artillery, he'd fired them all.

But his absolute favorite, and the weapon for which he was best known, was the twelve-round "Slingshot," first issued to American troops just three years before, and the source of the nickname Rallos acquired during a tour in the army: "Rocketman."

The launcher, which was extremely light and fired "minirockets," each the size of an old-fashioned number-two pencil, was the first weapon of its type intended for use against "soft" targets.

The Saurons were an interesting challenge. Partly because they were too close to use the heat-seeking guidance system without endangering his comrades, partly because they were falling, and partly because they were relatively small targets.

But so was a receiver in the end zone, especially when viewed from fifty or sixty yards away. Perhaps someone else would have thought about the angle of deflection, the fact that the wind was from the west, or any of a half dozen other factors. But not Rallos. He fired the Slingshot the same way that the younger version of himself had thrown footballs—quickly, instinctively, naturally.

The first rocket hit Rel-Dek, exploded, and showered the humans below with bits of raw meat and still-morphing chitin.

The second projectile struck Dor-Buk's right foot, sheared it off, and exploded ten feet away. What remained of the bug cartwheeled through the air, was shattered by three rounds of double-ought buck as it passed over the point where Farley stood, and crashed into the front of a Sauron tanker-truck. The windshield shattered and a terrified Fon peered out through the remains of the warrior assigned to protect him.

The last of the Kan had surrendered to gravity by that time, hit the ground, and been blasted before they could bounce. A woman known by the handle "Longlegs" had their range, and slugs from her M-18 tore them apart.

Suddenly the battle was over. A couple of Fon drivers had survived, but the rest of the Saurons were dead.

Deac Smith turned to look up at the point where Luis "Rocketman" Rallos stood silhouetted against the sky. The resistance leader offered a salute, which the other man returned. The right person, in the right place, at the right time. As with many battles throughout human history, that was the difference between victory and defeat.

The thought had no more than completed itself when a beam of incandescent light touched down a hundred feet away, a tanker-truck exploded, and concussion blew half a dozen people off their feet. There was a loud cracking noise followed by the stench of ozone. The Saurons were attaching from orbit!

Smith spoke while still flat on his back. "This is D-One to all teams. Withdraw according to plan. Rendezvous two . . . repeat, *two* . . . execute. Over."

The freedom fighters split into fire teams, ran like hell, and were clear by the time the second, third, and fourth energy bolts struck the ground.

Hit and run, hit and run, hit and run. It was the same approach the Vietcong had used against both the French and the Americans.

Slowly, using the existing network of reenactors, survivalists, and ex-military as a cadre, Smith intended to create a classic guerrilla movement.

There was a problem, though—one he would eventually be forced to confront. It's one thing to fight *against* something, such as the Saurons, but another to fight *for* something, such as freedom.

What the movement needed, and Smith couldn't supply, was political leadership. The kind Churchill supplied to England, the kind Mao supplied to China, and the kind Mandela supplied to

South Africa. All Smith could do was fight and hope for the best. The hawk, which still circled above, continued to hunt.

BELLINGHAM, WASHINGTON

In spite of the fact that considerable efforts had been made to furnish the cargo module with items appropriated from Bellingham-area houses, the interior was a good deal less pleasant than the hotel room back in Seattle, and Franklin was pissed.

The Saurons were on his ass to pacify the slaves, Jina wanted him to *help* the slaves, and now, his poncho dripping rain, his boots heavy with mud, his own chief of security was reading him the riot act. The issue at hand, a man named José Amocar, had been ordered to wait outside. Manning was in midrant. His eyes were filled with fire.

"Begging your pardon, *sir,* but if you want me to protect you, and Lord knows you're going to need it, I need the freedom to pick my own team. Not only did you choose Amocar without discussing the matter with me, you made him number two, a critical position, especially if I get killed. That was a very stupid thing to do—and I want you to reverse the decision."

Jina, who was sitting in a corner, winced. Alexander's decision *had* been stupid, that much was obvious, but confrontation was the wrong way to approach him. *Especially* with her in the room. Manning had left her husband with no way to back off, no way to save face, and the result was entirely predictable.

The truth was that Amocar had been forced on Franklin by Hak-Bin, who claimed the man had excellent qualifications. And yes, maybe he'd been a little bit wishy-washy, but so what? One security type was pretty much like another. He might have been willing to discuss the matter, especially the question of rank, but not now. Now it was *mano a mano,* and a precedent would be set.

Franklin, who had been seated behind a folding work table, stood, placed his fingertips on the surface in front of him, and leaned forward. His eyes were little more than slits. "Listen to me, Manning, and listen good. You may not like it, and you may not approve, but *I'm the president*. You will continue to select members of your team, but if I want to intervene, *I will*. Get okay with it or grab a shovel and head for the top of the hill. Do I make myself clear?"

Manning felt the blood rush to his face. He was about to accept Franklin's invitation when his eyes locked with Jina's. There was no mistaking the look there or the request to stay. Not for herself, but for her husband. He knew that, knew it was about Franklin, but the emotions were the same. What if this Amocar person screwed up? What if *she* were killed? No, he couldn't countenance that.

The security chief swallowed his anger, forced a blank face, and directed his answer to Jina rather than her husband. "Understood."

Franklin allowed himself to relax slightly. "Good. Now that we have that out of the way, let's take a look at my itinerary. There's a lot to do."

José Amocar was summoned into the room after that and stood with his back to the wall. He was short, and, in an attempt to make himself appear taller, had a tendency to walk on the balls of his feet. He had a barrel-like chest, though, thick arms, and a high tolerance for pain. Assets he had come to depend on.

It wasn't that Amocar *liked* the chits, they were too frigging weird for that, but it certainly didn't take a frigging genius to see which side of the frigging bread the frigging butter was on, and guide your actions accordingly. No sirree bob.

So, much as Amocar detested reports, especially *written* reports, he would dutifully memorize everything that took place, scribble it out, and turn it in.

The meeting droned on, Amocar listened, and kept one eye on Jina. It was fun to undress her. And it made the time pass more quickly.

HELL HILL

The slaves were hard at work by the time Hak-Bin landed in Bellingham Bay, shuffled up a ramp into a heavily guarded ground vehicle, and was carried up the hillside. The ground car's top had been retracted at the Zin's insistence, and he rode like what he was: a conqueror.

The sun was up, the clouds that had dominated the previous day were gone, and the land was bathed in gold. Everywhere the Sauron looked he saw slaves hard at work. Some dragged blocks of stone up paths cleared for that purpose; others dug drainage ditches conceived by the stonemaster; and some, so tired from the day's labors that they could hardly move, filtered down off the crown of the hill.

They were a scruffy lot, clad in layers of gray rags, hands and feet wrapped with strips of cloth, barely raising their heads as the Sauron vehicle approached.

Ah, but the looks they gave him! Looks that jumped the intervening space, looks that required no translation, looks that spoke to the importance of his mission. Because regardless of how tired they might be after a twelve-unit shift, the humans still had enough emotional energy to hate him. And that was dangerous. *Very* dangerous. Some sort of relief valve was necessary. A valve similar to the one furnished to the Ra 'Na.

Hak-Bin used a pincer to steady himself as the ground car took a turn and made its way up a heavily rutted side street. Like most of the structures on or around the hill—the "retreat," as its founder liked to call it—had been constructed with cargo modules. There were six of them, all pink, with three cubes on the bottom, two centered over those, and a single on top. The Sauron was struck by the fact that by coincidence or design the result bore an uncanny resemblance to what the central Temple of Life within the main citadel would eventually look like.

The individual who was responsible for the structure, who referred to herself as "Sister Andromeda," stood waiting on the recently swept plaza that fronted her church. She wore a handsewn full-length white robe. It had sleeves that allowed her hands to meet unseen. Sturdy-looking rope-and-tire sandals encased her carefully manicured feet and peeked out from under a nicely finished hem. Her posture, to the extent that the Sauron could interpret it, bespoke wary respect. Not as good as abject fear, but acceptable nonetheless.

The vehicle came to a halt. A detachment of Kan bodyguards stepped off the platforms secured to the ground car's heavily armored flanks and immediately took to the air. One landed on top of the retreat itself, another hit the ground not five feet from Sister Andromeda's left elbow, and a third disappeared to the rear of the complex. The warriors used their time in-air to survey the surrounding area, scan for threats, and orient themselves to each other. The nearest minaretlike security tower could provide additional fire support should that be required.

Sister Andromeda, who had endured the process several times before, still found the deployment to be more than a little disconcerting. After all, who in their right mind would want to harm a Star Being? The very idea of it caused the priestess to shudder. Still, not everyone shared her view of the aliens as fabulous beings sent to lift mankind to a higher level of consciousness. In fact, some of the less enlightened brethren saw the Saurons as *evil*, mistaking as they did the discipline required to establish a new order as a form of tyranny, and seeking to overturn it. A terrible error that she feared would cause the Saurons to withhold their knowledge and wisdom.

Not that Sister Andromeda was blind to the fact that each Sauron was an individual, meaning that some were less evolved than others. Hak-Bin being an excellent example.

Yes, the Zin had allowed her retreat to remain open, and more than that, freed her from the stone-cutting crew she had originally been assigned to. But he had also stopped short of granting the priestess the additional resources she so badly needed. Resources that would allow her relatively small band of believers to go forth and proselytize. Unless that was the purpose of the meeting, to tell her that the necessary permissions had been granted and that the religion was now free to grow.

Brightened by that possibility, Andromeda went out to meet the alien halfway. The priestess bowed, as she had seen the Ra 'Na do. "Welcome, my lord. Your presence enfolds us like the warmth of the sun."

Hak-Bin, who couldn't care less how slaves perceived his presence, scanned the area. "Improvements have been made."

"Yes," Sister Andromeda replied eagerly, "thank you for the cargo modules. We painted the interiors."

"Excellent," the Sauron said approvingly. "I would like to see them."

Thrilled by the alien's low-key demeanor and interest in even the most mundane aspects of her church, the woman struggled to stay level with her slow-moving guest. She babbled on about church services, new members, and her hopes for the future.

Finally, after what seemed like an eternity, the two entered the steel-walled structure and paused. The clean white interior was lit by Sauron-supplied lights—and a handful of acolytes scattered as the Star Being entered. Some because they were afraid of the Zin, some because they were afraid of Sister Andromeda. Hak-Bin took a long, slow look around. "You have no altar."

A lump formed in Sister Andromeda's throat. She managed to swallow it. "Yes, I mean no, not that we need one. Altars suggest some sort of deity, and in order to reach the next level of consciousness, we must abandon—"

"You need altars," Hak-Bin interrupted brusquely. "I will supply them."

Andromeda, who wasn't sure if she should be pleased or offended, nodded her head. "Thank you, my lord. Nothing could please me more. How many should we expect?"

"Let's start with six," the alien responded blandly. "One for each new structure."

The human's eyebrows shot upward. *"New structures? Does that mean I can—"*

"Yes," Hak-Bin replied. "I will order my staff to provide you with one hundred red ear tags—more than enough to meet your immediate needs. More resources will follow, but only if you and your adherents do everything within your power to encourage productivity, and thereby further the cause. Do I make myself clear?"

"Very," the priestess replied, well aware that her activities had been tolerated, *would be* tolerated, only as long as she said positive things regarding the aliens, encouraged the slaves to work harder, and supported the status quo. Something she was quite happy to do as long as her organization flourished.

"Good," Hak-Bin finished, already shuffling toward the door. "I will return in five rotations. The first altar must be installed by then."

Mystified as to why the Sauron wanted to supply her with altars but pleased with the additional support, Sister Andromeda watched the alien leave. "Yes, lord, thank you, lord." The Zin made no response. The interview was over.

Once back in his ground car, braced against the movement to come, Hak-Bin looked back at the church. The slaves needed something to cling to. Given the right sort of encouragement, it would flourish like a weed. But weeds can be dangerous, especially if they grow out of control, which was why each of the specially constructed altars would house a powerful remote-controlled bomb. Just the thing to kill this particular weed should it grow *too* strong.

Satisfied with the morning's work and just a bit hungry, the Sauron signaled his driver. A crow cawed, a breeze pushed in from the west, and the sun inched across the sky.

5

DEATH DAY MINUS 128

THURSDAY, MARCH 26, 2020

The problem of the twentieth century is the problem of the colour line—
the relation of the darker to the lighter races of men in Asia and Africa,
in America and the islands of the sea.
—W.E.B. Du Bois,
The Souls of Black Folk, 1903

EVERETT, WASHINGTON

The Sauron transport swung over the harbor, turned north, and
came in for a landing. The hull bounced three times, steadied,
and plowed a furrow through the pewter-gray water. A tug hurried
to meet it. There were wrecks to avoid—and wind gusts to contend with.

Everett, Washington, which was about sixty miles south of Bellingham, boasted a decent harbor and a well-equipped naval base.
Like most of the facilities the Saurons took an interest in, it had
been spared the sort of destruction visited on McChord AFB and
the naval command in Bremerton.

That being the case, and consistent with orders from the stonemaster himself, the Everett location had been set aside for use as
an assembly area where the pumps, filters, valves, and other
equipment necessary to accommodate "the change" could be
preassembled under his watchful gaze—a strategy that his inherited memory assured him would reduce the kind of costly errors
that ate resources and wasted time.

But that required slaves, *lots* of them, which was why Franklin had been ordered to go there, speak to the human workforce, and do what he could to address the steadily increasing incidents of vandalism and outright sabotage that plagued the facility of late. Activities that threatened not only the stonemaster's carefully conceived plan—but the construction process itself.

Of course, there were threats to security, many of which Manning had been unable to neutralize. Though much more organized than it had been one week before, the team was still rather thin. So, with the exception of a cursory check performed by José Amocar a few hours earlier, the dock area remained unsecured. While Franklin took the security chief's concerns seriously, there wasn't much he could do. The Saurons had ordered him to go, and he had little choice but to obey.

"Remember, Mr. President," Manning said over the whine of the ship's drives, "the security team leaves the ship first. You stay here till I give the all-clear."

Franklin nodded, as did his wife. Jina was breathtakingly beautiful. Manning tried to ignore her but couldn't.

The spaceship bumped the landing stage. Slaves hurried to secure shock lines to eyebolts, and the security team passed through the lock and out onto the floating dock. The wood was slippery, and the air smelled of brine. The pier was supported by pilings festooned with streamers of green seaweed and clusters of white barnacles. The tide was low, which meant the team faced a steep climb.

Manning led Rafik Alaweed, Morley Rix, and Jonathan Wimba up a series of metal gangways and onto the dock. It had been constructed to service warships, which explained why it was both spacious and well equipped. Though far from fully trained, the team instinctively put some distance among themselves. Rix remembered how his DI used to shout, "One grenade get you all!" and grinned.

A stack of the now ubiquitous cargo modules plus a pair of skeletal-looking orange cranes provided a backdrop for some three hundred slaves. They stood in ragged rows and regarded the newly arrived "reds" with a combination of curiosity, loathing, and fear. The presence of a dozen Kan warriors did nothing to put them at ease.

Manning ignored the almost palpable sense of resentment that hung in the air and eyed his surroundings. The crowd, which had been assembled under the no-nonsense supervision of the Kan, should be relatively safe. But what about the surrounding structures? Everything should have been searched, then sealed. *Would* have been, had there been enough time and people.

A Kan-mounted Ra 'Na caught the human's eye and gestured toward the crowd. His voice boomed through a saddle-mounted speaker. "We have a schedule to keep, so conduct yourselves accordingly."

Manning gave serious consideration to flipping the alien off, knew it was a waste of effort, and spoke into his wrist mike. "Snake One to Snake Team. The area is clear—but *not* fully secured. Proceed with caution. Over."

There was a series of clicks as the team acknowledged the transmission, Franklin was notified, and the presidential party left the ship's lock.

About twenty yards away, in the darkness under the pier, a dry-suit-clad diver floated just below the surface of the extremely cold water. His name was Mason Chix, and he, along with eleven volunteers, was there to assassinate Alexander Franklin. He whispered into a microphone: "The target is here."

Not far away, in the hull of the newly landed ship, Orvo Orvin sat up and took notice. What normally served as the ship's wardroom table was loaded with scanners—all of which were set to troll for scraps of conversation. Anything that might represent a threat. Difficult under normal circumstances but easy now, especially since the aliens liked to stick to the same frequencies, and humans were off the air. Or were *supposed* to be.

Orvin nearly jumped out of his skin when he heard the transmission. He hurried to warn Manning. "Snake Four to Snake One. Over."

Manning, who was still waiting for the president to arrive on the pier, did a slow 360. "This is One. What's up? Over."

"Keep your eyes peeled. Someone has a CB radio. Only one transmission so far—but it's a lulu: '*The target is here*.' "

Manning felt his gut go cold. "That's what they said? 'The target is here'?"

"That's affirmative, Snake One. Over."

"Shit."

"Roger that," Orvin said fervently.

Manning turned toward the point where Franklin would appear, realized the politician was already there, and yelled into the mike: "Abort! Get Big Dog back on the ship!"

But the order came too late. Boyer Blue, who had insisted on leading the team himself, kicked the door with his foot. Hinges squealed as the cargo module's hatch swung open. The resistance fighters were momentarily blinded by the harsh light but someone yelled "Fire!" and people did.

Blue, one hand held in front of his eyes in an attempt to shield them from the light, tried to stop them, but it was too late. Assault weapons chattered, the slaves started to scream, and the man to his right jerked spasmodically as Kell, almost kneeling on Franklin's chest, fired four carefully aimed shots. The range was somewhat long for a handgun, so the grouping was looser than the ex-Ranger would have liked, but the effect was the same. The would-be assassin fell over backward.

Blue, who had yet to fire a shot, half jumped, half fell out of the doorway, crashed onto the module below, and rolled off the edge. He heard the cloth-ripping sound of a submachine gun as the pavement slapped the bottom of his feet. A line of slaves fell like wheat in front of a combine. Those who hadn't been hit broke ranks and ran. Blue realized that the Kan had opened fire. The Saurons were perfectly willing to shoot *through* the slaves to kill the rebels.

Blue shouted, "No! Stop!" but no one listened. Shoes grabbed Blue's wrist, towed him to the edge of the pier, and pushed him off. He fell, made a hole in the water with his boots, and was shocked by how cold it was.

The diver surfaced behind the professor, grabbed Blue around the neck, and forced something rubbery into his mouth. The second tank, and the long hose, had been rigged for this very possibility. The academic knew that but didn't want to go. "No!" he wanted to say. "I should be up on the dock!" but the words never made it out.

Well aware of how cold the water was and how quickly hypothermia could set in, Chix towed Blue away. Shoes, who was equally vulnerable, swam alongside.

The diver gestured, Shoes nodded, and both men dived. Blue felt hands pull him down, saw the barnacle-encrusted hull loom ahead, and knew it belonged to a naval supply ship. One of many such vessels sunk by the Saurons.

The water shuddered and the fugitives felt the thump, thump, thump of grenades going off in the water behind them.

The hatch was just as Chix had left it an hour before. The opening was about halfway down the starboard side and had once been used to load stores. All three of them passed through with no difficulty whatsoever. The light thrown from the scuba diver's headlamp washed across a rather small and undistinguished fish, which flicked its tail and swam away.

Once inside the vessel's hull it was a simple matter to swim up a vertical companionway toward the point where a light glowed beyond the surface of the water. Blue broke through, felt hands grab his arms, and was hoisted up and onto one of the wreck's decks.

Shoes, who had been forced to hold his breath throughout the duration of the swim, burst through the surface and gasped for air. Hands seized his wrists and hauled him free of the water. Once that was accomplished, it was a race to get the unprotected men into sleeping bags and warm them up.

The storeroom was small but adequate to their needs. Blue wanted to look outside but saw that the windows, if that's what they were properly called, had been covered with black spray paint. What light there was came from a pair of battery-powered lamps. They threw giant shadows against the port bulkhead. Out there, beyond the protective steel, the Kan were hunting. Not with the fervor they would have demonstrated had the attack been targeted against a Sauron—but with enough energy to convince their superiors than an effort had been made.

"How many?" Blue demanded through chattering teeth. "How many people died because of my incompetence?"

The wardroom was silent for a moment. There hadn't been any radio reports, not yet, but the way the attempt went down, and the fact that only two of them made it off the pier, seemed to speak for themselves. Finally, after some sideways glances, it was Shoes who spoke. "It's too early to know what kind of casualties we suffered, sir. But regardless of the number, they weren't your fault. You did the best you could. We all did."

"That's right," Chix agreed as he toweled himself dry. He was a slender man with long, well-muscled arms and legs. The swim mask had left an oval-shaped mark around his eyes and nose. "Remember what you told us—'If we nail Franklin, then good. But if we scare the shit out of him, that's good, too. A combination of doubt and fear will slow the bastard down.' "

"That's right," the woman named Keesha chimed in. "And that goes for the bugs, too!"

Blue knew they were right, knew *he* was right, knew that these were messy details that history books, the kind *he* had written, usually left out. Still, innocent people had died in front of his eyes, not because of what the bugs did to them, but because of orders given by *him*. Would the sacrifice be worthwhile? Would the deaths make an important difference? There was no way to know. One thing was for sure, however: Like so many chapters in human history, this one had been written in blood.

■ ■ ■

The scene on the pier was one of utter chaos. Kan warriors jumped back and forth as they searched for would-be assassins. But they managed to stay well clear of the water, for which they had a marked aversion.

Kell, Amocar, and the rest of the team had formed a protective cordon around the president and his wife, weapons out, eyes scanning for trouble.

Manning, who no longer had any desire to chivy his charges in the direction of the highly suspect landing stage, waved his weapon at the same Ra 'Na who had spoken to him earlier. The human pointed toward a Sauron ground car. "We need that vehicle. Get it now."

The Ra 'Na, still riding high on the Kan's back, started to object but thought better of it. The human had a weapon, was clearly agitated, and capable of anything. Perhaps his mount would protect him and perhaps he wouldn't. Like most of his kind, the Kan took very little interest in what sort of mayhem lesser beings inflicted on each other.

Besides, the slaves who lay sprawled on the blood-spattered pavement were either wounded or dead. That being the case, there would be very little point in having Franklin talk to them. The alien radioed for the car, and it began to move.

Jina, horrified by what she'd seen, and determined to help the wounded, darted for a gap in the protective screen. It was Kell who brought her back. She struggled in his arms. "Let me go, damn you! They need help!"

Franklin came to Kell's assistance, whispered in her ear, and was still whispering when they loaded Jina into the ground car and sped the length of the dock. "There's nothing we can do, baby. We don't have as much as a Band-Aid with us. Besides, they need doctors, nurses, people with skills we don't have."

What Alex said was true, Jina knew that, but the words didn't help much. Nor did the knowledge that some of her fellow human beings hated her husband with such a passion that they were willing to risk their lives in an attempt to kill him.

She started to cry, and the sound of her sobs, plus the noise from the vehicle's engine, served to muffle the sounds the Sauron weapons made as the wounded were put to death.

Not everyone was spared those sounds, however, nor were they put out of their misery. Though hidden within the half-submerged ship's superstructure, Blue and his companions still could discern the dull thump, thump, thump the t-guns made, and, from the manner in which the shots were fired, guess what was happening.

Blue felt as if each projectile passed straight through his heart. Silence, when it finally came, fell like a shroud.

HELL HILL

The sun had nearly reached its zenith, and struggled to poke weak, ineffectual fingers of light down through multiple layers of gray clouds.

The day shift had been at work for more than six hours by then and swarmed over Hell Hill like an army of ants. There were ditches to be dug, stone blocks to carry, and walls to build. A process that relied on ramps constructed with picks, shovels, and wheelbarrows, staging bound together with wire and clothesline, and cranes made from recycled telephone poles. Some of the cranes were topped with the crow-picked remains of slaves who moved too slowly, made some sort of mistake, or were in the wrong place at the wrong time. Most seemed to be grinning, as if privy to some horrible joke.

Not that the living spent much time looking at them, since to do so was both psychologically uncomfortable and likely to get them in trouble. No, their days were spent in much the same way that thousands of ancient Egyptian workers had spent theirs—doing hard physical work. But that which had once seemed strange had become ordinary, accommodations had been made, and a strange sense of normalcy had settled over the construction site.

People went to work, strove to cope with whatever task they'd been given, found the means to slack off, schemed to improve their circumstances, engineered better ways to get things done, sabotaged their work, competed with each other, gained power, lost it, were both cruel and kind, fell in love, pursued feuds, wondered why, and didn't give a shit. All depending on who and what they were.

And, thanks to the rather laissez-faire attitude that the Saurons had regarding what slaves did when they weren't required to work, a crude but serviceable city had grown up on the artificial plateaus excavated from the lower flanks of the hill. Random piles of cargo modules had been transformed into neighborhoods complete with fanciful names such as Big Pink, Super Stack, and Flat Top.

It wasn't long until businesses started to open. Most catered to the average slave's need for extra rations, work clothes, and small personal comforts, such as soap, toothpaste, and toilet paper. Others peddled less wholesome products, which, if not connected with the burgeoning sex industry, were obtained with the connivance of Ra 'Na technical personnel who looted the merchandise from warehouses far and wide in return for the fresh seafood that enterprising humans harvested in what little free time they had.

The result of all this activity was a rich jumble of sentients, exotic odors, a wide range of colors, and plenty of noise, all of which swirled around the carefully screened sedan chair as four heavily built human males struggled to carry it up through the area which due to the hue of the cargo modules stacked there, had come to be known as Big Pink.

The sight of such a conveyance was no longer so rare as to turn everyone's heads, but still drew stares from newly arrived slaves, and obscene gestures from some of the more daring inhabitants.

Perhaps most notable was the fact that the contingent of Kan normally assigned to guard the overclass was nowhere to be seen. So firm was the Sauron grasp on their slaves that many failed to note this interesting fact, while those who did looked skyward, confirmed that the sedan chair would be visible to those in the nearest guard tower, and assumed the dignitary within considered such protection to be adequate.

Most of those who took a moment to consider the matter envisioned a fat, self-satisfied alien lounging among plump cushions and eating the Sauron equivalent of grapes. Nothing could have been farther from the truth.

The Zin named Lem Lak-Tal writhed in agony, bit down on the harakna hide strap, and stifled a scream. A scream that, were it to be detected by Kan guards, could eventually cost the Sauron his life.

Since the meeting in which Hak-Bin addressed the matter of early changers, and displayed the time-lapse video of Raz-Pak's gruesome death, Lak-Tal's previously mild symptoms had grown progressively worse until no vestige of doubt remained. Like the unfortunate Raz-Pak before him, Lak-Tal was fated to be an early changer. Or, if he possessed the courage, to commit suicide. Turning himself in, only to be murdered by way of thanks, held very little appeal.

The spasm passed, released its ironclad grip on the Zin's musculature, and granted a moment of blessed relief.

Lak-Tal removed the saliva-soaked leather strap from his mouth, took a moment to catch his breath, and cursed his rapidly changing body. The spasms weren't the worst of it. The Sauron's internal organs had started to swell, and his chitin was beginning to crack along previously invisible suture lines. There were other unpleasantries as well, such as a plague of headaches; the thin, mucuslike discharge that flowed from his axillary glands; and bouts of vertigo. The Zin knew the nymph was growing larger with each passing day, sucking nourishment away from his body, taking whatever it wanted.

All of which made it virtually impossible for the Zin to get around without the aid of the human-powered sedan chair, a blessing for which he was extremely grateful.

The conveyance swayed from side to side as the slaves rounded a corner and Lak-Tal peered out between heavy curtains. Humans broke like a fleshy river in front of the sedan chair and flowed to either side. Going to work, returning from work, or shopping for things they required. The species was amazingly resilient, a quality the Zin admired, since it was fundamental to their continued survival. The same imperative drove his brethren to construct citadels. By what right would his species or any other extinguish another? Because they were stronger? More cruel? If qualities such as these were the building blocks of superiority, then the structure deserved to fall.

Exhausted by even that small effort, the Sauron allowed his head to fall back against the cushioned seat. It seemed that the physical changes had stimulated mental changes as well. Or had they? What about his considerable respect for the Ra 'Na? A very un-Zinlike thing to feel. Weren't such thoughts indicative of a preexisting flaw? Yes, there was little doubt that the great Hak-Bin would think so, as would most of his peers. And if they knew what he intended? To not only make contact with the human resistance movement but also quite possibly give them aid? How would his brethren receive *that*?

The very thought of it caused the Sauron to laugh—a grating sound that leaked out through the curtains. The lead slaves looked at each other, rolled their eyes, and redoubled their efforts. The saloon known as the Square Hole was just ahead, and they would welcome a moment of rest.

EAST OF BELLINGHAM, WASHINGTON

With the passage of time, and sporadic rebel attacks, the Kan command structure had decided that it would be prudent to establish heavily fortified observation posts along those highways deemed most critical to the slave trade.

True to their military instincts, the Kan constructed their keep-like fortresses high atop hills, where actual eyes could be used to supplement the orbital surveillance conducted from above.

It was boring duty for the most part, a negative that was offset to some extent by the fact that the Zin rarely if ever made an appearance. Which meant less time spent on the sort of pomp, ceremony, and chitin-polishing that the ruling caste loved so dearly.

The file leader named Bla-Nor was relatively content as he inserted his boots into the kickspace at the bottom of the wall, used his elbows to form a bipod, and trained his high-powered lens on the ribbon of gray highway. He started where it topped a rise, and followed the concrete down between high-cut banks and through an ancient stand of trees.

Was that a hint of movement? Why, yes, the Kan believed it was. Not much—just a quick flash of color. There was mist, however, flat, wispy stuff that clung to the contours of the land the way steam hovers above freshly cooked kla. It served to obscure his view. It didn't matter, however, since there was a clear spot in front of whatever the object or objects were. He would wait. And why not? Truth be told, the Kan had nothing better to do.

Down below, conscious of the fact that the column was under surveillance, Jonathan Ivory followed the yellow line down past a clutch of half-slagged trucks, a sign that said "Keep Washington Green," and a stream that gurgled happily before diving into a culvert.

Ivory looked different. Hard, lean, and confident. A red tag dangled from his right ear. It had been "harvested" from a real honest-to-God slaver of the sort he now pretended to be. A hard, pitiless seller of human flesh.

True to the part he was playing, Ivory wore all-black clothing, a heavily laden weapons harness, and his trademark combat boots.

Behind Ivory, heads down, chains rattling, came a column of

twenty-four ragtag slaves. Guards, four in all, marched to either side.

To the casual observer the dejected-looking captives would have seemed virtually identical to more than a dozen such groups all crossing the mountains on that particular day. Pathetic creatures—most, if not all of whom, would die on the slopes of Hell Hill.

A more critical eye might have noticed some small but significant differences. Given the fact that the Saurons placed a high value on physical strength, most such groups included more males than females. But this particular contingent was notable for the fact that only *one* woman had been chained to the drag line, a leggy type who found it difficult to keep her eyes on the asphalt.

Then there was the fact that each and every member of the column was white, and with the exception of the woman's crew cut, had clean-shaved heads. Not to mention the fact that they were *too* well fed, *too* healthy, and *too* happy.

A search would have revealed that hidden beneath their ragged clothing, each of them carried two semiautos each, knives, explosives, and a variety of other weapons.

And, had the aliens known enough to look, they would have discovered that these particular slaves wore a lot of nearly identical tattoos, including the *Totenkopf* (death's head) symbol favored by Hitler's SS, the spiderwebs that many wore on their elbows, and the word "skins" spelled out across hairy knuckles.

None of those things was apparent to Bla-Nor, however, who watched as the humans emerged from the mist. He sent the necessary report and wiped his mind clean. There were other, more important things to consider, like the need to oil his chitin and the midday meal. He started to salivate.

ABOARD THE SAURON DREADNOUGHT *HOK NOR AH*

The compartment was almost entirely dark, lit only by the blue-green glow of the iconlike images that covered most of one bulkhead, and silent, except for the drone of the midcycle Honas as some of the more devout initiates managed to monitor the screens and say their prayers at the same time.

This was no chapel, however, this dark and somewhat foreboding space hidden deep within the warship's armored belly. It was more like an electronic lookout station, a place from which more than twenty-five tiny surveillance cameras could be monitored and "recovery" teams dispatched.

That's the way Fra Pol thought of it at any rate, except that there had been more watching than dispatching, a fact that threatened to ruin everything. The initiate had been accepted to the lowest ranks of the priesthood some three ship years before and had long since mastered the art of mouthing prayers while the rest of his hyperactive mind roamed where it would. Now, as his voice melded with all the rest, Pol scanned the monitors arrayed before him.

There were *sleeping* Saurons, *eating* Saurons, and *gaming* Saurons. In fact, every kind of Sauron one could possibly imagine except the kind Pol liked best: *dying* Saurons.

Or, more specifically, early changers, like the one Hak-Bin had focused on during his presentation. Video of such a death, combined with data gathered during an autopsy, would prove beyond any shadow of a doubt that Pol's assertions were true, and force some sort of action. That was the plan, anyway, but in spite of the fact that every single one of the subjects displayed at least some suspicious symptoms, none had undergone the change.

That was unfortunate, but even worse was the fact that each screen, each image, represented a serious crime, a transgression that if discovered could not only result in death for the perpetrators, assuming they were caught, but also for twenty or thirty Ra 'Na picked at random and publicly put to death.

Many of the prelates were understandably afraid, and eager to end the research as soon as possible. Fortunately, for Fra Pol as well as for the rest of the Ra 'Na race, a contingent of Dromas led by the likes of Dro Rul had managed to hold the line.

But for how much longer? The project had been under way for more than fifteen ship cycles by then, with nothing to show for it. Rul or no Rul, support was starting to fade.

Pol focused on a sleeping Kan, *willed* the Sauron to die, and listened to the prayer as it rolled off his tongue.

BELLINGHAM, WASHINGTON

The ranch-style house, which had been broken into and looted more than once, stood on a forlorn half acre. Once-immaculate lawns were covered with debris left by winter storms, a tree had fallen across a toolshed, and the remains of an American flag snapped in the breeze.

The mostly nocturnal and seldom-seen "Free Taggers" had left a ten-foot-high message across the front of the house. It read

"Free Earth!" and seemed almost whimsical given the circumstances.

Inside, beyond the shattered windows and the much-abused front door, Manning stood with his back to what remained of a Sony entertainment center. The family room was spacious, and though trashed, still bore traces of the people who had lived there. One such memento, a picture of a man, woman, and two children, hung crookedly on the far wall. They looked happy if somewhat askew.

With the exception of Kell, Parlo, and Orbin, the entire team was assembled before him. All were dressed in off-the-shelf black clothing that would provide an edge at night; make them more identifiable in a crowd; and, like any other uniform, bind the group together.

The basic components consisted of black baseball-style caps; loose-fitting Gore-Tex windbreakers; a weapons harness worn over a mock turtleneck top; a belt that most members of the team used to support more gear; Levi's; and military-style combat boots, many of which were home to wickedly sharp knives.

There were some new faces, including Se Ri Pak, a woman of mixed Indian-Pakistani heritage, who rarely spoke.

Morley Rix seemed to be enjoying himself.

Sanjiv Sidhu spent most of his time watching Pak and playing with his flick blade.

Sandi Taglio sat near an open window, and in spite of the early hour, was smoking her ninth cigarette of the morning.

Jonathan Wimba, his notebook open in front of him, was eternally taking notes.

Also joining the team were Lido Soolian and Mario Tokarski, both of whom were fixed-wing pilots, plus John Wu and Vera Veen, who flew the team's newly obtained choppers.

Many team members were talking with their neighbors but stopped when Manning cleared his throat. The security chief waited until the room was completely silent, until every eye was on him, before he spoke. "Some of you have performed this sort of work before . . . and some of you haven't. We won't have the opportunity to provide you with much training, so pay attention to what there is. It might save your life. Here's lesson number one: 'Expect the unexpected.' "

That was the cue the "assassins" had been waiting for. There were four of them, all ex-military types who, though qualified in many respects, had failed to make the final team. All were glad to get away from the hill, if only for one day—and they still hoped to make the grade. They blew the carefully placed charges, dropped through the resulting hole, and landed with their backs to Manning. Their weapons were empty but menacing nevertheless. Dust swirled as bits of plaster continued to fall.

The security chief shouted, "Hold your fire!" and stepped through the center of the group. The entire team sat frozen in place. Many looked embarrassed. Only two had managed to half draw their weapons. The smile on Manning's face was empty of humor.

"Some of you think that was a cheap trick, bullshit that would never happen in real life, and you are *wrong*. If you don't believe me, you could ask people like Archduke Franz Ferdinand; President Jack Kennedy; his brother Bobby Kennedy; Reverend Martin Luther King, Jr.; President Anwar Sadat; Prime Minister Yitzhak Rabin; and more recently, Grigory Chobias, president of the Russian Federation. Except that you can't, because all of them are *dead,* and in the case of Chobias, so are half a dozen people who happened to be with him. Three of them were bodyguards."

The security chief turned to one of the play-pretend attackers. "Good job. Thanks. There's some chow out back—plus a case of beer."

The ex-noncom nodded, motioned to her companions, and led them back toward the kitchen.

The movement provided Manning's team with an excellent opportunity to stash half-drawn weapons and regain their composure. After the last "attacker" had left, Manning resumed the lecture.

"All right, so much for the drama, let's get to it. As I said before, some of you have experience and some don't. Those who don't, and spent time in the military, may think this is some sort of special ops team. Nothing could be farther from the truth."

Manning allowed his eyes to roam the room. "Our mission is to protect the president, his wife, and members of his staff. Nothing less and nothing more. That means we will do everything in our power to anticipate potential threats and neutralize them *before* something goes wrong.

"Should someone make an attempt on the president's life, we will use the minimum amount of physical force necessary to stop the assailants and disengage as quickly as possible. The purpose of this team is to protect the chief executive, not win gun battles. Is that clear?"

Heads nodded, but no one spoke.

"Good. Now," Manning continued, "let's discuss the first line of defense: intelligence."

The rest of the day was spent on everything from threat assessment to ambush theory. In an attempt to ensure that no one got bored, Manning concluded each one-hour session with a ten-minute "clinic" on everything from takedowns to push-ups.

In fact, by the time the end of the day finally rolled around, the team was exhausted. Rix and Wu had just completed a three-mile run and were bent over fighting for breath when Manning rounded a corner of the house. He was about to greet them, but Wu spoke first. "I don't know which is worse—the chits or Manning."

"I do," Rix replied. *"Manning."*

The security chief backed around the corner and smiled. Then, whistling as he walked, Manning tried again. The team was starting to bond—and that was good. Jina was well worth protecting, even if her husband wasn't. Maybe, just maybe, he could keep her alive.

HELL HILL

The saloon known as the Square Hole had begun its rather brief life as little more than two bottles of "salvaged" bourbon sitting on an upturned crate.

Not much of a start, but sufficient for a woman such as Chrissy Brooks, who had taken the single restaurant inherited from her parents, turned the place into a chain known as "Chrissy's," and done very well for herself. So well that she owned two homes, had a collection of sports cars, and lived with a "companion" twenty years her junior. Until the Saurons arrived, that is, and Chrissy, like thousands of others, was taken into slavery.

Not for long, however, since the entrepreneur had the foresight to steal her gigolo's stash of coke, hide ten of the tiny bags in the lining of her expensive wool coat, and leave him behind.

As with most of the things Chrissy did, she figured to profit no matter what. Assuming things got bad enough, and it looked like they would, the businesswoman could use the coke to kill herself. Or, and this was the truly brilliant insight, she could use the stash as capital. That plan worked far better than she ever dreamed.

The coke bought the services of three women, all of whom used what free time they had to work Chrissy's shifts. Then the illicit substance paid for one, then two, then three, then *four* cubes, not to mention the inventory of booze that turned the Square Hole into an overnight success.

The Square Hole was more than a saloon, though; it also served as a sort of neutral zone, where Ra 'Na came for fa and seafood, and Fon, weary from their supervisory labors, could gather in a room reserved for their exclusive use. That made the place a brokerage of sorts, where information was exchanged and deals were done.

The coke was gone now, having been snorted up dozens of nostrils, but the business was self-sustaining, and Chrissy, like her customers, could take an occasional break. Which was what she was doing when she heard a commotion outside, saw two muscular slaves appear in the doorway, and decided that she liked the one on the left.

But then, as the first two slaves stumbled over the threshold, and her patrons turned to look, Chrissy realized what they were carrying and felt her blood run cold. A Zin! What did it mean? That the chits were cracking down? Had come to take her away? No, not without a squad of Kan to secure the place first. Chrissy instinctively knew this was something else, something weird, but something she could handle.

Chrissy patted her hair, slid out from behind the bar, and hurried forward. The long, sheath-style lime-green cocktail dress limited her movements, and high heels clacked on steel. "Welcome to the Square Hole, your lordship. How can I assist you?"

The slaves paused, and the curtains stirred. Black chitin appeared. Was that the glint of an eye? Chrissy thought it was. The voice was hard and grating. "You have a room? A place the Fon use?"

"Yes," the proprietress allowed carefully, "the Fon work hard and need the occasional rest."

Lak-Tal knew the human was putting the most positive spin she could on the Fons' often slothful ways but was in no mood to debate the matter. "Yes, of course. Please show these slaves the way. I wish to use the room for the next cycle."

Chrissy had no idea how long a "cycle" might be, but it didn't matter. She gestured to one of her bouncers, saw him disappear, and knew that two Fon, both of whom had been playing an electronic board game for the past three hours, would exit out the back. With that accomplished, she addressed the curtain. "Of course, my lord—we would be honored."

Lak-Tal was far too objective to believe that, but was momentarily grateful for the unquestioning obedience that his status elicited.

The sedan chair tilted as the slaves were forced to back and fill, jerked forward, and passed through a rough-cut door.

The rest of Chrissy's customers watched the conveyance go, laughed nervously, and wondered what the chit was up to. There were plenty of theories . . . but none of them was correct.

EAST OF BELLINGHAM, WASHINGTON

The rain fell in a mist so fine that it seemed more like heavy fog than actual precipitation. But it was still wet, which meant that with the exception of Jonathan Ivory, who was disguised as a slaver and therefore entitled to a long, heavily waterproofed duster, and the guards, who wore similar garments, the rest of the column was soaked to the skin.

Now, with wet clothes, sore feet, and hundreds of miles behind them, the skins actually looked like what they were pretending to be: slaves.

The idea, which was audacious to say the least, had originated with Ivory. Once expressed, it had been so firmly seized upon by the Howthers and Marta Manning that Ivory found himself trapped by his own creative imaginings.

Like it or not, he would have to disguise a group of skins as slaves and march them into the Sauron camp, where, assuming they pulled the deception off, they would fade into the population of real slaves, get the lay of the land, and come back together.

Once hidden within the monster's belly, he and his minions would draw attention to the manner in which whites were abused, use the resulting anger to fuel a general uprising, and displace both the muds *and* the Saurons. From the smoke and fire the New Order would emerge and the one pure race would rule supreme.

It was a wonderful idea, a *brilliant* idea, and one for which Ivory had already been lionized. Now, with a chit roadblock up ahead and the damnable rain floating like mist around him, Ivory was convinced that his plan was not only stupid, but *insanely* stupid. If it hadn't been for the presence of more than twenty heavily armed racialists with him, he would have run for the nearby woods.

But that was impossible, so with the reluctant tread of a condemned man, he closed the gap with the roadblock and steeled himself against what seemed like an inevitable death.

The barrier consisted of two slave-built bunkers, both constructed from dirt-filled ammo containers, and a line of fifty-gallon oil drums, all of which bore the Exxon logo.

The ranking Kan, an individual named Toh-Tah, eyed the approaching column with a profound sense of boredom. Then, more out of a sense of duty than anything else, he leaped high into the air. When he landed, it was not five feet from Ivory. His subordinates, a file of six heavily armed warriors, stayed where they were. Rain ran down the skirts of their poncho-style garments and dripped onto the ground.

The alien's feet made a slapping noise as they hit the pavement. Water splattered in all directions. Never having witnessed such a maneuver before, Ivory felt his heart jump into his throat. The human came to a halt and held up a hand. The gesture came too late. Boner, who had been walking a few steps behind, ran into Ivory's back.

True to the character he had chosen to play, Ivory turned and slapped the skin across the face. Boner looked resentful, started to say something, and found himself looking at Ivory's back. Toh-Tah used a grasper to gesture. "Step forward. You will wait while we check your tag."

Ivory, who was well aware of the crew-served weapons that covered him from both sides of the highway, did as he was told.

The Kan produced something that looked like a pistol, aimed it at Ivory's head, and squeezed the handle.

The human saw a brief flash of light and was pleased to discover that he was still alive. The Sauron had "read" his ear tag, and, if the deception worked, would soon receive a message confirming that the file leader was face-to-face with none other than Alan Dean Pesco, a Fon-certified slave trader who now lay buried next to Highway I-90 back in Idaho.

Marta had the impression that the aliens didn't much care which slave was which, and that being the case, didn't keep very detailed databases. Besides, what human in his or her right mind would attempt to fraudulently *enter* a slave camp? That being the case, she was nervous, but not really scared. No, the racing pulse was more the result of being so close to the aliens, of remembering what Hell Hill was like, and what they had done to her ear. Most of the damage was concealed by the improvised turban she wore wrapped around her head, but what if the chits noticed?

Odds were that they would pull her out of line and send her away. Like it or not, Ivory would be forced to let her go. She'd be all alone again, and the long, arduous trip to Racehome would have been wasted. More than that her place in the group, her *significance*, would vanish. The thought made her tense.

Toh-Tah heard a tone in his earpiece followed by a Ra 'Na voice. The tag was authentic, and though he was behind schedule, the slave known as Pesco was authorized to proceed.

The Sauron spoke, and the translator rendered his words into flat, inflectionless English. "You are late. Make all possible speed or suffer the consequences."

Ivory swallowed the lump that threatened to block his airway. "Yes, of course."

Ivory turned and waved the column forward. He wasn't even aware that he'd been holding his breath until the roadblock was behind them, and he finally let it go.

A large green-and-white placard welcomed the newcomers to Bellingham. The skull that sat atop the sign grinned knowingly. There was no turning back.

ABOARD THE SAURON DREADNOUGHT *HOK NOR AH*

Images flickered in the murk, the air was thick with the scent of incense, and what little bit of sound there was came from the carefully muted com set and one of Fra Pol's legendary snores. The initiate was a long ways off, frolicking on the shores of a planet he'd never seen, when Fra Wor shook his shoulder. "Fra Pol—wake up."

Pol, who didn't want to wake up, was forced to do so anyway. He rubbed his eyes. "What now? Even *I* deserve some sleep."

Wor, who worked just as hard as Pol did, felt very little sympathy. "You can sleep later—they took Nok-Tee away."

Pol sat up straight. Every vestige of sleepiness disappeared. "When? Where? Show me."

Wor did. More initiates were summoned from the slumbers, the lights came on, and all of them watched as a group of four Fon functionaries entered the unfortunate Kan's quarters, loaded him onto a self-propelled cart, and took the long-suffering warrior away.

The Ra 'Na initiates had watched for days as Nok-Tee fell ill, locked himself in his cabin, and underwent what Pol knew to be the change, an extremely painful physiological transformation that the Sauron obviously didn't understand.

All Nok-Tee knew was that his body was changing, that there was a tremendous amount of pain, and that he wanted to be alone. But the Zin were on the lookout for such behaviors, and sent the Fon to take him away. Soon, within the next few cycles, they would put Nok-Tee out of his misery. It was then, before the body could be ejected from a lock, that the initiates must act.

Pol stood. "All right! This is our chance. Let's get him."

A number of the initiates, especially those assigned to the "recovery" team, sketched signs in the air and whispered their spiritual names. Most expected to die.

HELL HILL

The sun was in the process of making one of its rare appearances. It washed the hillside in gold and summoned vapors from the ground.

The path switchbacked up the side of the hill. While it was intended for use by the stone carriers, it conveyed other traffic as well.

Jina, who seemed unaware of the pack on her back, went first. Manning followed behind. His pack weighed sixty pounds, but was light compared to the burden of guilt that also rode on his shoulders. He had encouraged Mrs. Franklin to enter the stacks with a single bodyguard, *and* killed the power to his radio, all so he could be alone with another man's wife. Worse yet was the fact that he *knew* it was wrong but did it anyway.

But there she was up ahead, scenting the air that he breathed, climbing with an almost magical grace, oblivious to the manner in which it moved him.

Still, even without any sort of encouragement whatsoever, Manning knew he would risk anything to be with her, no matter how stupid that might be.

For her part, Jina was torn between two selves, the one that felt the sun caress the right side of her face and enjoyed the cold, crisp air that filled her lungs, and the more reflective self, who saw misery all around and felt the dark pull of despair.

Beyond that there was an awareness of the man who followed, the memory of his hungry eyes, and the suspicion that he what? Wanted her? The way Alex had, the way Alex would, *if* he had the time?

Yes, Jina thought so, and the knowing of it made her feel guilty. It was *she* who had allowed Manning to manipulate the situation, to create a moment in which they would be alone, in violation of his rules and hers.

But his desire to be with her, the attentive manner in which he listened to her least pronouncement, and the way he looked at her were like water in an endless desert. Water that she should never allow herself to drink. But she was compelled to do so.

A voice shouted, "Make way!" and both Jina and Manning were forced to step off the path as a crew of gaunt, scarecrowlike men rounded a switchback and approached from behind.

They carried a stretcherlike contraption that supported a five-hundred-pound slab of freshly quarried limestone. Alien hieroglyphics had been burned into the sides of the block, indicating exactly where it would go.

One of the men met Jina's eyes, saw the red tag that dangled from her ear, and spit at her feet. Another grunted an almost unintelligible order, and they were gone.

Jina wanted to stop them, wanted to explain, but knew it was hopeless. The slaves had seen the ear tag, the color of her skin, and drawn what they believed were the correct conclusions.

A hand cupped her elbow, and Manning spoke into her ear. "They *think* they know you, but they don't. No one cares more than you do."

Jina turned toward her bodyguard. There was no mistaking the look in his eyes—or the emotions behind it. "Thank you."

Manning felt himself blush, hoped she wouldn't notice, and cleared his throat. "It's the truth, that's all. Come on, it's best to keep moving."

Jina glanced at the nearest observation tower and nodded. Humans, even reds, were never allowed to pause. They resumed their climb.

It took the better part of fifteen minutes to reach the next plateau and turn into a labyrinth of, twisting, mud-paved streets. Stacks rose to either side, and drainage ditches carried runoff mixed with raw sewage down into gullies so noxious not even feral dogs would venture near.

The stink made Manning gag. No wonder the cholera problem was so bad. The security chief knew Franklin was hard at work trying to get the Ra 'Na to find a couple of containerized military hospitals that could be dropped into the stacks. But he hadn't received much in the way of cooperation.

Much as Manning applauded the president's initiative, he continued to be suspicious of the other man's motives. The security chief couldn't help but wonder if Franklin was truly interested in the slaves, or the need to keep the workforce healthy so they could work for the Saurons.

Or, and Manning suspected such might very well be the case, was Franklin under pressure from Jina?

Whatever the case, one thing was for sure: Dr. Seeko Sool's makeshift clinic was the only medical facility in place at the moment. So the backpacks that Manning and Jina carried were stuffed with medical supplies.

Now, as the stacks closed around them, Jina was reminded of the descriptions of medieval cities she'd read. Narrow streets, most of which were just wide enough to accommodate foot traffic; slops and worse that were hurled from windows; people who yelled from one side of the passageway to the other; ropes festooned with stiff, wind-dried clothing; smoke that poured, dribbled, and puffed from all manner of makeshift chimneys; and, with the exception of the momentarily blue sky and the pastel cargo containers that lined the lanes, little if any color.

There were openings, however, clearings in the maze, nearly all of which stemmed more from happenstance than central planning. The clinic bordered one such "plaza." That was fortunate, since the open space provided a place where Sool's patients could assemble and join the line that continually turned back on itself before passing through a heavily curtained door.

Jina and Manning were on the receiving end of numerous dirty looks as they made their way to the head of the line, announced their presence, and were greeted from within. Dixie stuck her head out and waved the visitors in.

Manning was nervous, *very* nervous, since the slaves had no way to know that the reds were bringing supplies to the clinic, *not* cutting into the line.

Had the security chief brought a full team, the way he should have, their weapons would have been sufficient to intimidate the crowd. Now, with little more than his riot gun to control potential hotheads, the situation felt iffy. Still, they managed to get inside and out of sight.

Sool, who had just finished putting some sutures into a four-inch laceration, took time to greet them. The doctor gave Jina a hug and thanked her for coming, but her eyes sought Manning. It was stupid, she knew that, but she couldn't help herself. What was it, anyway? Looks? No, she was past that. Besides, while handsome, he wasn't *that* good-looking.

Odds were that it had something to do with a sort of world-weary strength, coupled with the fact that he cared about people, that appealed to whatever adolescent fantasies Sool still had left.

But if *she* had fantasies, then so, judging from the way Manning watched Jina, did he. That meant the two of them had something in common: Both of them were fools.

■ ■ ■

Half a mile away and more than a hundred feet in the air, a Kan named Xit-Waa peered down through a high-powered scope and considered his options. Today was the day he got to kill something, and he welcomed the challenge. Especially since his team was three points behind.

The parameters of the contest were relatively simple: Each tower had responsibility for the pie-shaped chunk of territory that surrounded it. At randomly chosen times of the day a warrior from each high-rise observation post would select a slave from the thousands below, take aim, and fire. Targets were chosen without regard to what they were doing at the time, what sex they happened to be, or any other criteria except one: Dark-skinned humans were spared, since to kill one of them without good reason would be to symbolically murder one of the Zin.

The purpose of the exercise was to instill terror, make it clear how powerless the slaves were, and ensure compliance.

The game, which had been invented to combat boredom, called for each tower to try for targets *outside* their area of responsibility, thereby scoring points. *All* the guards were required to participate, which meant that the better shots couldn't carry the load alone.

Xit-Waa who, though better than average, was far from the best shot in his particular tower, but still determined to succeed.

The Kan swung his weapon to the left, watched scenery blur past, and noticed an anomaly. He brought the weapon to the right, located the plaza, and paused. For reasons beyond his comprehension, the slaves often formed a line at that particular location, in spite of the fact that to do so was to risk death from the towers. Rain, fog, and the darkness of night made such shots difficult at times, but today was different. The sun had emerged from behind the clouds, and everything seemed to sparkle.

Perfect! the Kan thought to himself. After all, why shoot at moving humans when stationary ones were so much easier to kill?

Xit-Waa checked to ensure that the target-rich environment fell beyond his tower's zone of responsibility, confirmed that it did, and returned his attention to the sight.

A female stepped out of a storage module. The Kan allowed his crosshairs to caress her light brown skin, decided that she was too dark to kill, and centered the reticule on the white male who stood by her side. He wore a red ear tag, but so what? Assuming he successfully dropped the soft body, the watch commander would forgive him quickly enough. Especially given the rivalry with his peers in tower two. The range was long, very long, but that's how points were scored. Gradually, so as not to jerk the long-barreled weapon off target, Xit-Waa exerted pressure on the specially contoured grip.

• • •

The back room at the Square Hole was not especially large and felt even less so with the sedan chair occupying half of it. The single rough-cut window was covered with an ill-fitting shutter. Bright slivers of light did little to dispel the heavy murk within which the Sauron increasingly preferred to dwell.

Lak-Tal had ordered the slaves to wait outside, where they were no doubt busy consuming free food and drink while complaining about how cruel he was.

In the meantime, the Zin had extricated himself from the richly decorated conveyance and appropriated one of four Sauron sling chairs provided for the comfort of the malingering kog gum–chewing Fon. Now roles were momentarily reversed as *he,* a member of the ruling caste, waited for a slave. Would the human show? Fear, doubt, and common sense argued against it. Still, by working through a trustworthy Ra 'Na technician, Lak-Tal knew the message had gone out. All the Zin could do was wait as the toxins within his body started to gather.

Meanwhile, in a doorway nearby, the human for whom the Sauron was waiting stood frozen in doubt. The whole thing was too fantastic, especially on the heels of the Everett massacre. A Sauron who wanted to talk? Who might go so far as to provide the slaves with some form of aid? No, it was too far-fetched. Shoes said so, as did most of his other advisers, including Jared Kenyata and Dr. Orville Hamby.

Not Amanda Carter, though, or Leon Williams, or the white woman named Keena Caitlin. They didn't say anything. They were dead, killed by the Kan, and so was Franklin's security team. Trying to do something they hadn't been trained for. Because *he* told them it was important.

Now, chastised by his failure but no less angry than before, Blue was ready to try a different strategy. Not the absolute abandonment of force, but a step back from it, while he examined

other means—assuming there were any. That's why he had agreed
to come, was willing to meet with the Zin.

The historian was glad that none of his followers was present
to see his cowardice, the way his hands shook, or his reluctance
to leave a place of safety.

Blue forced all such thoughts aside, took a breath of acrid,
smoke-flavored air, and stepped out onto the muddy street. Now,
as he entered the flow of foot traffic, he was somehow transformed. Marked as he was by his dark skin and the phony red
tag that dangled from one ear, the resistance leader became one
of "them." An overseer, a collaborator, a traitor to the human
race.

White slaves hurried to get out of his way, a Ra 'Na technician
nodded politely, and Blue felt the pull of privilege. It was there,
eternally waiting to seduce the unwary. And once seduced, the
historical record showed that people would search for and find
the means to justify their seduction.

Head up, shoulders back, Blue strode up the middle of the
muddy thoroughfare. If this was a trap, if this was the end, then
so be it. He knew Loretta and his daughter were waiting. Death
would be a release—an escape from the hell that surrounded him.

Blue took a hard left turn, marched up the wooden steps, and
pushed on the door. Hinges squealed, Lak-Tal looked up, and
daylight speared his eyes.

■ ■ ■

Marta experienced a strange sense of inevitability as Ivory led the
column of skinheads into the very place that everyday logic dictated they should least want to go.

But these were strange days, when everyday logic didn't always apply and audacity did. The Howthers understood the fundamental brilliance of Ivory's plan and so did she: Power, the
kind required to change the course of history, lay at the epicenter
of human activity. And that, insofar as she could tell, was *here*
on the slopes of Hell Hill. The ZOG had been weakened if not
destroyed. The long-awaited Armageddon had arrived. This was
their chance.

The easy part was getting in. Now, as the column trudged up
one of the many roads cut into the side of the hill, the real challenge presented itself. How to stop short of check-in? To fade
into the stacks and successfully establish themselves? Would the

rank-and-file slaves take the skins in? Or rush to betray them? There was no way to know.

But at least some of the slaves had to hate the muds as much as the skins did, especially given the way some of them had collaborated with the Saurons. That made them a natural constituency. A fact Ivory was counting on.

The column turned a corner and two of the "slaves" split off. They faded into the crowd and quickly disappeared, something that would have been impossible if the guards had been guards rather than skinheads. The march continued.

Ten minutes later it was Marta's turn to surreptitiously unhook the drag chain, scurry into a narrow passageway, and pause to check her surroundings.

An observation tower stood no more than half a block away, but, like all such structures, offered a poor view of events taking place directly below it. So, ironic though it was, the closer one came to such a tower, the less dangerous it became.

Seeing no signs of pursuit, Marta pulled a counterfeit tag out of her pocket, secured it to what remained of her ear, and hurried up the path. There was good reason to believe that her brother was close by. The Saurons continued to drop talking leaflets wherever the "sheeple" might find them. One of them, a tract listing the benefits of slavery, showed Franklin with a white man standing almost behind him. The face was older now but unmistakably Jack's.

Marta had been surprised to see her brother in a photo with the collaborator, but she understood. Her brother wanted to survive, and with no other possibilities to choose from, accepted the situation he found himself in. But not anymore. Now there was a *new* choice—the *right* choice.

Marta imagined the look of surprise on her brother's face, the strength of his embrace, and the sound of his voice.

Somehow, in some way, he had freed her. Marta knew that now, even if she didn't know how. Now it was her turn to save him.

ABOARD THE SAURON DREADNOUGHT *HOK NOR AH*

The Sauron's chitin made a crackling sound as Fra Pol ran the heaviest knife he'd been able to lay his hand on along the suture line that started in the Kan's armpit and ran diagonally to the bottom of his thorax, where it met up with a similar seam that originated under the warrior's right arm.

The initiate looked up. Fra Wor was in charge of the documentation phase of the autopsy and had no less than three separate lenses focused on the operating table. One wide, one medium, and one tight so a report could be edited together for the benefit of the Dromas. Wor intercepted the look and nodded. Everything was under control, if any part of what he regarded to be a living nightmare could be referred to as "under control."

Thus reassured, Pol returned to his work. To have the camera equipment fail after they had waited so long, and taken such terrible risks, would have been more than he could possibly bear.

The initiate raised the knife for the second time. Pressured from within, and weakened by the superficial incision made moments before, the entire thorax was ready to burst open. Pol had two assistants, neither of whom was very happy.

Gases had already started to leak out, and Fra Dras, never one to investigate the more visceral aspects of life, had started to feel ill.

Pol's second assistant, the comely Shu, wrinkled her nose. The visuals didn't trouble her, but the odor was really gross.

Carefully, and with as much precision as he could muster, Pol brought the heavy knife down onto the left suture line. He applied pressure, felt the chitin give, and heard a prolonged cracking sound.

Both margins gave way at the same time, the Kan's chitinous chest plate bulged outward, and two sides of a thick, semitransparent sac boiled out of the Sauron's thoracic cavity. The stench was horrible.

Pol fought the desire to throw up, peeled the chest plate away, and revealed what lay within. The nymph, only barely recognizable as such, could be seen through the nearly transparent natal sac. There was no doubt about it—no doubt at all. The Kan had been pregnant at the time of his death.

"Look!" Wor said, pointing from behind a camera. "It's alive!"

Fra Dras fainted, Shu made a gasping sound, and Pol stared in stunned fascination. There, fed by a network of darkly pulsating blood vessels, a dark mass could be seen. It seemed to move to the same rhythm as the initiate's heart.

"You've got to kill it," Shu said thickly. "Kill it *now!*"

"Yes," Pol agreed numbly, "but this is one of what will soon become thousands. That's what the Saurons are preparing for. Can we kill them all?"

There was silence, and when it ended, the voice belonged to Wor. "I have no idea, but it's certainly worth a try."

HELL HILL
Manning said good-bye to Sool, then swore silently as Jina stepped out through the door into bright sunlight. What if someone were waiting? What if?

But nothing happened. Manning followed her out of the clinic, paused to let his eyes adjust to the light, and sensed motion to his left. A man darted out of the shadows. He held a piece of pipe in his right hand and appeared headed for Jina. His eyes were filled with hate, and nonsensical words spewed out of his mouth.

Manning felt his stomach go cold, swung the riot gun toward the left, and saw the man's head explode well before his weapon was in position. A mixture of brain tissue and shattered bone splattered against the front of the clinic. The sound of the report followed a quarter second later.

The tower! The shot had originated from the tower!

There was no time to wonder why as the security chief grabbed Jina's arm and started to run.

Meanwhile, high above, Xit-Waa clacked a pincer in consternation. Just as the projectile left the barrel of his rifle, a second slave had obscured his target and taken a bullet in the head.

That was *bad* news. The good news was that a point had been scored and there was no reason to share his misfortune with anyone else. The watch commander would be pleased. Xit-Waa was still in the process of accepting congratulatory insults from his comrades when the riot started.

Manning and Jina were more than halfway across the plaza when a man yelled, "The reds killed Clyde! Stop them!"

It wasn't true, but only a few people had any inkling of what actually occurred, and a cry went up. A group of slaves moved to cut them off, and Manning fired from the hip. The double-ought buck flew intentionally wide but caused the mob to pause.

Manning used the momentary respite to jerk his charge into a passageway between two neighboring stacks. Laundry flapped from lines that crossed above. The security chief turned to face his pursuers, pumped a shell into the shotgun's chamber, and prepared to fight. The narrowness of the corridor would prevent more than two slaves from attacking at any one time. Those who did would pay with their lives—till he ran out of ammo, that is.

Then all bets would be off. He yelled, "Run, Jina, run!" and waited for the first target to appear.

Jina grabbed Manning's collar and pulled him backward, through a half-open door. The light disappeared, and metal clanged as she slammed it shut.

The security chief produced a small hand flash and held it in his teeth as he helped Jina lower a bar into a pair of crudely welded brackets. Not a moment too soon. Metal rattled as someone tried the door, yelled something unintelligible, and was gone.

There were more attempts to open the hatch but none was serious, and the mob sounds faded away.

The flashlight provided a quick tour of the cargo container's interior. There was nothing much to see beyond four pathetic bedrolls, a circle of fire-blackened rocks, and a pile of garbage. Graffiti decorated the metal walls. The lines, squiggles, and "tags" reminded Manning of cave drawings. Jina pressed against his side as if taking strength directly from his body. He felt her shudder as the reaction set in. It seemed natural to extinguish the light, pull Jina close, and meet her in the darkness. Her lips were sweet, her hair smelled of soap, and time seemed to stop.

■ ■ ■

Because Lak-Tal had been content to sit in the dark, to savor a moment of relatively pain-free existence, he felt mixed emotions when the door opened to admit a bar of hesitant sunlight.

A human stepped into the doorway and threw a shadow across the none-too-clean floor. There was no way to see his face, but the voice was deep and strong. "Are you the one called Lak-Tal?"

The Sauron stirred. His body would betray him before long. He knew it and could do nothing to prevent it. Perhaps his reaction stemmed from that or from a desire to test the human. Whatever the reason, the Zin spoke harshly. "Slaves address members of my particular caste as 'lord,' or failing that, as 'master.' "

The voice was hard and mechanical. Blue was frightened but determined to die rather than show it. He probed the murk, searching for the other being's eyes. "*Slaves* can call you whatever they please. But *I*, like the rest of the resistance movement, refer to your kind as the invaders, murderers, and monsters that you are."

There was silence for a moment. It was the Sauron who broke it. "My name is Lak-Tal. That took courage. You are the one I have been searching for. Please take a seat."

Surprised, Blue accepted the invitation. Now, seated only a few feet away, his pupils adjusted to the dark, Blue realized that this particular Sauron was either elderly or very, very ill. Lak-Tal's chitin bore a grayish cast, and his face seemed bloated. When the Zin spoke, it was as if he could read minds.

"I have no way to know if you have seen other members of my race at close quarters, but *if* you haven't, I can assure you that most look better than I do. By *our* standards, at least, which has everything to do with this meeting. My body is undergoing a dramatic change, and, within a matter of what you refer to as days, weeks at most, I'll be dead."

Blue remembered his wife, his daughter, and the people on the dock in Everett. "Good. I'm glad to hear it."

The Sauron made a strange rasping noise. It could have been the result of respiratory difficulty, or it might have been laughter. "Well said. Please allow me to extend your pleasure by informing you that I, and a few like me, are but the first of nearly two million Saurons who will die within the next one hundred and twenty days."

Blue frowned. "But that's impossible. Assuming our estimates are correct, that means the entire race would be dead."

"Exactly," Lak-Tal agreed.

Blue started to speak, but the Sauron raised a pincer. "That, as you humans like to say, is the *good* news. The bad news is that with the exception of some carefully selected individuals, the entire population of slaves, and that includes the Ra 'Na, will be put to death the moment the citadels are completed. Then the rest of my race will enter the birth chambers and give life to a new generation of Saurons."

Blue sat in stunned silence for a moment. He was about to speak when the convulsions began.

■ ■ ■

Everyone, with the possible exception of wide-eyed "newbies," knew where President Franklin and his wife lived, which meant that Marta had little difficulty obtaining directions. It seemed the collaborators had made themselves at home in an area called Big Pink.

"You can't miss the complex," a street vendor told her. "It's the only one guarded by a detachment of Kan warriors."

What followed were rudimentary instructions of the "turn right, then left" variety.

Armed with that information, and the sure knowledge that Jack would live in the presidential complex or very nearby, Marta followed a succession of serpentine streets.

The sun was low by then, hanging behind a screen of clouds, ready to disappear. There were no streetlights as such, but a warm, buttery glow filled windows and doorways. Marta stepped over the body of a dead dog and followed the street to the right.

Things had changed since she had been expelled. The stacks rose like metal cliffs all around, slaves had more freedom, and there was a good deal of commerce.

A street urchin appeared out of nowhere and brandished an unlit torch. "Hey, lady! Hire me and I'll show you the way."

"How much?"

"Two aspirin, one vitamin, or a cigarette. Whaddya say?"

Marta shook her head. The boy flipped her off and scurried away.

Marta grinned and continued on her way. Strangely enough, she found herself enjoying the relative intensity of the stacks after the quiet, nearly stultifying sameness of Racehome.

Yes, that pleasure was lessened to some extent by the high number of undesirables on the street, but that problem would soon be remedied. Once the New Order was in place, the parasites would be eliminated and a new society would emerge.

Marta watched as a black woman emerged from one of the cubes and entered the flow of foot traffic. She carried a baby on her hip at a time when many were grieving for lost children. People scattered in their eagerness to get out of the way.

The sight caused Marta's hand to stray toward one of two handguns concealed beneath her Levi's jacket. She forced it down. *That* time would come. But not for a while yet.

The street turned and switchbacked down along the north side of the hill. Amazingly, almost unbelievably, the human tendency toward social stratification extended even here, as those who could, established themselves in cubes that looked up toward Bellingham Bay. That being the case, it made perfect sense that the "president" would make his home there.

Just as the street vendor had suggested, the first hint that Marta was nearing the presidential complex came when she, along with a steady stream of other slaves, passed through a loosely knit screen of Kan warriors. If ever there was an indictment of Franklin, here it was. After all, why would Saurons guard a human, unless he or she were useful?

The warriors stood in groupings of two or three, peered from cubetops, and clustered around armored vehicles. Marta was frightened at first, but less so when she saw how passive the Kan were.

She might have assumed the aliens were inefficient, or simply lacked enthusiasm, except for one thing: her brother.

Marta knew him better than anyone else, knew how pragmatic he could be, and saw his handiwork all around. Jack would *never* trust the chits, not in a month of Sundays, but had been forced to accept them.

So, saddled with troops he couldn't and wouldn't trust, her brother had deployed the aliens along the outermost ring of his defensive bull's-eye, where they could absorb the brunt of a massed attack, or failing that, serve as a reaction force he could call on for support. In either case they were about as far away from what the security chief cared about as he could push them.

All of this meant that the second ring of defenses, those over which he could exert more control, was coming up.

Marta paused to examine a mound of clothing only recently salvaged from a pile of dead bodies and pretended to listen as a middle-aged hag droned through her sales pitch, while she scanned her surroundings.

Yes, they were there, all right, a thin scattering of men and women who were just a little better clothed than those around them, and who, in spite of their best efforts to do so, couldn't quite blend in.

Good, Marta thought, but not good enough. There's not nearly enough of them, and they're way too static. Not because Jack would want it that way but because he's short on resources. The *real* team, the one he's counting on, will be in and around the complex itself.

And sure enough, having left the disappointed ragmonger behind, Marta passed into the third and most important defensive zone. It was marked by an awkward-looking cyclone fence, what Marta recognized as an unobstructed free-fire zone similar to the lawns around the White House, and pole-mounted floodlights. It was nearly dark by then, and the glare threw long, hard shadows back and forth across the open ground.

A man with a bullhorn challenged Marta from a nearby roof, ordered her to stay well clear "of the residence," and tracked her as she pretended to obey.

But there weren't very many eyes, not given the number of

pedestrians they were supposed to track, and nobody noticed when Marta sidestepped into a urine-soaked passageway just outside Defensive Zone Three and turned to watch the watchers. Only for a moment—or that's what she told herself—but the minutes ticked away. The chance that she might catch a glimpse of her brother kept her there.

Marta was still there some twenty minutes later when there was a sudden commotion across the street, doors flew open, and a tall, well-built black man stormed out. Three heavily armed bodyguards followed.

The man shouted at his flunkies and entered a mud-splattered SUV. The guards crowded in behind him, and the vehicle roared away. Semiliquid slop flew in all directions.

The man was Franklin, there was no doubt about that, and Marta wished she'd been closer. Two rounds to the head and the chits would be looking for a new nigger to kiss their pointy butts.

But there was no opportunity, not a *real* one, so that task would have to wait.

Still, another possibility had offered itself, and she was tempted to take advantage of it. Based on what she'd seen, it appeared as though Franklin's sudden departure had further stripped the complex of guards, leaving a porous perimeter. The kind of perimeter that prisoners dream of but rarely get to see.

The ex-con focused all her senses on the far side of the street, scanned for things suspicious, and wasn't able to identify any.

It was impulse that carried Marta across the street into a clump of shadows and from there up and over the fence. It swayed, rattled, and returned to normal.

The ex-con held a weapon in each hand, waited for signs of an alarm, and felt a profound sense of relief. She was in. The rest was easy.

ABOARD THE SAURON DREADNOUGHT *HOK NOR AH*

In contrast to the comfortable, almost opulent quarters maintained by Tog and most of his cronies, Rul's reception area was as ascetic as the prelate himself.

Rather than hide the steel bulkheads behind religious tapestries, bare metal had been left to make its own statement. In place of the customary table loaded with exotic protein, Rul's hospitality extended no farther than some vessels of water and a stack of dried seaweed cakes. The light, which originated from panels at-

tached overhead, seemed excessively bright, and better suited to
a surgical suite than a Dromary.

There was a low murmur of conversation punctuated by an
occasional squeak of rubber-soled slippers as the Dromas navi-
gated the highly polished floor.

Tog lowered his considerable backside onto a hard, unpadded
chair and sought to understand why Rul made him feel so uncomfortable.

Yes, the holier-than-thou righteousness of the other cleric was
troublesome, but the real difficulty lay elsewhere. Trust—the kind
Tog valued, at any rate—flowed from a sort of mutual venality
in which everyone was a little bit greedy and granted each other
some slack.

That was only natural, or so it seemed to Tog. So he was
suspicious of zealots like Rul. After all, the Droma asked himself,
if there is no handle, no way to open the door, how can one know
what lies hidden within?

Tog's question went unanswered as Rul counted heads, assured
himself that all of the Dromas were present, and brought the meeting to order. Given the need for security, it had been publicized
as a gathering ". . . to discuss the pressing need for spiritual out-
reach." Just the sort of boring nonsense that enabled Tog to take
a restful nap.

But not this time. Without so much as a "by your leave," Rul
called for the lights to be dimmed.

The video appeared on several bulkheads at once. Tog, who
had secretly hoped that Fra Pol's illicit activities would bring him
to the attention of the Zin, and thereby free him from a constant
source of annoyance, was forced to watch in open-mouthed astonishment as his wayward subordinate sliced a member of the master race open to reveal another Sauron growing within.

The prelate next to Tog vomited onto the heretofore spotless
deck, the room erupted into fractious conversation, and Rul demanded order.

He got it, but only after yelling for his peers to "shut up," a
serious breach of etiquette, and one for which Tog thought the
other cleric should be censured.

Then, after the meeting was back under control, the *real* fight
began. Opinions flew, narrowed, and coalesced into two opposing
groups.

The first contingent, led by no less a personage than Dro Rul
himself, advocated resistance, up to and including the use of vi-

olence to intervene in the Sauron birthing, and save the Ra 'Na race.

The second group, under the leadership of a Tog ally, the loquacious Dro Zar, advocated a more moderate course. He, and those who followed him, recommended that a "Commission of Ecclesiastical Inquiry" be formed and empowered to make a full investigation of the facts. Then, once that activity was completed and a detailed report had been written, the Zin would be notified and given an opportunity to present *their* side of the case.

That notion struck the heretofore silent Fra Pol as so insane that he was on his feet and speaking before the more cautious part of his brain could stop him.

"With all due respect to Dro Zar and his esteemed colleagues, the Zin will put your entire commission to death, and thus warned, murder the rest of us as well."

Pol looked around the room, met their eyes, and willed his superiors to listen. "Don't you understand? This is our chance, our only chance to be free, to take our people home. *Seize it* or prepare to die."

There was a long, bleak silence. It was Zar who finally spoke. His voice was tired. "Even if I agreed with you, which I certainly don't, I would still have to ask the following question: How? How could our people, none of whom are trained for war, fight the Kan and win?"

"Simple," Pol answered pragmatically. "First, the Saurons have become extremely dependent upon our race, a weakness we can exploit. Second, the humans are very warlike and have every reason to help us."

There was a sudden buzz of conversation as the Dromas discussed this new and somewhat radical concept. Some said the plan would never work, but others were more hopeful, and Rul felt the weight of opinion start to shift. He hurried to take advantage of it. Plans were laid, responsibilities were assigned, and the entire College of Dromas was sworn to secrecy.

Tog remained unconvinced. He made no effort to stop the tidal wave of enthusiasm, but had a hard time seeing how the lowly humans could be of much help. So he decided to bide his time. Knowledge is power—and well worth savoring.

HELL HILL

It was dark within the cargo module, dark but safe, which was good because the riot that began with a shot fired from one of the observation towers had continued in an on-and-off fashion for hours.

Crowds formed, surged through the streets, encountered resistance, turned one way or the other, and were forced to disperse. Then, within minutes, the whole thing started over.

The Saurons shot a few, but rather than quiet the crowd the way the violence should have, it made them even more angry.

Manning had turned his radio on by that time and called for assistance. Kell, along with a team comprised of Jonathan Wimba, Morley Rix, and Sandi Taglio, were waiting nearby. They were under orders to effect the rescue with a minimum amount of violence, a stricture imposed by Jina over Manning's objections.

The kiss, which ended all too soon, left both of them feeling awkward. Manning knew Jina loved her husband, or thought she did, and felt terrible about the momentary betrayal. So, rather than bring them closer, as the security chief might have hoped for, the kiss could drive them apart. Not that they had really been together, Manning thought regretfully.

The radio burped noise through the security chief's earplug. "Snake Three to Snake One. Over."

"Go Three. Over."

"The Big Dog is on the way—and he *is* pissed. Over."

Manning grimaced. "Roger that, Snake Three. Are you ready? Over."

"That's affirmative," Kell replied. "It looks like most of the rioters went home for dinner. We're on the way. Over."

The rescue team arrived four minutes later, formed a protective ring around Jina, and escorted her to a cul-de-sac about a thousand yards away. The towers had been notified and ordered to hold their fire. Whether they would actually do so was another question entirely.

Franklin, who had been ready to go in after Jina himself, saw the group and strode toward them. He'd been on an errand for Hak-Bin when Amocar passed the word: A riot had developed while Manning and Jina were at Dr. Sool's clinic, and now they were missing.

Suddenly Hak-Bin, the speech, none of it mattered. Franklin rushed back, stopped at the executive residence, and rushed out again.

Now, as she flew into his arms, and the politician kissed the top of her head, he raised his eyes. Manning looked tired, a little apprehensive, and something else—ashamed? Yes, that or something very similar. The two of them had been alone. Should he be worried? No, not where Jina was concerned. But the security chief was something else.

Perhaps, now that some time had passed, Hak-Bin would listen to him. A sentence or two and Manning would be back in the mines.

For one split second Franklin reveled in the knowledge that he possessed that kind of power. Then he realized how sick the thought was. The kind of sickness Jina worried he might succumb to. Striking out at Manning might feel good, but it could push his wife away. Were such thoughts too calculating? Too similar to the manner in which the political part of him operated? Yes, but that's how it was.

Franklin wrapped an arm around Jina's shoulders, marveled at how small she was, and guided her to the waiting SUV. They climbed in and were whisked away.

Kell, along with the other members of the rescue team, relaxed their vigilance, but only slightly.

Manning watched the taillights vanish from sight. There had been no recriminations, nor were any necessary. He was an idiot. The team knew it, *he* knew it, and Franklin knew it.

Kell offered Manning a ride, but the security chief chose to walk. It was a penance for sins committed, and he felt a tiny bit better by the time he passed through security and entered his combination office and bedroom.

The security chief hit the switch on a battery-powered camp light, dumped his weapons harness on a chair, and turned toward the plastic washbasin.

Something stirred, Manning's heart skipped a beat, and Marta stepped out of the shadows. She looked lean and hard, nothing like the young woman he remembered. "Hi, Jack. It's good to see you again. Don't I get a hug?"

■ ■ ■

Lak-Tal felt his leg and arm muscles start to spasm, knew what was coming, and managed to utter a single sentence before his entire body locked up. "Hide me from the Kan and I will help save your people."

Blue heard the words and was still thinking about them when the Sauron jerked violently, made a horrible choking sound, and started to thrash around.

Blue jumped to his feet, realized he didn't have the foggiest idea of how to help, and wondered if he should leave.

But what about the Sauron's offer? Should he take it seriously? Or simply walk away? The decision, which could have occupied a multidisciplinary panel of experts for weeks, was made by a single man. The nascent resistance movement needed every advantage it could get. If there was a possibility of help, no matter how remote that possibility might be, then Blue was obliged to do what he could.

Lak-Tal's head jerked spasmodically as Blue spoke into a small, handheld com unit. The cell phone part of the device was inoperable, but the CB band worked. The radio procedure that Shoes insisted on was foreign to him, but the resistance leader did his best. "Ivy One to Ivy Team. Over."

Shoes, along with a small team of heavily armed resistance fighters, was hidden nearby. All of them were African-American, which made it difficult to walk down the streets without attracting lots of attention. So they had barged into a ground-floor cube and taken over. A terrified white couple were huddled in a corner. A woman named Bates tried to put their fears to rest but wasn't having much success. Heads turned as the transmission came in. Shoes brought the com set to his lips. "Ivy Two here—go. Over."

Blue, sensitive to the fact that the transmission was far from secure, tried to be cryptic but nonetheless clear. "The individual with whom I am meeting would like to join our cause but requires medical attention. I need four—repeat, *four*—power lifters on the double."

Shoes frowned, eyed his team, and knew only three of them fit the bill. That meant he would act as the fourth. "Hawkins, Wambi, and Lother, you come with me. Bates and Purell will provide security."

Then, radio to lips, he sent his reply. "Roger that, Ivy One. We're on the way."

Lak-Tal heard his teeth clatter, wished it were all right to scream, but couldn't bear the shame of it. Not in front of a slave.

The part of the Sauron that dwelled outside the horrible supernova of pain and was still capable of thought half expected the human to leave in disgust.

But Blue stayed. Unable to ease Lak-Tal's pain, or truly understand it, he pulled his chair in closer; placed a hand on the Zin's hard, cold chitin; and spoke to the alien as if he were a child. "There, there, everything's going to be all right. This will pass. You'll feel better soon."

Lak-Tal, who knew the words to be false, found them comforting nonetheless. If nothing else, it was nice to have another sentient acknowledge his pain and take a moment to commiserate. Then, as if in response to Blue's sympathetic litany, the convulsions began to abate.

That's when the door flew open, Shoes entered with a .9mm clutched in each fist, and Blue jerked his head in the Sauron's direction. "His name is Lak-Tal. He's willing to help us. Load him in that sedan chair and let's get the hell out of here."

The rest of the team had entered by then, heard the order, and set to work. Lak-Tal, weakened by the seizures, did what he could to help.

Shoes stood next to Blue while Bates and Purell guarded both doors. The one through which they had entered *and* the one that opened into the saloon.

"I don't know, Doc," Shoes said thoughtfully. "We need some white guys to carry the chair. It's gonna look weird if we do it."

Blue shrugged. "If you have some white folks just itching to carry a Sauron all over the hill, let me know. Otherwise it's up to us. We'll keep it short, and move again the moment it gets dark."

Shoes nodded. "Yes, sir."

"And Shoes . . ."

"Yeah?"

"Don't call me 'Doc.' "

The sedan chair was removed ten minutes later.

There was a commotion out on the street as four African-Americans *and* a Sauron sedan chair seemed to materialize from thin air. But the conveyance soon disappeared and things returned to normal.

A full thirty minutes passed before one of the slaves who brought the chair to the Square Hole took a peek inside the room, discovered that the alien was gone, and summoned his buddies. "Look! The frigging chit is gone! What should we do?"

A man nicknamed Hog broke the ensuing silence. "I don't know about you guys, but I'm going to run like hell. What if the Saurons think we murdered him or something?"

The rest of the slaves looked at each other, nodded, and fought to be the first through the door.

Chrissy entered after that, but the room was empty. She assumed that the freeloading chairbearers had taken the chair out through the back door and was happy to get rid of them. The shift was about to change, which meant the bar would be busy soon. There was plenty to do.

■ ■ ■

The single source of light; dark, shadowy corners; and cell-like decor gave the room a strange, almost supernatural ambience. That being the case, Marta's sudden appearance was like a visitation from a childhood ghost.

Manning, still trying to adjust, heard himself say, "Marta?" and stepped forward to greet her.

Marta had been waiting in the unheated room for quite a while by then. She felt cold, like a marble statue, and he soon let her go. Manning stepped back. "You look good, stringbean—better than in the pictures they showed me."

Marta's eyes gleamed with a bright, almost fanatical light. "You got them to release me—*how?*"

Manning gestured toward his surroundings. "I agreed to protect Franklin."

"So he can keep the slaves in line."

Manning shrugged. "Yeah. That's the idea. Not that it makes much difference. Not yet anyway."

"He's black."

Manning raised an eyebrow. "Really? I hadn't noticed."

Marta's expression remained serious. "Listen, Jack. I appreciate the sacrifice you made, but that's over now. I'm free and so are you.

"There's a group, a *good* group, and I'm part of it. We're going to kill all the muds, kill the chits, and build a new order. You can be part of that—hell, you could *lead* that. We need good leaders, lots of them. All you have to do is pop Franklin and take a walk. We'll be waiting. The white race will be waiting. What do you say?"

Manning frowned and started to say something, but his sister raised a hand. "Wait a minute, hear me out. The white race has been forced into slavery, and *you* are part of the problem. It's time to strike a blow, Jack—it's time to free your people."

As Manning listened to his sister's words, he realized that she was right—yet horribly wrong. Yes, people *had* been enslaved, not just some of the people, but *all* of the people, since in spite of whatever privileges he might enjoy, Franklin was just as powerless as *he* was.

Even worse was the fact that his sister had chosen to associate herself with those who were as inimical to the human race as the Saurons were. It was as if his mother's angry alcoholism combined with his father's emotional emptiness had given birth to a living weapon. A gun others could hold, aim, and fire.

His voice was strong but gentle. "You're wrong, Marta. They *are* my people, Marta, all of them, regardless of what color they may be. Franklin may have benefited from the situation, but he didn't create it. You want to shoot someone? Fight the Saurons. Kill as many as you can . . . but leave our kind alone."

"Niggers aren't our kind," Marta said with a sneer. "Or maybe I'm wrong. Is that how things stand, big brother? Are you a *nigger* now?"

Manning shrugged. "There are no niggers. Just human beings."

Marta put a hand inside her jacket and backed toward the door. Her eyes burned with hatred. "You made your choice, Jack. Pop the sonovabitch or I will."

"Don't try it, Marta. I don't want to kill you."

"You won't, asshole. You're not good enough. I walked through your security once, and I can do it again."

Manning said, "Marta—" but she was gone.

The security chief should have raised an alarm, should have sealed the complex off, but couldn't bring himself to do it. Later, much later, Manning would wish that he had.

6

DEATH DAY MINUS 109

TUESDAY, APRIL 14, 2020

The moment the slave resolves that he will no longer be a slave, his fetters fall. . . .
—Mohandas Karamchand Gandhi,
Nonviolence in Peace and War, 1949

ABOARD THE SAURON DREADNOUGHT *HOK NOR AH*

The Sauron battleship was *so* enormous that it obscured a large segment of the star field as the small ten-place shuttle entered the dreadnought's inner defense zone, received the necessary clearances, and closed on the light blue force field. It rotated like the eye of a hurricane and filled Jina with dread.

Why had Hak-Bin summoned her husband into orbit? And why had *she* been ordered to accompany him? It wasn't social, she was sure of that, so what then? Did the summons have anything to do with the riots that Manning and she had unwittingly triggered? And what if her husband was punished for her stupidity? More than that, her infidelity? An almost overwhelming sense of guilt pressed down on Jina's shoulders as she examined Manning from the corner of her eye.

The bodyguard sat to her right. He was stoic, or seemingly so, though Jina believed she knew better. She had kissed him after all, had felt the gentle pressure of his hands on her back, had heard him say her name. Not the way he normally said it, but in a *special* way. A way that she wanted to hear again but shouldn't. Not ever.

The shuttle drilled its way through the center of the big blue pinwheel and popped out the other side. Both Franklin and Manning had experienced the transition before and recognized the cavernous flight deck complete with rows of atmosphere-scarred fighters.

The shuttle settled onto a brightly lit high-priority triangle. There was a noticeable thump as a tubeway extended and sealed itself to the ship's lock.

The Kan pilots, their eyes glassy, watched the humans leave the ship. Manning, the only bodyguard whom Franklin had been permitted to bring, went first. A squad comprised of six warriors stood waiting. They grabbed the human, took his weapons, and pushed him away. The security chief, who hadn't been roughed up for some time, felt a sudden stab of fear. Something had changed, and it wasn't for the better.

A single warrior, t-gun at the ready, placed the barrel against Manning's head. The Sauron wore a translator, but no translation was necessary. The weapon said it all: "Move and you die."

Jina emerged from the tubeway a few moments later, was seized and dragged away. She gave a cry of pain. Manning lurched forward, and went to his knees as something struck the back of his head.

Franklin yelled, "Hold it!" and charged out of the lock. The Kan had been expecting something like that and clubbed him to the deck. Blackness beckoned, but the politician forced it back. He attempted to rise, but a large podlike foot held him in place.

A pair of Ra 'Na boots entered Franklin's field of vision and stopped. Slowly, fighting the pain, the politician managed to look upward. Though he was still in the process of mastering alien facial expressions, the human believed that Lin Mok looked genuinely sorry. There was an unintentional trace of humor in what she had to say. "Lord Hak-Bin will see you now."

The subsequent journey was both painful and humiliating. The two men were pushed, shoved, and prodded from one place to the next. Saurons and Ra 'Na alike stared at them, and some laughed—assuming that's what the strange noises equated to.

That mattered little, however, since both men were thinking about Jina. Where was she? And why had the threesome been separated? Both questions gnawed at the men as they were herded through the corridors.

Franklin, who had traveled the route from the flight deck to Hak-Bin's private quarters on numerous occasions before, knew where they were headed, and was far from surprised when he spotted the now familiar entry hatch. Kan warriors stood to either side of it.

Mok, who had led the way, passed straight through.

Franklin was in the process of formulating an impassioned speech when the humans were ordered to halt. Then, rather than be shown into the Zin's cabin as had been customary in the past, the politician and his security chief were ordered to kneel, to face the steel bulkhead, and to lace their fingers behind their necks.

Up until that moment Franklin had harbored the hope that it was all part of some silly misunderstanding. Now, staring at the dull gray metal, he knew it wasn't. Hak-Bin was pissed, and this was *his* way of communicating that fact. That was bad enough, but the fact that Jina was involved made it even worse. It was his fault, *all* of it, and the knowledge ate at his gut.

Finally, after what seemed like hours but was actually little more than fifteen agonizing minutes, a series of orders was barked. The humans were jerked to their feet, ordered to behave themselves, and marched through the hatchway.

Jina had been stripped of her clothing and spread-eagled in the air. Four thin, nearly invisible steel wires held her there, each connected to a harakna hide cuff.

The light, such as it was, originated from the two identical globes that floated to either side of the suspended woman. A gag prevented Jina from speaking, but her expression was eloquent enough. She was terrified.

A Kan stood behind her and off to one side. The whip, which was connected to a t-shaped handle, lay snakelike on the deck. The threat was obvious.

Manning was sickened by what the aliens had done to Jina *and* by the fact that some primitive part of him enjoyed seeing her naked. He admired her firm, uptipped breasts; narrow waist; and long, finely tapered legs.

The fact that he was capable of thinking such thoughts, and could find the scene stimulating, told Manning what he already knew: He didn't deserve a woman like Jina—never had and obviously never would.

With no other authority figure in sight, Franklin turned to Mok. It was difficult to sound authoritative, but the politician did the best he could. "What's the meaning of this outrage? Order them to release my wife at once!"

The Ra 'Na fervently wished she were somewhere else, knew

better than to order Saurons around, and felt sorry for the human. That being the case, she spoke in an urgent whisper. "Speak when spoken to, be respectful, and do as you are told. Your mate is alive—that means hope."

Franklin started to object, thought better of it, and gave a nod instead.

Jina, who feared that her arms would be pulled from their sockets, applied pressure to one wire, then the other. The strategy offered some relief but not much. The pain was such that nothing else seemed to matter, not her nakedness, nor the fact that others could see.

The tableau remained that way for a good five minutes. Partly because Hak-Bin was busy dealing with an administrative matter and partly because the Sauron knew the wait would help put the humans into the proper frame of mind—frightened and therefore malleable.

The Zin took his own sweet time as he shuffled from one compartment to the other, lowered his weight onto the sling chair, and locked eyes with the only human who mattered. He neither looked at the female nor referred to her. "There were riots."

Franklin felt something akin to relief. He was in trouble, *deep* trouble, but at least he knew why. The key was to strike the right tone. Subservient, but not obsequious. "Yes, lord, started by the Kan."

An investigation had been carried out and a report had been written, which meant that the Zin knew the human's allegation was essentially true. The stonemaster had been reprimanded for allowing the forces under his command to entertain themselves in a counterproductive manner, and a Kan named Xit-Waa had been thrown off an observation tower. Not to placate the slaves, but as an example to his peers. None of which excused the human's failings. "What the Kan do is no concern of yours. The choice is simple—control your fellow slaves or prepare to join them."

Franklin eyed his wife and felt a lump form in his throat. "Yes, lord."

"Good," Hak-Bin replied. "Time grows short. The workers must double their efforts if the temples are to be completed in time. There will be no further warnings."

"Yes, lord."

"But an example must be made. Remember what you are about to see."

The Kan, who had been statue-still till then, flicked his wrist, waited for the tightly braided harakna hide to fall, and jerked the whip forward.

Franklin yelled, "No!" The whip cut through the air and made a cracking sound as it struck Jina's back. Her body wobbled, she attempted to scream, but the gag blocked the sound.

The whip had left a long red line across Jina's previously unblemished back. She fainted, and her body hung slack from the wires.

Hak-Bin touched a control, and motors whirred as Jina was lowered to the deck.

The Sauron waved a pincer. "Take the female. And remember this. Each time you fail, *she* will be punished."

Franklin gathered Jina into his arms and backed toward the hatch. Manning followed his example.

The Sauron watched the humans withdraw, and so, unbeknownst to him, did Fra Pol. The cameras, more than a hundred of them, none larger than the dot over an "i," had been wiped onto Hak-Bin's chitin along with the latest coating of oil. Each image was different from all the others, depending on what part of the Sauron's anatomy that particular device clung to, and the lighting involved. The Zin didn't know it, but a strange sort of war had been declared. Though smaller than the Saurons and therefore weaker, the Ra 'Na had some formidable weapons: their brains.

HELL HILL

As was the case with the other stacks, Flat Top was a universe unto itself. The Saurons had positioned the containers so all of the openings faced west, but changes had been made. New entryways had been hacked from solid steel, many of the old ones had been sealed to protect the residents from the storms that blew in from the Pacific, and a maze of internal passageways gradually came into existence.

Given the fact that there were no maps, one either knew their way around or had little choice but to hire a guide. Typically one of a small number of children, who, thanks to some phenomenal piece of luck, or a momentary indulgence by one of the Saurons, had been allowed to accompany a parent into slavery. Most were older rather than younger. One of them tugged at Blue's sleeve. He was ten, maybe twelve, and in need of a bath. "Bad things can happen in here, mister, especially to folks who happen to be black. I can show you the safe way, the *good* way. Whaddya say?"

"I say 'no thanks,' " Blue replied, handing the boy a miniature bar of soap. The words "Holiday Inn" were emblazoned across the wrapper.

The would-be guide made a face. "It's your decision, mister. Don't blame me if the skins get you."

"The who?"

"The Hammer Skins. They're here, mister, and they hate black people."

Blue swore silently. Here it was, the same old tribal bullshit. *We belong to a special race, we have the one true God,* or *we have a superior form of government.* Or, more often than not, all three of those.

Like cholera, and other communicable diseases that mankind had failed to totally eradicate, racism was there, hidden in the deepest recesses of the human mind, passed from one generation to the next like some sort of genetic defect, eternally ready to burst forth. And now, with humanity on the ropes, people were even more vulnerable than usual.

There had been many groups who called themselves "Hammer Skins," a name that had its origins in Norse mythology, and the god Thor. A potent symbol for those who believed in white supremacy.

The historian sighed, resolved to be more alert, and chose a different route than he had taken the time before. He paused now and then to check his back trail. There was no sign of a tail.

Finally, after passing through one of the hot, steamy communal kitchens that had popped up throughout the stacks, the resistance leader passed through a "friendly," one of the cubes controlled by one of his supporters, nodded to the white woman who sat soaking her feet, and knelt in the corner.

The "throw" rug, which had started its life as a Ra 'Na tarp, served to hide a floor-mounted trapdoor. Blue removed the rug, pulled up the door, and lowered himself through the newly exposed opening. He found the ladder with his feet and followed it downward. The hatch clanged as it fell back into place.

The ladder—or, to be more accurate, sequence of ladders— allowed the resistance leader to descend two additional levels before moving horizontally from one cube to the next. A heavily armed guard nodded and moved to one side. The door stood ajar.

Later, assuming the human race managed to survive, the documents Blue was creating would become part of the historical record. The historians who read it would be spared the stench of Lak-Tal's rotting body; the long, semicoherent ramblings; the harsh, autocratic demands. Get this, fetch that, as if the humans were Ra 'Na or Fon, having no purpose beyond service to the Zin. A habit that Lak-Tal genuinely seemed to disapprove of but couldn't seem to control.

The Sauron appeared to sag, as if his chitin had grown softer, or the makeshift sling bed had started to give way. When his lashless lids fluttered they were oddly reminiscent of a little girl's. He turned his gray-black eyes to Blue. They were clear this time, as was his voice. "So," the alien observed, "I'm still alive."

"Yes," Blue confirmed. "You're alive."

"Good," Lak-Tal replied. "That being the case, it is time for another lesson."

"I would welcome that," Blue replied, checking to ensure that all of the various recorders were on.

The Sauron shifted in his sling. "Have you ever wondered why the Zin rule in place of the Kan? Who are stronger than my kind? And born to the art of war?"

Blue realized that he hadn't. Yes, there were all sorts of explanations for that failure, including the need to survive. But the questions were so basic, so academic that he felt momentarily foolish. "No, strangely enough, I haven't."

"Then listen carefully," the Sauron admonished, "because our entire society hangs on one fact: Although the Zin pretend to be more intelligent than the other castes, they aren't. The *real* reason for their ascendancy is the fact that they have long-term memories, while the Kan and the Fon live in the eternal now.

"Oh, they can remember for approximately two of your years, which is adequate given the sort of functions they are asked to perform, but everything prior to that is viewed through a thick, nearly impenetrable 'fog.' They can 'see' shapes, 'hear' sounds, but aren't sure what they mean."

Blue's mind started to race. "Then what of the birthing? Do they know?"

The Sauron was silent for a moment. "No. They don't know that they are going to die, and they don't know that another generation is about to be born."

Blue remembered Buddy, the venerable black Lab that he and his family had for so long, and the dog's trusting brown eyes as he took the last ride to the vet's.

His daughter had been crying, tears streaming down her cheeks, and Buddy, tail thumping against the seat, had licked her hand.

But old age had claimed his once vibrant body, and disease had done the rest. Unable to lift his head more than a few inches off the seat, Buddy had been reduced to little-dog whimpers, pitiful sounds that issued from the back of his throat. The Lab could feel pain but none of the fear, regret, or anguish that humans experience when they know they're going to die.

Blue gestured toward their surroundings. "So what do the Kan and the Fon think this is about?"

Lak-Tal lifted a pincer. "They believe what they have been told. That temples must be constructed, and once built, will be left behind."

"But why? Surely they deserve to know."

"Not the way my fellow Zin see it," Lak-Tal replied bleakly. "They believe the 'lower castes' would be unable to deal with the knowledge of their own mortality, would abandon all work, and leave the next generation to be born in the wild. *Outside* the protective walls of a citadel and therefore vulnerable."

Blue was amazed by the arrogance of it, and reminded of what had once been referred to as "the white man's burden." The notion that all of the dark-skinned peoples who had been enslaved by the white race could simultaneously be regarded as a "burden" because once enslaved, they required some modicum of food, shelter, and medical care.

Still, such thoughts were highly ethnocentric, and Blue forced himself to put them aside. "So, how do you feel about that? About your progeny being born in the 'wild,' as you call it?"

Lak-Tal looked surprised. "How would you expect me to feel? He's trying to kill me. I hope he dies a painful death."

That's when Blue realized that by the standards of the human race, or *any* race for that matter, Lak-Tal was insane.

■ ■ ■

The cube was lit with dozens of candles. Some tall, some short, burning on shelves, ledges, and the floor itself. The space might have been reminiscent of a chapel or a church except for the racialist symbols and paraphernalia that decorated the room.

Ivory had discovered a couple of important facts about Marta Manning. The first was that her brother was a race traitor. And the second was that she gave the best back rubs he'd ever experienced. So good that they verged on sexual, to his mind at least, though he doubted she felt the same way. He had an erection, which he maintained via an almost imperceptible up-and-down movement timed to coincide with the thrust of Marta's hands. He lay facedown on a makeshift table while her fingers probed the musculature of his back.

The skins, those who were off-duty, napped, played cards, or cleaned their weapons. One or two watched Marta with hunger in their eyes, wishing she would massage *their* backs, but conscious of the fact that it would never happen. Ivory was the alpha male—for the moment, anyway—and to him went the spoils. Not sex, not as far as they knew, anyway—though some of them wondered.

As for Ivory, his thoughts had started to drift, back toward the problem at hand. He needed to take action, to move the cause forward, but how?

The skins had lived in the beast's belly for more than a week now. They had infiltrated work parties, hung out in bars, and talked till they were blue in the face. There had been converts, a trickle, but nothing like the wholesale conversion he dreamed of. He needed some sort of magnet, a way to draw people in and bind them to the dream.

Then Ivory remembered the clinic, Dr. Seeko Sool, and came in his pants.

PUGET SOUND, NEAR HELL HILL

It was night, the only time that the "Crips" dared to ply their trade, and the waves made a slapping sound as they hit the side of the sixteen-foot aluminum boat. It was cold, which meant that Wylie, Nok, Chu, and Nakambe were well bundled up. From Darby's position in the stern they looked like black lumps, rising and falling in front of the scattering of lights that marked Hell Hill. Lights for which the coxswain was grateful, since they helped to guide her in.

Due to the fact that it was impossibly dangerous to use any sort of motor, and that the organisms they sought lay inshore, where sails were a definite liability, the Crips relied on old-fashioned oars to move their boat forward. Oars, which in spite of the fact that they had been greased and wrapped with rags, still managed to squeak, an annoying sound that could travel a long way across water.

Still, there wasn't much Darby could do about it, so like all the other things she couldn't control, she tried to ignore it. There were other problems to worry about, like the fact that the tiller felt sluggish, and her crew had started to tire.

Their boat, a vessel that went by the somewhat unlikely name of *Sunshine,* was so heavily laden with bins of freshly harvested shellfish that it rode low in the water. That could prove dangerous if a southwest wind kicked up and waves broke over the transom. Add a few gallons of seawater to their cargo and the *Sunshine* would capsize. Not only that, but some of her crew, all of whom were physically challenged, were likely to drown.

Wylie was paralyzed below the waist, Nok had lost a leg to cancer, Nakambe had hooks where his hands should have been, and Chu had been born with one arm. These "disabilities" had saved their lives, because, with the single exception of Darby, every single one of them had been captured by the Kan and either released to starve or, as in the case of Chu, had managed to escape.

Now, having found each other, they were like a family, with Darby as the able-bodied "mother" and a group of twenty as a "family." A family that made its living by harvesting the seafood that the Ra 'Na doted on and selling it either to the aliens directly, or, as was the case that evening, to middlemen who found ways to close the commercial loop. It was an illicit trade carried out with the connivance of certain Fon, but still subject to interdiction by the Kan, or the kind of catastrophes that had killed fisher folk for thousands of years.

Darby heard something, or thought she did, and whistled a warning. The rowing stopped in synch, water dripped from oar-tips, and the boat surged through a succession of small waves. There was silence for a moment, followed by the throaty rumble of partially silenced engines. The oncoming boat, because there was little doubt as to what it was, appeared as a long, low silhouette. The gun mounts and missile launchers were plain to see. It slid between the Crips and Hell Hill, turned toward the southwest, and continued on its way. The *Sunshine* bucked as the larger boat's wake fanned outward.

Finally, when the mystery vessel had disappeared, it was Nakambe who whispered obvious questions. "What the hell was that? Some kind of Sauron patrol boat?"

Darby, who had last been employed as a third-class petty officer in the U.S. Navy, shook her head. "Nope, believe it or not, that was one of ours. A fast patrol boat or something very similar. It's hard to tell in the dark."

"That's bullshit," Chu whispered disbelievingly. "There *ain't* no navy, not anymore. Besides, the Saurons would see the heat and blow them out of the water."

Darby shrugged. "Maybe, and maybe not. Heat can be shielded, you know. Main thing is that they didn't see us. There's no telling what kind of agenda they have. Come on, let's get this baby to the beach. I'm cold and it's a long pull back."

Oars slid into the water, muscles contracted, and miniature whirlpools spun down both sides of the boat. The lights were brighter now, and a new one appeared. A second followed, as did a third. All stacked in a vertical line. The signal Darby was looking for. The ex–petty officer turned the tiller to slightly starboard, watched the bow swing in response, and felt the waves lift the stern as they pushed the *Shine* toward shore. Her other hand, the right one, slid under the peacoat. It felt good to wrap her fingers around the rubberized grip. The .357 was a whole lot of gun, but *she* was a whole lot of woman.

Sister Andromeda watched one of her acolytes hang the battery-powered lanterns in the correct sequence, nodded approvingly, and waited for the boat to appear out of the darkness. Payment, in the form of a box full of drugs provided by the Ra 'Na, sat next to her neatly shod feet. Rumor had it that there were more of the "Crips" beyond those who worked the boat, a whole colony of them hidden somewhere, and they needed drugs. All sorts of drugs, the kind only the Ra 'Na could scrounge, which explained why they worked so hard to harvest shellfish.

Well, more power to them, since the Star Com took a cut in both directions. Not to purchase *things,* but to buy *influence,* which was far more important. The kind of influence that could open doors, change work assignments, and channel scarce resources to the church. Yes, those were the things worth having, worth risking her life for. Because while some of the lower-ranking Saurons were on the take, thousands weren't, and took a dim view of black-market activities.

There was a crunching noise as the *Sunshine*'s bow ran up onto the gravelly beach, and Darby said, "Up oars."

Acolytes, well versed in how to handle such matters, dashed into the water, took hold of the boat's gunwales and carried the boat up toward the waiting tideline.

Darby, who had been expecting such a move, barely had time to remove the tiller-rudder combination from the pintles before they set the *Shine* down.

"So," one of the hooded figures said, aiming a flashlight into the boat, "what you got? Any clams?"

"Yeah," Darby said, swinging a leg over the side, "we've got clams, *and* oysters, *and* geoducks. But you keep your cotton-pickin' hands off 'em till we get paid."

"Oooo," the man said sarcastically, "I'm scared, *real* scared."

"You should be," Sister Andromeda said, stepping out of the surrounding gloom. "Darby has a .357 under that coat and she knows how to use it."

The acolyte raised his light, as if to see some sign of the weapon, and caught sight of Darby's face. Or what *had* been a face, back before the Saurons destroyed her ship, and the resulting fire consumed her flesh. The man gasped when he saw the heavily puckered scar tissue, said something about being sorry, and faded into the darkness.

Sister Andromeda found it difficult to look Darby in the eyes but took pride in doing so. "Sorry about that."

Darby shrugged. "Don't be. What is, is. You got the meds?"

Sister Andromeda motioned with her hand. Two of her acolytes moved forward, carrying the box between them. They lowered the container onto the beach and opened the lid.

Besides digging for clams and pulling the number four oar, Nok was an R.N. She spent a full five minutes checking the contents of the box, nodded her head, and stood up straight. "It looks good, Darb, release the protein."

The ex-sailor turned toward the waiting acolytes. "Unload the boat."

The full bins were removed, empties were loaded in their place, and Darby took her seat in the stern. The acolytes gathered around, lifted the *Sunshine* off the beach, and turned her bow toward Puget Sound. Fewer than twenty minutes after making landfall, the *Shine* was back in the water, and swimming out to sea.

The crew pulled hard, the now empty boat seemed to leap ahead, and water broke at the bow. Their camp lay a good forty-five minutes to the south. A long, difficult pull, but one that would be rewarded with bowls of tasty clam chowder, and chunks of crusty bread. Their cook, a man named Cecil, was there now, tending his makeshift oven.

Darby felt her mouth water, blinked salt spray out of her eyes, and stole a look at the luminescent compass strapped to her wrist. It was easy to get lost at night, and the crew would skin her if she caused them to row one more mile than was necessary.

Perhaps it was the noise from the oars, or the fact that she was distracted, but whatever the reason, none of the Crips heard the patrol boat, not till it was a hundred yards away. And that, as Chu commented later, "was way too frigging late."

ABOARD THE SAURON DREADNOUGHT *HOK NOR AH*

The walkway stretched ahead, passed between two of the ship's overarching ribs, and crossed a causeway. Below, in what had once served as a Ra 'Na recreational area, more than a thousand Kan stood in spiral formations and awaited an inspection.

Franklin, his features cast in stone, his wife cradled in his arms, walked the length of the thoroughfare as if it were rightfully his. Something about his bearing, about the anger in his eyes, jumped the species divide. Saurons and Ra 'Na alike moved to either side and watched the procession pass.

Lin Mok led the way, followed by Franklin and then by Manning. The security chief wondered who was the most despicable— the Saurons, Franklin, or he himself. The answer seemed obvious. The aliens were cruel, the politician was weak, but *he* was worst. It had been *his* selfishness, *his* perfidy that set the entire sequence of events into motion.

The solution was obvious. Marta was free, or as free as she wanted to be, and there was no reason to stay. Soon after the presidential party touched down, he would run. If the Kan caught him, then so be it. He would kill as many as he could.

Kell or one of the others would fill in behind him and prove a lot more trustworthy. Jina would be better off, and so, for that matter, would her husband. The plan, and the essential correctness of it, made Manning feel better.

Mok led the party of humans through a series of passageways and back to the same tubeway through which all of them had entered. The same Kan, or ones who looked just like them, were waiting. They remained expressionless as they returned Jina's clothing and gave Manning his weapons.

However, when the security chief checked, he discovered that the magazines for both guns had been removed, and the Saurons appeared to be grinning.

Then, in a departure from what had taken place in the past, Mok herded her charges into the shuttle, closed the hatch, and sealed herself in.

The shuttle lifted almost immediately, drilled its way through the ever-spinning force field, and was in space before Manning noticed that something was different. The Kan pilots had been replaced by a pair of Ra 'Na. The human turned to Mok. "What happened to the chits?"

The Ra 'Na produced something akin to a human shrug. "They were reassigned."

At that point the shuttle banked *away* from Earth, and Franklin quizzed the female. "Where are you taking us? What's going on?"

"There is nothing to be concerned about," Mok answered soothingly. "Dro Rul would like to speak with you."

Franklin frowned. "Dro Rul? Who is he? Or she?"

"*He* is one of our leaders," Mok answered patiently. "A very important person."

"I'd love to meet him," Franklin replied, "but some other time. My wife has been injured and—"

"Your wife is fine," Jina put in firmly, pushing her husband away. "Or *will* be. Hand me my clothes, please."

Manning turned his head as the president helped his wife get into her clothes. She winced as the cotton top touched her raw back. Most of the bleeding had stopped, and a scab had started to form. Franklin frowned. "Jina, let's see Dr. Sool first, and meet with Dro Rul later on."

Jina looked at Mok. Something that was female to female rather than alien to alien passed between them. "The meeting—it's important, isn't it?"

Mok made a sign with one hand. "Yes."

"Then that settles it," Jina said firmly. "Does anyone have an aspirin?"

HELL HILL

Blue steeled himself against the stench, which had already proven itself more powerful than a pan of slowly burning cinnamon, and fought the urge to gag as he entered the alien's quarters. He no longer ate prior to his visits, or immediately after them, for that matter.

Lak-Tal, who seemed to both hate and enjoy his status as invalid, was awake and momentarily lucid. The sarcasm and self-pity were typical of his better moments. "Ah, a visit from my jailer, confessor, and amateur physician. How nice."

Blue, who had been tolerant of that sort of comment during the early stages of their relationship, no longer had the patience to be so. A battery-powered lamp hung from the ceiling. The light pushed shadows down under his eyes. The Sauron, who had grown too large for the makeshift sling chair, squatted like some sort of obscene grub. "Hello to you, too. Wow, you're even bigger than last time."

"Perhaps I will explode and take you with me," the Zin offered, only partly in jest. "We could continue our conversations in the afterlife."

Blue knew a Sauron joke when he heard one and chuckled politely. "What a horrible thought! I'll have nightmares for weeks."

That led to a short discussion of dreams, the concept of "nightmares," and the "racial" dreams that all Saurons had in common. Dreams in which their ancestors spoke to them and passed along certain kinds of knowledge.

The conversation veered toward the precise nature of the Sauron language and a comment that grabbed the historian's attention.

"Yes," the Zin continued, "language is a very interesting thing. During the period while we assessed your civilization we were amazed by the diversity of languages employed by your species, and the number of individuals trained to read and write them."

The Sauron began to choke at that point, spat something into a bucket, and wiped his snout with a towel.

The human waited for the moment to pass before asking what he regarded as an obvious question. "Should I interpret your comment to mean that some portion of the Sauron population is sub-iterate?"

The question took Lak-Tal by surprise. "Of course. My caste, which is to say the Zin, would never allow the Fon or the Kan to read and write. Why bother? We perform that function for them. It's part of the burden we must bear."

"But they *could* learn?" Blue persisted. "In spite of the fact that they lack long-term memories?"

"Yes, I imagine that they could," the Sauron agreed thoughtfully, "as long as they used the skill frequently enough to hold on to it. That's the key, you see. Because of their comparatively short memory spans, the lesser castes must use a particular skill or lose it within eighteen to twenty-four of your months. Why do you ask?"

"Just curious, that's all," Blue replied.

"Curious about what?"

"What if the Fon and the Kan could read? What if we published the truth? What if they *knew* about the birthing?"

Lak-Tal felt something heave deep within his belly, as if the being who dwelled there had been listening and was trying to object. It hurt, and the words came in bursts.

"Then they would revolt—some would, anyway—and construction would be slowed."

Blue leaned back on his heels, and a predatory grin stole across his face. "Thank you. That's what I hoped you would say."

■ ■ ■

The citadel at the top of Hell Hill was higher now, two stories tall in most places, and more than that at the corners. A mixed group of Saurons and Ra 'Na stood on one of the battlements. The Fon, true to the instructions laid down in the Book of Life, stood in a rough semicircle, torches held high. A half-dozen Ra 'Na were under no such stricture and carried battery-powered torches.

Still, even with the combined illumination provided by both the torches *and* the alien flashlights, most of the ambient light was provided by the steadily rising moon, and beyond that, glittering like newly formed ice crystals, the stars themselves.

Below, gathered at the base of the partially built structure, a crowd waited. Most wore the hooded robes that identified them as members of Sister Andromeda's Star Com. The acolytes made a low humming sound as they gave voice to one of the vibratory mantras that their leader had taught them. The sound had a throaty, almost ominous quality.

Most of the cultists assumed that Sister Andromeda, resplendent in her crisp white robe, knew what was going on. She didn't, but the religious leader saw no reason to tell her followers that, and was careful to maintain a serene and seemingly knowledgeable countenance.

Meanwhile, up on the structure itself, the various functionaries, most of whom would have preferred to be somewhere else, stirred uneasily and stared at the heavily swathed stonemaster. His black togalike garment was held in place by a symbolic gold disk. It had been worn by *all* of his predecessors and would be passed to his successor.

The Sauron took a long, slow look around. His audience was attentive, there was no doubt of that, and would hang on his every word. More importantly—from *his* perspective, at least—they would repeat what he said to others.

Yes, a certain amount of distortion was inevitable, but hardly mattered. It was the effect that he was after. A sense of fear, wonder, and awe. Emotions that, when combined with the practical implication of his revelation, would boost productivity to new heights. Something he very much needed to do. Though not very understanding to begin with, Hak-Bin had become more irritable of late, even going so far as to threaten the stonemaster with premature entombment. The Zin leader didn't really mean it, of course, but the frustration was real.

Satisfied that everything was as it should be, the Sauron raised a pincer. A Ra 'Na named Ponz had been waiting for just such a signal and whispered into his com unit.

Others, high above, heard the technician's words, checked the displays arrayed in front of them, and touched a series of buttons.

The stonemaster launched into his speech. Like most of the things he said, it was short and to the point. "Half of each working day is lost to darkness, valuable time in which much could be accomplished. This is unacceptable and will no longer be tolerated. The slave population will be divided into two groups, each working a twelve-hour shift. To facilitate their labors, I hereby decree that light shall replace darkness."

With those words what appeared to be a new star popped into existence, and Hell Hill, along with a sizable chunk of surrounding territory, was bathed in amber light.

The onlookers gave a gasp of surprise, all except for observers such as Ponz, who knew what the light was and where it came from. Up in orbit, on the surface of an asteroid harvested for that very purpose, a flower had blossomed. Shiny metal petals had unfurled, tilted toward the sun, and redirected the incoming light.

The idea was far from new, even the humans had played with it, but context can make a difference. *Here, now,* the sudden wash of unexpected light had a sudden and dramatic effect.

Though not as bright as direct sunlight, the "bounce," as the Ra 'Na technicians referred to it, still provided more illumination than the fully visible moon. Enough to work by—which was all that mattered.

Sister Andromeda didn't know how the miracle had been achieved, only that it had, and was amazed by the extent to which one of her ad-lib prophecies had come true. Of course, when she predicted that aliens "would bathe the planet in light," she meant in the metaphorical sense, but so what? She had foreseen what would happen, and no one else could make the same claim.

Meanwhile, not far away, a group of four racialists, their white skin blackened to make them less visible, were caught out in the open. The sudden wash of unexpected light acted to freeze them in place.

Boner damned near shit his pants, a skin named Schultz swore, and Parker scanned the no longer darkened sky. Where was the light coming from? One of the observation towers? An alien spacecraft? No, there was no indication that either hypothesis was correct. Nor was there any indication of a threat. The light simply *was,* and Parker, who never spent much time on the "whys" of life, motioned the team forward. The skins had a mission, and he saw no reason to abort it.

The clinic had been closed for about twenty minutes. Dixie was asleep on a mat, and Sool was about to join her. The single candle flickered as the doctor splashed water onto her face, used the minimum amount of toothpaste necessary to get the job done, and went to bed knowing she would get fewer than six hours of sleep.

Sool lay down, pulled the scratchy wool blanket up over her shoulders, and felt sleep pull her down. The resulting loss of consciousness was so complete it felt as though she had been embraced by the arms of death.

The physician was deep in NREM-level sleep when a prybar was inserted into the gap between the door and the jamb, a significant amount of pressure was exerted, and the metal started to groan.

Dixie stirred, told the visitors "to go away" and turned on her side.

The crowbar was withdrawn, reinserted, and leveraged again. The bracket that held the makeshift throw bolt in place snapped under the pressure. Hinges squealed, Dixie tried to sit, and was buried under an avalanche of male flesh.

One of the men attempted to kiss her, took a size-twelve boot in the side, and rolled onto the floor, where Parker kicked him again. "What the hell's wrong with you? You keep those hands to yourself. Sorry, ma'am. We don't hold with that sort of nonsense. He'll be punished. Please remain where you are. We have no desire to harm you."

Dixie sensed that the man meant what he said, and had little choice but to watch as the invaders gagged Sool, and rolled the now conscious physician up in her own blanket. Then, hoisting the diminutive doctor onto his shoulder, one of the men carried Sool away.

"Don't worry," Parker said, his bulk filling the doorway. "We'll take good care of the doctor." That being said the racialist left.

Dixie's body trembled as it reacted to both the chemicals that flooded her bloodstream and the cold night air. She forced herself to the door, realized it was light outside, and wondered how such a thing was possible. Not that it mattered, as long as it helped her to see. The nurse grabbed her cloak off a hook by the door, slipped her feet into some muddy shoes, and slipped out the door. The men were still visible, still crossing the open square, and she would follow. Then, once Dixie knew where Sool had been taken, she would find help.

ABOARD THE SAURON SHUTTLE *MESSENGER* IN EARTH ORBIT

The Sauron shuttle banked away from the *Hok Nor Ah*, entered the flow of traffic that bound the fleet together, and wove its way among the myriad warships, transports, and support vessels.

During that time, and unbeknownst to the Fon who was supposed to track such things, the traffic control code initially assigned to the shuttle was mysteriously switched with that of another flight, while the ship assigned to the humans acquired a new six-digit mission designator and a vector to match.

Mok, who knew just enough about what was going on to be worried, sat rigid in her chair. Part of her was frightened, afraid that the bishops would lose what seemed like a dangerous game, but part of her was proud, delighting in the way that the Ra 'Na could defy the Saurons. *Had* defied the Saurons, though never so boldly, or in alliance with another race.

The asteroid designated as O Λ 2213 had been acquired many light-years away, equipped with external drives, and integrated into the fleet. The minerals for which it had originally been acquired had long since been removed, leaving it to be used as a spacegoing warehouse packed with Sauron booty—technology mostly looted from conquered worlds and stored against possible need.

Fra Pol, who had never guessed that such a place even existed, gaped in wonder as he followed Dro Zar and a party of his superiors down a narrow aisle. Alcoves opened to either side. Each one of them was packed with a jumble of machines, many of which were dead, or seemed to be, while others showed signs of life. One such device beeped intermittently, as if trying to alert its long-dead owner to the difficulty it found itself in, while another turned endlessly, like an animal in a trap.

The initiate longed to plunge into the metallic maze, to lose himself in the secrets hidden there. But Dro Rul, not to mention the bishops aligned with him, had other, more serious matters to attend to and weren't likely to tolerate any of what Tog would refer to as "his nonsense."

The ecclesiastical party rounded a corner and suddenly arrived in a fairly large compartment. Fifty or sixty storage modules, stacked in what seemed like a haphazard manner, lined the rocky walls. An ore crusher, left over from the mining operation, squatted to one side.

The humans, who had arrived only moments before, stood in front of a rather singular construct and were clearly interested in whatever it was. They looked up when the Ra 'Na arrived and seemed more than a little nervous. Not too surprising, given all they had been through.

Pol, whose duties had kept him aboard the ship till then, had never seen a human before, not in person, and was fascinated by how strange they were. Imagine! Bare skin! No wonder they were so fond of clothes. The black male spoke first.

"Hello, my name is Alexander Franklin. This is my wife, Jina. And my chief of security, Jack Manning."

Dro Rul bowed, named his companions, and gestured toward the space-scarred machine. "Interesting, isn't it?"

"Yes," Franklin agreed. "It bears a striking resemblance to one of our early spacecraft, *Pioneer Ten*. It was launched in 1972. I built a model of it when I was a little boy."

Something akin to pity appeared in the prelate's eyes. "You are correct. Come here. Look at this." The Ra 'Na pointed at something the human couldn't quite make out.

Curious yet a bit afraid, Franklin moved in for a closer look. Dust covered the plaque but fell away when brushed with his hand. The image was as clear as it had been on the day when the spacecraft was launched. A man and a woman stood in front of an outline of the spacecraft itself. The man raised a hand in greeting. A woman stood beside him. The sun was shown relative to the center of the galaxy. Franklin felt the bottom of his stomach drop out. The plaque was a road map, a spacegoing road map, pointing right at Earth. He took a step backward. "No, it can't be."

"Oh, but it is," the Dro said gravely. "It's your spacecraft, complete with directions on how to find your planet."

"You mean . . . ?"

"Yes. One of our long-range probes happened across your vehicle, took it aboard, and brought it back. The Saurons had been looking for a planet like yours, one with an oxygen-rich atmosphere and a ready-made workforce. The rest, as your kind would say, 'is history.' "

Manning and Jina were listening and experienced the same sense of shock that Franklin had. Jina, her pain momentarily forgotten, searched the Dro's face. "That's it? They found our spacecraft and came all this way to build some temples?"

"Again, yes, or so we believed," the prelate answered evenly. "But now, thanks to the investigative efforts of one of our more disobedient initiates, we know the truth."

Manning, who normally deferred to Franklin, heard himself speak. "Which is?"

"Which is that the temples are actually *birth* chambers, secure places in which the Saurons can die and a new generation can be born."

The security chief stared in amazement. "Holy shit."

"Yes," the prelate answered dryly. "I'm not sure that I approve—but 'holy shit' pretty well covers the situation."

HELL HILL

The boy waited in the bushes for a full fifteen minutes, swatting mosquitoes, and waiting for the oh, so predictable Kan to bounce past. His friends called them "chits," but Willie preferred "roos," after the way they jumped from place to place.

Then, quick as a rabbit, he was across the free fire zone that encircled Hell Hill's base, and up to the face of the newly constructed stone wall. The hole, dug over four successive nights, went straight under. The trick was to dive in and wiggle through without damaging the carefully planted weeds that hid the entrance. The fact that he was small and rail thin made that easier to do.

Like most of the Free Taggers, Willie had managed to make his way through the Sauron security perimeter on numerous occasions before. Why? Because that's where the eyeballs were—and graffiti without eyeballs amounts to a waste of time.

Getting in was relatively easy, but getting out—well, that was a bitch. Especially now that the suck-assed aliens had come up with a way to illuminate the hill at night.

Willie stuck his head up out of the hole, checked to ensure that his arrival had gone unobserved, and wiggled out.

Then, careful to brush the telltale clay from his clothes, the youngster clipped a counterfeit tag to his ear, climbed a recently terraced hillside, and followed a series of footpaths up into the lowest levels of the complex called Super Stack.

Not because he especially wanted to, but because that's where brother Shoes had *paid* him to do his thing. Which was cool, though kinda weird, since no one had ever encouraged Willie or his associates to tag walls before, much less compensated them for doing so.

Not that the concept was without controversy, since some of the taggers felt that the entire notion of paid graffiti was essentially corrupt. After all, they reasoned, traditional "street art" was both a protest and a statement of personal significance. Compensation threatened the purity of that.

But this was different, that's what Shoes said, and Willie believed him. This was about fighting the roos, driving the bastards into space, and saving the planet. That's when he would go looking for his mom. Logic dictated that she was dead, but he refused to believe it.

Willie made his way through a maze of passageways, emerged into a well-trafficked thoroughfare, and paused to look around. Laundry flapped from lines strung over his head, a crow cawed, and a dog barked in the distance. He fumbled with a piece of paper, removed a brand-new can of Krylon spray paint from under his jacket, and went to work.

The Sauron glyphs didn't mean much to the teenager, but he had a good eye, and he replicated each grouping of symbols on the wall next to a quick sketch of what they meant. For example, "O [] / Λ" meant "food," which Willie associated with a skillfully rendered picture of a Kan ration box. Not just any ration box, but one with steam shooting from the vents on top, which looked real enough to hold.

Passersby looked at the youngster with open curiosity, wondered where he had obtained the paint, but didn't care what he did with it. Willie could tag the entire complex, as far as they were concerned. It, like everything else, belonged to the Saurons.

But it wasn't long before a group of Fon appeared at the far end of the passageway, and people scattered in every direction.

Willie sensed the movement, used a few quick strokes to complete his latest word picture, and turned away.

The tagger was more than a hundred feet away by the time the

Fon drew abreast of his latest creation, paused, and started to gabble among themselves.

Though not perceived as such—not at the moment, anyway—a seed had been planted, a seed that given some more time would produce a crop of semiliterate beings. Something that Hak-Bin, had he been aware of it, would have done anything to prevent. But he *wasn't* aware of it, not yet, and words attacked fortress walls.

■ ■ ■

Sool struggled during the trip through the mazelike streets, but the blanket proved to be a surprisingly effective restraint system, and the gag prevented any cries for help. Not that such cries were likely to do any good, since no one wanted any more trouble than they already had, and the skins were spoiling for a fight.

Her brain was at work, however, tackling the problem in the same way it would engage a medical emergency. But a good diagnosis requires symptoms that point the way, and Sool had very little to go on.

Rape was a possibility, but didn't seem likely somehow, given all the effort involved. No, rapists would have assaulted her in the clinic itself, and Dixie, too, for that matter. What had one of them said? "We'll take good care of the doctor"?

Yes, she thought so, and that suggested something else. Something medical? A sick comrade, perhaps?

The logic of it, the likelihood that there was some purpose behind the abduction, didn't eliminate the fear that Sool felt, but helped her manage it.

Her bare feet hit something solid as the man who was carrying her turned a corner. Sool heard someone ask, "Is that her?" and heard another voice reply, "Who the hell else were you expecting? The tooth fairy?"

Then there were lights, *more* voices, and hands that lifted Sool up. The gag was removed. Sool felt her feet make contact with a cold steel floor and took the opportunity to look around. The cube—*two* cubes really, joined together—was filled with rough-looking white men.

The doctor wondered if she'd been mistaken, if they *were* going to rape her, when a woman appeared. She was tall and lean. There was something strange about her eyes, as if live coals burned within and might burst into flame at any moment. Her voice was feminine but hard. "I know what you're thinking, but there's no reason to be afraid. White warriors respect women, *white* women, and wouldn't touch a hair on your head."

A hand blurred and reappeared with a .9mm pistol in it. The barrel was pointed toward the ceiling. "Besides," the woman continued, her teeth white in the gloom, "they know I'd blow their balls off."

The men burst into loud laughter, as if that were the funniest joke they'd ever heard, and slapped each other's backs.

A new face appeared. It was male, handsome in a predatory sort of way. "Hello, Dr. Sool. My name is Jonathan Ivory. Please accept my apology for the manner in which you were summoned. Marta is correct, you *are* safe here. Safer than at your clinic. Your nurse is fine, by the way, or was when my men left. Please, take a seat. Are you hungry? Would you like something to eat?"

Food was something that Sool frequently went without, partly because of her tendency to give whatever nourishment that came her way to needy patients, and partly because there was so little time. Suddenly she was aware of a wonderful odor, felt her mouth fill with saliva, and heard herself say, "Yes, I think I would."

The words had an immediate effect. All tension seemed to drain from the room, the vast majority of the skins returned to whatever they had been doing, and she was shown to a makeshift table. A man with a large swastika tattooed across his chest stood, nodded, and drifted away.

The table consisted of a sheet of three-quarter-inch plywood on a couple of crudely made sawhorses. Skulls, swastikas, and jagged bolts of lightning had been carved into the surface and varnished into place with coffee and spilled food. The images were disquieting and seemed at odds with the homey feel of the place.

The stew, which was ladled out of an iron skillet by a man called Knees, was excellent. He watched with pleasure as Sool consumed one bowl and part of a second. She thanked the man. He grinned self-consciously and returned to his chores.

It was only then, as Sool wiped her mouth with an old washcloth, that both Ivory and Marta took seats at the other side of the table. "So," Ivory asked, "do you feel better now?"

Sool did her best to look strong and confident. "You feed your prisoners well, but they're still prisoners."

Ivory shrugged. "True, for the moment, anyway. But who knows? Hear us out and perhaps you will *want* to stay."

Sool looked from one face to the other. They were sincere, that much was plain to see, but there was something else, too: Both wore the self-satisfied smirks of people who think they know all the answers. Still, talk was cheap and would buy her some time. Sool forced a smile. "Okay, I'm listening. What's this all about?"

Ivory spread his fingers over a well-executed but nonetheless grotesque-looking skull. In a world where most hands were dirty, his were clean. "Do you know who we are?"

Sool looked beyond Ivory to the white swastika that had been painted on the opposite wall. Some trick of the lighting caused it to glow as if lit from within. "Some sort of white-supremacy group?"

"Yes," Ivory said with no trace of embarrassment. "We believe that the great Yahweh, our name for God, set the white race over all others, and ever since that time Satan, with the assistance of the Zionist Occupational Government, has worked to pull us down."

Sool was starting to feel sick. She hoped it didn't show. "Pull you down? In what way?"

"Through race mixing," Marta volunteered earnestly. "Take a look around. The muds are everywhere. And who are they aligned with? The Saurons."

"Marta's right," Ivory agreed. "But the Saurons are a gift sent by the great Yahweh to cleanse the planet. He did his part. Now we must do ours.

"That's why we're here, to rally our kind and take the world back. You could be part of that. We call ourselves the Society of the White Rose. Join and we'll feed you, have someone take care of your work assignment, and support your clinic as well."

Sool thought of her own mixed ancestry, realized that they believed she was white, and felt the pull of temptation. All she had to do was grant them what they wanted, allow them to believe that she was white, and reap the obvious benefits. White, not white, what difference did it make? It would be nice to eat regular meals and practice medicine without having to dig ditches as well. Or would it? Sool looked from one to the other.

"Let's say I agreed to your proposal and joined your group. My clinic is open to everyone. Would it stay that way?"

Ivory's chair creaked as he leaned against the back. "I know you mean well, Doctor, treating the muds and all, but it doesn't make sense. They're out to destroy our race. Why give comfort to the enemy? No, I think your services would best be reserved for white folks."

So there it was—a direct answer to a direct question. *If* Sool agreed, *if* she gave the racists what they wanted, she'd be forced to betray her patients and herself. The doctor sighed. Why couldn't anything be simple? Why was everything so hard? She met Ivory's dark, penetrating gaze. It was like looking down the barrel of a gun. "I think we have a problem."

"A problem? What sort of a problem?"

"The kind where I say 'no' and you get pissed off."

The man frowned. The front two legs of his chair made a clacking sound as they hit the floor. "What? The muds mean that much to you?"

Sool nodded. "Yes, as a matter of fact they do. Of course that might have something to do with the fact that I'm a mud myself. You don't know my name? It's Seeko Sool."

A look of disgust came over Marta's face. "My God. She's one of *them*."

Ivory, whose vision of an all-white medical clinic had just crumbled before his eyes, felt a quickly growing sense of rage. "Very well, then. Take the bitch outside and put her to work doing what muds do best: shoveling shit."

Sool was jerked out of her chair and pushed, kicked, and finally dragged out through the ground-floor door. Then, with her feet leaving twin lines in the three-inch deep layer of brown muck, she was towed through a narrow passageway into the foul-smelling lavatory that had been established in the courtyard between two steel cubes. A man, who had just risen from a plywood seat, hurried to pull his pants up.

The skins kicked Sool with their combat boots, took turns urinating on her, and pointed her toward a rusty wheelbarrow. "Use your hands to scoop shit from the trough, load it into the barrow, and ask the sentry for permission to take it away. Then, if you're *real* good, we'll shit you some more. Not just any shit, but *white* shit, which looks brown but really isn't."

The sentry, who had come back to watch the entertainment, laughed. The skins slapped each other on the back, delivered a couple of halfhearted kicks, and disappeared from sight. The sentry remained. He carried a submachine gun and used it to jab the air. "You heard the man—get to work."

Sool, barely able to move, was forced to crawl toward the trough. Then, having made it to her knees, she set about her task. But like any doctor or nurse, she was no stranger to feces, urine, and pus. She tried to call on that, to use it as a sort of psychological immunity factor, but the smell made her gag. The stew came up and added to the overall stench.

Meanwhile, not more than two hundred feet away, separated from Sool by the cubes, Dixie watched and waited. The nurse had witnessed the manner in which Sool had been dragged into the passageway and was relieved when there weren't any gunshots. Yes, there were other ways to kill someone, but deep down Dixie knew Sool was alive.

That feeling was confirmed twenty minutes later, when the physician was escorted out onto the street by one of the sentries and allowed to push a wheelbarrow toward a ravine a hundred yards away. One look was sufficient to see that she had been beaten.

Dixie waited till the strange twosome was gone, used a sleeve to wipe away her tears, and hurried off. The means weren't clear, but one thing was for sure: The skinheads were going to pay.

ON PUGET SOUND NEAR HELL HILL

Even though the patrol boat was small by naval standards, it looked like a huge black blob to Darby and her companions. The ex–petty officer heard the telltale whine as at least one deck-mounted weapon came to bear, and she knew that a 76mm gun was aimed at the thin-skinned aluminum boat. All the coxswain could do was whisper, "Up oars!" keep the bow into the waves, and hope for the best.

But all such hopes were dashed when a shaft of brilliant white light pinned the fishing boat to the dark, oily-looking water. It disappeared two seconds later and was replaced by an amplified voice. "Stay where you are and prepare to receive a line."

The voice was human, distinctly so, and Darby allowed herself to hope. Had some small portion of the navy managed to survive?

The fishing boat rolled dangerously as the naval vessel drew closer. A line snaked through the air, fell across the *Shine*'s square bow, and was quickly made fast. The patrol boat was still under way, and the forward motion acted to pull the flat-bottomed skiff up against a row of low-hanging fenders. There was a noticeable bump, and the two vessels were joined.

A silhouette appeared against the slightly lighter background of the sky, and a flashlight played across the faces below. Darby managed to remain expressionless as the beam fastened itself on her ruined face. The voice held no signs of pity, for which the sailor was grateful. "So, who's in charge?"

The Crips didn't spend much time on org charts and the like, but Darby was generally acknowledged as their unofficial leader. She looked the length of the boat, saw no sign of anyone else stepping forward, and squinted into the light. "I guess I am."

"Good," the voice replied. "Please come aboard. No one will harm you or your friends. Sorry we can't bring everyone aboard, but we need to keep this short. I'll send a thermos of hot chocolate down to your crew."

Chu said, "Hot chocolate?" and the deal was done. Hot chocolate was a special treat, one they could rarely indulge in, and well worth the delay.

Darby was hoisted up onto the patrol boat's deck while a thermos and a package of hastily assembled sandwiches were passed down to her crew.

Once aboard, Darby was shown into a small space designed to act as a lock in case of biological warfare but that now functioned to prevent light from leaking out.

After the outer hatch had been resealed, the young woman was invited to enter the boat's tiny fire-control center. A group of four men and women stood in a semicircle behind a computer-controlled plotting table. Landmasses glowed green, while multicolored deltas, squares, and circles marked other points of interest.

In place of the uniforms or civilian seagoing garb she might have expected, Darby saw 1890s-style trapper outfits complete with buckskin shirts and knee-high boots, mixed in with the latest in high-tech backpacking togs. All of the strangely dressed people smiled, none seemed put off by her face, and a fatherly looking man stepped forward. He held out a hand. It was as hard and callused as her own.

"Hello, my name is Deacon Smith, but most folks call me 'Deac.' The guy in the silly-looking boony hat is George Farley, sometimes referred to as 'Popcorn.' That's Buckskin Mary next to him, and the other lady has to put up with all sorts of nicknames. My personal favorite is 'Squid,' Farley likes 'Swabbie,' and Mary calls her 'Admiral.' However, given the fact that she's the only one who knows anything about how to run this tub, most people just call her 'ma'am.' "

The woman in question offered her hand. It was firm but uncallused. "Don't pay any attention to that 'ma'am' stuff. There isn't much navy left. You can call me 'Jane.' "

Darby released the other woman's hand, saw the U.S. Naval

Academy ring, and snapped to attention. " 'Ma'am' will be fine, ma'am. Petty Officer Third Class Stokes reporting for duty."

Lieutenant Commander Jane Simmons eyed the sailor who stood in front of her. "At ease, Stokes. I'm glad you made it. *Real* glad, since we need some intelligence, and there's nothing better than a trained eye. How well do you know these waters?"

"*Very* well," Darby replied. "My friends and I harvest shellfish from the beaches and sell it to the Ra 'Na. Mostly at night."

"Excellent," the naval officer said eagerly. "You're exactly the kind of person we hoped to find. How would you like to strike a blow for freedom? The kind that will hit the Saurons hard?"

Darby's hand went to the still-healing scar tissue that covered one side of her face. It was hard and rough. "I'd like that a lot, ma'am. Can I ask what you have in mind?"

Simmons looked at Smith, saw him nod, and turned back. "Yes, if you'll agree to stay. You'd be a security risk otherwise."

Darby looked doubtful. "I don't know, ma'am. My friends— that is to say, the civilians in the boat—have a variety of disabilities. They need me."

The naval officer considered ordering Darby to stay but thought better of it. The PO *wanted* to do the right thing; all she needed was some help. "Tell you what: How 'bout we tow your boat home, and take you back when the mission is over?"

"How long would I be away?"

Simmons shrugged. "One, maybe two days. This boat is equipped with the latest in stealth technology, but the Saurons are bound to spot us if we linger. We need to move, and move soon."

Darby looked at the fire-control panels. She was an electrician's mate and knew enough to appreciate what she saw. "Where did you find her? If you don't mind my asking."

Simmons gestured toward her strangely attired companions. "Deac and his people heard about Hell Hill and walked all the way up from Oregon. No small task, since they had to play hide-and-seek with bugs all along the way.

"They found the boat grounded down near Olympia, managed to work her off, and hid her away. Then, after they pulled me out of a scrape with some slavers, we hooked up. I figure we have a day, two at most, before they realize we're here."

Darby nodded. "You're right about that, ma'am. What's the target? The temples on the hill?"

Simmons looked toward Deac Smith, and it was he who answered. "No, we considered that, but ruled it out. That kind of attack would result in hundreds if not thousands of human casualties."

"That's right," the naval officer agreed. "That's why we chose a cleaner and more strategic target."

"Which is?"

"Are you familiar with the Sauron anchorage north of Hell Hill?"

"Yes, ma'am. We cut through the southern part of it at times but generally try to avoid it."

"Well, there were six good-sized Sauron ships anchored there last time we looked," Simmons responded, "and we plan to sink every damned one of them."

Darby gave a long, low whistle. It was an audacious plan—the kind that John Paul Jones or Lord Nelson might have favored. "That would put the hurts to the bastards—that's for sure."

"Yeah," Simmons replied. "And it's about time."

■ ■ ■

The president and his wife had an entire cube to themselves. The interior was furnished with *real* furniture, all of which had come from someplace called the Oak Store. Of course, this was more than most people had, but neither of them was complaining. Jina felt guilty about the queen-sized bed but had allowed Alex to talk her into it. Now, lying on her stomach, she was grateful to have it. She winced as her husband dabbed at the long, partially scabbed wound. "A nurse you are not."

"Sorry, hon, but there's some bleeding. Not much, but a little. That whip cut deeper in some places than in others. We should have come straight home."

Jina looked back over her shoulder. "You've got to be kidding! You heard Dro Rul—the Saurons have been lying! This changes everything!"

Franklin frowned. Jina was right, he knew that, and cursed the way his mind worked. She wanted him to accept the Ra 'Na offer, wanted the human race to join the aliens in a full-fledged alliance, and he was stalling. Why?

Was it because he needed time to build a consensus within the human underground, as he had claimed? Or was it something more sinister?

For example, how would Hak-Bin react if Franklin gave him Dro Rul and the College of Bishops on a silver platter? Would the Sauron give the humans some slack? Could they supplant the furry aliens as the more privileged slave race?

But no, faced with the very real possibility that the chits would kill *all* of their slaves, that consideration was meaningless. There was no choice, not a *real* one, and he might as well . . .

A half-inch Craftsman crescent wrench hung from a string next to the door. There was a clanging sound as metal struck metal. Franklin swore under his breath. When would they give him a break? The demands never seemed to end. "Yes? What is it?"

The reply was muffled. "It's Manning, Mr. President, and I have the nurse from Dr. Sool's clinic here with me."

Franklin felt a sudden sense of affection. Manning had gone to the clinic for help. A thoughtful thing to do. "Come in!"

Hinges squealed, and the door opened. Dixie entered first, followed by Manning. The nurse saw Jina, the long red mark, and the gauze in the president's hand. "Here, let me do that."

Franklin backed out of the way. "Thanks, it was nice of you to come. How's Dr. Sool?"

Manning cleared his throat. "I ran into Dixie on the way up to the clinic, sir. The doctor was abducted."

"Abducted? By whom?"

"By white supremacists," Dixie answered, her back turned. "I followed them to their headquarters. They took Seeko inside, beat her, and put her to work. She's cleaning their latrines. With her bare hands, from the look of it."

"But *why?*" Franklin wondered out loud.

"I'm not altogether sure," the nurse replied, running a disinfectant-soaked sponge the length of the whip mark. The patient grimaced, but Dixie didn't seem to notice. "It could have something to do with the clinic, though."

"It makes sense," Manning put in. "Assuming the supremacists are trying to recruit new members, which they almost certainly are, the clinic would make a nice tool. There's nothing like free medical care, especially now. They could use the facility to spread their hatred."

"Jack's right," Jina said through gritted teeth. "You must help her, but more than that, keep the clinic open."

Franklin, who was not altogether appreciative of the manner in which his wife and chief of security seemed to have joined forces, raised an eyebrow. "That's an interesting analysis, Jack. Of course you and your sister have quite a bit of experience where matters of racism are concerned."

It was a nasty crack. The blood drained from Manning's face. Franklin felt an immediate sense of guilt. He could feel Jina's disapproving stare but refused to meet her eyes. "I'm sorry, Jack, you didn't deserve that. Please accept my apology."

The security chief gave a short, jerky nod. "Apology accepted, sir, although I'm ashamed to say that my sister is a member of the group in question. She tried to recruit me, and I said no. I planned to tell you but never found the right moment."

There was silence for a moment as the politician searched for something to say. Manning's anguish was plain to see. Franklin cleared his throat. "There's an old saying, Jack: Actions speak louder than words. Your presence says it all."

Manning felt better, and Franklin allowed his eyes to drift into contact with his wife's. The pride he saw there was the kind of pride he'd seen only a few times before, on those rare occasions when he managed to live up to what she saw as his potential. No piece of paper or plaque had ever meant more.

"No offense," Dixie said as she applied a dressing, "but what does this mean for Dr. Sool?"

Manning knew what he was going to do, Franklin or no Franklin, but waited to see what his boss would say. A sanctioned raid would go a whole lot easier.

Franklin checked his chief of security, saw the eagerness there, and grinned. He turned to Dixie. "Judging from Jack's expression, it looks like we're going in. I'll notify the Saurons and ask them to stay out of it. How 'bout it, Jack? Is that what you were hoping for?"

The politician turned, but Manning was gone.

HELL HILL

The new day dawned bright and clear. Blue rolled out of his bedroll, wished it were located on something besides the hard floor, and worked his way to his feet. The arthritis had been little more than a minor irritation prior to the Sauron attack. But now, living as he was and without medication, the condition was much more noticeable. Perhaps this was the way Lak-Tal had felt at first—a little pain but nothing to worry about. Except that it *was* something to worry about, because it was the harbinger of death.

On that cheerful note Blue pulled his clothes on, downed two cups of black-market coffee, and thanked his hostess for her hospitality. Then, after peeking out the door, he stepped onto the street. Blue felt a momentary sense of well-being as the sunshine hit his face and knew why. He had granted himself two days off. Two days away from Lak-Tal, and two days away from Hell Hill. Time that would be spent with members of the original team. The feeling didn't last long, however, since there was no true escape.

The morning shift was about to begin. That being the case, most of the traffic was headed up the hill while Blue went down, a fact not lost on the slaves, most of whom were white.

Blue was bumped, subjected to racial epithets, and forced to walk next to the open sewer. Some tried to nudge him into the ditch, but the historian kept his feet.

There had been tension from the start, ever since the aliens either knowingly or unknowingly took advantage of the racial divide, but it was worse of late. Especially since the skinheads had arrived. They had burrowed into the hill like maggots into a corpse.

The crowd began to thin, the level of tension diminished, and Blue felt a little bit better. There were bright spots, such as the literacy campaign, which had already achieved some level of success.

So much so, in fact, that a Fon had been spotted writing some primitive half-literate graffiti on a wall! A twenty-first-century equivalent of cave drawings! What the Fon would think when *real* messages were posted was anyone's guess.

As Blue reached the bottom of the hill and followed the recently graveled road toward the main gate, fear settled into the pit of his stomach.

Yes, he had an appropriate ear tag, a *real* one, taken from a heart attack victim who lay buried on the hill, and yes, he had successfully passed out of and back into the camp on various occasions before, but this could be the occasion on which his luck ran out. It took all the courage he could muster to throw his shoulders back, keep his feet on the path, and march toward the checkpoint.

Two parallel rows of upside-down crosses served to funnel vehicles and pedestrians down to the wooden gates were Kan warriors monitored the flow of traffic.

As Blue came abreast of the first cross, he fought the desire to avert his eyes and forced himself to look into the woman's lifeless face. Doing so was important somehow, both in sympathy for the pain she had suffered, and as a trained witness, who, if he managed to survive, would attempt to write her epitaph.

He whispered the name of a man who had been crucified more

than two thousand years before, said a prayer, and continued to walk the gauntlet of pain. Some of the eyes blinked, begging him to help, while others stared into the next life.

But there was nothing he could do, so Blue forced himself to move forward, to pass them by, until he saw a face he knew. Not well, since Shoes had introduced the taggers as a group, but enough to know who the youngster was.

Willie's body was too small for the adult-sized cross, so the Kan had been forced to rope rather than nail it in place. A crow was sitting on one small upturned foot. It tore a strip of meat of the boy's instep, gulped it down, and flapped away. Another crow took its place.

Tears welled in Blue's eyes when he saw the way in which the can of spray paint had been forced between the youngster's jaws, and the look of horror in his staring eyes.

Heedless of what the Saurons might think or do, Blue stepped forward, closed the boy's eyes, and knelt in the mud. His words were pitched low, so low that only Willie could have heard them. "I sent you to your death and for that I will always be sorry. You were a soldier, a *good* soldier, and the human race is proud. May your soul rest in peace."

Then, getting to his feet, the tall man with the black skin walked through the Sauron checkpoint. He looked neither right nor left, felt no fear, and not one of the Kan tried to stop him.

■ ■ ■

There was no such thing as night anymore, not on Hell Hill, and most of the skinheads never worked on the so-called temples, so the timing of the raid was somewhat arbitrary.

Shift changes were to be avoided in order to limit the number of casualties suffered by noncombatants, an issue important to both the Saurons *and* the Franklin administration, but that was the only limiter.

That being the case, it was about ten in the morning when the team, led by Manning, began to enter the target area. The assault force included Vilo Kell, who wore two perfectly matched .45-caliber M1911A2 semiautomatic pistols; Morley Rix, who was armed with a long-barreled sniper's rifle; José Amocar, who carried a Heckler & Koch 9mm MP7 machine gun; Lucky Lu, who was equipped with an M16A3 complete with 40mm underbarrel grenade launcher; Se Ri Pak, also armed with an M16A3; and Jonathan Wimba, who, when he heard about the nature of the raid, insisted that he and his M62 7.62mm machine gun be included.

They were dressed in rags, covered in filth, and equipped with a variety of props. Kell carried a bucket as if going for water, Pak carried what looked like a bedroll, and Manning was disguised as a beggar.

The security chief was well aware of the fact that with the exceptions of individuals like Kell, his team hadn't been trained for military-style operations and might be in over their heads.

Manning was also cognizant of that fact that he had lectured them on the dangers of mission drift, the defensive nature of their ongoing assignment, and the importance of focus. All of which had momentarily gone out the window.

Not that the security chief regretted what they were doing. Sool was special, *very* special, which meant that Marta and her pet psychopaths deserved whatever they got. He hoped Marta was somewhere else, and therefore safe. But he was determined to succeed. Even if that meant his sister got hurt.

Manning jabbed his wooden bowl at a stranger, mumbled something about a bad leg, and realized that he had forgotten to limp. A metal disk containing some Glide dental floss fell into the bowl and rattled around the bottom.

It was a generous donation and one Manning could trade for food and drink. He inclined his head, said "Thank you," and limped up the street. He slipped his right hand into a pocket, wrapped his fingers around the radio, and felt for the transmit button. He pressed it three times.

About five miles away, in the cockpit of a CH-50 Chinook helicopter, John Wu heard three clicks, gave Vera Veen a thumbs-up, and lifted off. There was a slight jerk as the load came onto the cable and the chopper turned to the south.

The sentry, one of fifteen skinheads stationed in the area around headquarters, saw dozens of beggars each day. He was about eighteen years old, wore a goatee exactly like the one Ivory favored, and loved the weight of the twin "mud-killers" holstered beneath his armpits. They made him feel strong and damn near omnipotent. He leaned against the sun-warmed metal, spat into the street, and jerked his head to the left. "Keep it moving, pops. We don't need your kind around here."

Manning stopped, squinted, and looked the boy over. "Who the hell are *you* to tell *me* what to do?"

The skin took his weight off the cube and pulled his jacket

open. The handguns nestled butts forward. "I'm the guy who will shoot you in the gut and leave you for the crows. Now move along."

Other guards had watched the interchange and laughed. The sentry, unsure of *who* they were laughing at, frowned. Manning, still in his role of truculent beggar, stood his ground. He could hear the distant sound of an incoming helicopter and needed more time.

"Wait a minute—are you one of those racist guys?"

"We call ourselves *racialists,*" the skin answered primly, "but yes, I am willing to fight for my kind."

Manning drew himself up. "Me too! How can I join?"

"You can't," the sentry said disdainfully. "We need warriors, not beggars. The only thing lower than a mud is a white person who won't pull his weight. Now move it."

The Chinook was louder now, *much* louder, and the skinhead looked upward. Helicopters weren't that common anymore, so he held a hand over his eyes and took a second look. "What the hell?"

Manning, who had remained where he was, did likewise. "Well, I'll be damned, a helicopter. What's that hanging below it?"

The sentry had already observed the object dangling beneath the Chinook's body and knew what it was. The answer came automatically. "It looks like a Sauron cube."

"It sure does," Manning agreed mildly. "I wonder where they're taking it?"

The helicopter swept in toward the stack, started to slow, and hovered directly over their heads. Se Ri Pak spoke into her sleeve, and John Wu removed a safety. The skin found himself staring up at the bottom of a steel box. It was rusty and bore a series of Ra 'Na numerals. He frowned. Should he go inside? And interrupt the ceremony? Or remain at his post? Either action could be criticized.

"I think you should run," Manning said helpfully as he started to back away. "What if that thing falls?"

The hook had been released, the container was falling, and the sentry was centered in a large black shadow. He pulled the mud-killers out of their holsters, aimed them upward, and started to fire. Brass casings arced through the air and tinkled across the ground. The sun vanished. The sentry yelled, "No!" and his blood spurted outward as the container smashed into the ground. There was a brief moment of silence before Wimba fired his machine gun.

● ● ●

The cube, which had been specially decorated for the occasion, was brightly lit. The skins, each dressed in the best clothes they had, stood with their backs to the walls. The rest, some fifteen in all, were outside.

Fewer than 20 percent of them had served in the military, but every single one had assumed a position similar to attention.

Ivory, who stood at the center of the group, imagined himself as Hermann Goering or Heinrich Himmler. Not Hitler, since that would be presumptuous, but someone to be reckoned with. Perhaps there would be a painting, like the ones at Racehome, celebrating the moment.

The ceremony—from Ivory's perspective, anyway—was directed to a specific purpose: unit cohesion. As explained to him in boot camp and in books he'd read since, "cohesion" was the stuff that held military units together.

The "stuff" consisted of a clearly defined culture, a set of norms, common uniforms, key symbols, stories of past glories, and so forth.

Even the mention of Germany's Third Reich was sufficient to evoke images of peaked officers' caps, Iron Crosses, SS insignia, jackboots, Luger pistols, death's-heads, and the immortal swastika.

Ivory knew it would take a while to build such a highly integrated matrix of symbols, but the effort had to begin somewhere. That's why he was about to hand out some attaboys, make some promotions, and distribute a handful of medals. Trivial considerations really, but ones that many of the skins stood ready to die for.

The racialist had just opened his mouth, and was about to speak, when the ground shook beneath his boots. He thought it was an earthquake until bullets started to rattle across the front of the cube. Headquarters was under attack!

Ivory was one of the first people to the hatch. He grabbed the handle, turned, and pushed. The door swung about five inches or so, clanged against a metal wall, and could go no farther. A cube! Someone had dropped a cube right in front of the hatch! Why? To block the door, *that's* why. Ivory heard the crack of pistol shots overlaid by the cloth-ripping sound of a machine gun. His sentries were ass deep in a firefight. He slapped bare metal. "Damn it! Who are they? What's going on?"

Marta, seemingly unruffled, had appeared by his side. "Who indeed? The Kan are a possibility, but I doubt it. Their style is a good deal more direct."

Ivory, conscious of the fact that the skins were watching, took a step backward. It was important to look cool. "Who then?"

Marta's eyes seemed to roll out of focus, as if staring at something a long ways off. "There's no way to be sure, of course— but my brother comes to mind."

"But why?"

"The doctor," Marta said evenly. "He came for the doctor."

Given the fact that Franklin was a black, and seemingly uninterested in anything more than kissing Sauron ass, the possibility that the politician would use the forces at his disposal to launch a rescue mission had never occurred to Ivory. That being the case, he had taken no steps to defend against it. A feeling of shame washed over him, and he gritted his teeth. "Break out the cutting torch and make a new door."

He wanted to say something more, about how the attackers would pay, but knew it would be stupid. The battle would be over by the time the new opening had been cut. Not only that, but a single person with a semiauto rifle could keep them penned up the rest of the week if they wanted to. No, all he could do was hope that someone would have the good sense to blow Sool's brains out—and that the rest of his people would die bravely.

■ ■ ■

After cleaning the latrine, Dr. Seeko Sool had finally been allowed to sleep. The fact that she *could* sleep, while lying on the hard, cold ground not six feet from a communal toilet, was a testament to how tired she was.

She was in the midst of a dream when the Chinook arrived. A *wonderful* dream in which the sound of the helicopter's rotors was transformed into the Saturday afternoon drone of her father's lawn mower and she was safe in her room.

But that illusion was shattered when the steel container hit the ground out front, someone shouted, and weapons began to fire.

Sool's eyes popped open. She rolled over and came to her feet. It never occurred to the doctor that the battle might have something to do with her. What *did* occur was the possibility that the conflict might offer a distraction—an opportunity to escape.

She took two steps, heard a thump, and felt something hard ram the base of her spine. Sool knew without looking that one of the skins had jumped off the roof and landed behind her. Someone yelled, "There's too many of them! Pop the bitch!"

The first skin was about to reply when Morley Rix acquired the target he'd been looking for; let out a long, slow breath; and squeezed the trigger.

The Remington M42A1 sniper's rifle kicked his shoulder, sent a 7.62mm slug spinning through the air, and was soon ready to fire again.

However, there was no need, since the first bullet hit the skin between the shoulder blades and threw him forward off the top of the cube.

Sool heard the rifle shot, saw the body strike the muddy pavement in front of her, and twisted to the right. The movement saved her life.

The skin who had been standing behind the doctor had almost screwed up enough courage to shoot her in the back. When she moved, he swung his weapon accordingly.

That's when Manning, a .9mm in each hand, came around the corner, saw Sool turn, and fired both weapons.

Four of the slugs punched their way through the skin's chest, expanded to twice their original size, and blew large, overlapping holes out through his back.

Sool waited for the impact, didn't feel any, and turned to discover that she was still alive. She saw Manning, discovered that she couldn't generate the necessary words, and pointed instead.

The security chief saw the gesture, turned, and fired again.

The man, who had slipped in from the passageway that ran behind that particular row of cubes, looked surprised. *He* was the one who was supposed to kill people, not the other way around. His fingers went limp, the weapon clattered to the ground, and the sky seemed to wheel. The dirt came up to meet him.

There were more pistol shots from out front, followed by a burst of automatic fire from Wimba's machine gun and a squawk from Manning's radio. The voice belonged to Kell. "The area's secure, Chief. Well, mostly, so keep an eye out."

Manning acknowledged the transmission, returned one weapon to its holster, and slid a fresh magazine into the second. He looked at Sool. "Thanks, Doc, you saved my butt."

Sool, who was covered in filth and standing not ten feet from a bloody corpse, was surprised to discover that even under those circumstances she could feel attracted to Manning. Not only that, but there was time to think about how good he looked, even in rags, and to realize that to a large extent this was his kind of environment, just as a hospital was hers. Which meant that their functions were essentially opposed to each other. What was the attraction, then? Some sort of primitive alpha male thing? Or was she an overly analytical idiot with a run-on brain?

The physician opened her mouth to discover that she had regained the power of speech. "Thank *me*? No, I don't think so. I'd give you a big hug except that I doubt you'd want one."

Manning pretended to look her over. "You've got a point there, Doc. I'll take a rain check."

The radio burped static. It was Kell. "Time to amscray, Chief—the skins are cutting their way out."

"Casualties?"

"Pak got nicked—everyone else is okay."

Manning wanted to ask about his sister but resisted the temptation to do so. He held out a hand. "Come on, Doc, let's go home."

Sool stuck out her hand, saw how dirty it was, and tried to pull it back.

Manning saw the movement and stopped her. His hand was huge by comparison and seemed to consume hers. His eyes crinkled at the corners when he grinned. "Don't worry about it, hon. What's a little shit between friends?"

They left after that, and Sool, her hand still lost in Manning's, wondered how she could possibly feel so good.

ON PUGET SOUND NEAR HELL HILL

A few miles south of Hell Hill, where "night" still meant something, rain spattered against the patrol boat's windshield, and the vessel's engines burbled softly as one of the U.S. Navy's few remaining assets idled in a tiny bay known as Wildcat Cove. It was close to the hill—*too* close, really—but that was part of the charm. Who would look for something that wasn't supposed to exist in a place where it couldn't possibly be? No one, that's who. Getting there had required hours of painstaking navigation, working their way up the coast at what seemed like a crawl, often with no more than five or six feet of water under the hull, something that would have been impossible without the expertise supplied by the Crips.

Simmons stood on her tiny bridge and stared out into the darkness. She wore a bright orange dry suit in place of her uniform and was damned uncomfortable. Did that explain the rivulet of sweat that ran down the small of her back? Or was it the knowledge that this was *the* moment when the buck could no longer be passed, when officers, even *supply* officers, were forced to lead, and whatever would be would be? Was she up to it? At least three people believed that she was.

The crew, which consisted of only three people besides herself, were all volunteers. Darby had agreed to handle the wheel. A gentleman who went by the handle Lockjaw Joe was in charge of fire control, and a woman named Missy Jensen was their engineer.

One of the patrol boat's many virtues was the extent to which she was automated. Targets could be acquired, tracked, and destroyed all without human intervention. This was a real plus given the fact that Simmons had a crew who, with the exception of Darby, knew next to nothing about naval warfare.

The decision to attack during what should have been night, and mostly was, except for the area immediately surrounding Hell Hill's artificially lit topography, was no accident.

The first factor was the obvious matter of concealment, since high-tech detection equipment aside, there were still thousands of Kan eyeballs to consider. Eyeballs that, if given some daylight to work with, might deliver a warning.

Second, for reasons known only to the highly predictable Saurons, two of their supply vessels landed at about six o'clock each evening, were unloaded during the night, and lifted some eight hours later.

Those ships, plus the two or three that normally lay at anchor, made *very* juicy targets. So, given the fact that Simmons wanted to inflict the maximum amount of damage she could, there really was no choice. The attack would take place at night, before the patrol boat could be discovered.

The naval officer's thoughts were interrupted by the voice of the gaunt man who called himself Lockjaw Joe. He had once been employed as an air traffic controller. He was seated below and behind the bulkhead designed to protect the fire-control center from a direct hit on the bridge. The glow from the screens turned his normally white beard a sickly green color. His voice had the calm, seemingly neutral quality affected by pilots, surgeons, and military personnel everywhere.

"We have two bogies approaching from the north. They appear to be following standard Sauron landing protocols. Four blips are going out to meet them."

Simmons knew the "blips" were tugs. She reviewed the plan of attack for what seemed like the hundredth time. Deac Smith and his "trappers" had confirmed the fact that three Sauron spaceships lay at anchor. The trick was to nail the incoming vessels first and get in among the stationary targets before they knew what hit them. Wild though it seemed, she believed *that* part of the plan would work. But what about the Saurons lounging around in orbit? How long would it take them to react? And what would they do? The answers to those questions would make all the difference.

Simmons felt the desire to yawn, knew it was related to the fear she felt, and managed to suppress it. She had been trained for this—well, sort of—and now was the time to put that training to use. Never mind the fact that she was a supply officer, had never been in command of a ship before, and had never seen combat. She'd been to the Academy, had taken the necessary classes, and that should count for something.

"All right," the naval officer said quietly, conscious of the fact that she was addressing a mostly civilian crew, "if you aren't at your battle stations already, this would a good time to go there and strap yourselves in. All offensive and defensive weapons have been activated and are on-line. There is no such thing as a friendly, so we will attack anything that moves. Darby, take her out."

Darby felt her heart start to race as she braced her feet, advanced the throttles, and felt the bow start to rise. The dry suit chafed at her neck, but she didn't dare remove her hands from the chromed wheel. She was an electrician's mate, for God's sake, not a coxswain, and it would be easy to screw up.

The mufflers had been disengaged, the engines roared, and the petty officer kept her eyes glued to the display directly in front of her. The course, which had been entered by Simmons, appeared as a dotted line. All she had to do was follow it. Or, if everything went to hell in a handcart, do what she was told. The rest of it was there, including the coastline, the ships at anchor, and the incoming targets. The whole thing was like a video game, only real. Would she die? Yes, almost certainly, but there was an upside to the situation as well. Once dead, she'd never have to look in a mirror again!

The thought caused Darby to smile, but the scar tissue turned the expression into something that more closely resembled a snarl, and the boat started to fly.

OVER PUGET SOUND WEST OF HELL HILL

Perhaps if Tas-Teo had been making the landing for the first time, or if he had been slightly less arrogant, he might have taken the threat more seriously.

The information was certainly available on the screens in front of him. But it didn't seem threatening. Yes, some sort of surface craft *was* heading out into the bay, but so were the tugs. Just as they were supposed to be.

No, the Kan didn't know what the fast-moving target was, but there was no reason to be concerned. Haven had been pacified; more than that, it had been *crushed,* and the population enslaved.

Besides, if Tas-Teo made a big deal out of the unidentified surface craft, and it turned out to be something innocent, he'd never live it down.

Still, Tas-Teo was naturally cautious, and might have given the matter a little more thought had an especially strong gust of wind not chosen that exact moment to hit the tubby spacecraft from the west, forcing the pilot to take corrective action.

After fighting the heavily laden ship down through the last few hundred feet of rainswept atmosphere, all the Kan's attention was centered on the moment when the hull fell like a stone, and the supply vessel belly flopped into the water. Spray exploded upward and rained down onto the reentry-scarred hull.

A single glance at the screen to Tas-Teo's left was sufficient to confirm that the second craft, piloted by the taciturn Rog-Sre, had managed to land as well.

An audible alarm went off, Tas-Teo jerked his elongated head to the right, and lived just long enough to see himself die.

The missile's magnetron homing head was prewarmed, enabling the weapon's gyroscope to spin up. Then, with a target already selected, the missile's boost motor ignited; and the long, spearlike weapon shot out of its launcher, accelerated to just below the speed of sound, and pitched over into level flight. The radar homing head came on. The missile dropped to fewer than thirty feet above the water and raced toward its target.

Prior to impact there was one extremely brief moment during which Tas-Teo had an inkling of what was about to happen. But he lacked sufficient time to do anything about it. There was a crack of what sounded like thunder, followed by a flash of harsh, actinic light, and a myriad of splashes as debris.hit the water.

Up on the top of Hell Hill, the stonemaster looked up from his waterproofed plans; slaves paused in the middle of their tasks; and birds, no longer sure of when to sleep, fluttered out of the trees. The first shot had been fired.

ON PUGET SOUND NEAR HELL HILL

Part of Simmons' consciousness registered the explosion, felt the hull shudder as a second missile departed from the launcher, and knew that the first part of her plan was an unqualified success. There was satisfaction in that but no time to savor it. The patrol boat was doing more than twenty knots by the time it rounded what had once been known as Governor's Point and made for open water. There were more ships to attack, and it was her intention to destroy every one of them.

The plan by which Simmons intended to accomplish that goal was so venerable that Admiral Nelson would have understood and approved of it.

After rounding the point of land currently known as Hell Hill, the patrol boat would execute a high-speed turn to starboard and enter the bay where the remaining targets were moored to the south of Chuckanut Island.

Then, making use of the chain gun mounted on her bow, the naval vessel would pass between the innermost spaceships and the point, attack targets one and two, turn to port, and make a run from the southeast toward the northwest.

By doing so, it was the officer's hope that any shells that missed targets three and four would strike one and two, assuming they remained afloat.

Now, as Darby turned the wheel to starboard and as the deck started to tilt beneath her feet, the patrol boat entered the artificial light reflected down from orbit and she got a look at the area where the engagement would take place.

All of the ships had been secured to large white buoys, each of which mounted a mast and a blinking navigational light. They rode at their respective moorings like torpid water beetles, wallowing in the slight swell.

Echoes of the explosion were still dying away as dozens of tiny figures appeared on rain-slicked decks. Alerted by the noise that had penetrated even thick steel hulls, Kan crew members and Fon functionaries were eager to see whatever had taken place. An accident of some sort, most assumed, which would serve to break the monotony of their daily existence.

The oncoming patrol boat was clearly visible by then, but the majority of the aliens made the mistake of assuming that whatever the approaching vessel was, she had to be under Sauron control. Most stood where they were, sought to shade their eyes, and watched the naval vessel bear down on them.

There was an exception, however, a Kan who, due to the relatively low rank of his progenitors, was of low status himself. His name was Mor-Sud, and it took him little more than a single glance to evaluate the situation, draw the correct conclusion, and return belowdecks. In spite of the fact that the Sauron vessels had no secondary armament to speak of, the Kan had plenty of infantry weapons at grasper, including shoulder-launched missiles.

In the meantime, the oncoming patrol boat had pulled within what Simmons considered to be the kill zone. She grinned a wolfish grin, ordered Darby to "hold her steady," and gave the Gatling gun permission to fire.

What happened next had often been a source of amazement for those who had witnessed the sight before and most certainly impressed those Saurons fortunate enough to be watching from the summit of Hell Hill rather than from the decks of the cargo vessels below.

The chain gun roared like a mythical sea monster as it spit high-velocity slugs at the first target. Every sixth shell was a tracer, which drew a straight line between the patrol boat's bow and the alien spaceship.

The hull was strong, *very* strong, but not strong enough. Explosions sparkled across the surface of the ship's black hull, metal surrendered, and the shells forced their way inside, where they found the Sauron power plant. The resulting explosion was like a gigantic flashbulb going off as the stonemaster found himself temporarily blinded, and more than a thousand slaves put up a reedy cheer.

In spite of the fact that the cargo vessels were equipped with Ra 'Na–designed repulsor fields, they had never been intended for surface use, and were deactivated upon entering the atmosphere.

That didn't stop an enterprising Fon from activating the second ship's repulsor fields, however, an act that required the quick-thinking functionary to defeat no less than three safeties prior to pinching the correct control.

But, while stopping the incoming projectiles, just as the Sauron had hoped, the field also pushed the surrounding water away, proceeded to fail under a massive overload, and dropped the vessel into a hole of its own making. More than a dozen Saurons were swept from its decks. None knew how to swim.

The waters of Puget Sound rushed back in, found the open hatches, and gushed through. There were locks, however, strongbox-shaped compartments intended for use in space, which served to keep the water at bay.

With its hull still intact, the ship popped up out of the water like a superbuoyant cork, seemed to pause a couple of feet above the surface of Chuckanut Bay, and exploded when a pair of surface-to-surface missiles slammed into its fully exposed hull.

The bright orange and red flower had yet to fade when Lockjaw yelled, "Yahoo!" and Darby turned the ship to port. Two targets down—and two to go. They had been lucky, very lucky, but how long could that luck hold? And why did she care? Because she wanted to live, that's why—ugly face and all.

The sudden realization caused her to grip the wheel even more tightly and to squint at the rain-smeared windshield. She didn't need the computer display anymore, not with the bay lit up like hell's belly, and target three dead ahead.

Mor-Sud was back on deck by that time, the missile launcher resting on his shoulder, the firing bulb clasped within the confines of his right pincer.

The target filled the targeting grid, the missile's onboard computer memorized the image, and the Kan squeezed the bulb.

The launcher jerked as the missile leaped out of its tube, and the Kan watched it go. There had been no time in which to fetch a reload, or to recruit someone to help, so all he could do was hope.

The period between launch and impact was so short that the sounds of the buzzer and of the explosion melded. The patrol boat shuddered as the impact punched a hole through the lightly armored superstructure.

Simmons died instantly as a shard of metal tore her head off, and Lockjaw followed a fraction of a second later when the carefully shaped explosion destroyed the forward bulkhead and consumed the fire-control center.

Darby, her hands still on the wheel, felt cold rain pepper her face as it was sucked in through the badly shattered windshield. She was amazed to discover that she was still alive, glanced to the left, saw her commanding officer's decapitated body, and knew she was on her own.

Well, not entirely on her own, since Missy was babbling incomprehensible nonsense from the engine room, but essentially so, since there was no time to discuss the situation.

Deprived of computer control and locked in place, the Gatling gun continued to send a stream of slugs off to what the still-functioning compass said was the west. A long line of miniature geysers showed where the shells were wasting themselves on the surface of the bay.

Darby jerked the wheel to starboard, saw the tracer line up with target three, and watched with grim satisfaction as the Saurons fell like wheat to a scythe.

One of them, empty launcher still on his shoulder, was literally cut in half.

Then, before any of the shells could punch their way through the spaceship's hull, the chain gun abruptly quit. Not because of a jam, or a power failure, but because it had run out of ammo.

With nothing left to fight with beyond the hull itself, all Darby could do was line the bow up with target three and lock the course into the autopilot. The spaceship's crew were trying to cast off, but Darby didn't think they'd make it.

She yelled into the intercom, told Missy to bail out, and followed her own advice.

The Sauron vessel was no more than two hundred feet away when Darby left the patrol boat's wheel, dived through the half-slagged remains of the port hatch, and hit the fifty-degree water.

She was still under, still kicking her way to the surface, when the patrol boat hit the spaceship, punched a hole through its hull, and triggered an explosion.

The fireball seemed to rise, to float upward, before collapsing in on itself.

The stonemaster was still staring, his mouth open, when the communicators started to buzz and vibrate. Hak-Bin had been alerted, had seen the final denouement, and wanted some answers. Five ships destroyed and one badly damaged. How could something like that happen?

The conversation, if that's what the one-way diatribe could properly be called, would be anything but pleasant. The Zin steeled himself against the coming onslaught, brought the device to his ear hole, and said, "Yes, lord."

Meanwhile, out in the bay, protected by the dry suit, the sole

surviving member of the patrol boat's crew swam toward Chuckanut Island. Supplies had been pre-positioned there. Providing
that Darby kept her head down, she had a chance to survive,
something she now wanted to do. She put her head down, kicked
with her feet, and swam for shore. The Battle of Bellingham was
over—and the U.S. Navy had won.

7

DEATH DAY MINUS 98

SATURDAY, APRIL 25, 2020

Since a politician never believes what he says, he is quite surprised to be taken at his word.

—CHARLES DE GAULLE,
in Ernest Mignon, *Les Mots du Général*, 1962

ABOARD THE SAURON DREADNOUGHT *HOK NOR AH*

The sixty-foot-tall structure specially constructed for the occasion rose to occupy most of the space once used by Ra 'Na merchants for recreational purposes. It was gray and accessed via a spiral ramp that started at deck level and wound its way up to a flat top. There, an old-fashioned forge had been established and the steel rods nestled in their red-orange coals.

More than a thousand Saurons stood on the balconies, platforms, and galleries that overlooked the structure and waited for the ceremony to begin. The vast majority of the audience consisted of Zin, but there were representatives of the lesser castes as well, brought in to act as witnesses.

The ritual known as the "cleansing by pain" predated the time when the Saurons had captured their first ships and started the long journey through space.

Originally, according to racial memories, and the account found in the Book of Life, those subjected to the "cleansing by pain" had been required to make a long trek though a dangerous wasteland prior to their final atonement at the summit of an extinct volcano.

Now, in keeping with the realities of shipboard life, the ordeal was shorter but no less painful. This was a fact not lost on Hak-Bin, who, after putting no fewer than five of his most senior military officers to death for dereliction of duty, was honorbound to pay his own terrible price.

Had a human anthropologist been present, and privy to the proceedings, he or she would have been amazed to learn that the possibility of avoiding such punishment had not even occurred to Hak-Bin. In spite of the ordeal ahead, he preferred any amount of pain to the shame attendant to failure. How else could the slave attack and subsequent losses possibly be described?

It also hadn't occurred to Hak-Bin, not even for a second, that the five officers might have preferred the ritual to death. In his opinion, they hadn't deserved a second chance.

If some of the Kan considered that to be hypocritical, they lacked the courage to say so.

Hak-Bin, stripped of all clothing, stood at the foot of the ramp and waited for the deep, resonant moan of the great battle horn. Once it came, he started the long, shameful journey to the top of the artificial mountain.

The necessity to walk, to shuffle his way to the top, was part of the punishment, as was the knowledge that his nymph would remember the humiliation of the moment.

Slowly, leaning into the slope, Hak-Bin completed his first turn around the mountain and started the second. Some of the galleries were so close he could have touched them.

The sound, a sort of growl, was born at the back of a thousand throats and gradually built in intensity until the structure beneath Hak-Bin's feet started to vibrate in sympathy.

The Zin felt pleasure surge through his body. Here was the hatred, the disgust, and the contempt he sought.

A Kan stomped his foot, others joined, and the thumps came at three-second intervals. They were loud, very loud, and introduced a percussive element to the symphony of shame.

Now, as each circling grew shorter and as the Zin approached the summit, he could smell the acrid smoke produced by the ancient forge. He felt the first pang of fear. It was one thing to fail, and subsequently be cleansed, but another to reveal the slightest sign of weakness. Because, strange though it might have seemed to a race like the Ra 'Na, the ordeal now under way could actually *strengthen* Hak-Bin's position, depending on the manner in which he managed to endure it.

Could he handle the pain? Would he cry out? No, such a possibility was too awful to consider.

The painmaster stood with arms crossed while the tools of his horrible trade continued to rest in the forge from which so many famous blades had been pulled. Hak-Bin saw that the other Zin's glossy black chitin was pitted where sparks from innumerable fires had burned through the outermost layers of his exoskeleton.

The painmaster took pride in Hak-Bin's obvious strength and reveled in the knowledge that this precious moment would be passed to all of his descendants. Hak-Bin conquered the summit, shuffled the last few steps, and came to a halt.

The foot stomping grew even more frenzied as the painmaster waited for the noise to peak. Then, when the bedlam could grow no louder, the painmaster raised a pincer.

The Saurons, all of whom had been waiting for the gesture, brought their feet down one last time. The silence that ensued seemed to make the moment that much more dramatic.

There was no need for dialogue, no need for speech, since every being present knew the reason for Hak-Bin's journey of atonement. As did some who *weren't* present, such as the Ra 'Na Council of Dros, who, thanks to tiny cameras sprinkled all about the area, were watching from other parts of the ship.

One such group included Fra Pol, who, because of his role in the resistance movement, was accorded special privileges. Rather than the pleasure some of those around him evidenced, Pol felt a sense of fear.

How, the cleric wondered, could he and the rest of his race possibly hope to win their freedom from rulers so strong, so determined, that their leader would voluntarily submit himself to the most extreme sort of torture? The very notion of it suddenly seemed absurd. Perhaps the Saurons were superior, just as they claimed to be.

Unaware that his actions were being televised but conscious of the surrounding silence, the painmaster uttered the words everyone was waiting for: "The penitent will take his place."

Careful lest the fear in his belly somehow betray him, Hak-Bin ordered his feet to carry him into the waiting framework. Originally made of wood but now constructed of metal, the structure was intended to give the penitent something to hang on to.

Now, with something to grab with his pincers, and the waiting nearly over, Hak-Bin felt a bit better. All that stood between him and absolution were three ritual wounds, one for each branch of the Sauron race. Then, with his conscience clear and his authority intact, he would emerge victorious. The pleasure of that would be worth the suffering.

Satisfied that the necessary formalities had been observed, the painmaster turned to his forge. It was a crude device, like the society that produced it, but adequate to his needs. Heating the metal was relatively easy, but applying the instrument to a living, breathing subject—now, *that* required skill, something few if any of the onlookers could fully appreciate. It was the painmaster's task to push the implements through the subject's chitin with sufficient force to reach the underlying nerve fibers, but not so far as to cause permanent damage or result in death.

The Sauron grasped one of the rods, pulled it from the glowing coals, and waved it in the air. A tendril of smoke made S shapes over his head and served to prove how hot the steel really was.

Then, moving with precision born of long practice, the painmaster stepped forward. There was a hiss of indrawn breath as the onlookers imagined the agony of the first touch. Hak-Bin, muscles rigid, watched the painmaster's approach. Suddenly the crowd was gone and his entire being was focused on the red-tipped rod, the warmth that caressed the underside of his chin, and the pressure against his thorax.

Hak-Bin smelled the harsh odor of his own burned chitin, felt the hard outer covering give, and experienced a burst of almost unbearable agony.

It was worse than anything he had ever experienced before. It took his breath away and required every ounce of his self-control to contain the scream that tried to find its way out of his throat.

Then the pressure and the worst of the pain was gone as the painmaster withdrew the implement and dropped it into a pan of cold water. Steam hissed. Hak-Bin experienced a moment of vertigo and struggled to remain upright. One down—two to go.

Elsewhere, in another part of the ship, a contingent of Ra 'Na sat and watched. Dro Rul, who was seated to Pol's right, motioned toward the screen in front of them. "*If* we hope to win, *if* we want our freedom, we must be as strong as they are."

Pol knew the prelate was correct and nodded mutely, but couldn't imagine passing that particular test. In fact, somewhere deep down, the cleric knew that had it not been for what they had discovered regarding the Sauron life cycle, and the inevitable crisis ahead, he might have adopted the same collaborationist stance Tog favored. But they *did* know, and the hatching *would* come, which meant that the necessary strength would have to be found.

Hak-Bin watched as the painmaster turned, felt the weight of more than two thousand eyes, and braced his body against the pain to come.

This was the *second* rod, the one that symbolically belonged to the Kan, and that would be inserted into the opposite side of his thorax.

Chitin started to melt before the metal even touched the surface of his chest. Rather than wait for the implement's excruciating touch, Hak-Bin pushed his body forward, thereby taking the rod into himself.

Caught unawares, and concerned lest the Zin do himself permanent harm, the painmaster managed to arrest his forward motion.

The crowd, impressed by the extent of their leader's courage, stomped their feet in approval as the second rod was withdrawn and the third was removed from the forge.

Now, his body self-anesthetized by naturally produced painkillers, Hak-Bin came face to face with his own great-great-grandprogenitor, a much-storied individual who frequently appeared in dreams. "Take the third touch, my son, and with it the knowledge that life flows from death and that you will join us soon."

The Sauron jerked slightly as the last rod was forced into his body, waited for the hiss of the steam, and, in keeping with long-established precedent, allowed himself to go. Blissful darkness claimed the Zin as a thousand feet hit the deck in unison and the crowd expressed its approval. Had he been conscious, had he been able to hear, Hak-Bin would have been proud.

HELL HILL

The stonemaster stood in the harsh black shadow cast by five closely spaced crucifixes and stared at the slaves grouped in front of him. There were fifty, give or take, half male, half female, all dressed in filthy rags. Crow food really, or what should have been crow food, except for one important detail: This particular group of slaves had skills the likes of which were nowhere to be found. Not among the Ra 'Na, not among the Zin, and certainly not among the illiterate Kan and Fon.

When interrogated, this particular group of humans variously described themselves as engineers and architects, words that didn't translate into the Sauron language. But he had learned to associate those words with slaves who, truth be told, knew more about construction than *he* did, and had already proved their worth to such an extent that when they suddenly stopped working, the stonemaster had resisted the urge to kill them. A most unusual indulgence indeed.

The humans blanched under the strength of his stare but showed no signs of capitulation. That in spite of the fact that their demands were patently absurd. Not only did the thankless wastrels want a larger ration of food, they also wanted him to divide the day into *three* shifts rather than two.

The only problem was that with their help the Zin had been able to make up six of the thirty-seven days that the project was behind. Not only that, but the feat had been accomplished without resorting to proscribed technology. Simple levers, pulleys, and ramps had been employed to save labor and time.

The result was an impasse that the stonemaster was now attempting to resolve. Perhaps the slave that the Zin thought of as Hak-Bin's ruka, or pet, would be able to talk some sense into his fellow creatures. If so, then good. If not, it would be a simple matter to have the entire lot of them killed. The Zin turned to a Fon assistant. His tone was testy. "So where is he? Now means *now*."

The Fon, a somewhat dull individual named Por-Das, had already done everything in his power to summon the slave, up to and including the provision of ground transport. What more could the stonemaster want? Por-Das made a show of peering out over the rampart. Much to his surprise and delight, it appeared that the human had arrived. He managed to keep his voice flat as though the matter had never been in question. "The slave and his party have arrived, lord. I will go to meet them."

The Zin waved a dismissive pincer, and the lesser being hurried away.

Two terraces down, where the road looped around the base of what would eventually become a fifty-foot-tall monolith, Franklin, along with Jina, Manning, Amocar, and Kell left the confines of the vehicle sent to fetch them and prepared to ascend a long flight of stairs. The partially completed citadel loomed above.

Franklin squinted into the rising sun, wondered why the stonemaster had sent for him, and felt a tendril of fear snake into his stomach. There was no such thing as safety or peace. Not anymore. Every moment of every day was dangerous, and the reality of it wore on him.

Appearances *were* important, however, so Franklin plastered a look of self-confident calm on his face and tackled the stairs. The steps were made out of the same limestone as the structure above. They were both broad but shallow, to accommodate Sauron physiology. Franklin took them three at a time.

In the meantime, the slaves who had been working under the direction of human architects and engineers were momentarily idle. They lined both sides of the stairway. Though not clear on the details, they knew something was up, and were naturally curious. Why had work been allowed to stop? And when would it start again? There was no way to know.

Some of the slaves spit at Franklin as he made his way upward, but most simply stood there, too exhausted to be more than mildly curious, eyes empty of hope.

Manning, along with the other members of the security team, tried to screen Franklin lest someone throw a rock, or attack the chief executive with a shovel. But there were *hundreds* of slaves, more than enough to roll the presidential party under had the onlookers mustered the will to do so. No, it was the presence of Kan warriors that kept the workers under control, not the relatively puny force under Manning's command.

Franklin looked up and saw a Fon at the top of the stairs. Judging from the harakna hide whip in his right pincer, the functionary was an overseer. The Sauron acknowledged the human with a nod and used the whip as a pointer. The words were stiff and formal. "The stone master awaits."

Franklin was about to reply when someone shouted his name. He turned in the direction of the sound and saw a woman dash between a pair of warriors and run straight at him. Her physical appearance had changed, but the voice was unmistakable. "Alexander! It's me! Marie!"

Maria Alvarez-Santo had been the state superintendent of public works, a fine civil servant, and a good friend.

Franklin smiled and opened his arms to receive her, but Alvarez-Santo never made it that far. The whip, wielded with considerable skill by Por-Das, caught the woman around an ankle and sent her sprawling.

Manning, who had been ready to shoot her, returned his weapon to its holster.

The slaves, conditioned by weeks of cruelty, took a step backward.

But Franklin, angered by what the Sauron had done to one of his friends, stepped forward. It was only then, after he was committed, that the politician realized that the Fon had already flipped the whip back over his right shoulder and was prepared to strike again.

Franklin opened his mouth to object, but it was too late. The fifteen-foot length of neatly braided leather cut through the air and made a cracking sound as it struck Franklin's chest.

He staggered under the impact, heard himself grunt, but managed to keep his feet. Manning stepped forward, but Franklin shook his head and held his arms out. There were Kan all around, and the slightest hint of resistance could get everyone killed. The security chief obeyed but allowed his hand to hover over the holstered .9mm handgun.

Careful to maintain his balance, Franklin took three steps forward and held out his hand. Alvarez-Santo took it, allowed the ex-governor to pull her up, and managed a shaky smile. "Thank you."

The Fon, who was unsure of how the stonemaster would react to the unprecedented situation, coiled his whip.

The onlookers eyed each other in surprise. Franklin, the man many of them liked to refer to as "Frankenstein," had stepped in front of the overseer's whip. That took balls, *big* balls, the kind a real leader would have.

But to what end? There had been other acts of defiance, as evidenced by the triple rows of crosses that now encircled the top of the hill. Perhaps Franklin would join them.

Eyes shifted as a squad of heavily armed Kan emerged from the bottom of the citadel and jumped downhill. Once in place, they formed a loose circle. The crowd fell back.

The stonemaster completed the trip in two hops and landed on gravel. Stones skittered away from his pod like feet. If the Zin had seen the altercation, he gave no sign of it. His eyes met Franklin's. "So," the Sauron said with a growl, "you came."

"Yes, lord," Franklin said evenly, struggling to ignore the way his chest burned. "What can I do for you?"

"Some of the slaves are more useful than others," the Sauron replied, "but refuse to work."

"We *can't* work," Alvarez-Santo put in stolidly. "Not without more food and rest. A dart would be more merciful. Go ahead, order the Kan to kill us."

"You see?" the stonemaster demanded querulously. "They make demands! As if *they* are the overseers and *we* are the slaves!"

Franklin raised an eyebrow. Blood stained his otherwise immaculate shirt. Jina tried to come to his aid, but he waved her back. He gestured to Alvarez-Santo. "She has a point, lord. Look at her body; it's wasting away. In weeks, a month at most, she will die."

The politician gestured to the hollow-eyed crowd. "Hundreds, perhaps thousands will die, and to what end? Who will build your temple when they are gone? The Fon? The Kan? The Ra 'Na? No, I don't think so."

The stonemaster paid little if any attention to slaves under normal circumstances. But now, standing among them, it was easy to see the way in which some of his prime workers had started to lose a substantial amount of body mass.

Yes, more arrived with each passing day, and *yes,* most could handle unskilled tasks, but only a small minority had the kind of skills that could make up for lost time.

Still, there was his honor to consider, not to mention that of his race, and the stonemaster could never capitulate. Especially now, in front of so many witnesses. His predecessors, who so liked to dominate his dreams, were uncharacteristically mute. Opinionated though they were, none sought to advise him now.

A crow cawed, a Sauron shuttle etched a line across the sky, and someone coughed. Franklin knew he should say something, *anything,* to prolong the dialogue, but nothing came. It was as though the weight of all those stares had squeezed everything out of his mind. Time stretched long and thin.

"He *needs* us," Alvarez-Santo said from the side of her mouth, prompting the chief executive, just as she had during confrontations with the legislature. "Especially the engineers. See what you can get."

Something about the way the woman put it, as if the whole situation were part of the latest budget battle, put Franklin's brain back into motion. The arguments, plus the best way to present them, bubbled up from deep inside. He gestured to the translator that hung from the Sauron's neck. "That's a marvelous device, my lord, but machines are subject to malfunctions. In an effort to maintain their health, and thereby ensure that the temple is completed on schedule, the workers meant to make *suggestions,* nothing more. If the translation was flawed, and conveyed the wrong impression, they beg your forgiveness."

The peace offering bordered on the absurd, and would have been rejected out of pincer had it not been for the desperate state of affairs that the stonemaster found himself in. He pretended to consider. "There is some truth to what you say," the Zin allowed, glaring at the nearest technician, "especially where Ra 'Na machines are concerned. They fail with amazing regularity. Almost as if the miserable little fur balls *want* them to fall apart."

The technician who had been singled out did her best to look innocent, wondered how much the Sauron had managed to divine, and wondered if she would live to see the sun set.

"So," the stonemaster continued, "assuming some sort of malfunction, a *suggestion* of the sort that you describe might be tolerated, especially in support of Sauron goals. With that in mind I am prepared to grant the slaves another bowl of soup each day, together with two additional units of sleep."

An offer had been tendered, and, true to the culture he'd been raised in, Franklin was about to make a counteroffer when the stonemaster raised a cautionary pincer. "Careful, human, lest you push me too far."

The politician looked at the semicircle of Kan warriors and tried to remember when they had raised their weapons. Earlier? Or just now? He risked a nod in place of a bow. "Thank you, lord. I can assure you that the additional food and rest represent an excellent investment."

The Sauron latched on to the human phraseology with something akin to lust. *"An investment."* That's the way he would present the agreement to Hak-Bin. He glared at the slaves. "Well? What are you waiting for? Get to work."

Slowly, as if wading through gelatin, the slaves turned away. The truth was that they had received far more than they had expected to. Food, rest, but most of all, hope.

But the agreement had other implications as well. The tale of Franklin's bravery had already started to spread from one slave to the next, a Ra 'Na technician carried the story up into orbit, Amocar made his report, and a legend was born.

■ ■ ■

The Fon functionary hopped along the twisting, turning streets as if he owned them, which, along with the rest of his kind, he essentially did. Not *big* hops, mere fifteen-footers, which ate distance but conserved energy. Humans hurried to get of his way, even going so far as to jump into doorways, and in one case, dive through a window. The Sauron hardly noticed.

Bal-Lok was a traitor to his race, a fact that made him feel powerful one moment and terrified the next. Suddenly, after a lifetime of subservience, he, along with all the rest of his newly literate brothers, were on a par with the Zin.

Yes, the total number of Fon functionaries who had learned to read and write via the human-sponsored literacy campaign was relatively small, but that didn't alter the fact that their capacity to learn had been proven. And oh, what they had learned!

Not Bal-Lok, because his duties lay elsewhere, but brother Cal-Rum, who worked for the stonemaster himself. He had been able to surreptitiously gain access to most of the Zin's scrolls, tablets, and books.

By reading during the stonemaster's twice-daily naps, at great risk to his own life, Cal-Rum had uncovered any number of interesting pieces of information—including the fact that rather than being created by the Zin, as the ruling class had claimed for so long, alien missionaries had given the alphabet to the Sauron race as a gift. This was something that the Fon and the Kan had been encouraged to forget.

Of equal interest was the fact that the "missionaries" had actually landed on the Sauron planet looking for certain raw materials. Having located them, they quickly set about imposing their religion and values on the natives, whom they regarded as savages.

A bit of arrogance for which they paid when a sizable group of tan-colored natives attacked their settlement, killed their soldiers, and seized their spaceships. They were the *first* spaceships in the long, glorious journey that continued still.

Bal-Lok and his brethren realized that they would have to constantly relearn these facts lest they forget and lapse back into ignorance.

It was all very interesting but nothing when compared to the *real* news—the entire Sauron race was about to die, or be reborn, depending on how much of the Zins' carefully dispensed excreta one chose to believe. Rather than constructing temples, as they'd been told, the Fon were actually hard at work on vast death-birth chambers, which, if everything went as planned, would produce another generation of Fon destined to suffer a lifetime of servitude.

Well, not if *he* could help it. There was nothing Bal-Lok could do to prevent his own death. He knew that, but what of his nymph? *That* was another matter.

It—no, *he*—would be born into a world where Fon and Zin were equals, where his caste would no longer bear the brunt of the work, and the *true* slaves, beings like the humans, would shoulder the increased load.

But that meant taking steps to ensure that Zin nymphs were prevented from assuming control, that Fon nymphs were taught to read and write, and that enough members of the servant races would survive to take care of all the work.

Fortunately for Bal-Lok, not to mention his more enlightened brothers, a group existed that was perfect for the task. For reasons Bal-Lok couldn't understand, the Star Communion worshiped the very race that had enslaved them. Still, they were well organized, and, if provided with the right incentives, could monitor the birth process.

If he could connect with them, *if* they would agree, and *if* he could escape capture by the Zin named Xat-Hey—a frightening individual who, if his Ra 'Na informant was correct, had already been dispatched to the planet's surface.

Was his name on the enforcer's list? The informant thought so, and the fact that the enterprising Cal-Rum hadn't been seen in more than four planetary cycles seemed to support the assertion. Arrests, when they took place, were rarely announced.

Bal-Lok gave an involuntary shudder as he thought about the manner in which a Kan interrogator could peel chitin off, one segment at a time. He knew that no one could remain silent for long.

Yes, odds were that Cal-Rum had been apprehended by the stonemaster or one of his aides and subjected to torture. So Bal-Lok had deserted his job, and now, with help from the humans, hoped to live underground. No, *would* live underground, for the sake of all Fon to come.

A human appeared below, failed to detect the fact that an airborne Fon was falling out of the sky, and went facedown in the mud as Bal-Lok landed squarely on his shoulders.

Bal-Lok, his superiority affirmed, continued on his way. The next leap carried him fifteen feet down the street. He was a Fon, and for the first time in his life, the knowledge felt good.

■ ■ ■

Jonathan Ivory ducked out of the murky depths of the shop that he and his followers had established on the second level of Flat Top, and squinted into the bright sunlight. He heard the strange, high-speed whine typical of Sauron shuttles. A pair of heavily armed skinheads took up positions to his right and left.

Shading his eyes, just as many other bystanders were doing, Ivory peered in the direction of the sound. The Sauron aircraft came in from the north, lost altitude, and released a blizzard of white. It looked like the chit propaganda machine had been put into high gear once again. What now? Ivory wondered. Take a Sauron home for dinner day? Nothing would surprise him anymore.

Toilet paper was hard to come by. So even though the talkies weren't very absorbent, people nonetheless scrambled to capture the falling leaflets.

Rather than join the fray, which might have compromised his dignity, Ivory waited for a bodyguard to fetch a flyer. The touch activated a likeness of a stern Sauron who was halfway through the message by the time Ivory received it. ". . . Therefore President Franklin will make an appearance at Food Depot Three near the community in Hilman. He will visit Yakima after that, followed by . . ."

Ivory crumpled the sheet into a ball. The voice continued to speak but was muffled now. He wasn't even aware of it as his mind raced ahead. Now, like a gift from God, came the information he needed: Franklin would be in Hilman, Washington, on May 4!

By hitting Franklin, and doing so in a public place, the White Rose would not only eliminate the Sauron puppet, they would also lend support to the claim that racialist freedom fighters had destroyed the Sauron spaceships out on Puget Sound. An assertion which, lacking any evidence to the contrary, a significant number of people actually believed.

Certain of what he must do, and happier than he had been for a long time, Ivory handed the ball of paper to a needy-looking woman, patted her shoulder, and smiled. "Here you go, ma'am. Make good use of it."

ABOARD THE SAURON DREADNOUGHT *HOK NOR AH*
As Dro Tog emerged from the clandestine meeting and eased his way into the normal flow of foot traffic, he felt hungry, confused, and more than a little scared.

The first sensation was a familiar one, and the direct result of Dro Rul's parsimonious ways, but the other two were unusual. That's what he liked about the status quo, the certainty of it, the comfort associated with certainty.

Much to Tog's astonishment, it seemed as if the entire Council of Dromas had succumbed to Fra Pol's deluded rantings and were now prepared to risk their lives fighting an ill-conceived war for freedom. No, more than that, they were risking *his* life as well. And for no good reason. But what, if anything, could be done about it?

A Ra 'Na technician bowed respectfully as the cleric passed, and Tog raised a bejeweled hand by way of response. The interaction served to remind the prelate of his responsibility to the entire species, most of whom had no idea what the Council was up to.

Tog arrived at his quarters, said "hello" to the comely Mys, and headed for the tranquillity of his study.

Mys watched the Dro pass, smiled, and returned to her work.

Tog stepped through the hatch. But, in place of the peace he sought, the prelate discovered that P'ere Has was there, lying in wait. The Dro knew that Mys had not only neglected to warn him, but also that she enjoyed the omission. It was too late to escape, however—Tog had little choice but to drop into his favorite chair and treat his subordinate to a "What are you doing here, and you'd better make it quick" stare.

Has, who knew the look well, wasted no time launching into a litany of complaints. It wasn't long before it became apparent that every one of them had one thing in common: Fra Pol.

Not only had the wayward initiate failed to teach devotionals to the fourth form, as he had been instructed to do, but rarely attended church services himself, and when questioned regarding his dereliction of duty, refused to divulge where he had been and what he'd been doing.

Tog did his best to produce the sort of stern, judgmental expression that his subordinate had every right to expect. But he was far from surprised. Given the fact that Has wasn't privy to the supersecret deliberations taking place within the Council of Dromas, he had no way to know about Pol's activities on the Council's behalf and was understandably upset.

It occurred to Tog that he could sympathize and offer up some empty platitudes. Or, and the idea seemed to supernova within the Ra 'Na's brain, he could use Has to put things right. His frown, and the sigh that followed, conveyed deep concern along with something like paternal exasperation.

"I'm sorry to hear that Fra Pol has been such a burden for you, P'ere Has. Not often, mind you, but once in a while, we run into a brother or a sister who, in spite of our best efforts to guide him or her toward spiritual and moral redemption, decides to walk the path toward darkness instead. Unfortunately, based on the information provided by you, it pains me to conclude that Fra Pol falls into the latter category."

P'ere Has, who had fully expected to be ignored, and would have been happy to settle for nothing more than a little heartfelt sympathy, felt a sudden sense of alarm. While he was undisciplined, there was no evidence to suggest that Fra Pol had chosen "the path toward darkness." Whatever that meant. But he had made his complaints, and there was no way to retract the words without seeming disingenuous. They could be softened, however, and Has hurried to do so. "Well, yes, your excellency, but there may be extenuating—"

Tog held up his hand. "No, P'ere Has, while your attempt to intercede on Fra Pol's behalf speaks of a generous spirit, Pol *must* be disciplined. Besides, unbeknownst to you, I have evidence that the brother has dabbled in the darker arts, and even more distressing, has plotted to overthrow the Saurons. Why, on one occasion he went so far as to listen in on one of their most secret meetings! A subversive activity that could rain destruction down upon all of us."

Has was not sure what "the darker arts" were, but the phrase had an ominous quality, and he was afraid to ask. Not that he needed to; plotting against the Saurons was bad enough. "How can I help, your excellency?"

Tog made a tent with his fingers. "Rather than deal with the matter directly, I suggest that we provide the Saurons with the right amount of information and allow *them* to take the necessary steps. What do *you* think?"

The proposal was not as novel as it seemed. Though they never discussed it openly, the Ra 'Na hierarchy had taken advantage of the same strategy in the past, and to good effect.

Moreover, it was the first time that Tog had asked for his opinion, and the glory of the moment momentarily blinded Has as to the consequences of his words. "An excellent idea, your excellency."

"Good. We're in agreement then. Return in two units. I will provide you with the necessary documentation."

It was a clear dismissal, and Tog spoke as Has rose to leave. "One more thing . . ."

"Yes, your excellency?"

"This arrangement is to remain between you and me. You will share it with no one. Is that clear?"

"Yes, your excellency."

"Good. You may go. Tell Mys to fetch my lunch. I'm hungry."

■ ■ ■

Hak-Bin was naked from the waist up. He examined himself in the full-length mirror. Thanks to repeated applications of oil, most of his chitin had reacquired its glossy sheen, with the exception of the recently acquired wounds that is, which, thanks to a substance developed by the Ra 'Na, were sealed with blobs of artificial filler. The fact that the repairs served to emphasize the holes, thereby highlighting his bravery, was an enjoyable plus.

His attire consisted of the usual pleated black skirt, metal necklace, and utility belt. He looked good in it, or thought he did, which added to his confidence.

And confidence was important. Especially when dealing with the likes of Xat-Hey, one of the few Saurons of whom Hak-Bin was genuinely afraid. Though technically a Zin, Xat-Hey had the instincts of a Kan and a well-honed aptitude for violence. The latter made him both a tool *and* a threat.

Hak-Bin pushed the thought away, marched past a groveling Ra 'Na servant, and paused while the hatch whirred up and out of the way. Xat-Hey had been waiting for ten units by then, not much compared to what Hak-Bin put most visitors through, but sufficient to establish dominance.

Now, as he approached his work area, the Zin had already slipped into the cold, calculating persona that long-dead mentors had coached him to assume, and was prepared to bend another Sauron to his will. Something he did with almost boring regularity.

That was his plan, but Xat-Hey was different, *very* different—independent, unpredictable, and irreverent. As Hak-Bin entered his work area, he discovered that Xat-Hey had commandeered his desk *and* the controls integral to it. Now, as the silver spheres chased each other about the room, the Zin felt a sudden surge of anger—anger he would have to control if he was to obtain what he wanted.

Xat-Hey, who had very acute hearing—not to mention an equally acute understanding of how to manipulate his host's emotions—allowed one of the globes to collide with an intricately decorated bulkhead. It was a bulkhead that, in spite of its Ra 'Na origins, Hak-Bin secretly admired. Xat-Hey uttered the Sauron equivalent of "oops!" and spoke without turning his head. "You've got some nice toys, my lord. I should drop by more often."

Hak-Bin was about to say that the light globes weren't "toys," managed to suppress the comment, and looked for the means to gain control of the situation. "That's not very likely, given the kind of assignments you receive. How long was that reconnaissance mission, anyway? Ten standard years?"

The comment, a direct reminder that Xat-Hey had been sentenced to the Zin equivalent of prison, and been allowed to return only after Hak-Bin had decided to issue the requisite orders, was sufficient to bring the Zin around. For the moment, anyway. Xat-Hey backed out of the chair, rose, and moved toward a guest sling. "Mind if I sit down? Thanks. Yes, it's been a long time. *Too* long."

"You were lucky," Hak-Bin replied sternly as he reclaimed his rightful place. "Murder cannot be condoned. Especially where Zin are concerned. Zin may be executed, if absolutely necessary, but never murdered."

"The worthless piece of Dra deserved it," Xat-Hey replied easily. "He was a slave-lover—and a traitor to his caste."

There was more to it than that, of course, since the enmity that led up to the unfortunate Zin's death had been born hundreds of years before, and kept alive by the ghosts who haunted Xat-Hey's sleep. But everyone had ghosts, some of whom were quite unpleasant, and most managed to ignore such rantings. No, there was no excuse for what Xat-Hey had done, but little profit in saying so. "Perhaps," Hak-Bin allowed evenly, "but due process is important. Ignore it at your peril."

Xat-Hey allowed himself a long, slow smile. It was as if he already knew what he would be called upon to do, and in so knowing, could call Hak-Bin a hypocrite. His words were heavy with sarcasm. "Yes, lord, whatever you say, lord. What can I do for you, and through you, for the good of our species?"

Unable to find any wiggle room, Hak-Bin found that he was

forced to explain why *this* particular series of murders was different and therefore justified.

"With each passing day I receive reports of more early changers. We identify most before they realize anything is amiss, and having done so, are able to take them out of circulation. But some are so selfish as to run.

"As you know, Citadel Three is south of the planet's equator. Rather than turn himself in, an individual named Sil-Wat hid in the jungle and started to give birth. He radioed for help. Three Kan were dispatched, encountered the nymph, and called on the resident stonemaster for advice. He went out alone, managed to kill the Kan, but couldn't locate the nymph. We assume it died in the jungle, but there's no way to be sure.

"Such episodes are sad, and more than a little disheartening, but secrecy is paramount. There's no telling what the lesser castes might do if information regarding the birthing were to be prematurely released. Not to mention the effect it would have on the local slave population."

"Yes," Xat-Hey said, eyeing the wounds that decorated his superior's chest. "I hear they can be quite unruly."

Rather than confront the sarcasm, and the obvious reference to the destruction of the ships, Hak-Bin chose to ignore it. "I'm glad you understand. With that in mind I have a task for you, one you will find quite agreeable."

"How nice," Xat-Hey said lazily. "So, who should I kill?"

The words, plus those that followed, were picked up by dozens of tiny listening devices and sent to a distant part of the ship. From there they went to Dro Rul, and from him to others, and from them to the planet below. For information is power and, when properly used, serves as a weapon of war.

WEST OF HILMAN, WASHINGTON

The Chinook's dragonflylike shadow followed along behind it as the big chopper swept in from the west and flew over undulating fields of spring wheat. Manning crouched behind John Wu while Vera Veen handled the controls. The security chief felt the back of the copilot's seat vibrate under his arm as he peered over Wu's shoulder.

Most of the land they were passing over had belonged to big agrabusinesses prior to the invasion. There were some family farms, however, smaller operations marked by clusters of burned-out buildings. These buildings had been targeted from orbit and destroyed with the same precision a surgeon would use to cauterize a bleeder.

The purpose of the seemingly wanton destruction was to deny "feral" humans a place to sleep and thereby aid the slave trade.

The surrounding fields had been spared, however, not because of any generosity on the Saurons' part, but because slaves have to be fed. The wheat fields of eastern Washington were only a few hundred miles from the limestone quarry in what had been the city of Bellingham.

But the wheat had to be harvested and processed before it could be fed to the slaves, and now, thanks to the increased rations reluctantly authorized by the stonemaster, even *more* food was required. This meant that in addition to wheat, the slaves would be hard at work picking apples, beans, and corn. Meat was in demand as well, so much so that every cow, sheep, and goat the aliens could lay their graspers on was being rounded up for slaughter.

In an effort to increase production, Franklin had been dispatched to the Hilman area, where he was supposed to raise morale and convince the workforce to produce *more* food. A hopeless mission if there ever was one.

There was an upside, however, and that was the fact that the trip offered Franklin the perfect opportunity to make contact with those who functioned as leaders within the local population, and attempt to recruit them. It was his belief that so long as the human resistance movement remained divided, it was doomed to failure.

Yes, the destruction of five Sauron spaceships was something to be proud of, but without the context provided by an overall plan, it had little if any meaning. The ships had been replaced, security had been tightened, and the slaves continued to slave. Nothing significant had changed.

Manning happened to believe that the politician was correct, and figured that if anyone could bring the humans together, Franklin could. But he was determined to stay out of the political process. It was his job was to *protect* the president, not get him elected. Or so he told himself.

Others, Jina among them, knew it was more than that. They knew that the security chief was no longer concerned about his sister's safety, that if anyone could survive in the "wild" Manning could, and that in his own way he was a patriot. A word that would have made Manning nervous had he known that it had been applied to him.

Veen pointed with her chin. "The LZ is about five miles ahead."

Manning squinted through the windshield. Acre after acre of green slipped under the helicopter's belly. "Don't land. Circle first. I want to eyeball the place."

Veen nodded. "That's a roger—one three-sixty coming up."

The Chinook banked, and the security chief watched the ground. Hilmer's municipal airport consisted of a short ribbon of concrete, a pair of World War II–era Quonset huts, a white pylon from which an orange wind sock flew, a couple of work-worn yellow crop dusters, a Piper Cub with no wings, a dilapidated helicopter with "Joe's Air Tours" painted along the side of its fuselage, and a small tank farm.

Such strips were a common sight in this part of the country, and this one was no different—except for the presence of more than a dozen Kan, their chitin shimmering as it matched the soil's color. They, plus the Sauron equivalent of three armored ground vehicles, comprised the escort that Manning had requested. Heads swiveled as the aircraft continued a wide, sweeping turn. "Should I land," Veen inquired, "or take another spin?"

"Let 'em wait," Manning replied. "The sun will do them good. Follow the road toward town. Let's see what, if anything, is hiding in the bushes."

The pilot nodded, banked to the left, and followed the road. It dipped, crossed a creek, and wound its way toward a cluster of distant grain elevators, some buildings, and the stadium beyond. That's where the slaves would be—and that's where they were headed. A fact that, thanks to all the talkies dropped from the air, was available to anyone with the capacity to understand English.

This created a situation so bad from Manning's perspective that he had to wonder if Hak-Bin had grown tired of Franklin and was *trying* to kill the politician.

Though constrained regarding what technology could be used to build the citadels, the Saurons were under no such strictures when it came to feeding the slaves. The road passed a lot full of confiscated harvesters. Most wore John Deere green, a few were rusty orange in color, but all of them were *huge*—two stories tall in some cases, each having its own glassed-in control compartment. A flock of birds took to the air as the helicopter passed over, circled, and settled again.

Farther on, at the edge of the town, a church stood. The original building had burned down more than twenty years before, but the necessary money had been collected and a new structure had been raised. It possessed a steeple, complete with belfry, and that's where Ivory stood as the Chinook passed over. Manning was a cautious bastard, just as Marta said he would be, but it wouldn't make any difference. Not in the end. Eventually, after Manning had his look-see, the chopper would land. And so-called President Franklin would get out, ride into town, and give his speech. The last speech the sonofabitch would ever make.

HELL HILL

Thanks to a lot of elbow grease and support from the Saurons, the Star Com's most important retreat had grown to occupy twelve modules, and been glorified by the addition of some crudely carved wooden statuary, a number of colorful murals, and the beginnings of what would eventually serve as a circular reflecting pool in front of the structure itself.

Sister Andromeda stood there, her back to the edifice she had brought into being, waiting for the expected guest. She didn't know Bal-Lok personally, but she took all of the Saurons seriously, even members of the Fon. The caste, according to her extensive intelligence network, to which her visitor belonged.

There was a stir off to the left as some off-shift humans exploded in all directions. Then, like an emperor entering Rome, a Fon appeared. He landed easily, then jumped again. He looked neither right nor left as he arced through the air, bounced off the roof of a cube, and disappeared from sight.

Andromeda frowned. Was that Bal-Lok? Or another Fon on an errand of some sort? She had just concluded that the second hypothesis was correct, and resolved to keep on waiting, when an acolyte appeared at her side. She was young, and her eyes bulged with excitement. Her name, her *new* one, was Water Dance. "Sister Andromeda! There's a Fon to see you! He came through the back."

Andromeda resisted the temptation to turn and enter the retreat. Instead she looked up at the nearest observation tower, wondered where the Saurons were looking, and took the younger woman's arm. "Thank you. Come on, let's tour the plaza. Look! The night shift planted some flowers."

If Water Dance was confused, which she definitely was, the acolyte was careful to hide it. It was no secret that Andromeda had a temper, and the young woman had no desire to trigger it. That being the case, she played along.

So Bal-Lok was forced to wait for a good five minutes before the slave finally entered the small, dimly lit room where he had been instructed to wait. Bal-Lok's voice hissed with pent-up anger. "You took your own sweet time, slave. Do you know who you're dealing with?"

"A Fon," Andromeda replied coolly, looking the Sauron up and down, "who needs my help. Or did you sneak in the back purely for the fun of it? I've never been up in one of those towers, but I'll bet the view is excellent. Would you enjoy a visit from the Kan? I came as soon as I reasonably could."

The words hit Bal-Lok like a bucket of freezing cold water. Suddenly he was reminded of the fact that he had no justifiable reason for being anywhere near the Star Communion's retreat.

Concerned by the ease with which the human had discerned the truth, and reminded of how vulnerable he was, Bal-Lok suddenly became contrite. "My apologies. You are correct. The matter I wish to discuss *is* confidential in nature, which accounts for my roundabout arrival."

Pleased by the Sauron's conciliatory tone and eager to seize what she sensed might be an advantage, Sister Andromeda pointed to the handmade sling chair. "Please, have a seat. I'll ring for some refreshments."

Bal-Lok accepted the invitation, waited while Andromeda rang a little bell, issued some orders, and took a seat. "So," the human said, folding her hands in her lap, "what can I do for you?"

Bal-Lok was silent for a moment as he gathered his thoughts. Then, in what amounted to a monotone, he told the human how effective the clandestine literacy campaign had been, how quickly Fon such as Cal-Rum had learned to read, and how the truth was thereby revealed. "And so," Bal-Lok concluded, "the Zin took advantage of our forgetfulness to dominate the Fon. And now, as a *new* race is about to be born, we must take a stand."

Sister Andromeda, her mind churning as it attempted to deal with the implications of what she'd just heard, fought to maintain her composure. Everything she believed in and counted on had been turned upside down. The Saurons were as venal, corrupt, and self-serving as humans were. "And the slaves? What of them?"

"Dead, all dead," Bal-Lok replied, "except for a tiny number maintained as seed stock. That's why you must help us gain our rightful place. Unlike the Zin, the Fon will allow your kind to live."

"As slaves."

Bal-Lok waved a pincer. "Of course. Such is your role. But slavery can be rather pleasant. Consider the Ra 'Na. Do they suffer? I think not. Once the new race is born, and my nymph assumes its rightful place, the journey will resume. *New* slaves will be found and take their place at the bottom of the hierarchy. Your kind will move up. In the meantime there will be a place for an organization such as yours, an *honored* place, with privileges consistent with the service you are about to render."

"And what," Andromeda asked cautiously, "would that service involve?"

The Sauron shrugged. "The way things stand now, there are far too many Zin for the good of the race. Once they enter the birth chambers, their nymphs will become vulnerable. That's when you and your followers could do some judicious weeding."

Andromeda imagined what such an activity would be like, moving through an alien structure, murdering their young. Horrible, yet appropriate, given the manner in which the Zin had betrayed her. *If* Bal-Lok spoke the truth. But had he? Yes, she thought he had. But caution was in order. Acolytes would be assigned to check the veracity of his story. If an overseer had disappeared, people would be aware of it. In the meantime, she needed more information. "And the Kan? What of them?"

Bal-Lok tilted his head. "Who knows? Time will tell. Perhaps they, too, have discovered the secrets of literacy and are busy making preparations of their own.

"Or—and this seems more likely—you and your fellow slaves will be called upon to neutralize a sizable number of *their* nymphs as well. That precaution would prevent the possibility of a counterrevolution, and thereby secure the new order."

And why stop there? Andromeda wondered to herself. Why not kill some of *your* nymphs? Or *all* of them, for that matter? Had the Fon thought about that? Or was he so naive he believed the slaves would simply do as they were told? No, there must be an insurance policy of some sort. But what was it? The cult leader decided to keep such thoughts to herself. "And that's all?"

"Not quite," the Sauron replied somberly.

Sister Andromeda raised a well-plucked eyebrow. "Yes?"

"Yes," Bal-Lok allowed evenly. "I have reason to believe that one of my brothers was caught and tortured. Odds are that he revealed everything he knew to the Kan, including my role in the Fon resistance movement. In fact, assuming my sources are correct, an assassin has been dispatched to kill me."

"Really," Andromeda inquired, immediately concerned for her own safety. "What sort of an assassin?"

"A Zin named Xat-Hey."

"How interesting," Andromeda replied thoughtfully. "Perhaps we should eliminate him for you." And for ourselves, she thought, before he turns his attentions elsewhere.

Bal-Lok raised his head. "You could accomplish that?"

"Probably. For the right price."

Bal-Lok sensed danger but was powerless to resist. His very survival was at stake. "So tell me, slave: What price would you ask?"

Andromeda looked him in the eye. "In return for Xat-Hey's death you would become a member of my church, acknowledge me as your superior, and convince the rest of your caste to do the same."

There was a prolonged silence as the Sauron weighed the human's words. "Your proposal lacks merit. The Fon would become slaves to slaves."

"No," Andromeda replied smoothly, "quite to the contrary. The Star Communion *celebrates* your kind. Those who belong believe that in spite of the great cleansing, and the conditions they presently live under, better days lie ahead. Days in which they will live in peaceful harmony with the Sauron race. What I'm suggesting should be regarded as an alliance. One in which two groups merge their strengths for the greater good. Surely you see the wisdom in that? I would lead—but with advice from you."

Bal-Lok didn't believe Andromeda, not for a second, but he needed the human's help. The answer was obvious: He would lie, await the first opportunity, and then nail the human to a cross. She would look good there, her feet in the air, a crow perched on the bottom of her chin. He forced the Sauron equivalent of a smile.

"What you say makes a great deal of sense. Keep your part of the bargain and I will keep mine."

The conversation was interrupted as the refreshments arrived. Bal-Lok was hungry and wasted little time tucking into the rolled pancakes that the Saurons loved so much.

Sister Andromeda watched the alien gorge himself, sipped some slightly sweetened tea, and marveled at this latest turn of fortune. Now, with help from the Fon, the church could truly unfold. Wonderful were the ways of God.

HILMER, WASHINGTON

With a Kan vehicle ahead, unknowingly sweeping for land mines, and the Chinook circling above, Manning was entitled to relax. After all, the partially armored Suburban, plus seven heavily armed bodyguards, should be adequate to handle the most likely assassination scenarios.

But the security chief *couldn't* relax, not in a situation where everyone who cared knew exactly where Franklin would be and what time he'd be there. He was testy, perfectionistic, and, in the words of Sandi Taglio, the Suburban's chain-smoking driver, "one major pain in the ass."

Manning glanced left, checked to see if the woman had both hands in the preferred "ten to ten" position, and saw that she did. Taglio, who had excellent peripheral vision, detected the seemingly casual inspection but kept her eyes to the front. The fact that the chief was pissy didn't justify taking her eyes off the road.

Pleased with what he'd seen so far, Manning looked back at Franklin and saw that the president remained buried in his speech.

Amocar was something else again. Here, should the shit hit the fan, sat Franklin's last line of defense. A sloppy asshole who, in spite of countless reminders to the contrary, had chosen to place his twelve-gauge riot gun butt down on the truck's outboard side, a location that could spell disaster if the idiot had to bail out. Short though it was, the eighteen-inch barrel could still block the bodyguard's egress.

Manning gestured toward the weapon. "José, how many times do I have to tell you? Put the long gun on the *inside,* away from the door."

Amocar wondered if the gringo could see the hatred in his eyes, and remembered the sunglasses. Thank God for the sunglasses. He moved the shotgun from one side to the other. "Sorry, Chief, I forgot."

Manning bit off the words that waited to be said, turned his attention forward, and wondered how Kell was doing. The ex-Ranger and a team that consisted of Morley Rix, Jonathan Wimba, and Se Ri Pak had been dropped on the far side of town and left to find their own way in. *If* Hilman had been penetrated, *if* someone was waiting, it was their job to deal with it. *Before* Franklin walked into anybody's sights.

Taglio glanced into her rearview mirror and saw that the Kan vehicle assigned to cover their butts had fallen too far back. Not too surprising, giving their lack of mission-appropriate training, but dangerous nonetheless. The cigarette, which, thanks to Manning's orders, remained unlit, waggled when she spoke. "Hey, boss, tell the chits in Blocker Two to close it up."

Manning glanced to the rear, confirmed that the Kan had indeed fallen too far back, and brought the radio to his lips. It was of Ra 'Na manufacture and felt too small for his hand. As with all such communications, the order had to be translated into a request. "Snake One to Blocker Two. This is Manning. I respectfully suggest that you increase speed lest an interloper insert themselves between your vehicle and ours. Over."

As usual there was no response, but the limpet-shaped vehicle *did* move forward, and, because the driver felt ornery, or was just plain stupid, hung fewer than ten feet off Taglio's rear bumper. The security chief considered trying to do something about that but decided to let the matter drop. There were other things to worry about, such as the steeple off to the right and the grain elevators that loomed ahead. Either of the structures could house a sniper who, if he or she had the correct weapon, could put a cluster of bullets through the Suburban's unarmored roof.

The security chief kept his eyes glued to the church as he gave the order. "Mr. President, please pull the ballistic blanket up over your head. I know the damn thing is uncomfortable, but it could save your life."

Franklin looked up from his handwritten notes and frowned. Manning was genuinely concerned, that much was obvious, and the politician was glad that Jina had agreed to remain at home. He didn't like the idea of pulling the blanket up over his head, of cowering beneath it, but he could hardly object. Slowly, reluctantly, he did as he was told.

Not far away, Ivory watched from the darkness inside the belfry, wondered if he should have posted a sniper there, and concluded that he'd been correct not to do so. It was a long shot, down through what might be an armored roof, at a target he couldn't see. No, what his team required would come later, when Franklin got up to speak and his head was fully exposed. There wasn't a bulletproof vest in the world that would protect the president then.

Ivory grinned, descended the ladder, and went out through the front door. The motorcade had passed, the Chinook circled like a huge mosquito, and there was no one to watch. The walk—no, the *stroll*—would last twelve minutes. Ivory knew because he had timed it. Then, after the speech, everything would change. The last vestiges of the ZOG would die and the new order would take its place. Birds chirped, insects buzzed, and the sun crept across the sky.

ABOARD THE SAURON DREADNOUGHT *HOK NOR AH*

The compartment, lit only by the glow of multiple videoscreens, was one of the most vulnerable aspects of the Ra 'Na resistance movement since it was from there that a handful of volunteers monitored the Saurons and passed their reports to the Council of Dros. To work there every day, as Pol had, was to live in fear.

Someday a Ra 'Na would betray his or her kind in return for a special favor, one of the clergy would give way under torture, or the Saurons would simply stumble across the truth: Their slaves were actively engaged in a campaign of subversion and sabotage. They would cut their way in, the mass retributions would begin, and the cozy relationship would come to an abrupt end.

It was inevitable, and everyone knew that, but the information they continued to gather was too valuable to forgo. So Fra Pol faced each shift with the same misgivings that a foot soldier feels while marching toward a battle. Only it was worse because Pol was by himself. Was this the day when his luck would run out? When would the Kan come to take him away? There was no way to know—and not knowing was torture.

It felt good to reach the end of the shift, to check all 143 of the incoming surveillance feeds, confirm that they were operational, and lurch to his feet. The long shift was over, he could get some sleep, and by doing so escape for a while.

In spite of the fact that Pol had not been allowed to meet the next operator, lest he reveal her identity under torture, the initiate knew it was a female. Who else would wear perfume? But was she attractive? There was no way to know. The cleric had even considered lying in wait for her, in hopes that she would conform to his fantasies, but knew such thoughts were dangerous.

Besides, knowing his luck, the other operator was probably twice his age, and ugly to boot. No, it was best to leave, and do so quickly.

Pol slipped out of the compartment, made his way through a maze of small passageways, and approached the hatch that would serve as his exit. Once outside, in the flow of foot traffic, he could finally relax.

The Ra 'Na stepped up, placed his palm against the print-sensitive plate, and waited for the door to slide out of the way.

The Sauron equivalent of "access denied" appeared on the status display in front of him.

Sensors could be cranky at times, so Pol tried again. He soon wished he hadn't. A voice issued from a speaker over his head. It was both stern and unusually loud. In fact, given the way it sounded, it might even be live. A most unusual circumstance indeed. Someone—there was no way to know who—had turned him in. "Remain where you are! You are wanted for questioning! Remain where you are! You are wanted for questioning!"

Pol turned and ran. The voice dwindled in the distance. The initiate backtracked for a while, dived down a side tunnel, and angled away. Part of him wanted to return to the compartment, to warn the female. But he knew better than to do so.

There were Zin—not many, but some—with skills sufficient to track his progress through the maze of passageways by monitoring the heat sensors located at regular intervals along the way. If he returned to the compartment, they could follow. Then, instead of protecting the other Ra 'Na, he would betray her.

That being the case, Pol scuttled in the opposite direction and tried to think of a way out.

Should he call on Dro Rul for help? No, not if there was even the slightest chance that his actions would compromise the prelate or his peers.

That left two choices. He could commit suicide, or—Pol found the second option to be a good deal more appealing—he could leave the ship. But how? Access to the enormous flight deck was strictly monitored even under normal circumstances and would be even more so now.

Still, that's where the shuttles were, so that's where he would go. Not directly, via the public passageways, but through the maintenance tunnels. Yes, they could track him, if they could find one of the Zin capable of doing so, but that would take time. Or so Pol hoped. The cleric remembered the harakna—and started to run.

HELL HILL

Free to do whatever their leader thought best, chosen for their absolute ruthlessness, the Kan warriors swept through the half-darkened streets of Hell Hill like a new form of plague, grabbing anyone unfortunate enough to catch their eye, and demanding information before they moved along.

Not content to shuffle like those they had conquered, the Kan traveled in long, combat-style leaps. Leaps that carried them to the top of cubes, from one roof to the next, and back into the streets. Faster than humans could run and faster than rumors could fly. Speed plus surprise: Those were the keys.

In the meantime, caught up in the mad rush, Xat-Hey felt as if he had been reborn. To move about the surface of a planet, to fill his lungs with raw atmosphere, *that* was intoxicating.

Xat-Hey relished the tang of the wood smoke that hung over the hill, delighted in the countless droplets of rain that drifted down through the artificial daylight, and savored the sense of purpose extracted from his mission.

Now, for the first time in years, the Zin felt truly alive. There was irony in that, given the fact that only a limited number of days remained to him, but that, too, was a source of enjoyment. Here, at last, was the purpose for which he had been hatched. To fly through the night, to seize danger by the throat, to take what he wanted.

Water sprayed up into the air as the Zin landed in the center of a puddle. A group of humans scattered. Most escaped, but one proved to be just a little too slow. There was a series of thumps as a dozen Kan warriors dropped around him. One of them, a file leader named Uul-Tas, grabbed the unfortunate slave by his collar and prevented his departure.

Xat-Hey witnessed the byplay and jumped the intervening gap. The name of the saloon they were looking for had been extracted from a Fon chosen at random. The fact that such a place was allowed to exist served to illustrate how slack things had become under the stonemaster's questionable leadership. The Zin shoved his nose into the slave's face. "The saloon called the Square Hole. Where is it?"

The human's jaw worked but nothing came out. Urine trickled down his leg and pooled at his feet. He managed to point.

Xat-Hey looked, confirmed that there was a door with a sign overhead, and said with a growl, "Run."

The slave ran and the Zin grinned. He waved to the Kan. "Come, my brothers, there is work to do."

Chrissy Brooks was sitting at the bar, counting the day's till, when the Saurons burst through the door. Her first thought was for the back room, where a meeting was in progress, but it was too late. Before she could put her body into motion, or send some-one else, the door slammed open and a human stumbled out. More than half a dozen followed. A pair of Kan brought up the rear.

They shimmered as their chitin sought to match the saloon's questionable decor.

The saloon owner realized the invaders knew about the back entrance, realized the raid was serious. Fear oozed like cold lead into her belly.

Xat-Hey scanned the bar for a human who matched the description he'd been given, identified one who came close, and shuffled across the room.

Chrissy watched the Zin approach. She knew there was something different about this particular Sauron and wished she were somewhere else. But she wasn't, which meant that when his pincer closed around her wrist, she felt every bit of the resulting pain.

The Zin jerked Chrissy off her stool and dragged her to the center of the room, where he took control of the human's shoulders and forced her to turn. Faces, most of which she knew very well, passed in front of her. *"Look at them,"* the Sauron commanded, "and choose the ones associated with the human called 'Boyer Blue.' Point them out and you will live. Fail and you will die."

Chrissy looked into terrified eyes, realized that two of the resistance leader's followers were present, and tried to blank them from her mind.

Xat-Hey sensed the human's reluctance, and pointed across the room. "The juvenile—shoot her."

Almost faster than an eye could see, one of the warriors aimed and fired. The dart caught the teenage waitress in the chest and threw her back against the wall. Blood smeared the steel as she sank to the floor.

"Another," Xat-Hey commanded, pointing to a patron. "Shoot him."

"No!" Chrissy heard herself speak as if from a thousand miles away. "Stop, please stop!"

"Then tell us what we want to know," the Zin demanded calmly, "and do it *now*."

Chrissy, tears flowing down her cheeks, turned toward the resistance fighters. Their hatred was plain to see. Maybe, just maybe, she could save one of them. One happened to be white and the other was black. She hesitated, then pointed to the black man. He flinched as if Chrissy had slapped him, narrowed his eyes, and stood a little taller.

"Good," Xat-Hey said, and released the woman's arm. "Now shoot her."

The dart followed so closely that Chrissy barely had time to process the words before the projectile struck the center of her forehead and blew her brains out, spraying another woman who flinched but stayed where she was.

"So," Xat-Hey said, standing next to the dead woman's body. "Some progress has been made. *You*," the Zin said, pointing to the man Chrissy had identified, "come here."

The man's name was Chris Johnsón, and, given what he had just witnessed, he expected to die. He took five stiff-legged steps forward and stopped. He noticed that tiny flecks of Chrissy's blood dotted the front of the Sauron's black chitin.

Xat-Hey smiled but only the Kan recognized the expression as such. His voice, harsh till then, suddenly softened. "You are black—like me."

Johnson, his eyes focused on the far side of the room, forced himself to speak. "I'm black . . . but *not* like you."

"Of course not," the Zin replied casually, feet shuffling as he circled the human. "You are a slave . . . and I am a Sauron. *Boyer Blue* . . . where is he?"

Johnson made balls of his fists and screwed his eyes shut. There was no way to prevent what was about to happen, but there was no need to watch. "I have no idea who you're talking about."

The dart, fired at close range from Xat-Hey's weapon, hit the back of the human's right knee joint and blew bits of bone and cartilage out the front. Johnson collapsed, grabbed what remained of his leg, and screamed. Blood jetted from the end of a severed artery but stopped when a Kan knocked the human's hands out of the way and slapped a self-sealing battle dressing over both sides of the wound.

"Now," Xat-Hey said as he hunkered down, "let's try again. *Where* is Blue?"

This time, to Johnson's horror, he heard himself talk. And talk, and talk, and talk, until he started to babble and the Saurons grew bored and left.

After he had gone, Johnson felt for the battle dressing, found the edge of the patch, and ripped it off. Blood spurted onto the floor. The rest came easily.

HILMER, WASHINGTON

The town of Hilmer, like everything the Sauron deemed potentially useful, remained virtually untouched. Main Street, along with its hardware store, public library, city hall, banks, competing cafés, gift shops, movie theater, and fire station, looked exactly as it had prior to the invasion except for the weeds that sprouted up through cracks in the sidewalks, some broken windows, and storm debris that no one had bothered to clean up.

That, Franklin thought as the Suburban's huge mud and snow tires whispered down the street, was because those who had lived in the town, those who managed to survive, were slaves now. They were somewhere ahead, mixed with the crowd in the local football stadium.

Though not especially pretty to look at, the sports arena was a sizable structure, one Franklin had visited before. In fact, as chance would have it, the politician, in his official capacity as governor, had thrown the first ball out onto the field.

Now, knowing what he knew, Franklin realized he had spoken to the crowd that day about the importance of freedom, of treating everyone fairly, and had done so with only the most remote understanding of what those concepts truly meant. He wished he could go back and give the speech again but knew that was impossible.

What he *could* do was give the best speech possible today, and then, before Manning could whisk him away, meet with members of the local resistance, especially the group that referred to itself as "Deacon's Demons," who, depending on which rumors one chose to believe, might or might not be the ones who deserved credit for destroying the Sauron spaceships.

The Sauron vehicle passed a sign with a large Puma on it, turned into the crosshairs of a telescopic sight, and entered a parking lot. Marley Rix, who, along with Kell, Wimba, and Pak, were lying on a thick carpet of pine needles under a clump of trees, watched the vehicle disappear behind a maintenance building and raised his head. "Well, they're here."

"Yeah," Kell replied glumly, "but so is the opposition."

"We don't know that for sure."

"No, we don't," Kell agreed. "But I can *feel* it. The bastards are out there."

"But where?"

"That's the million-dollar question."

"I vote for inside the stadium," Pak put in, speaking for the first time. "That's where *I'd* be."

Kell turned to eye the normally taciturn woman. "Yeah? Why's that? Wouldn't an ambush be a lot easier? On the road to the airport, for example?"

Pak shook her head. Her black hair was so short it didn't even move. "No, I don't think so. If that was the plan, why wait? They could have attacked the Suburban on the way in. No, assuming that the opposition is human, they'll want to kill the president in front of as many witnesses as possible. That would maximize the impact, build their rep, and ensure the story would spread by word of mouth."

The theory made so much sense that Kell figured she'd been thinking about the matter for some time. "Why not mention your idea earlier?"

"You never asked."

"Yeah? Why now?"

Pak shrugged. "I got tired of waiting."

"Come on," Rix said, a grin splitting his sunburned face, "let's find the bastards."

Meanwhile, within the stadium itself, Franklin, with Manning in front and Amocar to the rear—and a Kan on either side— proceeded up three flights of stairs, through a fire door, and out onto a newly constructed plywood ramp. It bounced underfoot as the group made its way onto a specially built platform.

Like most high-ranking government officials, Franklin had given hundreds of speeches, some of which had been delivered to less than friendly crowds. But he'd never been involved in anything like this. As Manning stepped to one side and positioned himself to block a shot fired from the south side of the stadium, the audience—if that's what the slaves could rightfully be called—was fully revealed.

There were thousands of them, all seated on the ground. The stands, for reasons known only to the Saurons, remained empty. Row upon row of gaunt-faced men and women sat with arms around their bony knees, their eyes huge as they stared up at the well-fed politician. They were silent, completely silent, like ca-davers brought to life.

The odor of their unwashed bodies, the stench of the excrement they had deposited on the field while waiting for him, and the smell of disinfectant washed over Franklin like a wave.

The Kan, who had already tied pieces of cloth over the olfac-tory organs located along the undersurface of their arms, remained outwardly impassive.

The humans fought to keep from retching.

Franklin swallowed and swallowed again. Here, literally starv-ing to death, were the slaves forced to harvest food so *other* slaves would have the strength necessary to build the alien citadels. Not only that, but it was *his* job to encourage them, to urge the pathetic-looking scarecrows to even greater heights of production, absurd though the thought clearly was.

Franklin felt sick to his stomach as he approached the microphone. His voice echoed off the empty stands. "Greetings. I won't say 'good morning' because it certainly isn't. Some of you may recognize me as Alexander Franklin, former governor of Washington State.

"Regardless of whether you do or don't, I suspect that those of you who still have the strength, hate me. I don't blame you. Especially given the fact that I was sent here to urge every single one of you to work harder and longer. Something which, believe it or not, I'm actually going to do.

"*Not* because the Saurons ordered to me to do so, *not* because I care about their temples, but because I want each and every one of you to survive."

Franklin paused to scan the faces before him. "Some of you think I'm crazy, that there's no way you can survive, and that there's no good reason to do so. Well, you're wrong.

"Some of your progenitors, dead for hundreds or even thousands of years, were slaves to the Egyptians, to the Romans, or to the barbarians of northern Europe. *They survived—and so can you.*

"Some of your ancestors slaved to build the great temples of Central and South America or were captured by tribes here in North America and forced to accept a life of servitude. *They survived—and so can you.*

"My great-great-grandparents came to this country in the hold of a slave ship and were forced to work in the white man's cotton fields. *They survived—and so can you.*

"The proof of their survival, of the courage they had, is right here in front of me. *You* are the proof, *you* are what they lived for, *you* must survive. For them, for yourselves, for the future.

"So if you have the strength to work a little harder, or the knowledge to work a little smarter, then use it. Who knows? Maybe the Saurons will leave as they say they will. Or maybe, just maybe, something will break our way. Whatever happens, it won't mean much unless you're alive to benefit from it."

Franklin paused and Manning looked at the politician in amazement. The question of what the ex-governor would say, what he *could* say, had never crossed the security chief's mind. Now, having heard the words, he was amazed.

It was the best speech, the *only* speech, that Franklin could have given without coming across as a full-blown collaborator, or offending the Saurons so badly that they nailed him to a cross. Or worse, from Manning's point of view, nailed *Jina* to a cross.

Somehow, in some way, the wily bastard had actually turned into a genuine leader. A person actually *worth* protecting. The realization that things had changed, that he wanted to protect the *man* as well as the man's wife, was something of a shock.

Somewhere, out among the forest of skin-clad bones, someone responded. The clap was so faint, so weak, that it might have been a figment of Franklin's imagination, except that another pair of hands came together, and another, until hundreds of hands were clapping, and the noise bounced from one side of the sports stadium to the other.

One of the slaves, a man who appeared a bit healthier than those around him, clapped loudest of all. He was an old friend of George "Popcorn" Farley's, a regular at the annual rendezvous down in Oregon, best known to his buddies as "Hawk." A nickname that stemmed from the tomahawks he liked to make, the tattoo on his left forearm, and the shape of his Roman nose.

His *real* name was Paul Gulick, and it was *to* him, along with his wife, Tasca, that Deac Smith had entrusted leadership of the resistance movement on the eastern side of the Cascade Range, and it was *from* him, among others, that Smith would expect to receive some sort of recommendation. Should the resistance group informally known as "Deac's Demons" throw their support behind Franklin? A man many believed to be a collaborator? Or should they hold out, hoping to find someone better?

Those who believed in the man, and there were a few, pointed to the manner in which he had taken a Sauron whip rather than let it fall on a slave, to the way his wife worked to improve medical conditions on and around Hell Hill, and wondered what more the man could realistically do.

Still, until Franklin's visit, and the speech that not only acted to knit the slaves together but also hinted at the existence of a resistance movement, the Hawk had been one of Franklin's most vocal detractors.

But now, having seen what the man could do, having felt his presence, the Hawk was of a different opinion. He clapped, started to stand, and thought better of it. The slaves sitting to either side of him weren't about to waste any of their precious energy on something that frivolous and neither should he.

The Kan, unsure as to the exact meaning of the applause, stirred uneasily.

Meanwhile, in the announcers' booth, high above the other end of the field, Ivory shook his head in amazement. Like it or not, you had to give the politician credit. The tricky bastard had the audience eating out of his hand. They were buying his bullshit! Well, so much the better. When the old-fashioned .303-caliber slug tore the motherfucker's head off, the idiots below would witness what happens to niggers who get too big for their britches.

He turned to Boner, who was sitting on a chair behind the long, carefully tweaked rifle. It rested on a sandbag, had been preregistered, and was loaded with match-grade ammo. Ivory opened his mouth and was just about to give the necessary order when the skin named Jonsey held up a hand. "Take a look at this, boss. We got a mud with a scope-mounted M-16."

Ivory frowned. "So? What's your point? Manning has all sorts of scum on his security team."

Jonsey continued to look through the high-powered binoculars but shook his head. "No, I ain't talking about the bullet-catchers. This one is on her way up."

Ivory stepped over, grabbed the binoculars, confirmed that a woman had arrived on one of the two catwalks that provided access to the announcers' booth, and swore. Like it or not, he'd have to use his radio. He brought the device up to his lips. "Marta, shoot your brother. Parker, nail the mud on the catwalk. Jonsey, shoot the nigger. Kill them now!"

Marta, who had positioned herself up at the very top of the south side stand, was partially hidden by a steel girder. She looked down the length of rifle and cursed her luck. Motivated by who knew what, a Kan had stepped into her shot. She heard the order, put a bullet into the side of the Sauron's head, and worked the bolt. An empty casing flew free, and was still arcing into the seats below, when she fired again. Her brother had made his choice, the *wrong* choice, and would have to pay.

Manning saw the Kan jerk from the corner of his eye, saw blood mist the air, and charged the president. The sound of the shot followed a fraction of a second later.

The applause had died, and Franklin was just about to offer some closing remarks, when he heard the first gunshot. What felt like a truck hit him, and the politician was thrown from the platform.

Jonsey wasted a fraction of a second debating whether to try to fire through the red fog that momentarily enveloped his target, realized his mistake, and squeezed the trigger. The rifle slug passed through the place where Franklin's head had been a quarter of a second before. It hit a Sauron in the leg. The Kan screamed and created his own dance.

Pak heard Marta fire, saw motion in the announcers' booth, and raised her weapon. Parker, his .9mm at the ready, dropped from the girders above. The grating clanged as his boots made contact. Pak had just started to turn, just started to understand, when the bullet struck the back of her head. The lights went out and she toppled facedown. Parker spit on her body as he stepped over it.

Kell used the doorway into Exit 3-North for cover, heard Wimba's M-62 roar as the bodyguard applied counterfire to the area from which the first shot had originated, and yelled into the boom mike, "Snake Three to Ground One! They're taking fire! Prepare for immediate extraction! Snake Three to Air One! We could use some cover."

Veen, one hand on the stick, the other on the cyclic, turned the Chinook toward the stadium. "Cover?" From a big honking ship like hers? The only armament the ship had was a pair of door guns, one to port and one to starboard. There was no one to man them except for Wu, who had anticipated the problem, and was up out of his seat. He yelled over the noise from the rotors, "Put the target to starboard!"

Veen nodded her helmet. "Air One to Snake Three. That's a roger. Air Two requests something to shoot at."

There was an all-consuming roar as the huge helicopter passed over the south side of the stadium and hovered above. The slaves, frightened by the gunfire but surrounded by Kan warriors, huddled on the ground. Kell pointed. "The announcers' booth! Hose it down!"

Wu, who had plugged into the jack next to the Chinook's starboard door, felt the deck drop as Veen turned into position. What looked like red fireflies winked at the copilot as a cluster of bullets whipped past his right elbow. He marched his tracers across the front of the booth.

The center pane of glass had been removed by the White Rose Society the day before, but the panes to either side exploded into thousands of fragments that rained down onto the slaves trapped below. A woman screamed as a jagged chunk of metal plunged into her back, and a man, unfortunate enough to be looking up at that particular moment, lost an eye.

Ivory, more enraged than frightened, hit the floor and elbowed his way toward the door as the machine-gun bullets ripped Jonsey apart. Boner, his arms working like pistons, followed behind.

Maybe Franklin was dead and maybe he wasn't, but the important thing was to get away, a requirement into which a good deal of time and research had been invested. The key—in Ivory's judgment, at least—was not so much to escape as to drop completely out of sight. Regardless of whether his team had succeeded, a full-scale manhunt would begin the moment the attack was over.

If his assumptions were correct, and the Saurons behaved the way he thought they would, the sweep would focus on the area that surrounded the sports arena rather than on the facility itself. After all, the aliens would reason, what fugitive in his or her right mind would linger at the scene of the crime?

So Ivory low-crawled his way toward the catwalk and hoped he would get an opportunity to cross it.

Manning heard Kell's orders through his earplug, rolled onto his back, and saw the Chinook drop into the stadium. People screamed as the glass fell. Franklin scrambled to his feet and moved toward the crowd.

The security chief stood, looked for Amocar, but couldn't spot him. Was the sonofabitch down? No, more likely hiding somewhere safe. It was difficult if not impossible to hear Franklin's voice over the sound of the helicopter's engines and the machine-gun fire. But there was little doubt that his presence on the ground, motioning for the slaves to remain where they were, helped prevent what could have been a massacre.

Hawk, who had already started to extricate himself from the crowd, kept a wary eye on the Kan. Some of the warriors jumped from one place to the next, as if unsure of what to do, while others took potshots at the helicopter, and the rest threatened the slaves.

Manning, now intent on getting the president out of the kill zone, yelled into the mike, "Snake One to Air One! Put it down in the stadium! If the Kan fire on you, waste them! Over."

Veen looked down through the Plexiglas panel near her feet. A sea of terrified faces looked back up. "Air One to Snake One, no can do. Not unless you want me to grease a whole lot of civilians. I'll meet you in the parking lot. Over."

Manning swore, knew the pilot was correct, and said so. "Roger that, Air One, over."

The security chief pulled a quick 360. Amocar, who had been missing only minutes before, had magically reappeared. Not only that, but judging from his warlike pose, the errant bodyguard was the meanest, most hard-core sonofabitch on the entire team.

Manning growled into his mike, "Snake One to Snake Two, get Big Dog to parking lot."

Amocar nodded, grabbed the president's elbow, and directed him toward a set of stairs. Kell, Rix, and Wimba arrived from the far side of the stadium, wrapped him in a fleshy cocoon, and hustled him away.

Manning followed, walking backward for the most part, a .9mm in each hand.

The Chinook rose, the sound of its rotors slapping both sides of the stadium, and slipped across the roofline.

Ivory was surprised to be alive, gave thanks to the great Yahweh, came to his feet, and ran the length of the catwalk. Boner and Parker followed.

The riser, through which a cluster of heavy black power cables rose to supply the stadium's lights, was protected by a heavy-duty metal door. The words "Danger! High Voltage!" were prominently displayed on the front, complete with lightning bolts and a border of yellow-black tape.

Opening the obstruction was a snap, given the fact that the group had located all sorts of things in the maze of passageways under the playing field, including an office decorated with *Playboy* centerfolds, and a rack full of carefully marked keys.

Marta, who had arrived moments before, pulled the door open and motioned for the others to enter. "Where's Jonesy?"

"Dead," Ivory replied somberly, back in the announcers' booth. "The bastards damned near cut him in half. Still, we got Franklin, and that's what counts."

Marta, who was normally willing to say almost anything, found herself reluctant to speak. She swung out onto the vertical access ladder and started the descent. "Jonesy fired too damned late. He missed, which gave my brother an opportunity to push Franklin off the platform."

Ivory, who had no way to know that Marta fired early, causing

Jonesy to fire late, addressed the top of her crew cut. "And your brother? Did he escape as well?"

The voice was muffled. "Yeah, I took my shot, but he was in motion by then."

Ivory followed Marta down. "Shit."

"Yeah, that about covers it."

The rest of the descent was made in silence. A maintenance tunnel swallowed the racialists whole.

HELL HILL

There was a distinct shortage of meeting rooms on and around Hell Hill in which the newly literate Fon would be free to plot the next step of their revolution, especially with the Zin named Xat-Hey on the loose. He and his gang of Kan had already brutalized a number of the Fon, to say nothing of all the dead humans left in their wake.

However, thanks to the recently negotiated alliance with Sister Andromeda and the Star Com group, Bal-Lok and his brothers were allowed to borrow the retreat's central chamber—the very one that, unbeknownst to the organization's members, housed one of Hak-Bin's pre-positioned demolition charges.

Like the altars in the lesser retreats that Hak-Bin had encouraged the organization to build, this one had been constructed by Ra 'Na technicians. Though interesting to look at, it meant nothing at all. Nothing beyond its function as a bomb casing, since what appeared to be thousands of semiprecious gemstones were actually little bits of prepositioned shrapnel intended to rip flesh like miniature razor blades.

The top of the altar was shaped like a cradle in which a thousand multicolored lights floated like stars in space.

Sister Andromeda often told people that the yellow lights corresponded to suns, and that the red lights represented planets on which Sauron temples had already been constructed. It was complete nonsense, but people seemed to like it, and as time passed, Andromeda came to believe it herself.

The fact came to the rest of the chamber was bare of furnishings, was painted an eye-searing white, and was kept spotlessly clean served to make what was actually a collection of cargo containers feel like the temple they were supposed to be.

Having no model for how a meeting should be conducted, other than those occasionally held by the Zin, Bal-Lok naturally gravitated to a format in which he spoke and everyone else listened.

A quick count revealed that thirty-four Fon were present, all at least semiliterate. With no sling chairs to sit in, they stood in a rough semicircle. The majority were overseers, many of whom still carried their bloodstained whips tucked under their waist belts. But a few, functionaries with administrative assignments, wore the cross straps and pleated skirts appropriate for clerical duties.

Sister Andromeda, who, along with some key aides, had been permitted to watch from the rear of the chamber, made a note to have appropriate furniture constructed. After all, the more comfortable the Saurons were, the more likely they would return. Something she very much wanted them to do.

"Greetings," Bal-Lok said self-consciously, "and welcome to the first meeting of the Fon Brotherhood. You were invited here because of your proven intelligence, your ability to read and write, and your willingness to defy the Zin."

The words amounted to heresy. Some of the Fon shuffled their feet uneasily. Others looked back over their shoulders. Could the humans be trusted?

Bal-Lok understood their concern. Since he had no ethical standards to concern himself with, he proceeded to take liberties with the truth.

"Yes, slaves *are* present, but there is no reason for concern. It was Sister Andromeda, along with her followers, who risked their lives to free us from ignorance. *They* spray-painted the alphabet on walls and thereby planted the seeds from which literacy was able to bloom."

One of the Fon stomped a foot, others joined, and Andromeda bowed in response. Yes, the whole thing was a lie, but a *necessary* lie, and that made all the difference.

Now, with the brethren's fears at least partially allayed, Bal-Lok tackled the most important agenda item: the fact that every Sauron in the room was going to die.

A few, those who had been associated with the now-martyred Cal-Rum, knew the truth already. But many did not, and listened intently as Bal-Lok laid out the *true* purpose of the so-called temples, and the manner in which the next generation of Fon would soon be subjugated.

The response was mixed, running the gamut of shock, confusion, anger, and fear, a rather understandable reaction by those who had only recently learned of their own impending deaths. The conversation that followed progressed from the mechanics of death itself, to the ensuing birth process, to the options before them. At no time did the participants evidence the denial, confusion, or panic predicted by the ruling caste.

Some of the brethren felt that the entire caste should retire to the wilds, where they could meet death on their own terms, where their nymphs would be born free of Zin tyranny.

Others favored a more conservative approach. After all, they reasoned, a great deal had been accomplished. Why waste all that work? Rather than give birth in the wilds, where they would be vulnerable to animals and slaves alike, why not take refuge in the citadels, just as the Zin would eventually order them to do? Then, shortly after the nymphs hatched, *they* could stage a revolt. A rather nifty concept that shifted all the unpleasantness to the next generation.

Members of he first group objected at that point, indicating that the newly hatched Kan would put an end to any such revolt. At that point Bal-Lok chose to reenter the discussion.

"An excellent point, and one to which I have given a considerable amount of thought," he said judiciously. "It happens that I agree with those who wish to take advantage of the citadels, but with one important difference. Rather than terminate most of the slaves, as the Zin plan to do, we could arrange to spare some. A rather large contingent of specially trained humans led by Sister Andromeda. Once the birth process is over and the nymphs are ready to emerge, it would be their task to reduce the Kan to a more manageable number."

The Fon's proposal elicited an explosion of commentary. A great deal of it was positive. But there were detractors as well. One such individual, an overseer known to the workers as Nuu-Mak the Cruel, waved a blood-encrusted whip. "Are you insane? Why would the humans honor such a pact? What's to stop them from slaughtering *our* nymphs as well?"

Sister Andromeda, who had watched the discussion unfold with something akin to a sense of dread, looked at Bal-Lok. The Fon produced what looked like a sly smile. "Simple. Sister Andromeda will provide her followers with the necessary orders, allow herself to be imprisoned in a place known only to us, and our nymphs will release her!"

The plan, which was calculated to take full advantage of the memories that the Fon nymphs would inherit from their progenitors, was met with something akin to delight. Here was a plan so clever, so devious, that it was worthy of Hak-Bin himself.

Sister Andromeda, whose full cooperation was assumed, could only watch in horrified awe as the Saurons stomped their feet and Bal-Lok gloried in the applause.

But at least one individual remained unconvinced, and finally, after the noise died away, he raised a pincer. His name was Hoy-Dat. He was shorter than average, wore an immaculate white skirt, and favored a shock baton rather than the more traditional whip. "You speak of a time in the future. We live here and *now*. Even as we meet, the one known as Xat-Hey roams the hill. It's only a matter of time before someone in this room is caught and interrogated. What then?"

Bal-Lok looked toward the back of the room. He located Sister Andromeda, and his eyes locked with hers. "There is danger, *great* danger, and it would be silly to claim otherwise. As for Xat-Hey, he will precede us into the world beyond. Our loyal slaves will see to that."

Though not especially thrilled with continual use of the word "slaves" where she and her followers were concerned, Sister Andromeda reminded herself that it was important to be patient, and offered a respectful bow. "Bal-Lok speaks the truth. The Zin named Xat-Hey will die."

EAST OF THE CASCADE RANGE

Like the Maglev train preserved by the Saurons so they could transport slaves from east to west, the creaky General Motors SD70M 4000 HP Freight Locomotive and its complement of old Trinity Industries hopper cars had been saved for a specific purpose—to move grain and other foodstuffs from eastern Washington over the Cascade Range to the vicinity of Hell Hill.

Wheels clacked, metal groaned, and all manner of things rattled as two specially trained Ra 'Na technicians guided the train up through the steadily thinning evergreens, past a cliff of tan sedimentary rock, and toward the pass ahead.

It was hot in the locomotive's cab, and neither alien was very happy. The only thing they had to look forward to was some fresh seafood in the place that humans referred to as Everett, Washington. And that was many hours away.

Neither of them felt inclined to make the midjourney security check that their orders called for. The procedure involved walking the entire length of the train while jumping from car to car. The Ra 'Na weren't built for that sort of thing, and besides, what if they encountered a human? He or she was almost certain to be larger than they were and might be armed. No, it was much better to remain in the cab, let the slipstream blow in through the window, and fiddle with the air-conditioning controls.

So neither Ra 'Na was aware of the humans who had boarded the train about ten miles outside of Hilmer, Washington, roped themselves to a pair of hopper cars, and were along for the ride. Ivory, along with Marta, rode the rear of one, while Parker, along with Boner, occupied the front of the next unit back.

All four were exhausted. Ivory, who had the watch, sat with his back to hard steel. The defeat had been hard to take, especially against the backdrop of his fantasies, nearly all of which centered around a victorious return to Racehome.

But now, rather than the recognition he craved, he was going back to Hell Hill. The fact that he wanted to succeed so badly that he would voluntarily return there was something of a surprise. But that's how it was, and nothing less would do. When had he changed? At what point had he crossed the line from cynical member to fanatical leader? He supposed it made no difference. The problem was that time continued to pass—and opportunity with it.

The plan to kill Alexander Franklin was correct. Ivory felt certain of that. The problem was how.

The train pushed its way into a curve. Ivory allowed the rope to take his weight and let his eyes drift with the clouds. What was the old saying? "Where there's a will, there's a way"? Well, he *had* the will, so where was the way?

ABOARD THE SAURON DREADNOUGHT *HOK NOR AH*

Fra Pol stopped his headlong flight, listened for the rasp of harakna claws against steel, and heard nothing beyond his own labored breathing. Had he lost the ravenous creatures? Or never heard them in the first the place? Anything was possible within the steel capillaries that crisscrossed below the surface of the ship's skin.

He had made progress, though—*good* progress, given where he had started. He was close to the flight deck. In fact, judging from the coordinates engraved on the metal plate opposite his nose, only one layer of metal separated him from the cavernous space he so wanted to reach.

But it might as well have been twenty layers, for all the good it would do him. Given the fact that Pol was no longer allowed to access public thoroughfares, access to the flight deck and the shuttles there was completely out of the question.

A wave of self-pity swept over him. The future seemed clear. He would run for as long as he could. Then, weakened by hunger, and cornered by the harakna, he would die a lonely death. Later, while performing a routine maintenance check, a work party would find a scattering of bones. *His* bones, which they would sweep up, dump into a trash bag, and carry to the garbage disposal center.

The disposal center! Would the ship's security system allow him to access that? Maybe, just maybe it would. After all, why protect garbage? It wouldn't make sense, not to the cost-conscious merchant for whom the vessel had been built, which meant the facility might be open to everyone. Including him!

Filled with a sudden sense of hope, Pol returned to the last intersection and took the passageway to the left. A long line of blue lights curved with the contour of the ship's hull.

All he could hear was the rumble of the ship's life support system, the steady thump, thump, thump made by his feet, and the rasp of his own breathing. Then there was a shout, a powerful light threw his shadow forward, and a dart buzzed past his head.

Kan! Pol glanced over his shoulder, confirmed his hypothesis, and ran even faster. Though dangerous, the Kan were slow, especially in tunnels, where it was impossible to jump. The key was to take advantage of the hull's curvature, push his way beyond the area the Kan could actually see, and find a place to hide. To do otherwise was to lead them to the very place he wanted to go.

Pol spotted an intersection ahead, looked back to ensure that the Kan wouldn't be able to see him, and fumbled for the amulet he wore around his neck. His mother had given it to him, but he knew she would forgive him. He pulled the object over his head.

Skidding to a halt at the center of the intersection, the initiate threw the amulet down the passageway to the left, whirled, and continued along the path he had followed before.

He passed a set of small oval-shaped holes cut into an overarching girder and stopped. Then, using the foot- and handholds to climb as far as he could, the Ra 'Na swung onto the top of a duct, and lay flat.

Pol couldn't see from his hiding place, not without revealing himself, but he could hear. There was a shuffling sound as the Kan arrived, followed by muted conversation, and audible commands: "Check the side tunnel! Look for signs of passage."

Pol listened to the warriors shuffle away and prayed the ruse would work. It took fewer than twenty heartbeats for the Kan to locate the amulet, shout his victory, and summon his companions.

He waited, heard no more, and looked to make sure. The intersection was clear. He swung his feet over, felt for a foothold, and lowered himself to the deck.

Running with renewed vigor, Pol headed for the disposal center. He arrived at another intersection, checked the coordinates there, turned a quick circle, spotted the low, almost invisible access hatch, and hurried over. Chances were that the Kan had realized they'd been duped and were now on the way.

The hatch was equipped with a palmplate. Was it hooked into the ship's security system? Or could anyone with a sufficient amount of body heat trigger the mechanism? There was only one way to find out.

Pol held his breath, placed his palm on the plate, and heard a servo whir as the lid tilted upward. Light from the compartment below speared the metal above, and the thick, throat-choking odor of garbage wafted its way up through the hole. Pol grinned. Gross though it was, the disposal center was sweet indeed.

It took fewer than one unit to drop through the hole, slap the second palmplate, and close the lid. Pol had a story prepared should one of the Ra 'Na attendants have witnessed his arrival, but a quick check revealed that no one was around. Judging from the bins full of empty food containers, the chamber he was in had been dedicated to storing and sorting recyclables.

Pol consulted a wall diagram, verified that the part of the center he wanted was on the far side of the facility, and considered his options.

To reach his destination he could sneak from one place to another, which would almost certainly consume a considerable amount of time. Or—and this was the approach he favored—he could stroll through the halls, pretend he had every right to be where he was, and depart from the ship more quickly. *Assuming* the Ra 'Na who worked there allowed him to pass, *assuming* the Kan weren't lying in wait for him, and *assuming* the rest of his plan actually worked.

Pol took a deep breath, plastered what he hoped was a self-confident expression on his face, and stepped into the hallway. It was well lit and well scrubbed. The strong odor of disinfectant battled with the garbage and lost. The persistent rumble of machinery grew louder as he made his way down the corridor and paused next to a conveyer belt that carried garbage into a massive sorter.

An attendant, who was supposed to monitor the flow and use his long hook to remove unusually large objects from the belt, was leaning on the tool instead. He wore protective ear coverings, a breathing mask, and a badly stained smock. Clearly surprised and concerned lest the stranger accuse him of first-degree slackery, the technician hurried to look busy. The hook flashed forward, snagged a mass of twisted metal, and pulled it off the belt. Pol nodded approvingly and continued on his way.

Signs pointed the way, and he followed them. The whole thing was easy, *so* easy that he grew overconfident.

He rounded a corner, stepped into the pod bay, saw the Kan, and skidded to a halt. The Kan, whose back was turned, stuck his head into an empty pod, turned it from side to side, and pulled out again. His chitin seemed to oscillate from gray to silver. Then, shuffling as his kind were forced to do, the warrior moved to the next container. Someone, perhaps one of the Zin, had anticipated what the Ra 'Na would do and dispatched a Kan to prevent it!

Pol was too terrified to move. He stood and waited for the Sauron to discover him. Surely the warrior had heard him, would turn, and bring the entire escape plan to an ignominious end. But the Kan *didn't* turn, and Pol realized that the sounds generated by his movements had been obscured by those the machinery made. That being the case, perhaps he could back out of the compartment.

He took two backward steps before another idea occurred to him. The concept was audacious, outrageous, and thoroughly un–Ra 'Na–like, which meant it could possibly work!

Pol stopped, gathered his strength, and hurled himself forward. It wasn't until he was only a few feet away that the Kan heard the slapping noise made by the Ra 'Na's feet and started to turn his head. But it was too late by then. Pol hit the Kan's back with all the force he could muster, pushed the warrior forward, and had the pleasure of watching him dive headfirst into a half-filled disposal pod.

Then, moving with the alacrity of someone whose life depends on speed, Pol dashed to a nearby control panel, flipped a protective cover out of the way, flicked the safety into the "off" position, heard the hatch clang shut, and slammed his fist down on the firing button.

There was a pause while the ship's systems caught up with the quick sequence of commands. Pol listened as the Kan hammered the inside of the pod and watched as the cylindrical container dropped into the ejection port, where it would be readied for launch.

Fewer than five seconds passed before an airtight hatch slid into place and cut the tube off from the chamber above. Every bit of atmosphere was pumped out of the port, and the Kan was launched into space.

Not for long however, since rather than litter their valuable near-Earth orbits with thousands upon thousands of garbage pods, the Saurons ordered the Ra 'Na to let the containers fall through the planet's atmosphere and splash into the oceans below.

The very thing that Pol had in mind for himself. Except that unlike the Kan who had preceded him, he planned to survive.

Well aware of the passage of time, Pol hurried over to one of the thousands of emergency toolboxes placed throughout the ship, palmed it open, and grabbed a cutting torch.

He dashed to the control panel on the far side of the compartment, summoned a three-dimensional Earth, caused the display to rotate, selected a pod from the "ready" list along the screen's right-hand margin, clicked on the coordinates he wanted, glanced at the time, added thirty seconds, and entered the appropriate numbers.

Once that was accomplished, it was a simple matter to touch the final key, skitter across the deck, and jump into the appropriate pod. It was half filled with rotting food scraps. The horrible, stinking mess had risen all the way to his armpits before Pol's feet touched the bottom and he heard someone shout.

He realized that fifteen seconds of load time would have been sufficient, saw the Zin stick his snout into the container, and ducked into the garbage.

The Zin was in the process of reaching, his pincer only inches from Pol's body, when the hatch started to close. The Zin swore, jerked his snout out of the way, and disappeared as the lid fell into place.

His heart in this throat, Pol waited for the first jerky drop, the momentary pause while air was removed from the ejection port, and the sudden nearly fatal moment of acceleration as he, along with a large quantity of semiliquid garbage, was slammed from one end of the pod to the other.

But the slop served to cushion him, and though he was half

buried in garbage, Pol smiled. Short though his life might be, the rest of it would be free.

HELL HILL

Blue steeled himself against the inevitable stench, tied a bandanna across his nose, and entered the dark, fetid room. Absent the fittings that would be available within the citadel on the hill above and subject to his own runaway physiology, Lak-Tal's body no longer resembled that of a Sauron. He looked like a fleshy poached egg resting in a lake of its own excrement.

The room, always dark, seemed even more cavelike now, lit as it was by only a handful of guttering candles and cut off from the light of day. Blue entered, paused to get his bearings, then forced his body forward. "Lak-Tal? Can you hear me?"

The response, which could best be described as a wheezing noise, was faint but still audible.

Blue, who knew the Sauron must be nearing the end, forced himself to wait. One more try, he would give it one more try, and then he could leave. "Lak-Tal? It's me, Boyer Blue. Can you hear me?"

Now, as if woven into a long, steady exhalation of breath, a string of words was heard. "Yesssss, human, I can hear you." Only a third of the translator from which the words had been uttered still could be seen. The rest had been engulfed by a collar of blue-pink flesh.

Blue fought the nausea that threatened to engulf him, managed to swallow it, and chose his words with care. "Our plan, the one to teach the other castes how to read, it appears to be working."

There was silence for a moment followed by another reedy wheeze. "Not myyy plan. *Yourrr* plan. Not bad for a slave."

Blue was about to trade insult for insult when Shoes barged into the room and jerked toward the door. He wore the usual slave outfit and held a machine gun cradled in his arms. "Come on, Doc. It's time to haul ass. Somebody squealed, and the Saurons are working their way down through the stack."

Blue frowned. "Kan?"

"Yeah, but led by a Zin."

"The one they call Xat-Hey?"

Shoes shrugged. "Probably. Come on, we're taking casualties up top."

Blue turned, pulled his pistol, and addressed Lak-Tal. "We won't be able to return. Would you like to die?"

The response came more quickly this time. "Yesss, but not at the hand of a slave. Leave me and return to your people. They will need your leadership in the days ahead."

Blue heard the muffled thump, thump, thump of a shotgun being fired and knew that people were risking their lives in an effort to protect his. He offered an informal salute. "May your ancestors find and guide you."

"There'sss little chance of that," the Sauron replied softly, "sssince I betrayed them along with the rest of my species."

Blue might have replied except for the fact that Shoes chose that particular moment to grab his arm and jerk him out of the room. Together, running as fast as they could, they dodged through a succession of cubes and were ushered into a tunnel. A hanging made from a badly stained blanket dropped into place behind them, a rectangle of light lit the far end of the passageway, and a half inch of dark, fetid water splashed away from their boots.

Blue knew that he should have killed the Sauron, to shut him up if nothing else, and cursed his own weakness. How much information had the Zin managed to acquire, anyway? Could the local cell be compromised? And why hadn't he, the so-called leader, thought of such things earlier? Blue had started to slow, to think about going back, when Shoes shoved him forward. "Oh, no you don't! See that light? It's yours. All you gotta do is run a little faster."

Blue ran, and the light started to grow.

Less than a quarter mile away, Xat-Hey shot a woman in the face. Her body continued to fall as a Kan jerked the tarp out of the way and stuck a pincer into the grab hole. Hinges squealed as the trapdoor swung up and out of the way. The shaft was exactly where the immature male had promised it would be. A single glance was sufficient to confirm that the ladder had been constructed by humans for humans and would never accommodate the Saurons' long, narrow feet.

So the Zin dropped through the opening, absorbed the resulting impact with his legs, and looked for someone to kill. There was no one in sight. Not too surprising, given all the shooting.

Feet thumped as three heavily armed Kan fell the length of the shaft, bounced slightly, and moved out of the way. Xat-Hey signaled the closest. "The door—check on it."

It appeared to be dark beyond the opening, and a good deal less than inviting, but the warrior had no choice. He raised his automatic dart thrower, slid through the door, and gagged on the odor within. The movement of the otherwise stagnant air caused the candles to flicker, and the Kan realized that his initial impression had been wrong. There was *some* light, but very little.

Now, forcing himself forward, the warrior saw what looked like a pool of putrefied meat. Two additional Kan entered the chamber to back him up, saw whatever the thing was, and paused.

Xat-Hey made *his* entrance, saw the pulsating pod, and knew instinctively what it was. The words "Watch out!" had already formed in his throat when the creature exploded.

Finally stronger than its progenitor, and well aware of the danger it was in, the nymph had forced its way through the blood-rich birth sac. Now, thrusting its highly elastic neck to the full extent of its reach, the newborn applied razor-sharp teeth to the first Kan's throat.

Blood erupted like a fountain as the now lifeless body toppled to one side. The second warrior fired wildly, missed the target, and staggered backward as three of his own darts bounced off the metal walls and punched holes through his thorax.

The third Kan called for help and was backing away when Xat-Hey shot him in the head. It was unfortunate, *very* unfortunate, but there could be no witnesses. Other than himself, that is—and he knew even *that* might be questioned.

Careful to remain out of the nymph's range, Xat-Hey stepped forward, brought his weapon to bear on the pod, and prepared to squeeze the handle. The nymph spoke. The voice was quite similar to Lak-Tal's. "So you would kill your own kind in an effort to retain the power to which you are accustomed."

Xat-Hey held the weapon with both pincers. "I have no choice. By hatching early, you threaten us all."

"Not if the lesser castes were allowed to know the truth."

The Zin shook his head. "If the lesser castes knew what we know, then they wouldn't be 'lesser,' would they?"

The nymph was about to answer, about to make an important point, when the darts tore it apart.

Xat-Hey listened to the nymph's death scream, shuddered, and holstered his weapon. Suddenly, much to his surprise, the Zin wished he were elsewhere. It was a long climb to the surface, to the sun's clean light, and the fresh, salt-sea air. It was a strange world, an *alien* world, but the only one he had.

8

DEATH DAY MINUS 84

SATURDAY, MAY 9, 2020

You ask, what is our policy? I will say: It is to wage war, by sea, land, and air, with all the strength that God can give us; to wage war against a monstrous tyranny. . . . You ask, what is our aim? I can answer in one word: Victory, victory at all costs, victory in spite of all terror, victory, however long and hard the road may be; for without victory, there is no survival.

—WINSTON CHURCHILL,
Hansard, 1940

ON THE WESTERN SLOPES OF THE CASCADE RANGE

Though susceptible to attack from orbit, the upper elevations of the Cascade Range offered an excellent base from which the wilderness-savvy resistance fighters could interdict the columns of slaves who were funneled through the passes, ambush Kan patrols, and harass Sauron observation posts.

Abandoned mines, isolated cabins, and Forest Service watchtowers all offered shelter, as did the forests themselves, while a network of well-established hiking trails served to knit them together.

The resistance group known as "Deac's Demons" had elected to receive Franklin on *their* turf, where they could choose the terrain, control the area around the LZ, and ensure multiple paths of egress.

Here, a few hundred feet above the tree line, where the evergreen forest gave way to grassy meadows dotted with clumps of hardy trees, there was room not only to canvass one's surroundings but to also run for cover should that be necessary.

Deac Smith heard the big helicopter before he actually saw it. He was already looking upward when the Chinook roared over the treetops, turned, and disappeared beyond a clump of fir trees. That's where the LZ was, right next to a tiny lake, north of the old town of Monte Cristo.

The voice came from Smith's right. George "Popcorn" Farley had lost more than twenty pounds over the past few months and aged a couple of years. There was more salt than pepper in his hair now, the lines in his face ran even deeper than they had before, and a persistent sadness haunted his eyes. His voice was the same, though, as was the matter-of-fact attitude. "I don't know, Deac—remember that convoy a couple weeks back? What if the chopper is loaded with Kan?"

Smith remembered, all right. The convoy of ex-army six-bys had been disguised to look like it belonged to slavers. Then, after the Demons attacked, specially rigged canopies fell away so more than two dozen Kan could bounce up out of the trucks. The firefight lasted for the better part of half an hour, punctuated by carefully coordinated orbital artillery missions.

First there had been the roar of fractured air quickly followed by an explosion and a chest-thumping concussion as approximately four tons of dirt, rocks, and plant material geysered toward the sky. The exact nature of the technology involved was a mystery—but the results had been plain to see.

Eventually, after Smith and what remained of his attack force managed to break contact and pull back into the forest, the odds had improved. The Kan couldn't jump in among the trees, and while the sky eyes could detect heat, it was difficult to know what generated it. A human? A sun-warmed rock? A browsing deer? That being the case, the Saurons had eventually grown tired of blowing chunks out of the forest and given up.

The result had been eleven dead and fifteen wounded, heavy casualties for what amounted to a company of light infantry. So Farley was increasingly worried. The bugs had grown smarter and more aggressive of late.

Still, Smith knew that he and his forces could kill Saurons 24/7 and there would still be plenty of the bastards left. No, a *real* resistance movement, one capable of pushing the chits back into space, would require a coordinated effort.

Smith wrapped an arm around Farley's shoulders as they

walked through a scattering of wind-twisted trees. "Hey, that chopper could be carrying something even worse than the Kan."

Farley frowned. "Like what?"

Smith smiled. "Like a real, honest-to-God, dyed-in-the-wool human politician."

Farley laughed, and for that brief moment looked ten years younger.

■ ■ ■

The flight deck tilted to port, leveled out, and sent a shock up through Manning's combat boots as Wu put the Chinook down next to the tiny lake. The meadow was open in places, but there were still plenty of trees, rocks, and logs to hide behind. Judging from what the security chief had seen from the air, at least two platoons' worth of irregulars were scattered through the area. They were dug in, and judging from the way they were positioned, ready to put fire on the LZ. Manning didn't like the situation, not one little bit, but he had been overruled. Not once—*three* times.

The rotors made a steady whup, whup, whup sound as they wound down. Franklin appeared at the security chief's side and peered out through the open door. He had agreed to wear a bulletproof vest under his jacket, but that wouldn't protect him from a well-aimed head shot. Manning was about to say as much when the president raised a hand. "I know, I know. Don't worry, it'll be okay."

Manning edged to the right so that his body overlapped the president's. "I hope you're right, sir, but there's a whole bunch of white guys hiding in the area. I saw them on the way in."

Franklin smiled. "So? You're a white guy."

Manning refused to be placated. "You know what I mean. So far as we know, every single one of the Hilman assassins was white."

"Yes," Franklin agreed patiently, "and they were racists. *This* group is different."

"If you say so, sir," Manning conceded stubbornly, "but don't forget the plan."

"I know," Franklin replied, "run *away* from the chopper—not toward it."

"That's right, sir. If this is a trap, they will put a heat seeker or something similar into the Chinook right off the top. Our job is to hunker down, keep the bastards at bay, and wait for Air Two to show up. That should take about five minutes or so."

"Understood," Franklin said confidently, "but we won't need 'em. Come on, let's meet our new friends."

Kell, Amocar, Rix, and Wimba had deassed the chopper by then and were waiting on the ground. The moment Franklin's boots hit dirt, they closed in around him.

Smith, with Farley at his side, stood and waited as Franklin and his escort crossed open ground and entered the clump of trees. "I don't know," Farley said skeptically, "the Saurons can see everything we do from orbit. What's to keep the bastards from blowing the hell out of the entire meadow?"

"Nothing," Smith responded, "except that they believe Franklin is a full-blown collaborator. Plus his pilot reported a case of minor engine trouble and will pretend to fix it."

"That's bullshit," Farley replied contemptuously. "Most of the pilots I knew had a hard time zipping their pants, much less repairing an engine."

"Spoken like a true ground pounder," Smith said patiently, "but the Ra 'Na carry out most of the surveillance stuff *for* the bugs and, assuming Franklin is right, they're scanning the other side of the planet right about now."

Farley raised his eyebrows. "No shit? Frankenstein cut some sort of deal with the fur balls?"

Smith shook his head. "You're hopeless, George. Watch my back."

Farley grinned. "No problem, Top, I've got your six."

The two groups came together. Franklin plastered a professional grin on his face, shoved his hand out, and looked from one face to the other. "Hello, my name is Alexander Franklin. Which one of you gentlemen answers to Deac Smith?"

"That would be me," Smith replied, taking the politician's hand, "and this is George Farley, my executive officer. We served in the army together."

Farley, who still thought of himself as a sergeant, took the promotion in stride and shook Franklin's hand. The grip was good and firm. "Glad to meet you, sir."

Franklin shook his head. "Let's dump the 'sir' stuff. The Saurons call me 'President,' but that's bullshit and we all know it. The *real* president went down with *Air Force One* near Kansas City."

That was news to the resistance fighters. They asked the obvious questions. Franklin provided what information he could, and described the encounter at Spanaway Lake. "So," he concluded, "my wife thought I was wrong, but I accepted their offer. Partly because I thought I might be able to help any humans who managed to survive. But mostly because I was scared shitless."

Both statements were true, but even as he put them forward, Franklin knew there was more, a factor he had withheld. Even here, even now, the same desire for power that caused him to enter politics in the first place still coursed through his mind, body, and spirit. But it would never do to say so, not to his wife, and not to men like these.

Smith grinned. He liked Franklin's apparent honesty and waved the visitor in under the trees. "I don't blame you, Governor. Getting yourself killed wouldn't help the cause one little bit. Come on back. There're some camp chairs to sit on."

As the principals moved farther into the trees, their various bodyguards were left to sort themselves out. Slowly, as if by accident, five resistance fighters had drifted in to take up positions near Franklin's security team. The message was obvious: "One wrong move and you are toast."

Manning nodded to the woman who appeared to be in charge, instructed Rix, Wimba, and Amocar to take positions around the perimeter of the meeting area, and gestured to Kell. "We'll stay with the Big Dog."

With two resistance fighters in tow, the two men followed the principals into the clearing and took up positions facing outward. Both had twelve-gauge riot guns and two semiautos each. Even as they looked out, bored resistance fighters looked in, creating what amounted to a ridiculous standoff. A man dressed in buckskins but armed with an assault rifle winked, and Kell nodded. The official discussions, which had progressed beyond the get-acquainted stage by then, continued unabated.

"So," Smith said, settling back into an aluminum chair's somewhat tipsy embrace, "it's my understanding that we don't have a whole lot of time."

Franklin nodded. "That's correct. The Ra 'Na can protect us for an hour or so—but no longer than that."

"So it's true," Smith replied. "You really did cut some sort of deal with the Ra 'Na."

"Sort of," the politician acknowledged modestly, "although the argument could be made that *they* cut a deal with us."

"Really?" Farley inquired. "That's kind of surprising, given the fact that they seem married to the chits. They ride the Kan like horses, for goodness' sake."

"That's true," Franklin agreed, "but the cozy stuff is coming to an end."

Smith narrowed his eyes. The single-word response was part question and part challenge. "Why?"

Franklin examined one face, then the other. How would Smith and Farley react to the truth? To the fact that to survive, mankind would not only have to beat the Saurons, but also do so within an extremely short period of time. The reality of that might crush lesser men, but he had the feeling that nobody in his or her right mind would ever describe either of the resistance fighters as "lesser."

Franklin gave it to them straight, starting with the briefing by Dro Rul and concluding with some of his own observations. "I may be wrong, but based on the extent to which the Zin known as the 'stonemaster' was willing to compromise, and the general sense of urgency on and around Hell Hill, it's my guess that the birth chambers are running behind schedule."

Smith's chair made a creaking noise as he shifted his weight forward. His eyes seemed brighter, as if lit from within. The profanity, rare for him, served to highlight the strength of his emotions. "Damn! Let me see if I have this right. You're telling me that every single one of those bastards is going to die? So all we have to do is wait? Praise the Lord."

"What you say is true," Franklin agreed cautiously, "so far as it goes."

"Uh-oh," Farley said cynically, "here comes the rub."

"There *is* a rub," Franklin agreed reluctantly. "Based on intelligence gathered by the Ra 'Na, the Saurons plan to kill ninety percent of their slaves prior to the birthing."

Smith fell back into his chair. His voice was bleak. "It's over, then. Thousands will die."

"*No,*" Franklin said, with a certainty that surprised even him. "*Not* if we can bring all of the human resistance groups together, *not* if we can cement an alliance with the Ra 'Na, *not* if we move quickly enough."

"That's a whole lot of 'ifs,' " Smith said hollowly.

"And a whole lot of power for the man, woman, or fur ball who winds up at the head of the unified resistance movement," Farley added flatly. "And who might that be? *You*, perhaps?"

Smith looked at his friend and back to Franklin. "Don't let George bother you—he—"

"*He* has some legitimate concerns," Franklin put in. "An honest question deserves an honest answer. Yes, I think I'm the logical choice, but not at the expense of the movement. If either one of you has a desire to lead, then say so now. I will not only step aside, but throw my full support behind you."

There was a long, drawn-out moment of silence. Farley was the first to speak. "No way. I'd rather ram red-hot pokers through both my eyes."

"I wouldn't go quite that far," Smith allowed dryly, "but George is right. I know next to nothing about politics, and I don't plan to learn."

"So," Farley put in, "I guess that settles it: You're elected."

"Well, not *elected,*" Franklin said wryly, "*appointed.* Later, as we attempt to bring more groups into the fold, the issue will come up again."

"Good," Smith said intently. "You build the alliance—and we'll back you. Don't let us down, though. . . ."

"Or *what?*" Franklin asked, challenging the other man to say it.

"*Or,*" Farley repeated heavily, "bodyguards or no bodyguards, one of us will put you in the ground."

HELL HILL

Bone tired after the long, dangerous trip back from Hilman, not to mention two days spent waiting to penetrate the heavily guarded wall that encircled the hill's base, the White Rose was finally home. A rather strange word to apply to a death camp. But it was the one that came to mind.

It was dawn, just before the shift change, and a good time to move around. There were literally thousands of humans trudging along the paths, many more than the Kan up in the observation towers could ever hope to keep track of, and that made for excellent cover as Ivory, Marta, Parker, and Boner climbed steadily upward.

None of the slaves noticed them at first. And why should they? Tired, ragged-looking humans were a dime a dozen.

But many still possessed copies of the slick "talkies" distributed two days before, wanted posters that not only described the failed assassination attempt but also included video taken by the Kan. One such clip included a shot of the swastika on Jonesy's chest, and a surprisingly good shot of Ivory's face.

Nobody knew exactly what the humans had done, only that

they had the guts to attack the chits and that the aliens were pissed.

But that was enough to fill heads with hope and get people excited.

That being the case, it wasn't too surprising that someone noticed, pointed, and whispered to the person next to him.

Ivory, who walked head down, didn't notice at first, but it was only a matter of time till someone spoke more loudly. "Look! It's him! The one on the poster!"

Heads swiveled, people looked, and a man echoed the cry. "Look, it's them! The ones the bugs are after!"

Ivory and the others looked up, grabbed the weapons hidden beneath their rags, and prepared to defend themselves.

Marta swore as the crowd closed around them, Ivory nearly fell as someone slapped him on the back, and Parker accepted the poster that a woman jammed in his face. The skin took one look, saw Ivory's face, and tapped him on the shoulder. "Hey, boss! Take a look at this!"

Ivory accepted the poster, managed to read it as people continued to pummel him, and felt his spirits soar. The assassination attempt had failed, but, because of their less than perfect understanding of human psychology, the Saurons had provided the movement with the very thing it needed most: publicity. Now, thanks to the chits and the ever-faithful Yahweh, the White Rose was legitimate.

No longer tired, careless of what the Saurons might see, they marched like heroes through the streets of Hell Hill. Here, like the imaginary scenes hung at Racehome, was a moment of victory.

But even as Ivory luxuriated in the unexpected acclaim, he knew it to be false. The muds were gaining traction—he could *feel* it.

What the movement needed was some sort of new relationship, an alliance that would catapult the White Rose to the next level and secure their hard-won victory.

But with whom? The group called "Deacon's Demons"? No; word had it that the muds had infiltrated the organization. The Star Com? No; same problem. It seemed as if the remnants of the ZOG were everywhere, and that being the case, there was no—

And that was the moment when a milk-white Sauron appeared in the intersection up ahead, paused to examine some incomprehensible graffiti, and jumped onto a cube.

It was in that brief moment that Yahweh spoke. There *was* a group to whom Ivory and his followers could turn, a potentially powerful group, and one they should have looked at before: *the Fon*.

PUGET SOUND, SOUTH OF HELL HILL

In spite of the fact that the never-ending daylight made it difficult to ply their trade and forced them to operate farther to the south, the Crips continued to eke out a marginal living.

It was dusk now, down along daylight's edge, and the humans were pulling for home. They had enough shellfish to eat, but less than they had hoped for, well short of the surplus required to trade.

But, as with most less than desirable circumstances, there was a bright side, and Darby gave thanks for it. The less than average haul meant the boat had more freeboard than usual, an excellent defense against the waves that marched their way up from the southwest to slap the port side of the hull. Each assault produced an explosion of spray that blew back into the coxswain's face and chilled her skin.

But Darby was used to that and, with no danger in sight, allowed her mind to drift. None of the fantasies had anything to do with her brief career as a resistance fighter, the swim to the island, or the rescue that followed two days later.

No, her dreams were much more mundane. What she wanted was a little cabin somewhere, safe from prying eyes, with a plot of good dirt. That's where she would grow vegetables, put some flowers for the table, and—

Her reveries were interrupted as Wylie suddenly stopped rowing and pointed upward. "Darby! Look! A shooting star!"

The *Sunshine* slewed to starboard. Darby snapped, "Mind your rowing!" and scanned the sky. Whatever Wylie had seen was no longer visible, but she heard the roar of displaced air and saw water geyser ahead. Or had she? The strange half light made it difficult to be sure.

"It's the Saurons," someone whispered. "Let's get out of here!"

"Maybe," Darby allowed cautiously, "and maybe not. The splash was too small for a ship. Let's see what we've got. Together, now: Pull."

"Why?" Chu asked, her mind focused on the comforts of home. "I'm tired."

"Stop whining," Nakambe replied, "and pull your weight Maybe the thing is valuable. Let's check it out."

Grateful for the support and curious as to what they might find Darby steered for a point off the starboard bow. Had whatever it was already sunk? No, she could see it now, some sort of canister floating three-quarters submerged.

The rowers, none of whom could resist the temptation to sneak looks over their shoulders, jabbered among themselves.

"I wonder what it is?"

"Food! I hope it's food."

"Food? Are you crazy? What we need is medical stuff."

"Oh, right, like a whole bunch of medical supplies are going to fall out of the sky."

"Belay the bullshit," Darby said darkly. "Forward oars aloft Nok, make your way forward. See if you can get a line on that thing. I plan to take it in tow."

"Oh, great," Chu said. "*She* plans to tow it ashore. *We* row— *she* steers."

"Stow it," Nakambe replied curtly, "or get out and walk."

Chu started to reply but was cut off when the bow clanged against the canister, sheered away, and jerked back again.

"Got it!" Nok announced victoriously. "I'm passing the line back."

Darby swore as the *Shine* wallowed in a trough. They waited for the line to make its way aft, then secured it to the empty motor mount. "All right, you slackers: Pull!"

The Crips pulled, the line went taut, and the boat jerked to a halt.

"I said, '*Pull!*' " Darby said with a growl. "Or would you like to spend the night out here?"

There was grumbling, a good deal of which originated with Chu, but the Crips pulled, and dragged the canister behind them

Conscious of the hard work involved, and concerned lest he crew exhaust themselves, Darby steered for shore. The nearest beach was a good two miles north of the cove they called "home, but that was good enough. Once the Crips dragged their find into the shallows, they could assess its value and make a decision Should they leave it? Or take it home? The answer would be obvious.

A good fifteen minutes passed before the bow finally grated on gravel and those who could, jumped over the boat's side. The water was cold, *very* cold, and Darby swore as it rose to her thighs.

Reaching one hand over the other, the sailors pulled on the wet, slimy line till the canister bumped into the sharply shelving beach. The more mobile members of the crew rushed to inspect it. Chu got there first and shouted the news. "I hear a pounding noise! Like someone's inside!"

"There's a hatch!" Nakambe called. "I think it will open."

"*Don't* do it," Wylie cautioned from the boat. "It could be a Sauron."

"Sauron, moron," Chu replied. "Use your head. What chit in his right mind would land inside something like that? It'd have to be crazy."

Darby drew the big revolver from under her coat, pulled the hammer back to full cock, and waded forward. Chu hurried to get out of the way as the coxswain played a small flashlight across the top of the cylinder, took note of the alien glyphs, and saw the recessed lever. There *was* a noise, a sort of booming sound, as if someone were inside.

Holding the flashlight with her teeth and the .357 with her right hand, Darby grabbed the handle. It was stiff, as if seldom used. It took every bit of her strength, but the device finally gave.

There was a hiss as pressures equalized, followed by the overwhelming stench of garbage. Chu held her nose, Nakambe said, "That's gross!" and Darby took a full step backward. The small circle of light wobbled across the canister's hatch. The gun felt heavy in her hand.

A ratty-looking Ra 'Na stuck his head up out of the hatch, examined his surroundings, and spoke through a much-abused translator: "I smell bivalves. When do we eat?"

HELL HILL

The rain fell in a steady drizzle, not hard but consistently as if determined to impose its misery over the longest possible time. It was dark, or as dark as the Saurons would allow it to get, and that added to the gloom.

As usual, the line into Dr. Sool's Free Clinic snaked out across the plaza and down a side street.

Volunteers, people with a bit of medically related experience, constantly walked the line, searched out those who needed emergency assistance, and escorted them inside.

The rest, Boyer Blue included, had no choice but to wait as

the rain seeped through their ragged clothing or trickled down
their backs. Which was worse? they wondered. To have a condition that warranted being rushed inside the clinic? Or to be
healthy enough to wait out in the weather?

For Blue, who was fortunate enough to possess a worn but still
serviceable REI rain parka, the experience was somewhat different. One part of his mind, which the academic thought of as the
primate, knew that the Zin named Xat-Hey could show up at any
moment. It was that part of his beingness that was almost pain-
fully aware of the nearest observation tower and could feel Sauron
eyes crawling like bugs across the surface of his body. The primate gibbered and urged him to run.

Another part of his persona, what he regarded as the "higher"
him, stood outside his personal circumstances and focused on the
people around him. That's when he noticed something quite disconcerting—in a line where there should have been plenty of sick
children, many of whom would be crying, there were hardly any
sounds at all. Just the shuffling of feet, the low murmur of adult
conversation, and the occasional barking cough.

He remembered his daughter, the taking of uncountable innocent lives, and heard the primate whisper in his ear, "Kill the
aliens! Kill them! Kill them! Kill them!"

But Blue refused to listen. Not because he thought the primate
was necessarily wrong, but because the higher him had taken
notice of something important. Something he should have noticed
before. Though not obvious in many cases, either because the
women around him were dressed in loose-fitting clothes or were
intentionally trying to hide it, a significant number of them were
pregnant. Blue found himself nearly overwhelmed by both the
wonder and the horror of that.

Here, as the Saurons forced humans to build citadels so their
kind could survive, at least some of the slaves had intentionally
or unintentionally taken steps to replicate their species as well, as
if in response to the almost unimaginable number of casualties
suffered by humanity.

Was it the result of group carelessness? A sort of "let's live
for today" hedonism? Or did the otherwise almost unexplainable
decision to reproduce stem from something else? A yearning? An
undying hope? Instincts so deep they defied explanation?

Whatever the reason, the reality of the situation argued in favor
of action. Do something and he might fail. Do *nothing* and most
of the race, the human race, would die.

The voice came from behind and to the left. It was soft and pitched intentionally low, but it still caused him to jump. "Hello, Dr. Blue, my name is Dixie. I'm Dr. Sool's nurse." Please allow me to examine your left leg and accompany you to the clinic."

Blue nodded.

"And Dr. Blue?"

"Yes?"

"Remember to limp. There will be plenty of eyes—so give them a show."

Blue waited while Dixie ran her hands down his left leg, pretended to wince, and wondered if he was overacting. Was the charade actually necessary? Or was there some other means by which Franklin and he might meet?

Well, it didn't matter much, as long as they *did* meet and were able to get something done.

"Okay," Dixie said, "lean on me and favor your *left* foot."

Blue did as the woman requested, felt envious eyes probe his back, and wondered about Franklin. What sort of man was he? A self-serving collaborator, as many humans assumed? Or a self-sacrificing patriot, a sort of latter-day Zorro, who functioned as one person by day and another at night?

And what about Franklin's call for unity? Was it real? Motivated by a genuine desire to overthrow the Saurons? Or was the initiative part of the man's attempt to gain more power for himself? Or worse yet, a trap laid by the Saurons? Who was waiting for him, anyway? Franklin? Or Xat-Hey?

The door to the clinic yawned open. Blue pushed the raggedy curtain aside and slipped in a pool of blood.

■ ■ ■

Bal-Lok was dreaming. He wanted to stop, to break it off, but couldn't seem to disconnect. It felt as if hooks had been thrust through his chitin, each connected to an invisible wire, all connected to a being from the past. Ancestors who pulled, jerked, and tugged in different directions.

Some lectured, some pleaded, some stared through baleful eyes. All had one thing in common: They didn't want to lose their identities, to be forgotten forever, to die the final death.

And die they surely would if the Fon Liberation Front made a mistake, if his nymph, *their* nymph, were to die before it could truly live.

Bal-Lok tried to communicate with his progenitors, tried to tell them that they had nothing to fear, but most refused to listen. So the Fon was almost grateful when some unseen being pressed something hard and cold against the side of his head and made incomprehensible gargling sounds.

Bal-Lok opened his eyes, squinted into the bright white light, and realized he was surrounded by humans. Slaves, who under normal circumstances wouldn't dare lay an extremity on him, but who, by means unclear, had not only discovered his hiding place but also, judging from the weapons they held, were going to kill him.

There was movement, and Bal-Lok felt the sudden weight as something fell around his neck. A garrote? No, his translator. It appeared that the slaves wanted to speak with him. To taunt him prior to his death. One of them spoke, and the words came across in Sauron. "Sorry to wake you in this manner, but we had very little choice. My name is Jonathan Ivory."

The tone was much more reasonable than Bal-Lok expected, and that, combined with the sudden disappearance of human weaponry, acted to restore the Fon's power of speech. "How did you find me? What do you want?"

Ivory shrugged. The truth involved an abduction, followed by some carefully administered torture, and a tasty if somewhat greasy meal. Given the fact that it wasn't the sort of story likely to secure the Fon's cooperation, the human lied instead.

"One of your brothers told us about the Fon Liberation Front. We offered to help, so he told us where you were."

Bal-Lok made a mental note to find which one of his brothers had been so stupid as to trust slaves and find the means to punish him. In the meantime, he had little choice but to play along. In an effort to buy time and reclaim at least some of his dignity, he proceeded to back out of the Kan-issue field sling. The slaves made room. "You want to help? Why?"

Ivory directed the flashlight beam to those grouped around him. There was Marta, her eyes filled with determination; Parker, his face empty of all expression; and Boner, who pulled a finger out of his nose and blinked as the light hit his eyes. "Haven't you noticed?" Ivory demanded. "Black humans oppress *us* just as black Saurons oppress *you*. That's what the Liberation Front is all about, isn't it? Freedom?"

More fully awake by then, Bal-Lok felt his brain kick into high gear. Fantastic though it was, the slaves believed some sort of alliance was possible!

The absurdity of that was laughable, and the Fon was about to say as much when he remembered the illicit weapons the beings in front of him possessed. How had such things been obtained? How could the Kan be so lax? No wonder Hak-Bin had seen fit to dispatch the likes of Xat-Hey to the planet. The situation was out of control. "Yes," the Fon extemporized, "there is some truth in what you say."

"Damned right there is," Marta said hotly, "which is why we have a proposal for your consideration."

"A proposal?" Bal-Lok replied weakly, suddenly frightened by the speed with which things were moving forward. "What *kind* of proposal?"

Shadows shifted as Ivory waved the flashlight. "Summon your brothers, join us in an attack on the human known as Franklin, and we will shelter all who fight alongside of us."

The Fon was about to say "no," or find some way to stall, when he remembered Sister Andromeda, and the unreasonable conditions she was trying to impose on him. As if a Sauron would ever submit to a human! He chose his words with care. "The proposal you put forward is an interesting one. But my brothers and I need something more. . . ."

Ivory and Marta looked at each other. "Good," the woman answered cautiously. "What would you need?"

"You know of the human Star Com?"

"Yes," Ivory answered. "What about them?"

"Later," Bal-Lok said, "*after* the attack, you will kill the group's leader, but *only* their leader, because I have need of her followers."

"All right," Ivory replied slowly, "but why?"

The Fon considered telling the human the same truth he had already shared with Sister Andromeda—that the entire Sauron race was about to be reborn—but decided there was no need. Not yet. Not while he could play one slave against another. The answer seemed to produce itself. "Because she harbors blacks."

The answer was incomplete, Ivory knew that, but it was still everything he had hoped for. He smiled. "You know what? That's plenty good enough for us. Welcome to the cause."

■ ■ ■

The inside of the clinic smelled of disinfectant, sweat, and vomit. Blue slipped in a pool of blood, felt Dixie grab his arm, and managed to keep his balance. One section of the room had been curtained off and, judging by a woman's calm, unhurried voice, some sort of surgery was taking place within.

"Clamp that bleeder, thank you, four-oh on a stick, please. . . ."

"We get a whole lot of trauma stuff toward the end of each shift," Dixie explained. "People are really tired by then and they tend to make mistakes."

Blue wanted to ask a question but never got the chance. The nurse ushered him through a rough-cut doorway and into the adjoining module. Franklin was waiting there. As Blue entered, Franklin stood and offered his hand. "Greetings, Dr. Blue. Thank you for coming."

The moment stretched long and thin as Blue looked at the extended hand, paused, and finally took it. "I'm sorry, Governor Franklin, but I'm not sure what to say."

Franklin waved toward a chair. "Please, take a seat."

Blue accepted the invitation and sat with arms crossed.

Franklin grabbed a chair, turned it around, and sat facing the back. His smile was genuine. "I'm no expert on body language, but I sense a certain skepticism."

Blue shrugged. "Actions speak louder than words, Governor, and based on *your* actions, it seems safe to say that you are the worst sort of collaborator and a traitor to your race."

Blue's words cut deep. Franklin had expected to hear some of the same cynicism voiced by Deac Smith and George Farley, but nothing like this. Blood rushed to his face; he swallowed, and fought to maintain his composure. Blue, and the people who followed him, would comprise an important part of the proposed alliance. "I'm sorry you feel that way. Why did you come, if I may ask?"

Blue looked Franklin in the eye. "I came on the chance that my impression is mistaken. I came on the chance that you *are* who you say you are, or, failing that, have the capacity to *become* who you say you are. We need a leader who can tie the resistance together, and we don't have much time. Are you aware of the Sauron birthing?"

Franklin, amazed and a bit frightened by the extent of Blue's insight, nodded. "Yes, the Ra 'Na told me."

Blue raised an eyebrow. "Did they really? Now, that's interesting. Are they willing to join an alliance?"

"Yes, *if* we can deliver most if not all of the human resistance movement."

"Which is why you invited me to visit."

"Again, yes. The group called 'Deacon's Demons' has agreed to join, and I'm hoping that you and your people will do likewise."

Blue, arms still folded, leaned back into his chair. "Which brings us back to where we started. *If* the Saurons own you, *if* we make ourselves vulnerable, you could send each and every one of my people to their deaths."

There was a long silence as the two men stared at each other across the room. Finally Franklin spoke.

"There is nothing that I can say to prove my sincerity. All I can do is point out what you already know: The clock is ticking. The Saurons will kill most if not of all of us approximately eighty-four days from now. Our only hope is to band together.

"Since you can't trust me, then trust yourself, and lead the allied effort. You are a historian, a man who knows all the mistakes that human beings have made over the past two thousand years, and are therefore qualified to lead."

Was the offer genuine? Or some sort of ploy? Blue stared into Franklin's face as if it were a map that could lead him to the truth.

What came to mind, however, wasn't about Franklin. Yes, he knew human history, but rather than make him strong, as Franklin thought it did, the knowledge made him weak. Not as a historian—but as a leader.

The truth was that Blue's knowledge of history caused him to make simple decisions complex, to hesitate rather than act, and to worry about the manner in which future historians would measure what he had done. Which was a silly conceit given the fact that there weren't likely to *be* any future academics, given the way things were going.

Blue made a point out of uncrossing his arms and shifted his weight forward on the chair. He smiled. "Thanks for the offer, but before we turn to such desperate measures, let's talk for a while. I have questions. Quite a few of them."

Franklin, who felt as though he had passed some sort of test, allowed himself to relax a little. The ensuing conversation lasted for the better part of four hours.

■ ■ ■

Xat-Hey had no love of nuance, no tolerance for gray, preferring as he did the crisp, clean demarcations of black and white.

But here on Hell Hill, where the sun never seemed to set, and brothers like Lak-Tal could die in ignominy, his line forever severed, *nothing* was clear. Least of all his own emotions.

That's why the Zin allowed himself to be drawn back to the establishment called the Square Hole. Based on information gathered over the past few days, it was clear that the recently deceased proprietor not only encouraged Fon to make use of the back room but also supplied them with all the Ra 'Na–manufactured kog gum they could chew. A rather obvious ploy to purchase some protection.

Though constitutionally unable to approve of the corruption involved, Xat-Hey understood. Constant exposure to the slaves, not to mention pressure from above, left the Fon vulnerable to depression—the same sort of emotional low that he was experiencing now. . . .

Now, as one last jump terminated in front of the Square Hole's entrance, Xat-Hey saw a human enter and felt a sense of hope. The place was open. Did they have what he was looking for? A good, hard chew? He would soon find out. Humans scattered as he shuffled toward his goal.

Not far away, in the darkness sandwiched between two cubes, eyes watched the Zin enter the saloon. No sooner had the door closed than two dozen humans came scurrying out.

The acolyte waited for a good five minutes to see if the Zin would emerge before pulling the radio out from under his robes and holding the device to his lips.

"Starlight."

There was a pause followed by a burst of static. "Star Bright. Go."

"I have him."

"How long?"

"He entered the Square Hole five minutes ago."

"Stay where you are. Let us know if he leaves."

The acolyte nodded, realized that the com center operator couldn't see him, and said, "Understood. Starlight out."

■ ■ ■

With half the population at work on the temple complex and the other half asleep, it was midshift quiet on the hill, with only the distant clink of hammers, faintly heard commands, and the occasional caw from a crow to disturb the relative silence.

The Fon shuffled through the door like so many ghosts, the scent of wood smoke wafting in behind them adding its acrid note to the symphony of sweat, cooking, and eternally wet clothing that dominated the air within.

Once inside the cube, each alien was met and escorted back to an adjoining cargo container, where they were instructed to wait. Ivory and Marta had gone to considerable lengths to prepare the skins for the visitation, so the Fon were treated with the deference and respect to which they were accustomed.

And why not? Marta asked herself cynically. Few if any of them were likely to survive the upcoming battle.

Ivory deserved credit for the alliance itself, but Marta was the one who had figured out how to best take advantage of it. And now, as she prepared to lead the attack on the presidential complex, she was filled with a sense of pride. Finally, after all the years of nobodyness, her life had meaning and purpose. True to old man Howther's prophecy, the assassin had been born.

"That's number seventeen," Parker reported from his position next to the hatch.

"Good," Marta replied. "All of them are here. You can close it up."

The door clanged and Marta followed the last Fon back through the candlelit murk and into the makeshift armory. A row of plywood tables lined a wall decorated with racialist symbols. Each table bore the weight of at least five freshly oiled 12-gauge shotguns. Sauron t-guns would have been better, of course, but none were available, not at any price.

Because of that the human weapons, duck guns for the most part, had been retrofitted with grasper-friendly modifications that made the weapons easier for the Fon to hold and fire.

By hacking the trigger guards away, cutting the stocks down, and mounting a pistol-style grasper grip under each slide, the shotguns had been effectively "chitized."

Most were pump guns, which made training fairly easy. Jack a shell into the chamber and pull the trigger. What could be easier? Not that the course would take all that long. Fifteen minutes would be plenty.

Then, before the aliens could change their minds, or rat the operation out, Marta would lead them into battle.

The Fon would go in first, fire their weapons, and engage the Kan. Then, as the Sauron warriors revealed themselves, Marta's prepositioned snipers would do their bloody work.

At that point, having penetrated the outermost layer of her

brother's security cordon with few if any casualties, the skins would go in for the kill.

Then the *real* fun would begin. Once inside the presidential complex, Marta would look for Franklin, cap the bastard, and kill as many muds as she could.

As for her brother, maybe she would give him one last chance, and maybe she wouldn't. Either way, the job would get done.

Marta entered the armory, nodded to Ivory, and took her place at the front of the room. "Good evening. It's a privilege to fight alongside the Fon Brotherhood in their battle for supremacy. Please direct your attention to the arsenal of high-powered weapons lined up in front of you.

"From this time forward the Fon will take their place as Sauron warriors. The Kan, so arrogant before, will regard you with respect."

Bal-Lok, who stood front row center, thought how good that would feel, raised a foot, and brought it down.

The brethren joined in, and the skins did likewise. The same battle, the one waged so many times before, would be fought again.

■ ■ ■

Time had passed. The acolyte named Starlight wasn't sure how much, since the Saurons had taken his watch months before, but he guessed a couple of hours. *Boring* hours during which very little had occurred.

Off-duty humans entered the Square Hole from time to time, only to burst out through the front door seconds later.

Starlight could only imagine the scene within as the slave entered, saw the Zin, and wondered if he or she was about to die.

None did, however, because they always came back out, still looking back over their shoulders, afraid the Zin would chase them.

Eventually, when the door clanged, the acolyte realized that he'd been asleep on his feet. He fully expected to see another human scuttle out of the bar. But this patron wasn't human, far from it. He paused to look around.

Xat-Hey felt his senses whirl as he surveyed his surroundings and tried to remember which way to go.

How many strings of kog gum had he consumed, anyway? Five? Six? It made no difference. The answer was too many.

The Zin had gathered his energies and was about to jump when he sensed movement to either side of him.

At least two dozen white-robed humans emerged from the shadows. Many were armed with clubs.

Fear, along with the chemicals it helped generate, acted to cut through the kog gum–induced haze and prepare the Zin for action. The muscles in his hindquarters bunched, released, and propelled him into the air.

Starlight, who had just emerged from his hiding place, was in an excellent position to witness what happened next.

Two acolytes, stationed on the Square Hole's flat roof, threw the fishing net in concert. The yellow nylon web settled over the Zin's shoulders, arrested the jump, and brought him crashing to the ground.

The Zin bellowed a war cry and reached for the t-gun holstered at his side.

Someone yelled, "Pull the net tight!" and Starlight was there, pulling with all the rest, when a solid beam of light lanced down from above. The observation tower! They had been seen!

There was a momentary pause as the Zin struggled against the ever-tightening net, and the Kan, amazed by the sight below, waited for orders.

A watch commander, summoned from his meal, emerged onto the catwalk that circled the tower, took a look, and waved a tightly rolled pancake at his subordinates. "What are you waiting for? The slaves have a Zin! Shoot them!"

Starlight first became aware that he and his fellow acolytes had come under fire when the woman across from him acquired a third eye, threw her hands into the air, and toppled over backward. The crack of the long gun came like an auditory exclamation point.

Sunburst, one of Sister Andromeda's favorites, bellowed, "Hold!" and the acolytes held.

Xat-Hey had managed to pull his t-gun. Someone yanked on it, and the weapon went off. A male acolyte fell but another took his place.

An acolyte had a club. It cracked the surface of the Zin's chitin, and the alien grunted in pain.

Starlight released the net as the man to his right jerked under the impact of a high-velocity slug and fell to the ground. He had already turned, and was about to flee, when Sunburst grabbed his arm. "Oh, no, you don't. Grab a stick! Kill the Zin. *Then* you can run."

Suddenly ashamed, and determined to redeem himself, Starlight took hold of a fallen club and joined the circle of death.

The scene had taken on a surreal quality by then. The blood-stained sticks rose and fell as if wielded by machines. Xat-Hey bleated like a wounded sheep as the Kan fired bullet after bullet into the mob below. People fell in slow motion, or so it seemed to Starlight, who felt warm liquid splatter his face as the club next to him slammed into the Zin's now defenseless body, slumped to the ground.

"It's over!" Sunburst shouted. "God's work is done! Run!"

Starlight ran with all the rest.

Xat-Hey heard the call of distant voices, knew his name had been forever silenced, and marveled at the wonder of it. Slaves with sticks? Who would have thought? Then he was gone.

A few minutes later, when a hastily dispatched contingent of Kan arrived on the scene, the Zin's body looked like a flower of black ringed by petals of white.

Perhaps the noncom in charge would have felt more sympathy had it not been for the encounter the day before in which Xat-Hey and his toughs had accosted the Kan, pushed him around, and demanded information.

That being the case the noncom toed the body and murmured the only eulogy Xat-Hey was likely to receive. "So long, you nameless piece of excrement—long may you and your ancestors rot in hell."

■ ■ ■

The cubes formed a mosaic of light and dark squares lit from below where torches, can fires, and battery-operated lamps went together to produce a warm glow.

There were silhouettes, though, some stationary, and some that moved. One, a solitary Kan, shuffled from one end of the roof to the other. As with most military organizations, the Kan used various methods to punish relatively minor offenses, one of which was to pull sentry duty on the so-called presidential complex, an assignment that one wag equated to "standing guard over a pile of excrement."

A sentiment that the Kan named Duu-Bak couldn't help but agree with, since the very concept of protecting a slave was clearly stupid.

But what else was new? It sometimes seemed as if the Zin had nothing better to do than come up with absurd tasks, such as laying waste to worthless planets, constructing temples that nobody would ever use, and protecting slaves.

It was nighttime, which meant nothing really, except that work continued in a landscape of what looked like amplified moonlight.

Some of the Kan professed to like the sort of enchanted glow, but Duu-Bak wasn't one of them. There were too many shadows for his liking, too many places where assailants could hide, and too many humans about. Humans who, if the rumors could be believed, *hated* the slave named Franklin and might seek to kill him.

Which brought the Kan back to where the internal dialogue had started. Why protect the human? Especially if his own kind hated him? The whole thing was madness.

Such were Duu-Bak's thoughts as a human screamed, weapons began to bark, and a hail of double-ought buck rattled across the front of the cube on which he stood.

True to both instinct and training, the Kan launched himself into the air, activated his assault weapon, and scanned the area for targets.

What Duu-Bak and the other Kan warriors saw was so unlikely, so impossible, that even though many of them *could* have fired, they didn't, an understandable but deadly reaction.

Fon, at least a dozen of them, had emerged from the shadows and were advancing on the checkpoint below. They were armed, and more than that, firing on the Kan!

Even as Duu-Bak watched, one of his brothers stepped out from behind the safety of an armored vehicle, raised his t-gun, and paused.

A Fon terminated a short six-foot leap and fired his twelve-gauge. Duu-Bak saw his brother's face obliterated.

The nearly headless corpse was still falling when the Fon leader roared an inarticulate battle cry and waved his troops forward.

Though still baffled as to what going on, the Kan knew they were under attack, and did what they were supposed to do: Fight back.

"Shoot the Fon!" a noncom shouted, his voice blasting through Duu-Bak's radio just as the Kan's big platformlike feet touched down, and he again jumped into the air.

Higher now, much higher than the Fon below, the warrior fired his weapon. It was a difficult shot, triggered while in motion, but practice makes perfect, and the dart flew true.

Bal-Lok, his back exposed, felt the impact. T-guns, like weapons devised by most sentient races, had originally been designed to kill the same species that invented them.

The dart blasted a hole through Bal-Lok's chitin and exploded deep within his guts. He had just enough time to realize how treacherous the humans were and how stupid he had been. Most of the literate Fon would die in the attack; both the Zin and the Kan nymphlings would hatch unmolested and continue their tyranny.

But time was up. Bal-Lok experienced a flash of white light, an unexpected sense of warmth, and a lightness of being. Then he was gone.

Meanwhile, unaware that he had killed the Fon leader, Duu-Bak continued to fight. The Kan knew his particular unit had been in combat prior to landing on Haven but couldn't remember when or where. Not consciously, anyway, although there was something familiar about the keyed-up, superalert way in which his brain now functioned, as if some previously dormant part of himself had suddenly come to life.

Duu-Bak saw the first target fall, knew better than to waste time gloating over the victory, and waited for his feet to hit the ground.

But Parker was waiting, too, his rifle aimed at the spot where the Kan would land, his finger on the trigger. The skin knew that the key to shooting chits was to aim for the spot where they *would be*, rather than the spot where they *had been*. It was like hunting ducks.

Parker allowed his finger to tighten, felt the assault rifle nudge his shoulder, and squeezed again. By selecting semiauto rather than full auto, he would conserve precious ammo and still accomplish the desired objective. He liked the logic of it and watched the target fall.

Duu-Bak, wholly unaware of the trap that had been laid for him, continued to fall until his lower extremities entered the kill zone and the 7.62mm rounds started to eat him from below. The blows came in quick succession, as if delivered by an invisible club, each followed by a moment of exquisite pain.

Before he could even consider the nature or the meaning of his death, a bullet smashed its way through his side and penetrated his heart. Duu-Bak, plus all the Duu-Baks that might have been, was dead before his body touched the ground.

Parker grinned, released the spent magazine, and heard it clatter against the metal roof. The new mag made a satisfying click as it mated with the rifle, the action clacked when a round was chambered, and the weapon was ready to fire.

Everything was precious, so the empty magazine was halfway into the racialist's pocket when the light produced by an explosion strobed the side of the hill, and the resulting "boom" rolled across the nearby bay. Parker *knew* where the sound had come from and didn't bother to look.

Meanwhile, about half a mile away, the now empty rocket launcher still on his shoulder, Ivory stood to survey his work. The moment reminded him of the locker room in Denver, when he *could* have run, *should* have run, but hadn't. Not until Yahweh had time to witness the bravery, not until the fear had been controlled, not until the better part of him was ready. From pen to rocket launcher—all in months!

And now, there for all to see, were the results of his handiwork. The top of the tower, the part where the Kan kept watch, had been heavily damaged. One whole section of outside walkway had been blown away, smoke poured out of a black-ringed hole, and a Klaxon could be heard. He had done *his* part . . . and Marta would do hers.

Ivory smiled, faded into the alley behind him, and was absorbed by the dark.

Some of the Kan stood in stupefied amazement, still staring at what remained of the tower while Marta and her sharpshooters cut them down. Others, the more intelligent ones, realized what the assault on the tower meant. Rather than a freak occurrence, as most assumed, the initial attack had been part of a well-coordinated assault. One which had already cut their number in half and successfully neutralized the one place from which supporting fire might have come.

Had they been guarding something of value, something that made sense, the majority of the warriors might very well have stood their ground and sacrificed themselves.

But most, like the unfortunate Duu-Bak, saw little reason to guard a human and started to fall back.

All that a noncom such as Woz-Ful could do was attempt to control the extent of the rout and radio for help. Which he did with an admirable amount of clarity, in spite of the fact that he was wounded and unable to jump.

The ranking watch officer was more than two miles away. Conscious of the fact that a missile might strike his tower at any moment but determined to provide his troops with a good example, he stared at the area in question, listened to Woz-Ful's report, and wasted little time bumping the matter upstairs.

Hak-Bin, who should have been asleep but wasn't, was almost glad of the report, offering as it did a distraction from the mysterious aches and pains that plagued him of late.

He responded to the emergency with an uncharacteristic level of calm acceptance. So much so that his Ra 'Na servant was moved nearly to the equivalent of tears as he hurried to wrap Hak-Bin in a space-black cape and otherwise prepare the way.

It would never do to hurry, however, which was why no fewer than three of the more courageous Kan died during the time it took Hak-Bin to slide his feet into a pair of enormous slippers and shuffle to his desk.

Once there, another precious moment or two was lost getting settled behind the semicircular console before he was ready to review Woz-Ful's report along with others, which might agree or conflict with the noncom's observations.

Three Kan officers, all in full combat gear, stood waiting under the glare of the gently bobbing globes. Both their anger and impatience could be seen in the rigid manner in which they held their gently morphing bodies.

Aware of the Kan but determined to ignore them until all the relevant facts had been absorbed, Hak-Bin listened to Woz-Ful's report and watched the video that went with it. It was a *good* report, a *careful* report, and one that the Zin found interesting indeed. Even as the firefight continued and his forces fell back, Hak-Bin's highly analytical mind continued its work.

A contingent of Fon had attacked the Kan. Why?

Because they knew about the birthing. No other answer made sense. Never mind how, or what they intended to do about it, the idiots somehow knew.

The Fon were armed. Not with t-guns, as one might expect, but with weapons manufactured by the humans. Why?

Because the humans planned to manipulate the Fon—to use them for some greater purpose. Did *they* know about the birthing as well? Yes, quite possibly.

What purpose?

Franklin. It had to be Franklin. There could be no other reason for an attack on that particular part of the hill.

Conscious of the fact that his troops were dying, and unable to contain himself any longer, one of the officers shuffled forward. A globe followed. "Forgive me, lord, but time continues to pass, and the longer we wait, the more successful the slave revolt is likely to be. One round from an orbital energy weapon will be sufficient to sterilize that section of complex. Strike now and we can avenge our dead brethren."

Hak-Bin made a show of shifting his weight backward while seeming to deliberate. "You are correct, Los-Maa, and your counsel is sound, or would be were the situation as simple as it seems.

"That, however, is not the case. Tragic though it is, and for reasons I am not free to discuss, those particular Fon deserved to die. More than that, *needed* to die.

"As for your Kan, well, it seems that they lacked vigilance, a rather key quality where warriors are concerned. Or would you disagree?"

Los-Maa felt a burning desire to ask an obvious question: Why would anyone expect an attack by the Fon? But the officer knew that a lack of vigilance by his troops could be construed as a lack of vigilance on *his* part. He had no desire to endure a session with the painmaster, not if he had no shame for which to cleanse himself. The Kan bowed his head. "Yes, lord, I take your point. But the slaves are out of control. Surely we should stop them?"

"Perhaps," Hak-Bin agreed, pleased by the ease with which the Kan had been brought to heel. "*If* they exceed certain parameters. In the meantime, I suggest that you summon some reinforcements and surround the affected area. A momentary flare-up is one thing. But I wouldn't want the disease to spread."

"Yes, lord," Los-Maa was forced to agree, "but what of the human? The one we were assigned to protect?"

Hak-Bin stared off into the distance, as if he could see things denied mere mortals. "The human has a security force of his own. Let's see how good they are. Besides, humans attacking humans. What could be more amusing?"

The officers laughed at the jest, and while doing so, missed the *true* nature of Hak-Bin's thoughts. The reports obtained from the human called Amocar, while not entirely clear, were anything but comforting. They suggested the very real possibility that the ruka might turn on its master.

Should the charade be allowed to continue? Was the puppet

government worth the time, energy, and resources required to keep it in place? There was no way to be absolutely sure, but Hak-Bin found the notion of allowing the slaves to settle the matter themselves to be extremely appealing, and that was sufficient. Others could suggest, but *his* word was law. The interview was at an end.

■ ■ ■

Marta, her stomach muscles held tight, moved forward through the Ra 'Na–manufactured twilight. The sound of gunfire had grown less intense during the past few minutes so that now, as the White Rose picked its way through what remained of the Kan strong point, there was only the occasional distant "bang" as Saurons fired at shadows.

The way was open, or seemingly so, although Marta knew better. No, the real opposition—meaning that which her brother commanded—lay just ahead. Not only were they a helluva lot more dangerous, they also were heavily armed and knew she was coming.

What, Marta wondered, was her mud-loving brother doing at that particular moment? Shitting his pants? Or kissing Franklin's ass?

The image amused her, and she was laughing when the only surviving Fon, an individual named Hoy-Dat, lurched out of his hiding place and stood in front of her. His left arm had been blown off at the elbow and he had a bloody rag wrapped around the stump. "Please. Help me."

"No problem," Marta said as she blew the top of the Fon's head off. "Consider yourself helped."

■ ■ ■

Ex-governor Alexander Franklin and Professor Boyer Blue had been talking for the better part of two hours when the Fon Brotherhood launched their suicidal attack.

The muffled gunfire provided the first indication that something was wrong. It was quickly followed by the attack on the observation tower, the activation of searchlights that now swept the hill, and a sudden flurry of radio traffic.

Manning, who had stationed himself near the door to Sool's clinic and was busy trying to recruit Shoes when the fracas started, listened with a growing sense of disbelief as Orvin described the manner in which a contingent of Fon had attacked the outermost ring of defenses and been eliminated by the Kan. The assault was still being pressed by forces unknown.

It was the last part, the reference to "forces unknown," that helped the security chief leap to what he felt was the proper conclusion.

Deac's Demons were behind Franklin, and Blue was here discussing the matter. So who did that leave? The White Rose, that's who, and more specifically, his sister. But Franklin was not all snuggly inside the presidential complex; he was here, meeting with Blue. Manning had taken a dim view of the trip but had been forced to acquiesce to it.

But *Jina* was in the complex; Jina, and the men and women assigned to protect her. And what about his supposed number two? Would Amocar do his job? Or run like hell?

Kell, who knew Manning pretty well by then, materialized at his side. "Don't tell me—let me guess. . . . You want me to take the Big Dog and head for the hills while you commit suicide."

Manning looked at the blanket-covered door and thought about Sool. She was in there, as always, doing her job. Who knew where the White Rose would strike next? He could no more abandon Sool than Jina. He shook his head. "No, talk to Shoes. See if we can pull Blue's security people in to mesh with ours. Fortify the clinic and do everything you can to protect it."

"And Big Dog?"

"Tell him there's some sort of disturbance and I went to check on the complex."

Kell was about to reply, about to tell Manning how stupid that was, when Franklin burst out through the door. Blue was right behind him, pocket com still plastered to his ear. "Call for the truck!" the president bellowed, "and give me a gun! The complex is under attack and Jina is there by herself!"

It was an exaggeration, of course, but Manning understood and sighed. He turned to Kell. "Never mind the last order. Hold the clinic and protect Dr. Sool. Check?"

Kell's shotgun made a clacking sound as he pumped a shell into the chamber. "No problem, boss. That's a roger."

• • •

In spite of the name "presidential complex," the pile of cubes that the locals sometimes referred to as "Frankenstein's castle" was not especially attractive to look at. In fact, except for the much-repaired cyclone fence that surrounded the ministack, and the free-fire zone out front, it looked a lot like all the other "hoods" on the hill. Security "out front" consisted of the two guards on the main gate, plus José Amocar, who had been assigned as shift boss and was supposed to provide the "fronties" with backup while monitoring the rest of the defenses.

But that would be work, an activity that Amocar had no special affection for, and shirked whenever he could. So he was standing in the shadows, taking a deep drag on a black-market Marlborough, when the Fon launched their ill-fated attack on the outer defensive zone.

Amocar's first thought was for his own safety. He crushed the potentially telltale smoke under one of his thick-soled boots, drifted six feet to the right, and tried to make sense out of the sounds he heard.

First came the bang, bang, bang of human firearms, shotguns by the sound of them, followed by the staccato bark of Sauron t-guns. There was yelling overlaid by the resonant moan of a chit Klaxon and the sharp crack of an explosion.

The conclusion was obvious. Somebody, a group of humans judging from the sound of it, had a hard-on for Franklin and were coming to get his ass. So, the agent asked himself, what should a self-respecting survivor type do? Run around waving a gun? Or locate a hole, then pull it behind him?

The radio burped static as Orvin came on. "Snake Base to Snake Two. We have condition red—repeat, red. Over."

Amocar was halfway across the free-fire zone and had already pulled his sidearm by the time he brought the radio to his lips. "This is Snake Two. Send reinforcements! We have a group forming at the main gate. Over."

"Roger that," Orvin replied calmly. "We'll do what we can, but there's no one to send at the moment. Hang in there. Over."

The fronties, both of whom were waiting for orders, watched expectantly as Amocar approached. They had monitored Amocar's transmission, knew there was no such group, and wondered what the shift boss was up to.

One, a woman named Mona, noticed that Amocar had drawn his weapon but thought nothing of it, having pulled her own. She lifted her eyebrows and was just about to ask a question when Amocar, who knew all about her body armor, shot Mona in the face.

The other frontie, a youngster known to his friends as "Skate," tried to run.

A bullet in a leg was sufficient to bring him down, and a double tap to the back of the head put him away for good.

Amocar was already outside the fence and making his way down the street by the time he pressed the transmit button again. The lack of radio discipline was intentional, as was the desperate sound in his voice. "The bastards shot Skate! And Mona, too! Hey, you—hold it right there!"

Careful to maintain pressure on the transmit button, Amocar fired two shots into the air. Then, having uttered what he hoped was a believable scream, the shift boss ran down the street. The rest of Manning's half-assed clowns could do whatever they pleased. *His* shift was over.

■ ■ ■

Surrounded by steel walls and sealed within a matrix of cargo containers, Jina had no inkling of trouble until Morley Rix used the wrench to bang on her door. "Mrs. Franklin! It's me! Morley Rix. Please open the hatch."

True to Manning's training, Jina peeked through Juma Parlo's crudely bored peephole, confirmed her visitor's identity, and slipped the lock bar. The door squealed open and she backed out of the way. The cat named Mako wiggled through the opening and was gone.

Jina wore a set of dark blue Reebok sweats that doubled as pajamas. Cold air pushed its way in, and she crossed her arms by way of a defense. "Riley, what's wrong?" She could tell something was amiss. Her first thought was for her husband. Her *second* thought, be it right or wrong, was for Manning.

Rix, who held the submachine gun pointed up toward the ceiling, shook his head. "We aren't sure, ma'am. All we know is that someone hit the outermost layer of security and seems intent on working their way in."

"Have you heard anything from my husband?"

"Yes, ma'am. The presidential party is on its way back."

"No!" Jina insisted. "Tell them to stay where they are! It's too dangerous."

"Sorry, ma'am," Rix replied politely, "but I'd be wasting my breath. They're coming, and that's that. Best thing we can do is make sure there's somebody here to greet them."

"It's that bad?"

"Yes, ma'am."

"Where's José?"

Rix, who had little use for Amocar, offered an eloquent shrug. "Who knows? Orvin thinks somebody took him out, but I wouldn't count on it. Come on, let's get out of here."

Jina, unsure of what to do, allowed Rix to lead. "Where? Where are we going?"

"Anywhere, as long as it's somewhere else. Come on, let's go."

Rix left, and Jina followed.

■ ■ ■

The flat metal roofs, which stretched sideways, also stair-stepped up the side of the hill and created another dimension in which attackers must attack and defenders must defend.

Not only did the surrounding cubes crowd the presidential complex from every side, they were covered with shacks, piles of debris, clotheslines hung with gray laundry, chimneys from which smoke dribbled, wire mesh chicken coops, and stacks of scrounged firewood.

Manning, who understood the danger posed by the neighboring cubes, had pushed for and finally obtained what amounted to a twenty-five-foot air moat between the complex and the surrounding stacks.

So, given the organic manner in which the hill-spanning slave quarters continued to grow, streets quickly emerged to box the complex in so it sat like an unmarked island within a sea of graffiti-covered metal.

Twenty-five-foot planks were in very short supply, so the "roofies," as the operatives on the roof were known, didn't have to worry about an infantry assault. Not from humans, anyway. But they *did* need to concern themselves with rocks, bottles, bullets, grenades, and rockets, any and all of which might and probably would come their way during a full-scale assault on the presidential complex.

A parapet made of sandbags, handsplit logs, and scrap metal had been built all along the roof's perimeter, and a young man named Dylan, along with six of the other roofies, was hunkered down scanning the surrounding rooflines, trying to make sense of the situation.

Dylan had joined the security team only three weeks before and knew he had a lot to learn. But he still couldn't understand how the attackers had managed to break through the cordon of Kan warriors, and having done so, were free to advance. Where were the chit reinforcements? The Sauron airships? The orbital weapons everyone talked about?

When a bullet spanged off the metal plate to his right, Dylan saw the unsuppressed muzzle flash and fired the shoulder-launched multipurpose assault weapon, or SMAW, at the heat blob that had appeared on his scope. He didn't have a positive ID on the shooter, but didn't think he needed one.

The small, candle-size missile shoved the launcher backward, accelerated away, and hit a skin known as Hog square in the chest. The device didn't explode—it hadn't traveled far enough for that—but it did pack enough force to blow Hog's sternum out through his spine.

Dylan confirmed the kill on his scope but knew he'd been lucky and might be criticized for firing the launcher. The target had been too close and too insignificant to justify a SMAW round. Still, he had managed to kill the bastard. He went facedown as a hail of retaliatory bullets swept the parapet.

Dylan looked left and right, saw that the more seasoned members of the team had taken cover as well, and wondered what Amocar knew about the overall situation. He pressed the "send" button on his radio. "Snake One Four to Snake Two. Do you read me? Over."

There was a moment of silence followed by a burst of static. Parlo was positioned on the far side of the roof. His voice sounded like a meat grinder. "Don't waste your batteries, son—or SMAW rounds either, for that matter. Your job is to hold this friggin' roof, and there ain't no need to worry about nothin' else."

Dylan was still evaluating the older man's advice when a rocket-propelled grenade exploded and cut Parlo to ribbons. The roofies returned fire, and the assault continued.

■ ■ ■

Marta, with Parker, Boner, and two others in tow, rounded a corner and paused across from the presidential complex as a firefight raged above and tracers crisscrossed the sky. She smiled. Everything was going as planned. As long as the White Rose kept the rooftop security forces engaged, the muds couldn't reinforce the ZOG troops on the ground. And it was on the ground where entry would be made and the final phase of the assassination attempt would be carried out.

But before that could be accomplished, Marta and her assault team would have to cross the heavily rutted street and cut their way through the fence, or deal with the guard station.

No simple task, or that's what Marta assumed, except there was a lot less activity than she had expected. She looked and looked again. Where the hell were Franklin's ground forces, anyway? In hiding? No, not with her brother in charge. He would never fold so easily.

Still, something was wrong. Logic dictated that the front of the complex would be the most heavily defended area of all. But something had come along to change that. What didn't matter. What *did* matter was her willingness to exploit the opportunity.

Cautiously, lest she and her companions walk into a trap, Marta sent a skin named Zipper across the street, waited for him to wave, and led the rest of the team after. They maintained their spacing, just as they'd been trained to, and arrived unopposed.

"Look!" Zipper said excitedly, pointing toward the ground. "Somebody popped the guards!"

A single glance was sufficient to confirm that the skin was correct, that someone *had* "popped" two of the president's guards and departed for parts unknown. Jack would be pissed, *very* pissed, assuming he lived long enough to find out.

Marta frowned and looked up toward the front entrance. The hatch was closed. Marta crossed the free-fire zone and pushed on the door. Hinges groaned as the barrier swung inward. Still another pleasant surprise! A gray cat dashed between her legs. She pushed her way in and paused to look around.

Inside, Rix, with Jina in tow, heard boots on metal. Unaware that Amocar had not only murdered the fronties but left the front entrance unsecured, he assumed that other members of the team had entered the front foyer, and he hurried to greet them.

His submachine gun was pointed at the ceiling as he rounded the corner, saw the intruders, and realized his mistake. The weapon fired as Rix sent a message to his finger . . . and Marta shot him between the eyes.

Rix fell as a stream of .9mm slugs bounced off the metal ceiling. Some of them struck Zipper in the chest. The skin jerked like a marionette on a string and fell out through the front door.

Marta, who was untouched, saw Jina recoil in horror. "It's her! The president's wife! Get her!"

With no other place to go, Jina ran back the way she had come—around the corner, down the hall, and up the wall-mounted ladder. She climbed quickly, her legs working like pistons, her back braced for a bullet.

Meanwhile, out in front of the complex, a black Suburban bounced to a halt. Its flanks were covered with mud, half its windows had been shot out, and there was damage to the front right fender. Taglio, a cigarette dangling from her mouth, bailed out and used her General Motors Guide Lamp Division .45-caliber M3A submachine gun to cover the far side of the street.

Warned of the vehicle's imminent arrival, the "roofies" put a withering fire on the roofline opposite the front of the presidential complex and forced the attackers to put their heads down.

The volume of incoming fire dropped as Manning, closely followed by Franklin, left the relative safety of the hulking SUV, ran through the unguarded gate, jumped the bodies that lay there, and sprinted for the entrance. Having no other information to work with and no time to check the scene, Manning was forced to assume that the guards had been killed by snipers.

He was still running; still charging the entrance, when a face lurched into view. An unfamiliar face, left to secure the door.

The skin took a step backward, tried to bring his pistol up, and fell as Manning's shoulder struck his chest. He was skidding backward on the floor when the security chief opened fire. The first slug took the luckless guard in the crotch, the second put a period over his belly button, and the third took him in the throat.

Manning saw Rix, knew what the body signified, and turned toward Franklin. "The bastards got inside! Search the first floor! I'll go topside."

Manning disappeared, and Franklin, his heart trying to beat its way out of his chest, thrust the pistol's unfamiliar weight in front of him. "Jina? Can you hear me? It's Alex."

Fearful of what he might find, Franklin held the weapon the way movie cops do and moved in short, determined bursts. Look, listen, and move—they felt like the right things to do.

For reasons he hadn't bothered to analyze, Manning believed he *knew* where the intruders were, and was glad to have Franklin out of the way. Assuming his guess was correct, and the bad guys were on the second floor, the situation would be hairy enough without having the president to protect.

Figuring that speed was more important than stealth, Manning peeked around the corner, assured himself that the next stretch of hallway was empty, and sprinted for the ladder.

He approached the ladder with weapon raised, verified that his path was clear, and started to climb. It wasn't easy, given the need to devote one hand to the .9mm, but well worth the effort.

He was halfway up the ladder when he heard a familiar voice. "Hosky, what the hell are you doing? I told you to guard the ladder, not stare at my ass. Go back and do your job."

The reply was somewhat muffled, but Manning got the impression that Hosky was pissed. Thanks to the warning, he was waiting when the disgruntled skin stuck his blank, moonlike face out into the shaft. Hosky barely had time to register what his eyes were seeing before a .9mm slug entered under the chin and exited through the top of his skull.

Manning hugged the rungs to his chest as a mixture of blood and brain tissue rained onto his head. The skin nose-dived toward the metal below. The body brushed the security chief's back, and he thought it had cleared, when the metal-capped combat boots struck his shoulders. The force of the impact damn near pulled him off the ladder. It also hurt like hell.

But Manning held on, heard someone yell, and clawed toward the top. The ladder, which had been salvaged from the outside of a Bellingham apartment house, extended two feet above the floor. That enabled the security chief to climb all the way to the top and step off without maneuvering on hands and knees.

Boner had heard the gunshot. He was closest to the ladder, so he was ready when Manning appeared. The skin held a Glock in each fist and was already in the process of squeezing both triggers when Jina, who had been watching through her peephole, unlocked the barrier and shoved as hard as she could.

Hinges squealed as the slab of steel slammed into Boner's side. The Glocks sent brass casings tumbling through the air, but the slugs flew wide. Some exploded into tiny fragments, others made bright metal smears, and the rest buzzed like angry bees as they flew this way and that.

Manning, the .9mm held with both hands, fired twice. Blood spurted as the hollow-point ammo blew divots out of the skinhead's bony chest.

Jina saw the man collapse, stepped through the doorway, and looked to her right. That's when she saw Manning and heard him yell, "Jina! Behind you!"

But the warning came too late. Having tested the locked door, the remaining racialists had continued the length of the hallway, and entered Franklin's office. That's where they were, rummaging through the materials on the Chief Executive Officer's desk, when Hosky took a bullet.

Now, having burst out into the hall just as Boner went down, they saw Jina emerge and were quick to react.

Jina had just absorbed Manning's warning when Parker wrapped an arm around her chest and brought the razor-sharp hunting knife up to her throat.

Manning, his shot blocked by Jina's body, had no choice but to remain where he was.

Marta stepped out from behind Parker.

The security chief swung his weapon to cover her, and she smiled thinly. "So, big brother, funny meeting *you* here."

Marta held a Steyr O Series chambered for .40 S&W ammo. She waved the weapon like a baton. "Choices, choices, choices. First you chose to betray your race. Now you get to choose again. So what will it be? You could shoot *me,* or, if that doesn't appeal to you, us being siblings and all, you could shoot my friend Parker.

"He's big, but that .9mm should be able to punch some holes through the black bitch and still put him down.

"Then, if you're *real* lucky, or I fuck up, maybe there will be enough time to pop little sister."

Jina, her head bent forcibly backward, her hands pulling on Parker's forearm, still managed to speak. Her voice was hoarse but determined. "Jack, listen to me—Alex isn't perfect, but who is? He can do it, he can lead humanity back, but *only* if he's alive. I can't protect him, but *you* can. If you care about me, if you *really* care about me, pull the trigger."

The tone of Jina's voice, plus the look on Manning's face, told Marta everything she needed to know. Her smile widened. "Oh, my! So *that's* how it is! Can't say as I blame you, big brother. She's a fine piece of ass. Assuming you *like* niggers, which you obviously do."

A lot of things happened during the next fifteen seconds. Jina released Parker's arm, kicked a shin, and clawed at his eyes.

Reacting to the pain, Parker drew the blade across her throat. He felt the rush of hot blood, the way her body jerked against his, and he held her up.

Manning fired three shots in quick succession, each of which passed through Jina's torso and struck the man beyond.

Parker jerked spasmodically, looked surprised, and felt Jina pull him down.

Parker was still dying, still falling, when Manning began the long, impossible turn. The turn that would put Marta in his sights, that would avenge Jina's death, that would pay his family's debt.

But it wasn't to be, *couldn't* be, given the seconds already consumed. The Steyr would come into position, Marta would fire, and it was *he* who would feel the slugs plow through his body.

What then? Light? Darkness? It *wouldn't* matter, not unless Jina were there, and . . .

Franklin, his feet still planted on the ladder, held the pistol with his right hand and squinted through the open sight. Because Manning blocked most of his field of vision, he couldn't see Marta's face, or the weapon in her hand. But what he *could* see, and aimed for, were a pair of muddy boots. *They* were visible through the inverted V formed by Manning's widespread legs. The trigger was easy to pull. Leather, bone, and blood sprayed the floor as the .9mm slugs hit Marta's ankles and cut her feet out from under her.

That would have stopped most people, but as Marta fell, her brother turned sideways, and the *real* target came into view. Not much, just his head and shoulders, but enough. Ivory would have been proud of the way Marta fired as she went down, the first bullet striking metal, the second finding flesh.

But Marta didn't live long enough to see that. The last thing *she* saw was the look of hatred on her brother's face, the red sparks that flew from the barrel of his gun, and an ocean of darkness. Marta's head bounced off metal, her weapon skittered away, and the assassin was dead.

Franklin, his arm bleeding where a bullet had sliced the skin, staggered down the hall. He made a sound that married Jina's name to a long, anguished groan. He dropped to his knees, gathered his wife's body into his arms, and started to sob.

At least half a minute passed while Manning, unable to do anything else, stood and stared at the woman he had loved.

Then the *other* man, the one she had loved first, turned to meet his eyes. Nothing was said, not then, and not later. But both men knew what they had shared, what they had lost, and what Jina would want them to do.

Franklin, who had been marked by his wife's final words, and knew how they would haunt him, looked up into the eyes of the only man who could possibly understand. "Help me, Jack. Help me make the bastards pay."

Manning used a sleeve to blot the tears. "You have my word, Mr. President. The bastards *will* pay."

• • •

Later, in a high, clean place, on a sunny day, in a meadow covered with wildflowers, Jina Claire Franklin was laid to rest.

Outside of her husband, his security chief, and a respectful helicopter crew, the only other being to witness the ceremony was a Sauron named Sebo Hak-Bin. Because he was watching from orbit, he couldn't read the words that had been chiseled into a slab of limestone. The *same* limestone quarried for use in the Sauron citadels.

But had the alien been able to read the words, and had he been able to understand the passion behind them, he almost certainly would have called for the destruction of the humans, the helicopter, and the meadow itself. The marker read:

In memory of Jina Claire Franklin
1984–2020
She gave her life in the sure knowledge that the people of Earth
will rise again.

The countdown continues
in *EarthRise*!

NOW AVAILABLE IN HARDCOVER

WILLIAM C. DIETZ

EARTHRISE

THE SEQUEL TO *DEATHDAY*

**AVAILABLE WHEREVER BOOKS ARE SOLD OR
TO ORDER CALL 1-800-788-6262**

ACE
2003
50TH
ANNIVERSARY